THEY FOUND ATLANTIS

D1364381

DENNIS WHEATLEY

DENNIS WHEATLEY

THEY FOUND ATLANTIS

Frontispiece Portrait by
MARK GERSON

Original Illustrations by
IAN MILLER

Distributed by
HERON BOOKS

Published by arrangement with
Hutchinson and Co. (Publishers) Ltd.

2888

CONTENTS

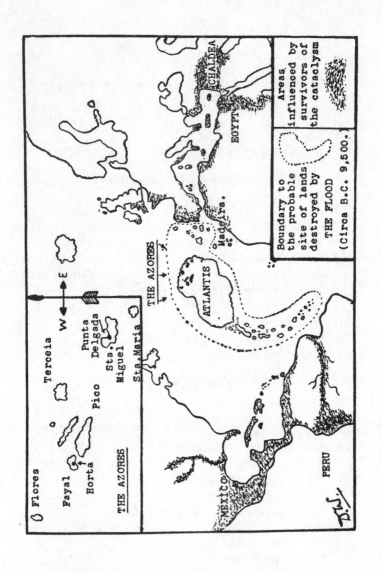

CHAPTER I

A STRANGE CRAFT

FUNCHAL, the capital of Madeira, is on the south coast of the island. Its leisurely dealings in wine and sugar, lace and basketwork, hardly disturb the serenity of the little town. Its buildings, straggling out along a wide blue bay and up the foot of the mountain which rises steeply from the shore, white, cream, and lemon among the greenery of vineyards and cane brakes, face a limitless waste of sparkling waters and for the most part lie sleeping in the sun.

The western end of the bay is dominated by a high cliff upon which stands Reids Palace Hotel. That is the real centre of the island's life. Often, when a calling liner allows its passengers a few hours in which to stretch their legs ashore, two hundred extra places are laid for luncheon there, and all the year round holiday-makers come and go, basking for a week or two in certain sunshine, since the climate of the fortunate island rarely drops below seventy or rises above ninety in the shade.

Palms, oleanders, bougainvilia and magnolia trees rise from the semi-tropical gardens to screen the lower balconies of the hotel, then the cliff drops almost sheer, and a cactus-fringed stairway leads down to a rocky promontory upon which the hotel guests sunbathe between dips in the blue waters of the Atlantic.

The McKay had had his morning swim and baked the lean body, to which he was pleased to refer as "the imperial carcass," a slightly deeper shade of golden brown. Now, with his Chinese robe girt tightly round him, he stood with his eyes glued to a pair of binoculars, watching a ship that had just come to anchor in the bay.

He was a shortish man but very upright, square-shouldered and square headed. His hair, thick, wiry and close cut, except

1

where it was brushed up from his broad forehead, had once been a violent red but was now only faintly sandy, the colour having been bleached from it until it had become almost white.

A girl with candid grey eyes and ripe-corn coloured hair was seated on the rocks near him.

"What do you make of her?" she enquired. "I've never seen a queerer-looking yacht."

"She's not a yacht, m'dear." The McKay lowered his glasses and offered them. "Take a look yourself. Fine feathers make fine birds they say but for all her brass and paintwork she's a tramp—or has been. It takes more than the addition of a few deck houses to deceive your old sailor man."

"Thanks." Sally Hart took the glasses and focused them upon the gaily painted ship with its unusual super-structure of white cabins forward and even stranger tangle of cranes, and massed machinery aft. "But why," she went on after a moment, "do you persist in referring to yourself as if you had captained the Ark?—you're not really old at all."

An appreciative grin spread over the McKay's face. It was lined from exposure to cutting wind, driving spray, and torrid sun-glare on the bridges of the many ships in which he had served, but the webs of little wrinkles which creased up round the corners of his blue eyes were due to an irrepressible sense of humour.

"That's nice of you, m'dear," he murmured, "but I'm old enough to be your daddy and too old at forty-six to be given another ship. At least, that was the opinion formulated by their noble lordships of the Admiralty when they retired me last year—the blithering idiots."

She shook her head. "I'll bet that wasn't the real reason. The British Admiralty like their sailors to be respectably married and have money when they reach captain's rank, so they can throw parties when they're in foreign stations. Naturally they axed a professional bad man like you who refuses to grow old and has no money or official wife—but a girl in every port."

"If you're not careful I'll run you for infringing the official secrets act," he countered quickly. "You know too much young woman—especially for a Yankee."

Without removing the glasses from her eyes she shot out one bare foot and kicked him on the behind. "How dare you call me a Yankee you ill-bred oaf. I come from

California and don't you forget it. Now tell me please, what's that great ball thing hanging out from the rear of the ship?"

"Starn, dearie, starn, the word 'rear' makes a sailor blush. I'm not certain what the ball thing is myself. It looks like the grandfather of all the buoys that ever were at this distance, but judging by photographs I've seen I'd hazard a guess that it's a bathysphere."

"And what's a bathysphere Nelson Andy McKay?"

"A bathysphere, oh child of ignorance and sin, is a hollow steel ball constructed to resist enormous pressure. Adventurous souls like Dr. William Beebe, who invented it, climb inside; then their pals lower them into the depths of the ocean so that they can make long noses at giant octopuses through the super-thick portholes."

"Of course—I remember hearing about Beebe's book 'Half Mile Down'. Would this be his research ship, then, I wonder?"

"No, I don't think she's Beebe's hooker. His bathysphere is quite a small affair. It holds only two divers and it's hoisted on and off the deck with a fair sized derrick—whereas that thing could hold half a dozen people and must weigh a hundred ton. That's why they ship it on those steel girders abaft the starn right down on the waterline I expect. It is about one third submerged already as you can see and they probably run it straight off the steel tracks so that the water carries part of its immense weight before it has to be taken up by that complicated system of cranes overhead."

"Oh look!" Sally turned and pointed suddenly. "Camilla and her boy friends are going off in the speed-boat to investigate."

As she followed the foaming track of the speed-boat in its graceful curve towards the anchored mystery ship the McKay settled himself on his lean haunches and studied her excited young face at his leisure.

Sally's skin was good, her nose straight, her mouth full and red, her teeth excellent, her eyes wide set but not large enough to give her face distinction. She was attractive but not a real beauty.

Her cheeks were just a shade too full and nothing, she knew, could alter that any more than the most skilful plucking would ever convert her golden eyebrows from semi-circular arches to the long narrow Garboish sweeps which she would have

3

liked. Besides, shame of all shames, her otherwise quite perfect figure was marred by thick ankles.

The McKay was not thinking of her ankles, only that she was a darned decent healthy little girl, and a thundering sight more fun to be with than her really beautiful multi-millionairess cousin, Camilla, newly divorced Duchess da Solento-Ragina, née Hart, who was speeding out to the strange vessel in the bay with a little bodyguard of would-be second husbands.

"Wonder which of 'em will hook her?" The McKay remarked, airing his thoughts aloud. "If I were her I'd pick the Swede—at least he's got *some* brains."

"Oh, but Count Axel's so old!" Sally protested.

"Nonsense, he's not much over forty, just the age to deal with a fly-by-night young creature like your lovely cousin. Still she hasn't the sense to see that's he's worth three of the Roumanian Prince—or ten of that little filth Master Nicolas Costello."

"Nicky's not so bad. He's rather fun I think, and quite a famous film star. You've only got a hate against him because you don't like crooners—you said so the other day."

"I'd croon him if I had him in a ship with me," said the McKay grimly. "I took a dislike to that young man before I even knew what brand of idiocy he indulged in. I suppose the odds are really on the Prince. Vladimir is a handsome looking bounder and she'd like another title, wouldn't she?"

Sally shrugged and regarded the McKay with mild amusement. "She doesn't tell me much. I'm only the female counterpart of Rene P. Slinger—just a paid companion she trots round with her to do her chores. I don't think she'll be in any hurry to take a second husband though. We only unloaded the Duke three months ago and her experience with him would last most girls a lifetime."

The McKay began to chuckle to himself.

"What are you laughing at?" Sally asked suspiciously.

"Just the story of Camilla and her Duke," he confessed. "Most men in his situation would have spent the rest of their lives tagging round after wealthy wifey like a kind of super footman on any pocket money she cared to dole out to them, but Ragina had the sense to fix things up properly before taking her to church. Then, when she started her tantrums, he was able to quit the party with enough cash to keep him in clover for the rest of his days as some compensation for the trouble she had put him to."

4

"Trouble!" exclaimed Sally hotly. "Not many men **find** it any *trouble* to make love to a pretty girl."

"True," the McKay agreed slowly, "but Camilla's **got a** temper and her education is pathetic, despite all the **thousands** her guardians must have spent on it, whereas Ragina, **I'm** told, is a peace-loving cultured sort of chap so he probably found her a most awful bore to live with after the first fortnight."

Sally flushed and hastened to the defence of her cousin. "How can you! He was a rotten little blackguard who trapped her into that wicked marriage settlement by trading on the fact that she had fallen for him."

"Fiddlesticks! Camilla wanted large coronets on her silk undies and the Duke was getting a bit weary of ye ancient family overdraft so they made a deal of it."

"That's not true. Before she was twenty-one her guardians would hardly allow her to see a man so she was horribly inexperienced and developed one of those wild short-lived passions the very moment she met him, just as any girl might who had been cooped up that way. He was terribly in love with her too—to begin with."

The McKay's blue eyes twinkled beneath their bushy, sandy-white, caterpillar brows. "Steady m'dear, you're getting almost as excited as if it had happened to you."

"Well I certainly feel that way at times. You see, I've been with Camilla ever since she left school, and I'll never forget those months that she was married. D'you know that little swine used actually to beat her—with his braces."

The McKay suddenly sat back and roared with laughter.

With an angry frown Sally stood up but he stretched out a detaining hand and caught at her bathrobe. "Now, now, don't run away. Camilla doesn't seem to have had any bones broken and lots of girls enjoy a playful hiding sometimes. It probably did her a power of good to learn that she could not carry her millions into the bedroom. Besides, you must admit that there's a funny side to it. Just picture the little dark Duke chasing that great hoyden of a girl round the room to give her a leathering."

"You brute," exclaimed Sally her grey eyes wide with indignation but as he struggled to his feet she had difficulty in repressing a smile.

"Come on young woman," he said firmly. "It's time for the odd spot before lunch so if you will deign to accompany the imperial carcass up to the hotel I'll buy you a sherry cobbler.''

"Thanks." She turned with him, then paused as she saw the speedboat hurtling towards them across the water. "Here come the others. They haven't been long have they? Do let's wait for a moment and learn the mystery about this queer ship."

They stood silent until the speed-boat drew alongside. The tall, dark, Roumanian Prince sprang on to the landing steps. Nicolas Costello, the film star, jumped out beside him. The Swedish Count took the golden-haired Camilla's hand to assist her ashore. Rene P. Slinger, a bald-headed thin-nosed man who was the Duchess's confidential adviser, followed and after him came a fat puffing stranger who mopped his bare head, from which thick fair hair sprouted like the bristles of a brush, with a red bandana handkerchief.

"Darling!" shrilled Camilla as she landed, "meet *Herr Doktor* Tisch. We just caught him leaving his wonder-ship and brought him ashore to lunch with us."

The perspiring German thrust his handkerchief into his pocket and bowed stiffly from the waist.

"Isn't it too thrilling," Camilla hurried on. "The Herr Doktor is out to rediscover the biggest hoard of gold there's ever been in the world. With that ball thing on his boat he plans to go a mile deep in the sea and dig up all the vast treasure from the lost continent of Atlantis."

CHAPTER II

THE SUNKEN CONTINENT

THE Duchess da Solento-Ragina was certainly a lovely young woman. In face and figure she was very like her cousin Sally and, in the distance they might easily have been mistaken for each other but, close to, Camilla's better breeding showed in her slim wrists and ankles, the more delicate bone construction of her face and larger eyes, the blue of which against her golden hair gave her a slightly more attractive colouring than Sally.

However, slim ankles do not guarantee a good temper or fine eyes a kindly consideration for the feelings of other people and Camilla, without being by any means an ill-natured girl was a little inclined to abuse the power which her millions gave her. She took an almost childish delight in watching her lovers quarrel for her favour and liked to tantalise them by withdrawing herself unexpectedly at times.

Now therefore, having introduced herself to Dr. Herman Tisch immediately on his ship's arrival and secured him as her guest for luncheon, she did not invite what the McKay cynically termed her 'circus' to join her table, so only Sally and Rene P. Slinger were privileged to share with her the Herr Doktor's account of his projected descent to the bottom of the ocean.

None of his auditors knew more of Atlantis than the bare legend that it had once existed as an island in the centre of the Atlantic, but the fat little German was an expert on his subject so it needed neither the two girls' eager questioning nor the bald sharp-featured Slinger's mild scepticism to release a positive spate of facts and figures, geological, botanical, and ethnological from the Doctor between the mouthfuls of a very hearty lunch.

Afterwards he asked to be excused in order that he might attend to his letters, which he had collected from the Hotel bureau, but promised to join them again later as they went out to drink their coffee on the terrace.

Nicolas Costello, his sleek fair hair brushed flatly back, and resplendent in a pale blue flannel suit, that no man other than a film star would have dared to wear, had already secured a table and ringed it with basket chairs. He held one facing the lovely prospect of the bay for Camilla and then, without a glance at the others, plumped himself down beside her.

Count Axel Fersan placed his long delicate hand on the back of another and drew it out for Sally, then he settled himself with leisurely ease between her and Slinger.

"Where is the Prince?" enquired Camilla with a little frown.

"Here, Madame!" The tall Roumanian appeared in the French window behind her. He was a magnificent figure of a man and his velvety eyes held a ready smile as he bowed to her.

"Come on now, Camilla," Nicky urged. "What's all this business about getting to the bottom of the Atlantic?"

The McKay appeared at that moment on his way down to the garden and Camilla called to him. "Come and join us, Captain, you know all about the sea. What are the chances of getting to the bottom of it?"

"Remarkably few if you happen to be in the British Navy —thank God!" he replied drily as he pulled up a chair. "I've managed to avoid it for twenty-eight years."

"Oh, stop this fooling," cut in Nicky impatiently. "Didn't the little German say there was a whole heap of gold to be got? Let's hear about it then."

The Roumanian's black eyes flashed with an antagonism that he did not attempt to conceal. "I have heard a rumour that you are bankrupt stock, but thought that you seek an easier way than a gamble with life to make whole your balances."

Nicky went scarlet. "See here!" he began but Count Axel's gentle laughter mocked him into a furious silence.

The Count was older than the other two. Slim, elegant, of middle height, he had neither the Roumanian's military swagger or the Greek-god features which had made Nicky's profile world famous, but he possessed the quiet distinction which scholarship lends to nobility. His face was long, his nose a little pointed, his eyes a quick intelligent hazel. His lightish brown hair was already thinning on his delicately moulded skull.

"Now children," Camilla held up her hand to quiet his impish laughter. "Be good, and Rene shall tell you all the Herr Doktor said at lunch of what he plans to do."

Slinger hunched himself forward, gave a twirl to the butt

of his cigar, and began in a high reedy voice: "I didn't understand half the scientific stuff he talked, but this is how I get it.

"Thousands of years ago there was land right in the middle of the North Atlantic—an island as big as France and Germany put together. There were chains of small islands too, one running from it down to Brazil and the other across to Portugal. According to the Professor that's the only way so many plants and animals that are common to both continents could have got across the ocean."

"How about their migrating round the Arctic?" Nicky cut in sceptically.

Count Axel shook his head. Like the majority of educated Scandinavians he spoke perfect English. "Many of the plants which are known to have existed independently in both hemispheres, such as the banana palm for example, could never have lived north of the temperate zone."

"Anyhow," Slinger went on, "the Herr Doktor postulates that this island was the original Garden of Eden as far as the White Races go. Fertile, fine climate, about like this in its southern part and, above all, isolated for thousands of years by its sea barriers on either side—so completely protected from invasion. That enabled its inhabitants gradually to develop in peace and security until they achieved a wonderful civilisation, the remnants of which are the basis of all the other cultures which have come down to us."

"That's interesting enough as a theory," agreed the McKay.

"The Doctor maintains that he can prove it a hundred times over by similarities between the root language of the Central-American Indians and various Mediterranean peoples; by the fact that they had the same hierarchy of Gods, the same system of astrology, the same methods of agriculture, and the same style of architecture. It seems that the Mexicans once went in for Pyramid building just like the Egyptians."

"That is so," Count Axel's thin mouth twitched at the corners and his rather sad face was lit by a quick smile. "Some of the pyramids built by the Aztecs in Mexico are very large and exactly similar to the early efforts in the valley of the Nile, although they got no further than the step pyramids which the Egyptians achieved as early as their Fourth Dynasty."

"You seem to know quite a lot about it already, Count," Slinger remarked.

"The rise of ancient civilisations has always interested me, and many people believe that they all owe their origin to trading colonies which were established by the Atlanteans before their island was submerged in some stupendous upheaval."

Slinger shook his bald pate. "The Herr Doktor was arguing that if that were the case those colonies would have carried on where the Atlanteans left off and reached a similar high plane within a few generations. His theory is that the Atlanteans held no communication with the outside world at all and that in one frightful day and night of earthquakes the whole continent went down. It must have been a catastrophe utterly unparalleled in the history of the world, but out of the several million people who probably inhabited the island it's likely that some who were in boats and so on would have been saved and washed ashore alive here and there in the huge tidal waves. A few reached Egypt and started that maybe; another lot struck northern Palestine and got going in Chaldea; a single man perhaps fetched up on the coast of Mexico and another in Brazil. If the Doctor's right that would explain why the new centres took so long to develop—only a little of the original knowledge would have survived with each man or group you see. Just as to-day, not one of us could carry a thousandth part of modern scientific knowledge and culture with us if we were suddenly dumped down among a barbarous people."

"I've often wondered just how much we could do if half a dozen people like us were washed up on a desert island," said Sally.

"It's an interesting speculation," agreed Slinger, "but to get back—the Doctor thinks that some of these folk who reached Cornwall and Brittany were simple fishermen who could do little more than carry their great religion of sun worship to the natives they found, just as any of us would know enough of Christianity to preach it, however ignorant we might be about electricity and machines. He holds that they founded the Druid's cult, whereas others, the batch that got to Egypt for example, had educated people amongst them, which would account for the Egyptians worshipping the sun god Ra, but in a more sophisticated way, and coming on with regard to the amenities of life more than all the rest."

Count Axel nodded. "That theory fits in very well with the story of the Flood. In addition to the account of it in our scriptures, the Celts, the Babylonians and all the tribes of Central-American Indians preserved legends of it too. I do not think anyone can doubt that the Deluge was an actual historical occurrence and a catastrophe of such tremendous magnitude would naturally be embodied in the race memories of all the people who knew of it. The Herr Doktor's idea of separate groups surviving is supported too by the fact that all legends of the Flood, although agreeing in their main particulars, differ in their account as to how their central figures were saved. Some, like Noah, had arks, others took refuge in caves on high mountains, others again were washed ashore clinging to great trees, and so on. The most curious thing of all is that Flood legends are very strong among the races of the West Indies and Mediterranean basin, vague if you go further north or south, and practically non-existent if you investigate the folk lore of the Pacific Islands, China, Australia, Malay and Japan. That points so very definitely to the calamity having occurred in the North Atlantic about where the Azores are now."

Slinger stood up. "I see you know more of this than I do Count, so I'll leave you to entertain the party while I find Doctor Tisch. He must have gotten through his mail by now."

"Let's cut out the cackle and come to the gold," Nicky suggested as Slinger left them.

"By all means." Count Axel smiled lazily beneath half lowered lids. "The case for the actual existence of Atlantis before the Deluge rests principally, for its historic foundation, on certain passages in Plato's *Critias* and *Timœus*. According to these a scholarly Greek named Solon visited Egypt about 450 B.C. and a learned Priest of Sais gave him an account of the marvellous island. Atlantis, according to the ancient tradition was preserved in the memory of the Egyptians as the place where early mankind dwelt for many ages in peace and happiness. It was the cradle of all civilisation and, when submerged some nine thousand years before Solon's time, inhabited by a powerful, wealthy, and cultured people.

"The capital of Atlantis was a mighty city beneath a great mountain in the northern part of the island. It was ringed by three broad canals, and three defensive zones each of which had high walls strengthened with plates of brass and copper. In the city itself stood the vast temple of Poseidon which was roofed and walled in pure red gold and contained life-size

11

images fashioned from the same precious metal so that——"

He broke off suddenly as Slinger and the German came out on to the terrace. The latter had lost his cheerful look. He now appeared a fat, hunched, dejected figure while Slinger exclaimed:

"The Doctor's had a rotten break. He feared it from a radio message he received a week ago but now it's been confirmed by mail. Klemo Farquason, has crashed on Wall Street, so the whole show's off."

"Seven years I prepare," bleated the little Doctor, "then for three more years I search for a rich financier who will back my great exploration. Everyone says I am a mad hatter but at last I convinced Mr. Farquason that I am not. Another year while we manufacture the super-bathysphere and have the ship outfitted. He is to meet me here—then I get a radiogram that there may be delay—now this."

A general murmur of sympathy went round and Slinger remarked. "I'm afraid it's not going to be easy for you to find another man with sufficient cash to finance a thing like this where the results are so problematical."

"But the loss to science," moaned the Doctor.

"Never mind the science," said Nicky, "how about the gold? Though I don't see how you'd ever find it. Even if it's get-at-able, and not buried under five hundred feet of mud, it might be anywhere between Lisbon and Miami. There must be ten thousand square miles of ocean where that continent was before it sank. You might go diving for a life time and not hit the spot where that city was."

"No—that is not so," protested the Doctor angrily. "Eleven years ago, when I was an archæologist on the Euphrates, I dug up a scroll at Eridu which gave me the great secret. The bearing of the stars which fixed the position of the city. The stars in ten thousand years do not vary more than a fraction. I will get within a mile of the temple at the first dive, then I dredge and within a week I will come to it."

Nicky stared at him. "That makes all the difference," he said slowly, then he looked sharply at Camilla. "How about it? People have staked worse bets than this. Why don't you cut in on it?"

Camilla straightened and they all watched her in silence for a moment, then: "It would be rather fun," she said slowly.

"If the expedition succeeds it will make history," remarked

12

the Count, "and you, Madam, as the leader of it, will remain famous long after you are dead."

It was a subtle piece of flattery and tickled Camilla's vanity. "Chartering the yacht wouldn't harm the trust any," she said thoughtfully, "but I'd have to cut various engagements. How long is it going to take, Doctor?"

"The work of excavation may go on for years, but I will find the city in a fortnight—less *Gnädige Hertzogin*."

"That means I'll have to cancel my visit to Scotland," Camilla hesitated, looking round at the ring of intent faces.

"Oh let's—do let's, please!" Sally exclaimed.

"All right," Camilla smiled and exclaimed suddenly: "Will you all come as my guests on this party to discover the lost continent?"

Only the McKay's voice rose above quick murmurs of acceptance that greeted her invitation. "If you're including me I hope you don't expect me to go under water in that bathysphere?"

"No, we'll let you play with a sextant on the bridge, but it would be nice to have the British Navy with us!"

"Well, what could be fairer than that," he laughed. "I'd love to come."

"Ach! Himmel!" the Doctor cried. "You mean this? You will finance my exploration with your money?"

"Certainly I will," Camilla assured him a little pompously.

An ecstatic smile spread over the German's face as he grabbed her hand in his pudgy fingers and kissed it.

Half an hour later the party had broken up. Only Rene P. Slinger and the Doctor remained on the terrace. The latter no longer smiled. His pink face showed doubt and distress.

"I haf agreed to do this only to save my exploration," he said heavily.

"Sure," nodded Slinger cheerfully, "but haven't things panned out just as I said. The moment I heard Farquason had fallen down on you a month back I knew that if you brought your outfit here Camilla would jump right into it. Once we get her up to the Azores in that ship of yours and the big boy comes on board you'll see things happen. Then you can go hunting your lost Atlantis until it rise out of the water again to hit you in the pants."

The Doctor ignored the gibe and nodded gloomily. "But there must be no bloodshed mind—no bloodshed—you haf promised me that."

CHAPTER III

SIGNS, SOUNDS, AND A WORRIED
LITTLE MAN

THAT night, the lovely Camilla, Duchess of Solento-Ragina—née Hart, expended some infinitesimal portion of her millions by giving a party to those friends and retainers who were to accompany her on Doktor Herman Tisch's mystery ship.

The retainers, her cousin Sally and her man of business Rene P. Slinger, were in excellent spirits. Sally because she felt that however mad the quest might appear it should prove amusing and Slinger, because he had succeeded in his secret design of getting Camilla to undertake the expedition for his own dubious purposes.

The McKay punished the champagne and blessed his luck that he had chanced to be present when Camilla offered the invitation to her intimates. As a Naval Captain, just retired, he was already finding it a difficult business to live in comfort on his pension and his inclusion in the party meant a few weeks free keep in pleasant company.

Camilla's three would-be second husbands—the Roumanian, Prince Vladimir Renescu, the film-star crooner Nicky Costello, and the Swede, Count Axel Fersan—were equally cheerful at the prospect of this voyage, which meant that the heiress to the Hart millions would be safe for some time from the pursuit of other suitors who might arrive upon the scene at any moment; moreover each was visualising in advance the delightful opportunities which might occur to get slender, blue-eyed, Camilla alone upon a moonlit afterdeck, persuade her to accept him, and thus finally rout his rivals before Doktor Tisch's ship returned to port. The little German doctor alone remained morose and uneasy, tortured by his secret thoughts.

When dinner was over the whole party migrated to the little Casino which lies half way down the hill between Reids Palace Hotel and Funchal. It was early yet and only about fifty people were scattered about the low cool rooms. The young Roumanian carried Camilla off to dance and Nicky

14

secured Sally solely because he knew that by dancing with her he would be able to keep an eye on Camilla without actually giving his rival the pleasure of seeing him lounge sulkily in the doorway of the dance room. The others passed through the far door and sitting down at a table on the terrace, ordered drinks.

The night was fine, the air soft and scented by the semi-tropical moon flowers which open their great white bells only after the sun has set. A sheer cliff dropped from the terrace to the bay, now shrouded in darkness, but out on its gently heaving waters the lights of the shipping, riding at anchor for a few hours after having dropped their passengers and mails for Madeira, twinkled cheerfully. To the left they could catch a glimpse of the lights on the foreshore down in Funchal town, and to the right those of Reids Palace Hotel glimmered from its eminence on the headland of the bay.

When they had finished their first drink Slinger suggested a stroll to Doktor Tisch leaving the McKay and Count Axel on their own. The sailor immediately broached the topic which was foremost in all their minds and asked:

"Well, Count! What do you think of this Atlantis trip we are to take together?"

"That it is one of the most interesting upon which any party of people can ever have embarked and I consider myself highly fortunate that chance should have made me a member of it," replied the Swede affably.

The McKay's thin lips twitched as he suppressed a disbelieving smile. "You don't really think though that we shall succeed in dragging up the gold from this temple a mile deep in the ocean?"

"Ah, that I do not say, but if we can secure even one small stone from the ocean bed, which bears an inscription, we shall have proved the one-time existence of this lost continent and all the histories of the world will have to be rewritten. Think of the romantic thrill in actually being present at such an epoch making discovery."

"Come now." The McKay shook his head and gave a low chuckle. "I thought all you told us of the Flood legends to-day extremely interesting—but then you are an admirable raconteur and, although your stories served their purpose, you can hardly expect a hardened old sinner like myself to believe them."

"Why should you think that I was not in earnest?"

15

"Isn't that rather obvious. Forgive me if I seem rude and of course your private affairs are none of my business but it must be an expensive pastime pursuing Camilla round Europe from one luxury hotel to another in the hope of making her your Countess. Surely this is a heaven sent opportunity to be certain of her company for several weeks to come at her sole charge. I would not put it to you so bluntly if I were not devilish hard up myself and willing to confess that the prospect of the trip at the expense of this lady, who can so well afford it, tempted me to accept her invitation."

Count Axel's eyes narrowed a fraction but his smile was lazy, tolerant, good natured. "I see," he murmured after a moment. "You thought that I was distorting facts in order to persuade her to undertake this voyage and, perhaps, considering it offered excellent opportunities to divert her attention from my empty headed rivals to myself by frequent displays of my erudition. I might resent that suggestion most strongly —from some people—but, as it happens, I like you sufficiently to let it pass. Actually it is true that this venture comes as a boon in the present state of my finances, yet I assure you that I distorted nothing, and meant every single word I said this afternoon."

"Then you honestly believe that this fabled continent did exist?"

"I do indeed and if you like I will endeavour to prove it to you."

"Right. Go ahead, the night is young but let's repeat the drinks before we settle down to it—hi, waiter!"

The man paused at the table and took their order, to which Count Axel added: "Bring me a few sheets of scribbling paper, will you." Then he turned back to the McKay.

"Am I right in supposing that you have no knowledge of ancient languages,—Sanscrit, Hebrew, Maya, Phoenician and so on I mean?"

"Perfectly." The McKay's lined face broke into a quick smile. "Even my Latin is pretty rusty now."

"Then my dear Captain I must ask you to accept my word for the truth of all that I am about to say. I will give you nothing which is not accepted as a fact by all serious students of archaic languages."

"Certainly, Count."

"Good. The study of words and their origins has been one of my hobbies for many years and although of course I could

16

not carry on a conversation in these long dead languages which hold the roots of modern speech, I know quite a considerable amount about them. Did you know that from all the thousands of tongues in which men convey their thoughts to one another only two *original phonetic* alphabets had been produced?"

"I don't know the first thing about it," the McKay admitted, "but never mind that."

"Well, it is so. All writing originated in the picture drawings left by primitive people who were on the march from one territory to another so that the other portion of their tribe, which was following, perhaps days later, might learn from their markings on stones and trees the direction they had taken and the good or ill fortune that they had met with in their migration.

"A crude drawing of a sun meant a day, of the moon—a month, rippling lines—water, crossed spears—a battle with another tribe, the horns of a buck—plentiful game, and so on. In time these signs became simplified or conventionalised so much as often to bear no further resemblance to their original. The Chinese script is an excellent if exaggerated example of the latter case. Each of the thousands of characters which are utterly meaningless to us, or even to all but the highly educated among themselves to-day, originally represented a picture of something—a peach—a cart—a tree bent in the breeze—or a state of emotion shown by the posture of a human figure. Egyptian hieroglyphics were the same although less obscured, because in quite early times the Egyptians decided to retain them as they stood for all sacred writings while bringing in an easier abbreviated set of forms, called the demotic, for every day use. The great Maya race of Central America however retained their hieroglyphic system until the Spanish Conquest.

"Think now how laborious it must have been to convey a message by this picture writing once you passed out of the realm of material things into that of ideas. The number of drawings you would have to chip out of a piece of rock to convey even one sentence such as 'The chief in this neighbourhood is a fool but his nephew the witch doctor is cunning, therefore propitiate and flatter him while tricking the chief into agreeing to your demands.'" Count Axel paused. "But perhaps I bore you with all this?"

"No, no," the McKay lied politely, "do go on."

"The time came when some long-forgotten genius conceived

17

the possibility of utilising already established symbols to convey sounds instead of ideas. The human throat, lips and tongue are capable of producing about twenty distinct sounds and these formed the basis of the alphabet. The letters which have been added since, bringing the total number up to twenty-six, are more or less variations of the originals or interchangeable with them. T and D for example, or V and F, or I and J.

"The alphabets of all European languages are, as you will know, derived from the Phoenician which, up to about four hundred years ago, was the only known *archaic* writing in in the world based on sound and not picture drawing. If you will pause to think for a moment you will realise that the difference between the two—as a medium for the exchange of ideas—is stupendous."

The McKay, more interested now, nodded. "Yes, I see that. It must have been as big an advance as from sail to steam in shipping—bigger in fact."

The waiter arrived with their drinks and the paper for Count Axel, who thanked him and went on:

"Very well then. Now we come to a very interesting fact. A decade or two after Columbus discovered America Diego da Landa, who was the first Bishop of Yucatan, took the trouble to enquire from the Mayas he was seeking to convert to Christianity the meaning of the grotesque hieroglyphics which decorated all their monuments. They told him that it was a form of writing which their predecessors had handed down to them and, to his utter amazement, he found that they were not picture drawings conventionalised *but the letters of a phonetic alphabet.*"

Now it was curious enough to find such a system in existence among the Mayas of Central America at all when all the great civilisations of Asia, Europe and Africa together had only succeeded in producing one—the Phoenician—but what is stranger still is that these two alphabets—the only ones of their kind—should bear an absolutely striking resemblance to each other.

"Say you were faced with the task of selecting sixteen signs to represent the sixteen principal sounds—for that was the number in the Maya alphabet—the variety of combinations of lines and curves which you might use to denote each are almost inexhaustible. If a hundred men sat down to the job separately it is hardly conceivable that two of them would select the same sign for the same letter. Yet I can prove to you that thirteen signs out of the sixteen in the two original phonetic alphabets have a distinct similarity of form.''

The Count took up a pencil and drew rapidly on the paper before him ⬚ . "That is the hieroglyphic for **H** as given by De Landa in his Maya alphabet. Simplify it a little as people would do in the course of time if they were in a hurry and you get ⬚ which is the hieroglyphic representing the sound CH in the Egyptian or this, ⬚ an even nearer form, which appears for H, in the archaic Greek and Hebrew. From that it is but a step to our modern symbol **H** for the same sound.

"Take the Maya C which was drawn like this ⬚ What is the essential characteristic of it which would come to be employed alone in course of time. Obviously the large single lower tooth ∧ . Well that is the form in which the letter C was found by Dr. Schliemann in the inscriptions which he unearthed from the ruins of Troy. The archaic Greeks shortened one limb and wrote it ∧ . Later when the Greeks changed their manner of writing from right to left to our modern method of left to right they turned round all such signs as were reversible and altered it to ⌐ . The Romans made it ⟨ then time and swifter writing curved its point so that we use it thus C .

"Now N which is an even clearer case. That sound in Maya was drawn ⟂ . In early Phoenician we find it ⟂ and later ⟂ . The Greeks wrote it ⟂ and when they

19

reversed their writing it became 𝘕 as we use it to-day.

"The Maya O bears little resemblance to our own at first

sight 🐚 , but what is the essential characteristic about it?

Surely the circle within a circle at the bottom, ◉ which was the Phoenician form for that same sound. Later the inner circle became a mere dot ⊙ . Then people began

to say, 'Why bother about dotting your O's!'

"One more example which we will approach from a slightly

different angle. What, to your mind, does this represent?"

The McKay leaned over. "A foot or footprint I should say."

"Precisely and the Maya word for footprint or path is pronounced '*Be.*' Now see their hieroglyphic for the letter B. This time we have secured the essential characteristic by working from the opposite direction. It is the foot sign with the toes separated from it as a series of dots. Now behold the Egyptian hieroglyphic for the letter B — It is viewed from a different angle—but again we have a foot."

The Count leaned back and smiled. "I could give you many more instances of a similar nature, but I feel that these are enough to prove my point."

"You mean that it would be quite impossible for these two alphabets to have so many things in common and yet to have originated among two completely separate peoples."

"Exactly. It is utterly inconceivable that these, the only two systems in the world of conveying vocal sounds by written signs, did not spring from the same original source."

"Well, I'll grant you that." The McKay's lined face broke into a broad grin. "But what's all this got to do with Atlantis?"

"Good God! My dear Captain. Think for a moment. If the two had a common origin where was it? Although both

sets of hieroglyphics embody ideas which are common to both
alphabets, no archaeologists in their diggings from Iceland to
Cape Town or the jungles of Assam to the barren rocks of
Patagonia have ever discovered the common root from which
both must have sprung. Yet it must have taken thousands
of years' thought and experiment among a highly civilised
people to build up this unique system of vocal signs. Where
did they live? Why have we found no single trace of their
efforts to perfect this staggering invention when we can find
cave drawings which must be of a far earlier date in every
continent. They were the people of Atlantis of course, and
when their whole country was submerged in some terrible
cataclysm all the evidence of their gradual development to
this high state of culture perished with them. That is the
only possible explanation."

"It's a very forcible argument," the McKay admitted,
"but——"

His objection was cut short by Sally who arrived at that
moment with Prince Vladimir behind her, Nicky having now
secured Camilla from him.

"Nelson Andy McKay, come and dance with me," she cried
gaily.

"I'm too old for dancing," he protested, "you ought to
know that by now."

"You're not too old to dance with me," she laughed. "We
got on famously the other night. Come along—Admiral's
orders."

"Drat the girl!" he exclaimed pushing back his chair and
standing up with mock reluctance. His plea of advancing
age was a well-worn pose. Actually he loved dancing and,
given a good partner, could put up a very passable performance. With an old-fashioned little bow he offered Sally his
arm as he said: "Well, the result to your feet must be upon
your own head, m'dear," and they passed into the dance room.

When they returned to the terrace Camilla and Nicky came
out with them, and they found that Slinger and Doktor Tisch
had joined the Roumanian and Count Axel at the table so the
whole party was assembled again.

Camilla now devoted her attention to the Count and, as the
other two had basked equally in her favours, the latent
jealousy which was ever liable to flame into bitter anger
between the three was temporarily at rest. Sally and the
McKay had laughed a lot during their two long dances together

and the bald-headed Slinger, urbane as ever, was super-intending the icing of two fresh magnums of champagne. Camilla's party was undoubtedly proving a great success. Only the little German Doctor remained silent and depressed.

During his stroll with Slinger he had pressed for particulars of the dark business which was to be carried out on the trip, but Slinger had put him off with vague generalities and finally, the abrupt admonition that, once the job was done, he could go ahead with his scientific stuff—all expenses paid for as long as he liked, but if he wanted that, he'd best stay in his cabin and forget that Camilla and her friends even existed once they reached the Azores.

It was eleven years since Doktor Tisch had dug up and deciphered that little cylinder of baked clay at Eridu on the Euphrates which, by bearings on fixed stars, gave the actual position of the great city that had once been the capital of the lost continent. With all the fanaticism of a scientist who lives for his work alone he had slaved ever since on the compilation of vast folios which would prove to an unbelieving world that Atlantis had actually existed in order that he might persuade some millionaire to finance an expedition for its rediscovery. After three years' search he had found Klemo Farquason. All preparations had been completed and then, a month ago, when he was waiting for Farquason to join him in Paris he had received a cable reporting the financier's collapse.

His long cherished hopes completely shattered by this blow he had poured out his woes to an old friend, who had suggested that the millionaire Duchess might be persuaded to take Farquason's place, and provided him with an introduction to her satellite, Slinger. The shrewd confidential secretary had seen, in this projected expedition, just the opportunity he had been seeking for the carrying out of a plan which he had conceived in concert with a certain very powerful person in New York. Long cables had been exchanged in private code. New York approved. Slinger and the Doctor had met again, and the latter, in abject despair at the wrecking of his life work for the mere lack of money had been tempted into agreeing to bring his ship down to Madeira, to which the Duchess was proceeding, and where Slinger promised to persuade her to undertake the enterprise provided that the doctor was prepared to close his eyes to anything unusual which might happen once she was on board.

The Herr Doktor sipped his champagne and glanced across the table at his hostess. What did Slinger and his friends mean to do, he wondered, when they got this slim golden-haired young woman to his base in the Azores. The men of the party would endeavour to protect her, that was certain, and there were four of them—no three, the crooner could be counted out. Doctor Tisch did not take a good view of Nicky despite his Greek god profile: but the tall dark Roumanian appeared to have the strength and temper of a bull, the Swedish Count might prove a dangerous antagonist despite his frail scholarly appearance and the square-jawed British sailor looked the sort of person who would jump into a fight for the sheer love of the thing.

Slinger had promised faithfully that there should be no bloodshed but the little Doctor found it difficult to place much trust in his word.

Herr Doktor Tisch took another, longer, pull from his big goblet and coughed a little. Then he endeavoured to solace himself with the thought that there were 1,600,000,000 men and women in the world's population so if the worst happened and there was a fracas, of what real importance was it that half a dozen of them might get hurt—providing that his epoch-making expedition was enabled to go on.

CHAPTER IV

THE MC KAY MEETS HEAVY WEATHER IN A BULLO-CARRO

SHORTLY after, the party on the now moonlit terrace broke up once more. The two girls wished to dance again before the band stopped playing and the little Casino would be closing soon. Night life in Madeira is not prolonged into the small hours.

Nicky grabbed Camilla before Prince Vladimir Renescu could ask her, and Sally insisted on the McKay taking her for another turn. Doktor Herman Tisch excused himself on the plea of fatigue and Slinger decided to return with him to the Hotel so the Roumanian and Count Axel Fersan were left to keep each other company.

"It has been a day of excitements," declared the Prince pouring himself another goblet of champagne.

"It has indeed," Count Axel agreed politely. He had little in common with either of his rivals to Camilla's hand and millions, but while he regarded Nicky as a nasty little bounder, the transparently simple good nature of the broad shouldered young giant opposite rather appealed to him. He smiled his lazy, faintly supercilious smile into the Roumanian's flashing black-velvet eyes and went on amiably:

"I consider this expedition to rediscover the lost continent of Atlantis a thing of quite exceptional interest."

"By crikey! You cannot believe in this sunken continent except as a thing of the imaginations surely."

"I certainly do."

"Mon Dieu! Count, no! It is a story for cocks and bulls only."

"You think so? Yet you were as eager as the rest of us to persuade Camilla into financing this expedition after lunch to-day."

The Prince threw back his dark curly head and gave a great guffaw of laughter. "And for why not?" he asked spreading out his enormous hands. "My bankers pester me ever with stupid cryings that I have not enough money. That would matter nothing if they would make remit—but they do not,

24

pigs and liars that they are. This invitation from our so adorable Duchess comes my anxieties for remits to relieve. Am I a half-bake that I should say no. Besides—what opportunities! Before we reverse to harbour Camilla will be affianced to myself."

"Aren't you rather counting your chickens before they are hatched," observed Count Axel mildly.

"By crikey no!" exclaimed the Prince with cheerful boast-fulness, his dark eyes sparkling and his strong white even teeth flashing in a glorious smile. "Myself I know. Our so adorable Duchess I know also. Behold then, it asks only time and place—you will see. When all is done I will make a great presentings to you, to show my esteems, for I like you Count. As for that Nicky I will give him a great kick in his so colourful pants." Upon which declaration he happily tossed off a further ration of his so adorable Duchess' champagne.

"Thanks, that's nice of you," Count Axel murmured, then he added with mild cynicism: "Since Camilla will have to pay for it in any case I am delighted to promise you a similar gift should my own fortunes with her prove better than you are inclined to think."

Vladimir shook his head. "Ah, Count you are pleased to joke—but you will see. The wedding it shall be in my dear Roumania. There will be much dancing and many flowers. We will roast an ox for the people of my lands and get drunk ourselves on sweet sparkling wines—also the Tokay which my grandfather bring back when he was Ambassador to Vienna Court. This folly of Camilla's that she takes us all to seek a place that is not, in the Doctor's ship, is just what I have need to make settled my good plans."

"You are quite convinced that Atlantis never existed then?"

"No, no. Be wise—how could it?"

Count Axel had no intention of going over the long exposi-tion upon ancient languages to which he had treated the McKay. He doubted if this nice young giant had the brain to understand its importance, so he contented himself with saying:

"The assumption that it did is no more wild than that the Sahara was once a great inland sea, a fact upon which all the leading geologists are now agreed."

"Ah, but that differs. If the coast barriers were broke

25

down the desert Sahara might become sea again. Somewhere I have read that to be so—but it would alter no how the levels of the land. To make believe that great pieces of territory can all suddenly jump out of the ocean or fall down beneath it is a story for cocks and bulls."

"Not at all," declared Count Axel stung into argument despite himself. "At one time the entire surface of Great Britain was submerged under water to a depth of at least 1,700 feet. Over its face was strewn thick beds of sand, gravel, and clay, which the geologists term 'The Northern Drift.' The land then rose again from the sea bearing those water deposits upon it. What is now Sicily once lay beneath the waters of the Mediterranean yet it subsequently rose to 3,000 feet above sea level. Even in modern times there have occurred vast upheavals and subsidences. In 1783 Iceland sustained a colossal earthquake which killed one fifth of its population and the disturbance in the whole area was so great that an entirely new island with high cliffs was thrown up near by. Its size was so considerable that the King of Denmark considered it worth claiming officially and he named it Nyoe. The Andes mountains in South America have sunk 220 feet in the last seventy years. The fort and village of Sindra on the eastern arm of the Indus were submerged by an earthquake in 1819 together with a tract of country *2,000 miles in extent*. Such radical changes in the distribution of land and water have occurred throughout every century in the world's history and because the cataclysm that destroyed Atlantis chanced to be far greater than any disaster which has happened since that is no earthly reason for maintaining that the occurrence was a myth."

The Prince shrugged his broad shoulders. "Really Count, it would be an ugliness for me to make argument facing as I do your high knowledge. Atlantis did exist then if it please you. To myself it counts nohow except that from the strong interest the fat German holds in fossils I am given opportunity to speak of my mind to our so adorable Duchess. Permit me to brim your glass."

"You are incorrigible Prince." Count Axel smiled as he pushed his goblet across the table. "Almost you make me envious of your youth."

"Ah my poor Count—how I understand that for you."

"Almost, I said," submitted Axel, "but not quite. With age comes wisdom and experience and persons of my temper-

ament are apt to value that—more than they should perhaps
—but we are just made that way."

The band blared out the Portuguese National Anthem and
then, in deference to the British visitors who are the mainstay
of all entertainment enterprises on the island, God Save the
King. The two girls, Nicky, and the McKay joined the
others on the terrace. Ten minutes later the attendants began
to put out the lights so Camilla's party decided to return to
the Hotel.

Sally insisted on going back in a Bullo-carro, one of those
strange square curtained contraptions like a four poster bed
on sleigh runners—a form of conveyance peculiar to the island
of Madeira. Camilla told her that she was certain to pick
up fleas from the cushioned seats, but the McKay volunteered
to accompany her so they set off in their musty chariot while
Camilla and the others, disdaining to walk the half mile
through the scented night, were whirled away in a big car.

Beside the Bullo-carro walked its tattered driver urging on
his lazy bullocks with a constant stream of profane Portuguese
and frequent prods from a long bamboo cane. Occasionally
he ran forward and threw a sausage-like sack filled with mutton
fat beneath the runners to grease them and facilitate the
progress of the vehicle as it slithered and jolted over the
thousands of closely packed little round pebbles which formed
the surface of the road.

"What do *you* think our chances are of finding this lost
city?" Sally asked idly.

"About as good as of the King sending a boy scout to tell
me that he is recalling me from my retirement to make me an
Admiral of the Fleet," grunted the McKay. "The Doctor's
a nice little man but he's nuts, m'dear—nuts!"

"Count Axel doesn't seem to think so."

"No, the Count's got all sorts of bees in his bonnet. I like
him but he's gone cranky from too much learning. He treated
me to a long dissertation on ancient languages this evening
and made quite a good case of it too, but hieroglyphics
are like figures in a balance sheet, you can make 'em
prove anything provided you juggle with them cleverly
enough."

"What he told us about the Flood legends after lunch fitted
in with the Doctor's theory perfectly."

"Fairy tales m'dear—all of 'em. As well believe in the
Gorgon's head or the one-eyed Cyclops. If there were any

27

truth in these old wives' tales the scientists would have got on to it long ago."

Sally was silent for a moment. If the McKay was so sceptical about the motive for the expedition why was he so keen to come on it? Perhaps—Sally's mouth curved into a pleased smile in the darkness—because he welcomed the chance of spending several weeks in the same party as herself. Till now she had refrained from examining her feelings about him and her thoughts were vacillating like the needle of a compass on a merry-go-round. True he was no handsome young gallant but he had the high spirits of youth coupled with the poise of a man of the world—moreover he never even glanced at Camilla. Sally was jealous, bitterly jealous that an unjust God had created her so like Camilla in colouring, face, and form yet denied her just that millimetre of difference in features which made her only good looking where Camilla merely had to look at a man to turn his head. She never quite succeeded in cheating herself into the belief that Camilla's adorers were only after her money, but now, here was a very personable man who paid no attention whatever to Camilla—instead he quite unostentatiously, but persistently, sought her own company. Sally gave a little secret chuckle as she felt him put out a hand gropingly in search of hers.

Even if he was right in his belief that they were setting out on a fool's errand she felt that the party would be fun, if he was going solely to be with her and, wishing to make him admit that she sought to give him a lead by labouring its possibilities.

"I don't agree with you," she said softly as he took her hand. "For hundreds of years all the learned people scoffed at the local folk tale that there were two buried cities at the foot of Mount Vesuvius. They changed their tune though when a farmer sunk a well one day and went slap through the roof of a building twenty feet under ground which led to the discovery of Pompeii and Herculaneum. Look at the ridicule all the wiseacres used to pour on that poor old Greek Heroditus too. They laughed at his account of his travels in ancient Egypt and Asia Minor for over two thousand years and dubbed them sheer romance, but we know now that his descriptions of the countries that he visited were true, and marvellously accurate. Why shouldn't Plato's account of Atlantis be the same?"

"Because he never visited it m'dear. He got the story from

some old boy who got it from someone else and even then it was a nine thousand year old chestnut. If Camilla expects to find any lost cities under the ocean she's just pouring her money down the drain I tell you."

"But——"

"Now stop it," he interrupted quickly. "I've had my fill of erudition for one evening. You just be a good little girl and don't bother your head with such nonsense. We're all going to have a darn good trip at Camilla's expense, and she'll get plenty of fun herself exercising her 'circus.'"

As he squeezed her hand Sally's heart gave a thump. She waited a little holding her breath and then asked with deliberate casualness, "Well if that's all there's going to be to it why are *you* so keen to come?"

"That's easy," he replied without hesitation. "I'm poor, I love the sea, and it amuses me to watch the 'circus.'" Then, like a bolt from the blue he added meditatively: "I don't think I've ever seen a better looking woman than Camilla."

Sally pulled her hand away as if she had been stung. "I thought you didn't like her!" she snapped angrily.

"Yo ho!" he laughed. "Sits the wind in that quarter. You're jealous m'dear. Interested in one of the 'circus' yourself, eh? But believe me jealousy's a great mistake—even in a pretty woman."

There was a sudden silence in the Bullo-carro. Sally thanked God for the friendly darkness. Her cheeks were scarlet and her face burning. Only the creaking of the springless box broke the uncomfortable silence. The stuffy air behind the thick curtains was charged with emotions as heavily as is a battery with electricity.

It even began to penetrate the McKay's weather-beaten skin that Sally might resent his last speech and he searched clumsily in his mind for words with which to comfort her.

"I'm afraid that wasn't very polite," he said nervously. "I'm sorry m'dear. You know I'm looking forward to seeing a lot of you on board. I always thought you had a rotten time with Camilla. It can't be any fun seeing her get away with everything. Now be sensible and the old man will do his best to console you——"

"And himself I suppose," she flashed, then her eyes filled with angry tears as she hurried on, "But don't worry—the trip isn't coming off. Camilla's not all that set on going to sea for weeks on end if there's no real excitement of finding

29

lost cities to be had. We're due in Scotland at the end of the month and she was looking forward to that.''

"Hi! Half a moment, you're not thinking of trying to persuade her to back out, are you?" the McKay exclaimed in some alarm.

"I am."

"That would be awfully hard lines on the little doctor."

"Oh, you needn't concern yourself about him," said Sally bitterly. "Nothing's signed yet but I don't doubt she'll compensate him. She has so much money that she wouldn't miss it if she financed him to set off on his own. Anyhow I might just as well save her from being sponged on by people like *Captain* McKay."

"Tut—tut," he murmured. "Naughty, naughty temper. However, you were saying only this morning that Camilla never consulted you about anything and she's keen on this trip, stupid as its object may be, so the chances are all against your being able to get her to alter her decision now."

"You think so? Well you've provided me with ample reasons for its cancellation and taken special care to point out how dull it's going to be for me. I haven't lived with Camilla all this time without learning how to handle her, so you might as well resign yourself to the fact that she'll cut it out.''

"Thanks," replied McKay stiffly, "I'll believe that when I hear it from Camilla—not before."

"All right—wait and see!"

At that moment the Bullo-carro halted before the door of the hotel. Sally jumped out and, to avoid displaying her flaming cheeks and angry eyes, she flung a curt "Good-night" over her shoulder then, while the McKay was still paying off the man, dashed straight up to her room.

As he walked thoughtfully upstairs behind her the McKay was a little worried by this apparently senseless quarrel. Certainly he admired Camilla. She was good to look at like any other well executed work of art and, having a simple old-fashioned belief in God, he had always considered really beautiful women to be the high watermark of the Great Master's efforts in the creative field. She was probably quite a nice girl too, he felt, if one happened to care for her type of outlook and conversation but personally she bored him stiff. Whereas he liked Sally. There was no nonsense about *her* in the ordinary way and she gave a fellow a comfortable companionable sort of feeling which it was nice to have. He had been looking forward to this cruise with her even more than he had realised up to that moment and he knew that he was going to be distinctly disappointed if she blew it up.

By the time he climbed into bed he had assured himself that she couldn't be such a young ass as seriously to resent his chipping and that anyhow she hadn't sufficient influence with Camilla to outweigh the interest of all the others who were so obviously keen to go.

In the morning therefore he was somewhat disconcerted to receive, on his breakfast tray, a neatly typed note—which read:

> "Camilla, Duchess Da Solento-Ragina presents her compliments to Captain N. A. McKay, R.N., and regrets that, owing to unforeseen circumstances, she has been compelled to cancel the party which she had arranged to cruise in search of the lost continent of Atlantis on Doktor Herman Tisch's yacht."

CHAPTER V

THE ISLAND OF THE BLESSED

RENE P. SLINGER was not a handsome man. His bald polished skull and beaky nose were vaguely reminiscent of a vulture. But he had an easy manner and a shrewd, witty, way of summing up events and people that made him an acceptable companion in the most diverse company. Moreover, his tact was only equalled by his efficiency and he had a genuine flair for getting things done with rapidity and ease.

It was this latter quality in him which had appealed to Camilla when, three months before, her previous man of business had gone down with a duodenal ulcer. Slinger had been an international lawyer practising in quite a small way in Paris. The slump had robbed him of his only two really important clients and the fall in the dollar had driven two thirds of the expatriate Americans, who gave him their casual business, back to their own country. To save himself from bankruptcy he had been angling for some share of the work which Camilla had to give, when her manager was taken ill, and had taken over her arrangements, to begin with, apparently in a purely friendly way. She had been surprised, not knowing the state of his finances, but pleased when he had proposed himself as a permanency. A cable to her lawyers in the States had revealed nothing questionable in his past history and so she had taken him on.

His task of dealing with her accounts and charities, arranging her accommodation as she moved from place to place and organising her parties might appear an easy one in view of the almost limitless funds behind him but, as Camilla had a habit of altering her mind every second moment, the job required real ability and the utmost diplomacy. However, Rene P. Slinger was not the man to be content with such a dependent position despite the very handsome salary which she paid him, and would never have considered it, except as a makeshift during temporary difficulties, had not a certain very powerful person in New York urged him to take on the job with a view to arranging a highly secret enterprise which would prove far more remunerative.

Rene was completely unscrupulous and saw in this person's suggestion a reasonably safe way to permanent affluence. He had agreed at once, seized upon Doctor Tisch's misfortune as offering the very thing he needed to further his plan and, with his usual skilful handling of people and situations juggled the Doctor into acquiescence and Camilla into financing the expedition to rediscover Atlantis without appearing to be in any way responsible for her decision himself.

Now, the whole thing had blown up on him at the last moment and it was a very angry Rene P. Slinger who lured the miserable little Doctor out into a secluded portion of the hotel garden immediately after breakfast.

His thin beaky nose was rather red but that was indigestion. He did not display any signs of the intense irritation and annoyance that he felt but inside he was cold, hard, venomous and determined, as he faced the fat bristly-haired German scientist beneath a great bougainvilia bush covered with purple blossoms.

"See here," he opened up, "that darned British ex-Naval Captain doesn't believe in your lost Continent. He told his tale to Sally last night and she got at the Duchess after, so the whole party has been called off. Maybe the fool's right but whether he is or not I don't give a dime. What matter's is that this show's got to go on."

The Doctor's sandy eyebrows shot up into two arches, his fat red face showed surprise and dismay. "But I thought it was all settled," he protested. "I brought my ship to Madeira—I promised to close my eyes to what may happen when the Duchess is on board. . . . I need the wages for my crew. I shall be sent to prison if I cannot pay."

"You've said it," agreed Slinger laconically, suppressing for his own purposes the handsome offer of financial compensation which Camilla had charged him to make the little man when he broke the news.

"But this is terrible!" exclaimed the Doctor. "And what case have I, for nothing is signed yet."

"No nothing's signed yet," Slinger repeated with an unhelpful stare.

"The Captain is a liar and a fool," burst out the Doctor suddenly. "The continent is there—sunk beneath the ocean—also the gold. I will talk with the Duchess and give her proof."

33

"Can you?" asked Slinger with apparent scepticism.

"Proof and again proof! I can convince anyone who will listen."

"Well you'll be in a fine mess if you fail. But you know I'm out to help you and I've been counting on it that you'd be able to put up a show so I've fixed a meeting for eleven-thirty in Camilla's private sitting-room upstairs. Are you prepared to come and say your piece?"

"Ja! I will come and she will be convinced."

"That's the idea. Don't make it too long though or too mighty scientific. Just think up a few really telling facts."

"Leave it to me. I haf argued with damn fools before."

Slinger at last permitted himself the shadow of a smile. He felt that he had manœuvred the little Doctor into fighting trim and could trust him to do his utmost to persuade Camilla. He nodded encouragement.

"That's the stuff—but remember if you fail to put it over the expedition is definitely off."

"That must not be. To save my exploration I have already agreed to things which my conscience hates."

"Sure," Slinger agreed and they turned to stroll back to the hotel.

In the lounge at that moment four disappointed men were holding an unofficial conference. The McKay and Camilla's "circus". He found that all three of them had received similar notes to his own cancelling their invitation for the trip and, although Count Axel was the only one among them who understood the scientific possibilities of the venture and had been looking forward to it on that account, Nicky Costello, and Prince Vladimir were equally dismayed that the expedition appeared to have fallen through.

The two latter were now saying that, after all, the Doctor was a very clever man and, wild as his theories might be, it was a darned shame not to give him a chance to try them out since Camilla could well afford it.

The McKay was generally regarded as an interfering fool, as it was in the nature of the man to confess that his scepticism the night before had been mainly responsible for the party falling through. He still stoutly maintained his complete dis-belief in the whole fantastic story, but readily agreed to adopt a benevolent neutrality if the matter was reopened.

When they were summoned to the presence an hour later therefore, the Doctor had everybody's sympathy and backing.

Even Sally's interest had been reawakened, for she had just received an unexpected parcel from the town. It contained a table cloth and a dozen mats embroidered in the local Madeira work. A strange gift, to be sure, for a girl who always lived in hotels, but enclosed was a scribbled note from the McKay, "Souvenir of some very pleasant hours you were kind enough to devote to an old man in Madeira."

It must have cost him a lot she knew, probably more than he could really afford, and on thinking it over she saw that his choice of a gift was a subtle suggestion that she would soon be married, a pretty compliment. He evidently felt very contrite about the night before to go to such lengths to make his peace.

The Doctor gave a jerky little bow and addressed Camilla with a certain awkward dignity.

"*Gnädige Hertzogin.* It was with great distress that I heard the reversal of your decision yesterday."

Camilla smiled her golden smile. "I'm sure I owe you an apology, Doctor, but things were fixed up in such a hurry. When it was pointed out to me last night that, after cancelling lots of engagements to which I've been looking forward, maybe we'd be weeks at sea without finding anything after all, I felt I'd rather not go, but I'm willing to hear anything you have to say."

"Thank you. I hope to convince you that my proposition is no dream but a practical exploration which will bring results." As the Doctor plumped himself down in an arm chair the others settled themselves, then he began:

"The principal historical evidence for the one time existence of Atlantis is based on an account by Plato. He lived in Greece during the fourth century B.C. and received his particulars via his compatriot Solon who had travelled to Egypt half a century earlier.

"While in Egypt, Solon visited the city of Sais which lies in the Delta. There he conversed with an Egyptian priest and recounted to him something of Greek beliefs and what we now term their mythology; upon which, to quote if you permit, the Egyptian replied:

" '*Oh Solon, Solon, you Greeks are but children . . . in mind you are all young; there is no old opinion handed down among you by ancient tradition, or science which is hoary with age.*'

"The priest then went on to say that the reason for this was that there had been many partial destructions of mankind both by fire and flood, which had wiped out whole races and their histories with them; leaving nothing to prove that they had ever existed except vague legends among the distant peoples who had escaped these calamities. He instanced the story of Phaeton who, unable to manage the steeds of his father's chariot, the Sun, was said to have burnt up all that was upon the earth, and explained that this Greek myth was really a memory of a distant time when a declination of the bodies moving round the earth and in the heavens had caused a great conflagration."

"What's all that got to do with Atlantis though?" Nicky asked.

"Be patient please," the Doctor reproved him gruffly. "This Egyptian Priest then gave Solon an account of the last great natural occurrence which had decimated a large portion of the human race, the Atlanteans, nine-thousand years before; and I shall now give you the salient facts which emerge from Plato's written version of the story which came to him from Solon.

"There was once an island situated in front of the Straits of Gibraltar. It was larger than Lybia and Asia Minor put together and was the way to other islands from which one could pass through the whole of the *opposite continent surrounding the true ocean*. By that he meant America of course and he actually refers to the Mediterranean as being no more than an inland sea.

"In this island there was a great and wonderful Empire, founded so legend relates, by the god Poseidon—or Neptune if you prefer—who begat children by a mortal woman. The centre of the island was a plain which is said to have been the fairest of all places and very fertile. Near the plain was a small mountain and this was enclosed with alternate zones of water and land equidistant every way and turned, as with a lathe, out of the centre of the land. This district the god gave to his eldest son named Atlas; and to his twin brother, Gadeirus, who was born after him he gave the extremity of the island nearest the Straits of Gibraltar, and to others of his children other regions were given.

"Atlas was made King over them all, giving his name to the whole island continent and the surrounding ocean; and the royal line descended from him direct for many generations. The wealth of these kings and their kingdom is stated to have been greater than that of any known before or since—that is, to Plato's time. The Atlanteans were great miners and dug out of the earth every kind of mineral including orichalcum, of which there were large deposits, and this they considered more valuable than any other metal except gold. There were great forests which supplied them with all sorts of woods and sheltered many species of wild animals including elephants which furnished them with ivory. Flowers, cereals and fruits both wild and cultivated grew in great abundance and variety including one fruit which is spoken of as having a hard rind and providing drink, flesh and ointment.

"They employed themselves in building temples, palaces, and docks and bridged over the zones of water which surrounded the ancient metropolis; also they dug a canal three-hundred feet in width and a hundred feet deep which they carried about six miles in order to link up the capital with the open sea, thus making the circular zones of water into a great inland harbour.

"The central island upon which the Palaces and Temples stood was surrounded by a high stone wall with towers flanking its approach across the bridges, and the two zones of land also had stone walls protecting the whole length of their outer circuits. The stone which was used in the work was of three colours, white, black and red. It was quarried from underneath the outer as well as the inner sides of the land zones and they removed it in such a fashion as to hollow out covered docks having roofs formed out of the native rock. The wall which went round the outermost canal they covered with a coating of brass; the next wall they coated with tin, and the third which encompassed the citadel flashed with the red light of orichalcum.

"Within the citadel was the great temple of Poseidon and this was ornamented with increasing splendour by many generations until the whole of the outside, with the exception of the pinnacles, had been plated with silver, and the pinnacles with gold. In the interior of the temple the roof was of ivory adorned everywhere with precious metals, and the temple contained many solid golden statues, together with that of the god himself which was of such a size that it touched the roof of the building with its head. This huge statue of Poseidon represented him standing in a chariot drawn by six winged horses and surrounded by a hundred nereids riding on dolphins.

37

"Between the buildings of the capital there were pleasure gardens containing fountains of both hot and cold water supplied from underground springs; also cisterns, some open to the heavens and others roofed over which were used in winter as warm baths. In the grove of Poseidon, which appears to have been a very beautiful park, many rare trees flourished owing to the excellence of the soil. The surplus water was carried off by means of aqueducts passing over the bridges to the outer canal. There were many places set apart for exercise and in the centre of the larger land zone there was a race course a stadium in width which circled the whole island.

"The country outside the capital is described as a level plain surrounded by mountains which descended towards the sea. Those to the north were very lofty and precipitous, but to the south the plain spread out through the centre of the land measuring at its broadest 3,000 stadia in one direction and 2,000 in the other, which is about 345 miles by 230. The whole region of the island was said to lie towards the south and be sheltered from the north.

"There were many villages in the mountains with rivers, lakes and meadows which supported them independently of the towns, and the great plain had been scientifically cultivated during many ages by many kings. The plain was entirely surrounded by a circular ditch and Plato says of this:

" 'The length and width of this ditch were incredible, and gave the impression that such a work, in addition to so many other works, could hardly have been wrought by the hand of man. But I must say what I have heard.'

"It was a 100 feet deep, 220 feet wide and about 1,150 miles in length. It received the streams which came down from the mountains, wound round the plain, and was then let off into the sea. Smaller canals a hundred feet in width intersected the plain at intervals of a hundred stadia, roughly eleven and a half miles, and by these wood was brought down from the mountains to the city and the fruits of the earth were conveyed in ships from one place to another. Twice a year the crops were gathered since in winter they had the benefit of the rains and in summer they were able to irrigate the whole plain by means of their canals.

"Plato goes on to say that for countless generations, as long as the divine nature lasted in them, the Atlanteans were obedient to the law, rejoicing in all the blessings that sacred island, lying beneath the sun, brought forth in such abundance, and that their wealth did not deprive them of their self control; but that the divine portion of their nature began to fade away by becoming diluted too often, so that human nature got the upper hand. They became base, corrupt and evil. Then the father of the gods wished to inflict punishment upon them that they might be chastened——

"Here to our great loss Plato's story abruptly ends and it is believed that he died before the completion of his manuscript."

"It sounds almost too wonderful to have been true," said Camilla doubtfully. "Is all that you've told us in Plato's book?"

"Every point that I have touched upon," the Doctor assured her with his little bow. "Also many other marvellous descriptions. I have a copy here if you would care to verify."

"No, no, Doctor, we'll take your word. Go on please do."

"Very well then." He sat forward with his pudgy hands planted firmly on his fat bent knees. "Consider please the following facts.

"How could Plato have invented a story correctly describing the *opposite continent* of America which he speaks of as surrounding the *true ocean,* meaning of course its semi-circle from the Cape of St. Johns, Newfoundland to the north eastern point of Brazil.

"Atlas's brother Gadeirus was given the extremity of the island towards the Straits of Gibraltar, which in Plato's time was still called the region of Gades. We still have a memory of this in the Spanish city of Cadiz. Moreover, it is a curious fact that the Basque people differ from all other European races. Their language, which has preserved its identity in this western corner of Europe between two mighty kingdoms, resembles in its grammatical structure no other language of the old world in any respect, but it has incontestable affinities with the aboriginal languages of America and those alone.

"The fruit, having a hard rind, affording drinks, flesh and ointment, which Plato speaks of, is obviously the cocoanut, and the existence of Atlantis and other islands could alone account for the migration of it, and countless other examples of semi-tropical flora from one continent to the other.

"In all the hundreds of systems of writing which have been evolved by different races all are based upon picture drawings with two exceptions only, these are the Phoenician alphabet and the Maya alphabet of Central America. Both of these

39

are based upon the expression of vocal sounds by written signs. These correspond to such a remarkable degree that it is impossible to doubt their common origin.

"In view of that it is particularly interesting to note that when the Phoenicians founded their great colony at Carthage they constructed their harbour upon precisely the same principle as that which Plato tells us was the Atlantean plan used many thousands of years before. Both were inland and circular in formation, both had islands in their centre containing the most important buildings of the city. Moreover, we find that both peoples used covered docks for their shipping so that each harbour must have presented the appearance of a great ring of airship hangars right down on the waterline.

"Plato speaks of three kinds of stone being used in the construction of the Atlantean fortifications. In the Azores we find rocks red and white in colour and also great lumps of *black* lava. He also mentions hot springs and these too are abundant in the Azores.

"The metal termed by Plato 'orichalcum' is undoubtedly pure red copper. The importance of the stress which is laid upon this metal is enormous. In both hemispheres we have ample evidence of a Bronze Age and in both, weapons and utensils formed from this compound of approximately nine parts copper and one part tin are almost identical in appearance. The tin is added to give hardness and durability, but it is inconceivable that this fact should have been discovered in both continents simultaneously. *The Bronze Age must have been preceded by a Copper Age of several thousand years during which men worked copper alone without the addition of tin.*

"Where are the traces of this Copper Age? There is no evidence to be found of its existence in any portion of the known world. The explanation therefore is that it developed in Atlantis, and the barbarous peoples of the outer continents passed straight from Stone to Bronze upon the arrival of the cultured survivors from the Atlantean disaster."

"Just as the Arab countries to-day are passing straight from the horse to the aeroplane having entirely missed the era of roads and motor cars," put in Count Axel.

"Exactly—you make my point Count," the Doctor agreed with a throaty chuckle. "Now, to proceed:

"In Plato's description of Poseidon's temple he tells us that the god was represented as standing in a chariot with six

40

winged horses. In every representation of Neptune we see him thus. Why should the god of the sea always be pictured driving a chariot or mounted upon horseback? Because he was not, in fact, a sea king but a landsman, who ruled the great island in the centre of the ocean, the survivors of which filled all other peoples with awe because, when they came up out of the ocean, they had already achieved the domestication of the horse.

"Further, in connection with this domestication of wild animals. In all our history we have no evidence of fresh species of animals being tamed and made to serve human convenience. Such a development would take many thousands of years experiment and practice. Atlantis, safe in its island security from invasion by barbarians, alone supplies a satisfactory territory in which this tremendous work for humanity could have taken place.

"This also applies to the conversion of wild plants and grasses into cultivated flowers, orchards, and reapable crops. It is a singular fact, that despite their great range of species, we owe hardly a dozen useful plants to Australia, South Africa, America north of Mexico, New Zealand, or America, south of the River Plate. What is even more strange is, that of more than one third of our cultivated species we have no trace whatever of the wild originals. All our great cereals— wheat, oats, barley, rye and maize—must have been first domesticated in a vast antiquity or in some portion of the globe which has disappeared carrying many of their parent wild plants with it.

"Where could such a place have been. Have we a pointer to it? Yes, for we find the homes of many others which we *can* trace to be in the mainland regions bordering on the central Atlantic. Innumerable trees and plants are common to Europe and the Atlantic states of America yet are not to be found west of the Rocky mountains. Upon the Pacific coast there are no hollys, burr-woods, lindens, gums, elms, mulberrys, hickorys or beeches. How, if they could not cross the comparatively narrow mountain barriers could they have passed from one side of the great ocean to the other unless, at one time, there had been fertile land and chains of islands between."

"Seeds are carried by the sea and by birds," suggested the McKay.

The Doctor stared at him. "That is true and it might have happened in a few rare cases, but not more—over such a great distance, and why please did not the sea and the birds carry the same seeds to the fertile sunny shores of South Africa? No. A central Atlantic continent is the only practical solution to the problem. That was the nursery where, through countless generations, from a state of primitive husbandry up to that of trained horticulturists, men must have laboured to produce and perfect practically every cereal, fruit and vegetable which we eat to-day."

"All right, I'll give you that," grinned the McKay.

"Good. We go on then," the Doctor leaned forward again:

"The description of the wealth and magnificence of Poseidon's temple may at first seem overstrained in Plato's account, but we have its parallel in the great temple of the Sun god of the Incas at Chuzco in Peru. When this was first visited by Pizarro thirty years after Columbus discovered America he states that it was a veritable mine of gold. Images, pillars, cornices, and even the flowers in the sacred garden being fashioned from the precious metal. The gold from that astounding temple was shipped home in the Spanish treasure fleets and, although it has been reminted many times in various currencies, its bulk was so great that it still represents a considerable portion of the gold currency in circulation in the world to-day.

"To leave Plato now and note various other correspondences. Our biblical legend states that Noah was the hero of the Flood. The ancient Mexicans had a similar story and a similar hero, they called him Nata, or Noe. In yet another aboriginal American tongue he is known as Hurakan, which has a strange resemblance to our own word *hurricane*, and they may well have christened him that on account of his coming up out of the great tempestuous waters.

"The Mandan Indians, although an inland people, preserve amongst them as the central focus of their religion an Ark, which they term the Big Canoe. Each year one of their witch doctors is painted white all over and comes among them as the white man who arrived from the waters bringing them peace, civilisation and prosperity.

Our Bible story tells us that Noah caulked the seams of the Ark with asphalt and we find the greatest pitch lakes in the West Indies. Further we are told that God gave the rainbow as His sign that He would never again destroy the earth by a deluge. This is also the belief of the Peruvians.

42

"The Mexicans, like ourselves, baptised children with a view to cleansing them from original sin. They mummified their dead as did the Egyptians; and many curious unnatural customs with regard to childbirth are common to both hemispheres.

"Even the place names of Central America and the earliest civilised regions of the Mediterranean bear a resemblance which it is almost impossible to explain except by the Atlantean theory. Chol, Zuivana, Colua and Cholima are four ancient Armenian towns. In Central America we have Chol-ula, Zuivan, Colua-can and Colima. The gods Pan and Mais of the Greeks are to be found as Pan and Maya in Central American mythology. The god of the Welsh, Hu the Mighty is found in Hu-natu, the hero god of the American Quiche Indians. Bel or Baal, the Phoenician deity whose cult is to be found in all parts of Europe, is represented almost as strongly by Balam among many tribes of American aborigines. And perhaps more important than any of these the great Sun god Ra of Egypt is identical with the Peruvian Sun god Ra-mi.

"Examine resemblances between the Chiapenee American Indian and Hebrew. 'Son' in one is *Been*, in the other *Ben*, 'daughter' *Batz* in the first and *Bath* in the second, 'father' *Abagh* in one, *Ahba* in the other. 'King' is *Molo*——"

"Hi stop!" exclaimed Nicky. "This is getting too much for me. Let's get on to something else."

"I regret Herr Costello if I bore you," the Doctor said frigidly, "but these explanations are necessary to prove my case. I shall not detain you much longer."

"I'm sorry," Nicky apologised, "forget it please and go right on with what you want to say."

"I thank you. The very word *Atlantis* speaks for itself. *Atlas*, we are told, was the first King of *Atlantis* and gave his name to the *Atlantic* ocean, the Mexican word *Atl* means water. There is an *Atlas* Mountain in Morocco, a town called *Atlan* on the shores of Central America. The *Atlantes* were a people well known to the Greeks and Romans who lived on the North West coast of Africa. In Central America we have the *Aztecs*, whose history states that they originally came from a country called *Aztland*. What can be clearer than the association between these two opposite points in the *Atlantic* ocean.

"In Plato's account of Atlantis he speaks of a vast canal system, great harbours, bridges and fortifications. The

43

Peruvian roads and bridges through the passes of the Andes were feats of engineering which have hardly been surpassed in the modern world. The canal system in Egypt alone enabled a sufficient area to be placed under cultivation for so great a population to exist in the restricted valley of the Nile. The artificial lake of Moesis, which they created as a reservoir, was 450 miles in circumference and 350 feet deep with subterranean channels, flood gates, locks and dams by which the wilderness was reclaimed from sterility. The Mexicans and the Egyptians both erected stone structures, similar in type, which are larger and more durable than anything modern civilisation has yet produced—their Pyramids. Owing to their inaccessibility to the ordinary traveller it is not sufficiently recognised that those in the New World are greater than those in the Old. The base of the pyramid at Choula covers 45 *acres* of land compared to the 12 *acres* covered by the great pyramid of Cheops in Egypt. The masonry of both people had reached such a degree of accuracy that the joints in their stone work are scarcely perceptible and not wider than the thickness of silver paper. Both had astrological systems showing a degree of scientific exactitude with which we have caught up only in the last century *yet, neither of these amazing cilivisations had any infancy and their art has no archaic period.*

"Ten thousand years would be but little for man to develop from a cave dwelling savage to such a high state of culture, yet all trace of that 10,000 years has been blotted from the face of the earth. Suddenly, from nowhere it seems, this race who must have appeared like gods to the barbarians, arrived in countries thousands of miles apart; and in a few generations they are creating marvels that have never been surpassed. Where did they come from? Where is the evidence of their long struggle against nature? The only conceivable explanation is the acceptance of Plato's record—that it lies beneath the waves that cover the lost continent.

"If further evidence is needed we have abundant historical memories to confirm the belief embodied as mythology in the religions of these races which had been completely separated for thousands of years until the rediscovery of the New World in the fifteenth century. The Incas and the Aztecs trace the foundation of their empires to a fair-haired, blue-eyed bearded stranger, who came up from the waters out of the East. This god-like figure is found with many names but all accounts agree that he brought with him infinite knowledge, peace and prosperity, teaching them husbandry, metallurgy, weaving, and to live in houses instead of rude tents and caves; then, after giving them a new code of laws his spirit returned to the island Paradise in the *East* from which he had come.

"It was on account of a similar fully accepted belief, so Cortes relates, that he was able, with a handful of white men, to subdue the legions of the Mexican Emperor Montezuma. They believed that their bearded myth heroes had come again from their island Paradise in the *East* and they fell down in their thousands before the Spanish lord, Alvarado, worshipping him as a god in human form because he possessed the white skin, the blue eyes, the magnificent golden hair, which tallied in all particulars with those of his predecessor who had brought them the blessings of civilisation.

"Turn now to the Mediterranean side of the Atlantic. The ancient peoples of the Euphrates believed that Ea, god of the Ocean, first brought civilisation from out of the great waters of the *West* to Assyria. In the Osiris legends of Egypt we get an exact parallel of the Mexican belief. The fair-skinned golden-haired Osiris arrived among the dusky primitive Egyptians, taught them the arts of agriculture, architecture and to observe a new highly civilised code of laws. Then his spirit departed to the islands of Sekhet-Aaru in the *West*, which are specifically stated to be intersected by canals filled with running water, which caused them to be always green and fertile. Wherever we turn in the mythologies of the Mediterranean peoples we find constant and persistent mention of this antediluvian world, the Garden of Eden, The Elysian Fields, The Gardens of the Hesperides and the Islands of the Blessed. Invariably this happy state is situated towards the *West* in the great open ocean that lies beyond the Straits of Gibraltar; so that the belief is even perpetuated in Europe to this very day in that colloquial expression for death 'to go *West*'.

"The ancient universal belief in the spirits of the dead going to an underworld is part of the same tradition. It was not until comparatively recent times that the expression was taken to mean a world under the earth. It signified originally the world beyond or *under the horizon*.

"The only possible explanation therefore of the American Heaven being placed in the *East* and the Mediterranean peoples' Paradise being universally in the *West*, is that it lay

45

somewhere between the two and is a race memory of that great peaceful island where all civilisation was first born, in the centre of the Atlantic.''

As the Doctor ceased there was a moment's hush then, his lined face breaking into a boyish smile, the McKay exclaimed:

"Doctor, I owe you an apology. I had no right to express an opinion without knowing more about the subject. I couldn't attempt to confute a single one of your arguments if I racked my brains for a month.''

"There are more—details—checkings up, a hundred points I have not yet touched upon," the Doctor burst out determinedly. "Take the mound builders——"

"Take nothing!" Nicky interrupted, "I've had enough. Once I was through College I took a vow against learning. We've heard all we want to of this mystic isle. What about it now Camilla?''

"The Doctor has convinced me about his theory all right," Camilla hesitated a moment. "But is the expedition practical —that's what I want to know?''

"That's it," echoed Sally. "Is there a chance in a hundred of our finding this place that's been eleven and a half thousand years beneath the seas?''

"Yes, yes, Fraulein," the Doctor insisted. "Ten years ago, even with the secret of the latitude and longitude which I possess—no. Five years ago—no. But now that Dr. William Beebe has invented his bathysphere for deep sea-diving—yes. In my model which is much larger I will take you to the very place where is the sunken gold.''

"In that case I'm all for it," Sally agreed, and Camilla smiled round at them.

"All right then—the party's on if you wish.''

Thus the final decision was taken which led this diverse group of people into the strangest adventure that has ever befallen men and women in our time.

CHAPTER VI

THE THREE LOVERS OF CAMILLA

D OKTOR HERMAN TISCH'S mystery ship was steaming almost due North-West towards the little coast town of Horta on the island of Fayal in the Azores. He had chosen it for his base in preference to Punta Delgada on the larger island of Saint Miguel because it lay nearer to the spot which was indicated on the precious cylinder of baked clay that he had unearthed from the banks of the Euphrates.

Eleven thousand four hundred years is but a split second in astronomical time and it needed only decimal corrections in the bearings of the fixed stars to give him the exact site where the mighty capital of Atlantis had once stood.

37° 52″N. 27° 8″W was the all important cypher which he kept locked in his own brain. He had an almost morbid dread that some one might steal his secret and forestall his great discovery so he would not even make a jotting of the map reference in his note book. When Camilla had pressed him, as her right through financing the expedition, for details of their destination, he had refused to say more than that the place lay between the latitudes of Richmond, Virginia; and Lisbon; which still left him sixty miles leeway, and he refused to give any indication of its longitude at all so they still knew only that it was somewhere to the southward of the Azores.

This uncharted point upon the map which held all the Doctor's interest lay well within the 1,000 fathom line. There might be pockets of a greater depth, of course, but he had 10,000 feet of cable on his drums, and so enough to reach bottom in the bathysphere, even if it was nearly double the depth that he anticipated, for the few miles round that area in which it was his unshakable conviction that the Golden Temple of Poseidon had once reared its flashing pinnacles to the sky.

All thoughts of Slinger's sinister designs upon Camilla which, at the last, had alone made his expedition possible, had left him. He was consumed with impatience now to reach his destination and get to work so on their first morning

47

out from Madeira he paced the deck oblivious of his surroundings while the others explored the ship.

It was an ex-cargo vessel of 2,500 tons, its forward part and midships converted to the semblance of a private yacht. Below the bridge a wide lounge with comfortable furniture and gay chintz curtains opened on to the sun deck where what had formerly been the forward hatch was boarded and canvassed to form a swimming pool. The dining room lay beneath the lounge and on either side of it were the cabins which accommodated the guests. To Camilla's annoyance the ship had no deck cabins but she had one which contained a private bath and sitting-room forming the owner's suite. Contrary to usual arrangements the entire accommodation abaft the bridge below decks was given over to the crew, while above, all the available space was occupied by the huge drums which carried the cable of the bathysphere and the massive machinery for lowering it into the depths. The bathysphere itself, supported by two huge steel girders locked into the hull of the ship, rode on the water line astern.

Captain Ardow took Camilla and her party round. They were, at first, uncertain of his nationality but on enquiry found him to be a Russian. He was a tall, lean, grey man, courteous but silent and unsmiling. Camilla invited him to dine that night but he asked her to excuse him with a firmness that discouraged her from pursuing the suggestion and went on to request that she would not extend similar invitations to his officers during the voyage or encourage them to mingle with her guests. As his reason for this lack of sociability he stated that the crew, which had been scraped together at the last moment, was a mixed one; so his officers would need to supervise it closely if the ship was to be kept neat and trim and he preferred that they should not be distracted from their duties.

Slinger congratulated himself upon his choice of Captain, for when he had made his arrangements with the Doctor in Paris he had insisted on selecting his own man for the job with power to pick his officers and crew. Evidently Captain Ardow meant to earn the very considerable sum he had been promised for his complaisance. He was taking no chances that any of his people should warn Camilla that something queer was afoot or cause trouble at the last moment through having formed a pleasant association with any member of her party during the trip.

48

For a few moments they all stood in the stern of the ship staring at the great spherical steel bathysphere with its row of small round protruding windows like flat eyes on short thick stalks.

"I should have thought that the glass in those portholes would have been liable to burst, however thick they are, under the immense pressure they will have to sustain at any considerable depth," remarked Nicky.

"They are not glass but fused quartz," replied Captain Ardow.

"How can you see through quartz?" enquired Camilla, "the bits I've seen in museums are all misty even when it's the kind that's supposed to be lumps of crystal."

"This is fused," Count Axel informed her with his quiet smile. "Not only is it far stronger than ordinary plate glass but infinitely clearer. So clear in fact that when you look through it things appear to be nearer than they are."

"That's fair enough," agreed Nicky, "and I don't doubt we'll see the ocean bottom plenty but we can't get outside that thing once we've been screwed into it so what I don't get is how we're to pick up the gold when we find it."

"There are dredges underneath the sphere which can be operated by electricity from inside it," Captain Ardow told him. "You cannot perceive them now for they are under water, but they are like the claws and pincers of a great crab."

Prince Vladimir Renescu stood by, a faintly supercilious smile on his firm lips. The arguments of Count Axel and the Doctor for the existence of Atlantis had passed right over his head. He still regarded the whole trip only as a heaven sent opportunity to get Camilla on her own. That afternoon he succeeded.

Count Axel Fersan, who was employing his very considerable brain to counter the physical attractions of his younger rivals, had decided to allow them to expend their powder and shot, since he was reasonably certain that Camilla enjoyed playing with all three of her suitors so much that she would not get engaged to any of them before the voyage was nearly at an end.

Little as he had in common with Nicky therefore, he buttonholed him after lunch in order to give the Roumanian his chance. Prince Vladimir took it and rushed Camilla off to have another look at the bathysphere since that was at the secluded end of the ship.

49

No sooner had they reached the stern than he shot one contemptuous glance at the big ball and said: "So we do divings in that round iron house eh? Wait here and we will talk of pleasant things far more."

Then he disappeared among the masses of machinery, to return a few moments later, red faced and breathless from his haste and the fear that one of the others might find Camilla on her own, with a pile of cushions and rugs. These he spread carefully on a few feet of open deck and with a smiling bow invited her to be seated.

Camilla was an artist at reclining gracefully and now she disposed her delicious limbs to their utmost advantage on the couch he had prepared; but her charming pose was rudely disturbed a second later for, with amazing speed and dexterity, he suddenly snatched at both her shoes and pulled them from her feet.

"Vladimir!" she exclaimed sharply.

He only laughed and his great deep healthy booming merriment drowned the hissing of the waters as they foamed from the screws, beneath the bathysphere, out into the white wake of the ship.

"You escape me not at all—now or hereafter," he declared. "Prisoner most precious I have you mine."

"Vladimir don't be stupid," she smiled. "Give me back my shoes."

He shook his dark curly head. "Not so, while I have you are compelled here to repose. Also your feet so small are godlike to behold. I could eat them for pleasure," then suiting the action to the idea he took one in his great fist, and carrying it up to his mouth, bit her big toe.

"Vladimir!—you idiot! Stop I say!" Camilla insisted, but she felt a sudden thrill run through her as, releasing her foot, his white teeth flashed in a quick smile, and he declared:

"This voyage I shall persuade you of myself and we will make happiness together. When we are so put, I will bite you all over."

"We are not going to be 'so put'. You'd better understand that Prince," she said a little nervously. "I don't approve of that sort of thing unless people are married."

"But you have me misunderstood," he protested, and his black velvet eyes stared into her with sudden seriousness. "As my wife I will bite you all over—not before. Think

50

upon it—all the happiness we will make morning, noon and by night."

"Is that another proposal of marriage?"

"Why yes. I am to you loving with desperateness. Take then my homage heartfelt so deep. The rank which should be by right with your so marvellous beauty I delight to give. Think of it. Prince Vladimir Renescu and his Princess. No couple so handsome would be in Europe. Young marrieds, as you say, very rich, very chic—everywhere most welcome. Also any man who speaks that you are not the most beautiful woman in the world—I strangle with these two fists." He held out his leg of mutton paws.

Camilla smiled and shook her head. "I can't decide just yet. Nicky and Count Axel both want me to marry them too."

He shrugged his vast shoulders. "Count Axel is a man of rank but not enough—also he is old. He must be fifty at the smallest, and he could not make happiness as I, who have no fatigues—ever. As for Nicky—no. You could not. He is one indivisible cad. Presently I kick him in his so colourful pants."

"You will do no such thing. You'd find Nicky a dear if you tried to understand him."

"For me that can never be. I am a Prince and he is a cad," declared the Roumanian with simple logic.

"You are a *snob*," smiled Camilla lazily, "but nevertheless I like you Vladimir—awfully."

"You like me eh!" His black eyes sparkled as he bent above her. "In that case—by crikey—we will kiss." And they spent the remainder of the afternoon that way.

After tea Vladimir tried to follow up his advantage but Camilla refused to be drawn away from the forward deck. Slinger had organised a deck-tennis tournament and, in the intervals between sets, those who were not playing either watched the others or the waves peacefully dissolving one into another on the limitless expanse of ocean.

Despite the sea's apparent emptiness there was always something of interest to observe. A school of round-backed porpoises leaping and diving as they ploughed their way to the south-eastward across the bows of the ship; a huge solitary sea turtle, floating idly in the waves, far from his home upon the Moroccan shore; the fate of a bucket of refuse that one of the cooks shot without warning from the galley below, and the graceful swoop of the screaming gulls from the mast-head as they dived to secure the floating crusts. Cocktail time came and went, then the party dispersed to change for dinner. The lazy hours of the day had drifted pleasantly by as they are apt to do in fair weather upon a ship at sea.

Dinner was cheerful but uneventful and after the meal Count Axel, pursuing his subtle policy of letting his rivals do their worst, suggested bridge. He knew that neither Camilla nor Nicky cared for the game whereas Vladimir not only prided himself upon playing a fine hand but being a born gambler in addition could not resist the lure of a pack of cards.

The Prince hesitated only a second. He did not consider that he had anything to fear from Nicky. It was inconceivable to him that his so beautiful Duchess could seriously contemplate marrying the crooner; whereas he regarded the clever, polished, Count Axel, whose age he exaggerated, as a really dangerous competitor. If the Count was willing to tie himself to the card table for the evening why should he not do likewise and enjoy his favourite recreation. Immediately he learned that Sally and the McKay were willing to make up a four, he agreed at once.

Slinger, as usual when his presence was not required, tactfully disappeared upon his own concerns so Nicky, quite unaware that Count Axel had arranged matters for his especial benefit, shepherded Camilla out on to the starlit forward deck.

"Sing something for me Nicky," she said as soon as they were settled.

"No," he shook his smooth fair head, "let's talk. I've got a heap of things I want to say to you."

"Presently. Sing something for me first. They'll be cooped up in there over their bridge for hours—so we've got lots of time." Her voice held a gently intimate note which flattered him. One of Camilla's many great attractions as a woman was her ability to make anyone whom she wished to please at the moment think that she really wanted to be with them *all* the time.

"All right," Nicky agreed and sitting on the deck at her feet, his hands clasped round his knees, he threw back his head and began to sing.

Some people like listening to crooners. Obviously many people must, for the records of the theme songs from Nicky's pictures sold in their millions all over the world. Camilla certainly did, and lay back with half closed eyes savouring to the full the primitive emotionalism of "Dear Baby God Gave Me I'm holding your hands", and "In all the world Mother—there's no one like you". Not so the McKay, who fifty feet away in the deck lounge, trumped his partner's trick, apologised and muttered fiercely: "God! how I'd like to tan that youngster's hide." Prince Vladimir only smiled darkly, recognising that it is impossible to sing and make love at the same time. He felt that he had less reason than ever to fear Nicky as a rival and that he had been wise to settle to his beloved cards while Camilla amused herself with her pet clown.

Ordinarily Nicky was extremely averse to giving free performances either in private or public. For one thing he very wisely took the greatest care of his voice, and for another he quite seriously thought of himself as the successor to Caruso who had developed his talents in a slightly different field. Having once got going however he did not stint his numbers. The soft night air, the illusion of being alone with Camilla on the face of the great waters, the ceaseless hissing of the wavelets as they rustled past the ship's bows, the faint starlight, all worked upon his artistic temperament and as time slipped by he sobbed out song after song with ever increasing pain and emotion. Suddenly he ceased and buried his face in his hands.

"What is it Nicky?" Camilla enquired gently.

"I love you," he muttered, "I'm miserable because I love you so."

"Are you?" Camilla smiled. "But I like you Nicky—awfully."

"Then why won't you marry me," he shot out sullenly.

"But my dear—I said I'd think it over."

"Words! words!" he exclaimed tragically, now visualising himself in the role of betrayed lover. "Camilla, you're driving me to despair. I love you! I want you! We were made for each other. What is it that has come between us? You were so sweet to me only two nights ago—and now—" he paused dramatically as though choking on a sob.

"Nicky dear, I haven't changed I——"

"Don't lie to me! Not that! I couldn't bear it!" he interrupted, passing a hand across his eyes as all the old clichés from a hundred parts he had played in the past came tumbling from his tongue. "Tell me the truth. I'm brave and I can bear *that* although life will never be the same again. I'm not a Prince. I'm not even a Count. I'm only a man who has worked his way up from nothing—I know that— but I love you Camilla. I love you more than words can say."

"Dear Nicky," cooed Camilla happily, allowing her hand to rest lightly on his bowed head. She was very gentle about it though knowing that he hated to have his fair, slightly wavy hair disturbed or ruffled.

He turned and caught her hand, bringing it quickly to his lips as he instinctively changed his role to that of the Other Man who has just come into the life of the woman with the drunken husband. "Camilla—dearest—you must leave all this! Let's go away together! I'll take care of you—I swear it! We'll start life anew. Just you and I in some place where no one knows us. It will be heaven to have you with me always. Poor little girl you've had a rotten deal—but I'll make up to you for everything."

Nicky had got himself so wrought up by this time that he made the unfortunate mistake of unconsciously dropping into the lines of his last big part which Camilla recognised. Angrily she jerked her hand away, and cried: "I haven't had a rotten deal and I don't want to be taken anywhere."

"Ah!" Nicky stared at her with a pained look as she hurried on: "In another moment you would have broken into your theme song and I don't care about being made fun of that way."

Just as though a bucket of ice cold water had been slung over him Nicky came out of his highly emotional state. The hard practical side of his nature reasserted itself instantly and he saw that he had slipped up badly. Without the flicker of an eyelid he passed from unconscious to conscious acting and gave a sad little laugh.

"Camilla how can you be so unfair to me just because I happened to use the same words to you that I had in that fool part. In this case I *meant* them. You *have* had a rotten deal and I *would* like to take you away from all this."

"I don't quite see what you mean," Camilla confessed intrigued despite herself.

"Why all this money you inherited. Money's not everything you know."

"Oh that."

54

"Yes. It prevents you knowing who your *true* friends are. Surely you don't think this Roumanian Prince and Count Axel would be running after you if you hadn't got a cent—do you? And I'm sorry for you Camilla. Sorry to see you deceived by all this flattery and hypocrisy just because of your wealth. That's why I'd like to take you away because I know that *we* could be happy together even if we were poor."

"I don't think I'd care much about being poor," said Camilla doubtfully.

"Well not poor exactly. My expenses are mighty heavy. Advertising costs a lot and my business manager takes a pretty useful cut but I'd have enough to keep you with all you'd need outside a yacht. That's what I'd like to do, and I'd be a sight happier if you hadn't got this great pile of cash."

"Would you really, Nicky?"

"Sure I would. Besides I hate to see you wasting your life among this crowd of spongers—doing nothing. You're worth better things than that. I'd like to see you doing something, making a big name for yourself you know."

Camilla's blue eyes brightened. "D'you think I could Nicky. How would I do that?"

"Why in the film game of course. There's not a girl in Hollywood that's got half your looks."

"That's the one thing I've always longed for—to be a film star," she said dreamily. "But it's no good—you see I can't act."

He shrugged disdainfully. "You don't have to. Film stars are not born but made these days. It's just a matter of a little preparation and a first class director does the rest."

"Is that true—really? Do you think then that someone would take me on and make me a star?"

He shrugged again. "They might, but the competition's something frightful and most of the big men have their own axe to grind when they're out picking stars. However—"

He paused feeling that now was the time to bring up his heavy artillery and produce the scheme he had hatched for his own benefit while holding out the bait of fame to dazzle her.

"However—what," she prompted leaning forward.

"Well. There's no denying that big money has its uses now and then. In this case for instance—say you set your

55

mind on becoming a star. What's to prevent you forming a company. I've made a useful packet and I'd put in all I've got. If we were married we could go some quiet place for a six months honeymoon where it would be fun instead of work for me to teach you all I know—and I know plenty. Then we'd get Markowitz to tune you up before directing you in a real big picture where we'd play opposite each other. Camilla if you were really game to do your bit by this time next year you could make Garbo come off her silent stunt and scream with jealousy."

For a moment Camilla sat spellbound fascinated by the supreme crown to a lovely talentless woman's ambition that Nicky was offering her. Then a gay voice broke in behind them.

"Have you any more so marvellous stories Nicky for the cocks and bulls?"

The bridge party having just broken up, Prince Vladimir had come silently across the deck and caught the drift of Nicky's last sentences.

Furious with indignation Nicky stumbled to his feet and confronted the Roumanian.

"You damned eavesdropper! Get to hell out of here!" he cried, his face dead white his hands clenched but trembling.

Vladimir's teeth flashed in a contemptuous grin. "Hold your peace whippersnap," he sneered, "or with one fist I will lift you overboard."

"You lousy wop!" screamed Nicky temporarily blinded to fear by his almost maniacal anger at having had his attempt to get control of Camilla's fortune exposed and ridiculed.

The Prince's eyes suddenly went blacker than the night, his smile became fixed and terrifying. He lifted one huge fist.

"Stop!" Camilla threw herself between them as the McKay seized Vladimir's arm from behind.

"How dare you," she stormed at the Prince. "How dare you start quarrelling in front of me." Then she swung on Nicky. "You've been abominably rude—you'd better apologise I think—both of you to each other."

"All right, I'm sorry," muttered Nicky sullenly.

The Prince shrugged. "In deference to my hostess I express regret."

Camilla turned to Count Axel, who was standing by, and almost instinctively took his arm. "Why is it," she asked

56

sadly as he led her back to the lounge, "that those two cannot remain civil to each other for five minutes?"

"Alas Madame," Count Axel's tone was filled with pained regret, "the Prince is still very young and unfortunately possesses a most unreliable temper coupled with very few brains; while Nicky has the misfortune to have been deprived during his youth of those social advantages which are, after all, the most important part of a gentleman's education." Thus, in one sentence, Count Axel disposed of any headway which his rivals might have made during the day.

The following morning the weather was again bright and clear. The sea, if anything, was even smoother, and the rise and fall of the water in the canvas swimming pool barely reflected the slight pitch of the ship as she held steadily on her course.

Camilla had not quite forgiven Vladimir. She did not resent his interruption of her tête-à-tête the night before so much as his tactless assumption that the possibility of her outgarboing Garbo, if she put her mind to it, was a story for cocks and bulls. Nicky did not put in an appearance when the rest of the party assembled round the swimming pool at ten o'clock. He was still under the impression that the Prince had shown him up for the fortune hunter that he was and unaware that Camilla's vanity had been so tickled by his proposals that she had failed to see his obvious self interest at the bottom of the scheme. As he remained, like Achilles, sulking in his tent, Camilla selected Count Axel for the target of her smiles.

Feeling that he had many days before him the Count did not seek to press his advantage in the least but slim, supple and enchanting in her sunbathing suit she came to sit beside him after they had had their swim.

"You are neglecting me shamefully Count," she declared. "I hardly saw you yesterday."

"Madame that was my loss," he inclined his scholarly head in a little bow, "but we have all to-day before us. Let me see if I cannot win your good graces by suggesting a new entertainment for you."

She liked the way he called her Madame. It lent her the dignity that she was never quite sure that she possessed. Smiling at him as she dangled her long legs over the side of the pool she said: "Now's your chance then Count. I'm all for new amusements."

"You will give me your promise then to play this game with me?"

"Well," she hesitated. "If it's to be with you alone I think I'd like to know first what it is."

Count Axel's blue eyes twinkled under their half lowered lids. "It is a game for three," he reassured her. "You, I, and one other."

"All right then—fire away."

"We will get the good Doctor to stop this ship and take us down for a trial trip in his bathysphere."

Camilla paled a little. "But—but do you think that would be quite safe?"

"Certainly. We shall send it down empty first to see that its windows and door resist the pressure of the water. If all is well there should be no danger after."

"I think I'd be scared of doing that."

"A little perhaps—but not too much," he encouraged her. "After all you do not mean to miss the wonderful thrill of seeing the sunken city if we find it surely—so you must make your first dive some time. Why not now?"

"But would there be anything worth seeing here in the open sea?"

The Count raised his mental eyes to heaven at the stupidity of the question but his placid smile remained unchanged. "Why yes. All sorts of fish, octopus perhaps, and all the teeming life of the great ocean. No aquarium that you have ever visited could compare with such a sight. If you will come I promise that you shall not have one dull moment and will thank me ever after for being the first to introduce you to such marvels."

It was an invitation which many men might have hesitated to accept, but Camilla was no coward and although her voice was a little breathless she nodded. "All right let's."

Doctor Tisch was furious when he was informed of her decision. His only thought now was to reach the Azores as quickly as possible in order that Slinger and his confederates could get through with whatever dubious business they meditated against Camilla and her party—and leave him free to proceed with his scientific investigation.

He protested in vain that the bathysphere had already been tested in European waters, that the dive was pointless, and that oxygen would be wasted to no purpose. Count Axel met his every objection and, since there was not the faintest indication of bad weather approaching, the Doctor was compelled to give in.

By eleven o'clock the whole party and a good portion of the crew had assembled aft. The ship was hove to facing the gentle swell. The tackles attached to the winches hauled the bathysphere to the extremity of its runners, the great crane rumbled into motion and took up the slack of the cable. Then, with no perceptible drop, the big sphere, already one third submerged, slid from its steel guides into the water.

At a signal from Captain Ardow the cable was paid out, the empty bathysphere sank from sight to a depth of fifty feet, then the great arm of the crane swung round until, further forward, the cable was brought almost to the ship's side.

As the bathysphere descended a group of men under the second officer had been paying out the thick rubber hose containing the triple telephone and lighting wires which entered the top of the sphere through a stuffing box. Now, this was attached to the cable by a rope tie in order that it should not break under the strain of its own weight. Captain Ardow gave another order and the bathysphere was let down a further 200 feet.

Another tie was fixed attaching the communication hose again to the cable. Both were paid out once more and so the business proceeded, with a halt at every 200 feet for fresh ties to be attached, until the empty bathysphere hung 2,000 feet beneath the ship.

The Doctor then gave orders for it to be hauled up again, and the reverse process was followed. As the cable wound in on the drums the communication hose was coiled down by hand, the machinery stopping every two minutes to enable the second officer to remove the ties which attached the hose to the cable.

At last, eighty-three minutes after the bathysphere had sunk from view, it reappeared again and now the ticklish task of getting it back on its runners was undertaken. A boat having been lowered guy ropes were attached to ringbolts in the sphere's surface, the winches were brought into play and the guy ropes tightened until the great steel ball had been brought into correct alignment. The crane clanked, the bathysphere lifted a fraction, and slid gently back into its original position.

The whole operation had occupied an hour and fifty minutes

so it was now nearly one o'clock but Camilla feared that if she put off her dive until after lunch she would lose her courage and told the Doctor that, if all was well, she was quite prepared to go down.

A ladder was lowered to the special platform which supported by the steel runners of the bathysphere, filled the gap between it and the ship. The Doctor and four of the crew descended to it.

For ten minutes they worked with great wrenches on the bolts that sealed the circular door in the side of the sphere. At last they got it off and Doctor Tisch, having made a careful examination of the interior, reported that everything was perfectly satisfactory.

Sally kissed Camilla impulsively and cried: "Oh do be careful darling! Are you sure you wouldn't like me to come with you."

Camilla bit her lower lip nervously, but shook her head. "No, dear," she said. "I promised to make the first trip alone with the Doctor and Count Axel—so here goes."

The Count handed her down on to the platform and helped her in the awkward business of scrambling through the small round opening in the sphere, then he turned, waved to the others and followed her inside.

At first there seemed hardly room to turn round in the strange spherical chamber in which they found themselves and except in its centre, it was impossible to stand upright. The concave walls positively bristled with instruments, cylinders, gauges, wires, and the searchlight apparatus occupied a good portion of the headroom to their right. However, it was actually constructed to hold eight people and climbing over the backs of the canvas chairs which were screwed to the wooden floor they settled themselves opposite the row of fused quartz portholes.

The Doctor climbed in after them and then his telephonist, Oscar, a pale pimply young man whom they had not seen before. A derrick lifted the circular solid steel door from the platform and swung it into place, the crew pushed it home over the ring of bolts that held it in position, and then began to screw it down.

Oscar squatted on a stool near the door and put his instruments over his head, while the Doctor wriggled into another of the canvas chairs from which he could control the searchlight. Suddenly there was a thunderous, ear-splitting crash.

Camilla and Axel both ducked but the Doctor shouted to them. "Do not be alarmed! It is only the crew who hammer home the bolts," and stuffed his fingers in his ears.

They followed his example but it was impossible to shut out the din and for the next five minutes the sphere reverberated as though giant projectiles were constantly being hurled against it. Then the noise ceased as suddenly as it had begun and gave place to an utter eerie silence.

"I'm frightened," said Camilla breathlessly.

Count Axel took her hand and pressed it. "No you're not," he told her confidently. "You are just missing the sound of the waves—that's all."

"All right, I'm not then," she smiled faintly but clung tightly to his arm.

The telephonist was speaking to his opposite number on the deck. The Doctor opened up his trays of Calcium chloride for absorbing excessive moisture, and Soda lime for removing the poisonous Carbon dioxide from the used air. Then he turned on the precious life giving oxygen, and the circulator fan. The telephonist spoke again, and the bathysphere began to move.

Up on the deck the McKay leaned over the rail with Sally beside him. "By Jove," he murmured, "I've often thought Camilla wanted her bottom smacking, but I'll give it to her that she's a darn brave kid. I wouldn't go down in that thing for a thousand pounds."

As he spoke the waters closed over the bathysphere and it began its journey to those grim regions where strange life dwells in perpetual night.

CHAPTER VII

DIVE NUMBER ONE

CAMILLA stared nervously out of one of the portholes. As the bathysphere sank below the waterline bubbles of air obscured her view and she could see nothing for a moment, then the chamber dimmed to a gentle green and she found herself facing a barnacle encrusted surface which had long streamers of greeny-yellow weed waving gracefully from it—the hull of the ship.

They seemed so near that she started back, fearing that they were going to crash against it, but Count Axel gave her hand another reassuring squeeze. He knew that, fused quartz being the clearest and most transparent material in the world, distances are apt to be deceptive when judged through it, and that the streamers of golden weed which appeared near enough to touch by stretching out a hand were actually fifteen to twenty feet away at the least. Another moment and the hull had slipped from view, their last visible link with the upper world was gone.

Almost at once the water took on a bluish tinge but the interior of the bathysphere remained light and bright. A thousand little motes drifted past the windows as they sank—the insects of the sea. Then a shoal of aurelia jellyfish drifted by pulsing gracefully along as they passed their level and, as they were halted for the first tie—attaching the communication hose to the cable—to be fixed, they saw their first fish.

"Oh look," exclaimed Camilla, "aren't they lovely!" It was only small fry but the irredescent light upon their scales made them seem like living jewels.

The telephonist muttered, the sphere descended again. All trace of red and orange in the light had disappeared, the yellow tinge was now scarcely perceptible and instead they had been replaced with a more brilliant blue. A dozen prawns came swimming by graceful, silver, fairy like, and then three fishes in a row. The bathysphere stopped and the Doctor murmured: "We are now at 400 feet. Deeper than any submarine now made can go."

A long string of siphonophores making a pattern like the most delicate lace slipped past. Then came another fish, a small fat absurd looking puffer, who peered with round expressionless eyes at them through the window, but he flashed away with a swift thrust of his tail as a ghostly pilot fish, pure white with black upright bands, came into view.

As the sphere moved on its downward journey two big silvery bronze eels came swimming by and now Camilla sat entranced. All sense of fear had left her under the fascination of this marvellous ever changing spectacle. The sight of all this teeming life beneath the ocean with its myriad colours and thousand different forms held her spellbound as she gazed.

Now the last trace of green had faded from the spectrum and the brilliant blue was tinged with violet. Yet the light had not perceptibly darkened, only its reds, yellows, and greens had disappeared leaving a strange unearthly brightness which had a queer effect upon them. It held excitement and exhilaration something similar to the effect of mountain air or a draught of iced champagne. There was a tenseness in the atmosphere and their senses seemed tuned up to a greater, almost unnatural, degree of vivid receptivity.

A lantern fish, their first sight of a real inhabitant of the deeper seas came sailing by, his scales ablaze with his full armour of irredescence. A squid, goggle eyed, pouch bodied, his tentacles waving in a deep sea dance pulsed on his way, then some pinkish fish, semi-transparent so that their vertebræ and food filled stomachs were clearly visible, and next a great scarlet snapper.

"Now 600 feet," announced the Doctor as the sphere stopped in its descent again. "No man has been so deep except in a bathysphere."

The light had darkened to a deep violet blue and still had that eerie unearthly quality about it. In the distance now they could see some pale flashes as fish from the deeps, carrying their own lights, moved to and fro. The Doctor switched on his searchlight but although it seemed dark outside the yellow glare had, as yet, little effect, so he turned it off.

Again the steel chamber in which they crouched together slipped gently downward. Two irredescent eyes suddenly appeared at the porthole, then as they moved a long pale ribbon like transparent gelatine undulated by, the larva of some great sea eel. Black jellyfish, a shoal of shrimps, a

63

pale blue fish and then a great dark form moving slowly in the blue black distance. More sea snails looking like dull gold shields, another squid, larger this time, and next a lovely silver hatchet fish glowing faintly in the deep blue murk.

At 800 feet it seemed that the limit to light penetrating from that far upper world of sun and wind and sky, had come. Only a grey blue blackness now filled the steel chamber yet the remaining suggestion of light still had that strange brilliant quality about it and when they tried the searchlight it made little impression on the darkened waters. As the Doctor switched it off everything went dead black for a moment then the intensely silent blue black twilight wrapped them in its folds again.

As they sank still lower, twinkling lights moved all the time in the distance palish green, lemon, pink, yellow, and blue. A big jellyfish slopped against one of the portholes its stomach filled with luminous food, a great deep sea eel came slithering past and then a cloud of petropods momentarily shut out everything else from view.

"1,000 feet," announced the Doctor. "We shall see now with our light," and as he switched it on they saw that it had at last become effective. The bright yellow beam cut a sharply defined path through the inky blueness of the waters. Then they were able to witness a most curious phenomenon. Outside the beam lights of all colours were visible like the fairy lamps in some enchanted garden; as a row of them moved forward they suddenly went out and the head and body of a strange looking fish appeared like a brilliant colourful painting in the yellow ray. Sometimes a fish would remain half in half out, its head and fore-part clear and beautiful but cut off as though with a sharp knife in the middle, the rest of its body and tail only indicated by a row of tiny lights like the portholes of a ship.

At 1,200 feet a great cloud-like mass came into view again but the extreme range of the searchlight only just showed it so their intense curiosity regarding this mighty inhabitant of the lower seas had to remain unsatisfied.

At 1,400 feet, there was an inexplicable empty patch. For some unknown reason not a single organism of any kind was visible, but at 1,600 they passed into teeming life again. Squids, jellies, deep sea prawns, rat-tailed macrourids and golden-tailed serpent dragons all carrying their own illuminations drifted or swam by. Even Count Axel who had expected

64

wonders was staggered by the thought of all this brilliant multi-coloured life spreading over the thousands of miles of sea that cover two thirds of the earth's entire surface.

When they reached 1,800 feet the Doctor switched off the light again. After the first almost physical blow of darkness had fallen an intense unutterable loneliness seemed to chill their hearts. The ship above seemed as far away as England. It was in another world, distinct, apart; their present life did not even seem to be a continuation of that which they had known; years back as they felt it at that moment, where moon and stars alternate with the daily rising and setting of the sun.

Gradually, into that vital bluish darkness a faint, faint greyness seemed to penetrate, and they knew that even here the last tenuous suggestion of the brilliant sunshine above could just reach them.

Spellbound they gazed from the ports. The blackness tinged only by palest grey was lit by an absolute display of fireworks. Green, red, yellow, blue, in rows of dots, singly, in pairs, in long tenuous streamers, they flickered and moved, some going on and off as though under the control of their strange owners. Something seemed to burst in the near distance giving off a million tiny sparks. The Doctor switched on the light; there was nothing to be seen but a shoal of incredibly thin fairy like fish and a big octopus half in and half out of the beam.

As they moved downward again more lantern fish appeared, and a shoal of hatchet fish, then a great blunt nosed monster at least three feet in length who carried a large green light waving above his head upon a single fin.

"We register now 2,000 feet," announced the Doctor. "The sun's light never penetrates to this depth. Here is the region of perpetual night." Again he switched off the searchlight. The pyrotechnic display outside continued but not the faintest glimmer of greyness now came to light the stygian blackness of this uncharted world.

"We ascend now," said the Doctor, and Oscar, who had been keeping up an intermittent mutter, mumbled again into his mouth piece.

"No, no!" cried Camilla, "let's go further down—please." It was the first time she had spoken for nearly three quarters of an hour.

"Not so!" The Doctor shook his head. "It is enough.

65

The sphere has only been tested for this depth to-day. We must not go deeper," and as he spoke they felt the pull of the cable carrying them up to daylight once more.

For the forty minutes of the upward journey they witnessed fresh scenes in the ever changing life which flourishes beneath the seas, from the self-lighted creatures who roam the depths, to a ten foot shark at 400 feet, and the floating jellies of the shallow waters. From out of the pitch black depths they rose by stages through the faint grey lighting of the bluish murk into the deep black-blue, then experienced again, for a thousand feet, the weird exhilaration of that staggeringly brilliant blue light growing brighter and brighter as they came near to the surface and, at last, passed into the area where green still penetrates then yellow and finally, just beneath the surface orange and red.

As the crew began their preparations for hoisting the bathysphere back on to its steel supports Count Axel smiled at Camilla.

"You enjoyed it?"

"Oh immensely." She squeezed his arm, "I never dreamed that such things could be. Thank you a thousand times for persuading me to come."

He leaned towards her: "There are many other wonderful things in the world which I could show you if you wished."

"Are there?" she raised one eyebrow with a little smile.

"Yes. You have hardly travelled at all yet and travel needs more than just money and a guide book to be undertaken successfully. It is an art."

"Of which you are a master Count—I suspect."

"And you Madame an apt pupil—as you have proved."

"But travel is not the only thing in life."

"By no means. I am a poor man and so have little choice but to wander as economically as I can from one pleasant spot to another. If I were rich I should spend at least half the year in London, Paris, and New York. In each—if I were very rich of course—I should keep a fine house in the old tradition. It would be no more expensive than occupying luxury suites at the big hotels and infinitely more comfortable. I should stock my cellars with great wines and appoint three Cordon Bleus to be my chefs; for the lure of a superlatively fine table rarely fails to attract the great brains of the world. Artists, scientists, men of letters, diplomats, statesmen, great beauties, prima donnas and all the men and women who are moulding the world that we shall know to-morrow would be my guests in carefully selected parties where each would be invited to meet some other that they wished to know.

"As I am blessed with a tolerant disposition I should doubt-less make many real friends among them and learn much of their hopes and fears, also perhaps something of those fascin-ating hidden motives, of which the great public never know, but which actuate the policies of men of power and often change the whole lives of many million people. Especially too I would seek for struggling talent among young people and by my introductions bring it to the light. That is a selfish thought perhaps but few pleasures can be so harmless or bring such satisfaction as being the means of helping people of ability to recognition. Then, when I tired of all their chatter I should be more selfish still and, leaving them for a period, sail away to refresh myself by visiting the marvels of India, Egypt. China or Peru."

Camilla knew that he was really speaking of the life he would make for her if she would marry him. It would be wonderful, she thought, to be a real Grande Dame, and a personality among the people who mattered in the world instead of just a rich girl throwing costly parties for hordes of nonentities whom she hardly knew. She saw herself receiving at the head of a great staircase in some old ducal mansion, accepting the homage of the writers and painters who, by her patronage, she had brought from poverty to fame, or listening in her *salon* to inventors and explorers as they told her of their latest discoveries before disclosing their secrets to the common world.

Axel was not boasting about his genius for friendship, she felt sure of that. His personality and breeding would secure him a place on equal terms with people of any rank, his brain and learning enable him to converse with the most intelligent, and his sure taste gave him a ready sympathy towards all creators of real beauty in any form. Given the money to pay for the right setting Camilla was certain that he was capable of carrying his wife to almost any height of influence and importance. It would be fun to travel too with a man who possessed such a wide knowledge of the world yet never laboured his learning and, in addition, was such an even tempered and amusing companion. But there was one thing he had not mentioned so Camilla asked with a sly smile.

"Is that everything you want in life Count?"

"No Camilla," he answered softly. "As a connoisseur of all things beautiful I want you for my wife."

Truly Count Axel was an artist in other things besides travel. The very syllables of her christian name coming so firmly but unexpectedly from him, was more effective than a score of platitudes.

There was a slight jolt as the bathysphere landed on its runners and next moment pandemonium reigned as the sailors on the platform attacked the bolts of the steel door with their heavy hammers.

Five minutes later Camilla was on deck again surrounded by her anxious friends.

"It was marvellous," she exclaimed breathlessly. "Absolutely wonderful—you've no idea."

"Tell us," they cried, "did you see any fish!"

She threw back her golden head and gave way to peals of laughter, then still gurgling she turned to Axel. "Listen to them! Did we see any fish! Scores my dears, hundreds, and every colour of the rainbow."

"Do tell us about it," pleaded Sally.

"I can't darling. It's utterly impossible. It's another world, fairyland, heaven, I don't know. And the light—the brilliance of it—that amazing blue."

"Light!—down there?" expostulated Nicky.

"Yes, yes, I can't explain it but it almost makes the sunshine look pale by comparison, and it's not the tiniest bit frightening. I know one thing. Every time the bathysphere goes down again I'm going too. But I'm ravenous. It's getting on for three—have you all had lunch?"

They confessed that they had not, but had been hanging about on deck for the last hour and a half wondering if they would ever see her alive again.

Even the taciturn little Doctor was cheerful over the belated meal that followed. It was his second descent in the sphere and, as on the first occasion off the Scillies, his apparatus had worked splendidly. Only a pint and a half of water had been found in the bathysphere's concave bottom after the dive and he saw no reason that he should not descend in it to much greater depths with equal safety.

After lunch Nicky cornered Sally. "Look here," he said "I want to talk to you."

"All right," Sally smiled. "It's a free country—ship

I mean. Come on deck and don't look so serious about it."

"But I *am* serious," he announced as soon as they had settled down. "It's about Camilla."

"How disappointing, I thought you were going to make love to me."

"You didn't!"

"Of course I didn't. You *are* a fool Nicky. But quite apart from any question of making love you'd be far wiser at least to pretend a friendly interest in people for their own sakes when you want something out of them."

"I didn't say that I wanted anything out of you."

"But you do."

"Well yes—in a way—but I've been thinking a lot lately and what I want to talk to you about will benefit you too."

Sally glanced suspiciously at his fine regular features and rather weak mouth. In a way she was sorry for Nicky, most women were when they did not fall desperately for his rather feminine good looks. She knew that his vanity and egoism were not entirely his own fault. Success had come to him when he was still too young to keep any sense of proportion. The flattery of the insincere but anxious to please artists who wanted minor parts in his pictures, and the adulation expressed in his feminine fan mail had gone to his head. Like others among the more sensible of her sex she remained quite untouched by what he believed to be his irresistible fascination for women, but had an instinct to mother him, and make allowances for his shortcomings which men, who mostly loathed him on sight, were quite unprepared to do.

"All right," she said, "fire away."

"Well you don't have much of a life—do you?"

"How exactly do you mean?"

"You're entirely dependent on Camilla—and at her beck and call all the time."

"Yes—I suppose I am. Anyhow for the moment."

"Why for the moment only."

"Well I might marry you know."

"Yes," he said slowly, "you *might* but not before Camilla."

"Thank you Nicky."

"Oh no offence, but the odds are all on her—aren't they."

"Yes, I suppose they are."

"I'd hate to see her marry this rotten dago Prince," he exclaimed with sudden venom.

"Now Nicky don't be naughty. Vladimir is just a nice large healthy animal. He's a gay and affectionate person too but if you will persist in sticking pins in him and making fun of his quaint English you can't expect him to be nice to you."

"I don't give a dime if he's nice or not. Do you think Camilla is likely to fall for him?"

"I've no idea. You'd better ask Camilla."

"Not very helpful are you?"

"Well, I don't think there is any immediate danger of her becoming Princess Renescu."

"Good. Well the Count's out of it anyway. He's far too old. Now about me? What do you think of my chances?"

"Honestly I can't say Nicky. She likes you a lot I'm sure and last night she was talking to me in her cabin about your idea of making her a film star. She seemed terribly intrigued by that but——"

"Did she," he interrupted joyfully. "That's fine! Now look here Sally this is where you come in. She thinks a lot of you. Just back me all you know and I'll see you right. Tell her I'm the Katz pyjamas and do everything you can to sheer her off that rotten Prince. Then, the day she marries me I'll give you a cheque that will make you independent of her for life—get me?"

Sally got him so thoroughly that for a second her mouth hung open with sheer amazement at his audacity in trying to bribe her, but she shut it slowly and murmured: "Yes—I get you Nicky."

"Well—is it a deal?"

"I don't quite know," Sally hedged. "Do you really love her?"

"Sure," Nicky declared airily, "I love her lots and I'm not after her cash like those other two. I make the sort of big money that most folks would be mighty glad to have."

"Even then I hardly like to influence her judgment, besides —after all—I might get married myself and then I wouldn't need the cheque—would I?"

"Oh nuts. It's always good for a girl to have her own income. She can tell her old man where he gets off if he

70

starts any rough stuff then. And who could you marry any-way unless—" He paused suddenly.

"Unless what?"

"Unless you've got your eye on that old Naval bird. He's not interested in Camilla—but you're always cooped up in some corner with him." Nicky swung round to face her with a jerk. "By Jabez! Sure enough that's why he was brought along on this fool trip."

Sally flushed scarlet but she kept her grey eyes steady as she shrugged. "What nonsense! Nicky you do get the most absurd ideas. The McKay is old enough to be my father—almost. Besides he's an arrant coward and I've no time for men who're as spineless as all that."

"Coward my foot! You can't put that over on me." Nicky grinned. "Everyone knows he's a V.C. and that's the highest buttonhole they dish out for glory in the British Isles."

"How do you know that?" Sally asked with veiled curiosity.

"A fellar back in the hotel told me before we started out. He won it at Zeebrugge or Jutland or some place where they cut each other's throats when I was in my pram. For jumping on a dock I think it was and shooting down ten Germans while his pals fixed a ladder from their ship. Murderous old devil, the thought of all those fools slaughtering each other makes me feel absolutely sick."

"Yes Nicky I suppose it does," murmured Sally thought-fully.

"Now what about our little arrangement eh? If you've got a fancy for old square face that makes no difference to our deal, so can I consider it all fixed?"

"I'll think about it Nicky," she replied standing up. "For the moment I'm just remaining neutral if you don't mind. I've got some letters to write now so I'm going below."

"You won't say a word about this eh?" he asked anxiously.

"No," she shook her head, "I'm good at keeping secrets; and I'll let you know later if I feel I need that cheque."

Sally's letters were of no immediate importance and she was much more anxious to have a few words with the McKay. When she found him however he was deep in a discussion with Count Axel about New Zealand, for both had visited the country and they discovered that they had mutual friends living there.

The moment being unpropitious Sally left them and it was not until after dinner, when the ship had dropped anchor off the little town of Horta, their base in the Azores, that she managed to get him on his own.

He was leaning on the rail placidly smoking a cigar as he watched the lights of the tiny port when Sally came up and said abruptly: "I owe you an apology."

"Oh that's all right m'dear," he replied casually turning to smile over his shoulder at her. "Children are always apt to be impetuous but aged people like myself get accustomed to making allowances for the error of their ways."

"You're not aged—and I'm not a child," she protested sullenly.

"Yes, you are m'dear—and a very pretty one."

"You brute." Sally felt her cheeks glow in the darkness. "You would choose a moment like this to say things like that—wouldn't you? But I had no idea you were a V.C."

"Oh that! Who's been telling tales out of school eh?"

"Nicky—he heard it from a man in the hotel. He says you did terribly brave things at Zeebrugge. Won't you tell me about it?"

He wrinkled up his nose in faint mockery and began to sing in his deep bass voice:

> "What shall we do with a drunken sailor?
> What shall we do with a drunken sailor?
> Hoist him up with a running bowline
> Early in the morn-ing.
>
> Hi! Hi! up she rises
> Hi! Hi! up she rises
> Hi! Hi! up—she—rises
> Early in the morn-ing."

"No seriously," Sally said in a wheedling voice, "do tell me?"

"There isn't much to tell. It was a dark and stormy night and the Captain said to the First Mate. 'Mate, tell us a story Mate' and the Mate began as follows: 'It was a dark and stormy night and the Captain said to the First Mate. 'Mate tell us a——' ''

"You idiot!" Sally interrupted. "Please. I've never met a V.C. before. What *did* you do?"

"I wasn't joking. It was just like all the other shows of

72

its kind, thousands of which received no recognition at all. I happened to be first off my ship when we were alongside the Mole and created a bit of trouble for the Bosch; then I helped a few of our wounded back just before we sheered off again. My Captain happened to see me so he put in a report. I thought I might perhaps get a mention in despatches and I was 'struck all of an 'eap dearie' when the Cross came through. Honestly there was no conspicuous bravery in what I did."

"Of course there was," Sally insisted. "Leading the attack and saving wounded under fire. If that isn't bravery —what is, and I was fool enough to call you a coward this morning because you said that you wouldn't go down in the bathysphere."

"You are probably right m'dear. If it were a matter of duty it would be different although I'd be scared stiff all the same, but nothing would induce me to go below in that death trap just for the fun of the thing."

"But if you're a V.C. you must be brave so I can't understand why you should be frightened of a little trip under water."

"Can't you? Have you had a look at the chart in the lounge by any chance?"

"No."

"All right—come on then." He took her arm and led her back to the brightly lighted deck house. A map of the Azores was pinned to the bulkhead and he pointed a square stubby finger at a dark spot on the southern side of Fayal Island—the town of Horta.

"That's where we are now, and the Doctor is being very secret about where we're going next, but I can give a pretty shrewd guess. If his theory is correct the whole group of islands are the mountain tops of the sunken continent. Now you remember what it said in that account of Plato's—that the *whole* region of Atlantis lay towards the *south* and was sheltered from the *north*. Further that its capital was on a low mountain no more than sixty miles from the sea. Pretty obviously that meant on one of the foothills of the range which formed the northern coast so the canal which connected it with the open ocean must have been either between the island of St Maria in the extreme west and St Miguel further north or between St Miguel and the big island of Pico north east of us. The odds are anyhow that it lies somewhere about

73

equidistant between all three and the Doctor would have used Pico for his base if it hadn't been practically uninhabited as you can see from the fact that there are no towns marked on it."

Sally nodded. "That seems all right, but what is all this leading up to?"

"Now take a look at the soundings," said the McKay, "and you'll see that practically the whole of that area is nearly a thousand fathoms deep."

"Well?"

"One thousand fathoms is six thousand feet and Camilla only went down two thousand to-day. Have you any idea what the pressure will be on that tin can of the Doctor's when they start trying to touch bottom?"

"No," said Sally.

"Well at two thousand feet it's very nearly half a ton to the square inch. Think of that on those windows, and the ratio of pressure increases the further you go down, so at six thousand, it's going to be something that doesn't bear thinking about. Ever heard of implosion?"

"No."

"It's the opposite of explosion and even more horrible. When something explodes near you there is at least a sporting chance of being blown clear and suffering nothing worse than concussion, but from implosion there is not the faintest hope of escape. If one of the ports of the bathysphere gave way under the immense pressure at six thousand feet the implosion would be so terrific that anyone inside it would be crushed as flat as a piece of tissue paper before they could flicker an eyelid. That's why the old sailor man prefers to stay on deck and smoke his pipe."

"But the bathysphere has been specially made to resist pressure at that depth."

"Maybe—still all sorts of things might happen. Say the cable snapped. Where would they be then . . . Down in Davy Jones' locker for keeps."

"I don't understand you," Sally shook her head. "They will send it down empty before each dive so where is the tremendous danger—and after all—to have any fun in life one's got to be prepared to take a little risk."

"A little risk eh! Well I've only survived to this age because I've always refused to take *any* risks that weren't strictly necessary."

"And yet you got the V.C. The highest decoration for valour that your country gives. I can't make up my mind if you're really brave or not."

"Nor can I m'dear," smiled the McKay. "It's a thing that I've often wondered but never been quite certain about."

The gallant McKay was still in doubt upon the point when, five hours later he woke with a start to see his cabin door swing softly back, and beheld two men silhouetted against the light of the passage both of whom held pistols which were pointing at his head.

CHAPTER VIII

THE GENTLEMAN IN THE
"OLD SCHOOL TIE"

THE McKay raised himself on one elbow. From years of responsibility in the ships he had commanded he was by habit a light sleeper. It was that which had brought him wide awake the second his cabin door had been unhooked and swung softly open. It was that too which had half roused him a little time before to the knowledge that a launch had come alongside and that people were moving about on the deck above. He had wondered vaguely then what they were up to at such an hour, but put it down to a shore party among the crew returning late from a binge in Horta. As a passenger such things were none of his business so he had dropped off to sleep again, but this was a very different affair.

"What the hell!" he exclaimed sharply.

"Get up!" said the taller of the two men, switching on the light.

The McKay blinked for a moment and stared at the intruders. They were hard-faced looking fellows clad in flashy, striped lounge suits.

"What the thunderin' blazes—" he began, but the taller man cut him short again.

"Get up," he repeated tonelessly.

The McKay proceeded to show a leg. He was far too old a bird to contemplate any heroics against these purposeful looking gunmen.

"Hurry!" said the man. "You're wanted in the deck parlour."

"Who wants me?" enquired the McKay, struggling into his slippers.

"Oxford Kate wants you."

"Does she indeed. Well I'd hate to keep a lady waiting."

"Oxford's no skirt an' he'll make it hot fer you plenty if you don't make it snappy."

The McKay did not like the look of things at all. He was thinking that Sally and Camilla would get a very nasty shock if they received a similar visitation. However he could do nothing for the moment except save loss of 'face' as far as possible. It would never do to allow these raiders to suppose that he was scared so, as he ran a comb through his crisp sandy greyish hair that had once been fiery red, he said curtly:

"If one of you care to take a message you can say that Captain McKay presents his compliments to Mr Oxford Kate and will be with him in two minutes."

Both men ignored the remark so he took his silk dressing-gown off its hook and handed the garment to the man who had so far remained silent.

The fellow stretched out his free hand and had taken it by the collar before he realized quite what he was doing. Then, as the McKay turned his back and slipped one arm through a sleeve, the man's mouth dropped open.

"Well!" he exclaimed, "can yer beat that?"

"It'll be a great laugh for the bunch," the other's lip curled in a sneer. "Jeff the Razz turns clothes help to English society man."

"You'd better! You spill that an' I'll—" the smaller man began venomously.

"Aw can it now," his friend cut in harshly. "Kate's up above."

The McKay hoped for a second that they might go for each other but seeing that there was no likelihood of the quarrel becoming violent he tightened the girdle of his robe and said:

"Now I'm ready to go and see the owner."

"The who?"

"Your friend who has apparently taken control of this ship."

"Oh sure—come on then." The taller of the two jerked his head towards the door. "Get in front and head fer the deck parlour. Any funny business an' you're for it—see!"

The McKay had *seen* several moments before, that from the way they handled their guns his two visitors were evidently accustomed to using them so, without further comment, he preceded them along the passage and up the hatchway.

The lounge was fully lit and as the McKay glanced round it he took an even grimmer view of the situation.

At the doorway stood two more gunmen, impassive but watchful, with their weapons prominently displayed. To the right, Nicky, clad in silks which for their colours would have rivalled the plumage of a bird of paradise, lounged sullenly upon a settee, his legs stuck out before him. Beside him was the Doctor, swathed in thick flannel night attire and looking more worried than ever while, at their feet, Prince Vladimir, breathing stertorously, was laid out neatly with a pillow beneath his head—unconscious on the floor.

Opposite this unhappy little group stood Slinger and Captain Ardow, both fully dressed, but the figure who immediately engaged the McKay's attention was a well made man of about forty, with a broad forehead and shrewd blue eyes, who sat behind a desk that occupied the middle of the apartment. His fair hair was a trifle thin, parted in the centre and brushed neatly back. The striped tie of a well known public school lent a patch of colour to his admirably cut lounge suit. Something about him suggested a combination of racing motorist, banker, and dandy, all merged into one strong personality.

"Captain McKay." It was a statement rather than an enquiry which came from the man at the desk and even the intonation of those two words spoken with quick assurance were enough to suggest the reason for his soubriquet "Oxford".

"Guilty," replied the McKay. "Mr Kate I imagine?"

The other smiled although his blue eyes remained hard and cold. "A somewhat vulgar witticism on the part of my henchmen, derived perhaps from my preference for silk shirting and my choice of socks. The ancient firm of Seal and Unman who supply them would be quite horrified if they knew that I think—don't you?"

"I've never heard of 'em," replied the McKay abruptly.

"Never mind—the name serves as well as any other—sit down." Mr Kate carefully ticked the McKay's name on a list which he had in front of him and, as he looked up again, Count Axel was marched in between two more of his men.

"Count Axel Fersan?" he enquired sharply.

"That is my name," Count Axel regarded him steadily from beneath half lowered lids.

"You, I am sure will have heard of Seal and Unman—am I right?"

The Count's face went blank with surprise for a second then he smiled. "Of course, when I can afford such luxuries I still get my things from them."

"Do you? In that case my people will probably call you Maud—be seated please." Despite the cynical jest Mr Kate's

78

blue eyes still remained cold and unsmiling as he ticked off the Count's name on his paper.

The McKay's two captors had disappeared and, after a few moments of almost electric silence, they reappeared with Sally between them.

"Miss Hart I think?" the man behind the desk rose to his feet politely as he asked the question.

Sally stared at him angrily. Her hair was scraped back from her forehead and, below her dressing-gown which she clutched tightly round her, portions of her seductive pyjamas were visible.

"Yes," she snapped, "what's the meaning of all this?"

"A little meeting to save you inconvenience to-morrow. Will you be seated—to the left there next to my friend Mr. Slinger. You know each other of course."

"So he's your friend, eh?" Sally cried bitterly, "and he's up and dressed so *he's* let us in for this." Her glance flashed murder at Slinger, then it fell on the still form of the Roumanian Prince.

"Oh, what have you done to him!" She started forward but Oxford Kate waved her back.

"Don't worry please, Miss Hart. He very foolishly resisted when I sent for him, so my men were compelled to hit him over his thick skull with their rubber truncheons—he will come round in a minute."

"You brute!" Ignoring his signal she fell on her knees beside Vladimir just as Camilla was brought into the room.

'Kate' turned to her at once. "La Duchessa Da Solento-Ragina?"

Camilla's face was pale but her eyes steady. "What is this?" she asked in a low voice. "A hold up?"

Vladimir groaned and Camilla, catching sight of Sally bending over him, ran to them without waiting for an answer.

"Oh my poor lamb!" she exclaimed, slipping her arm gently beneath his head.

His painful grimace gave way to a sudden smile. "Camilla, it is you! I was sprung upon too much but to see you safe is my reimburse for all distresses."

"He was the only one who had the pluck to put up a fight," said Sally, glancing indignantly at the others.

"My brave Vladimir," Camilla whispered and, with tears filling her blue eyes for a second, she stooped and kissed him swiftly on the cheek.

79

"Very pretty," sneered the big man at the desk. "Now, if you've quite finished I should be glad if you would give me your attention."

The two girls stared angrily at him but he motioned to a couple of his men. "Get the Prince up into a chair and if the ladies won't sit down kindly persuade them."

As the gunmen advanced Prince Vladimir staggered to his feet unaided and collapsed next to Nicky on the settee. The girls did as they were told without further argument. 'Kate's' eight men took up positions at the entrances of the apartment and he sat down heavily behind the desk again.

For a moment he remained silent, his hard eyes travelling without a flicker of emotion over each of their faces in turn, apparently assessing and registering the qualities of his prisoners, then he said quietly:

"My business concerns only the Duchess, but it occurred to me that if I saw her alone, she would pass on some garbled version of our interview to the rest of you immediately she got the opportunity. It is better therefore that you should hear what I have to say then there can be no excuse for any of you men attempting any heroics under the impression that you can prevent me carrying out my decision regarding her.

"I hope it is obvious to you all that my word is now law on board this ship. Anyone who endeavours to interfere with my wishes will be summarily dealt with. Captain Ardow and his men are in my pay so you need not imagine that you will receive any assistance from the crew——"

"Damn it, man!" the McKay broke in, "this is worse than piracy!"

"Thanks," Oxford Kate snapped with equal sharpness. "If you are thinking of treating me to a dissertation on the punishment meted out to seafaring criminals at Execution Dock in the years gone by you may save yourself the trouble."

"It's a kidnapping hold up," cried Camilla. "But you're making a big mistake if you think you can extort money from *me*."

"I don't," he replied evenly. "That would be crude and my plans have been worked out with considerable care. To begin with, *you*, my dear Duchess, are going to die."

The effect of his words was electric. The whole party stiffened with a cold positive horror. Camilla went deadly white and clutched at Sally. Axel's thin lips contracted in a sudden spasm, Nicky jerked back his legs and sat forward with staring eyes, while the Prince staggered to his feet and let out a roar like a bull.

One of the gunmen jabbed him in the ribs with an automatic and he fell back with a choking cough on to the settee but, his eyes night-black with rage, he would have struggled up again if the McKay had not held him down by the shoulders from behind for fear that they would shoot him.

"You can't!" cried Sally wildly. "You can't!—you can't! Oh, you inhuman devil. She—she'll pay—of course she will," and she threw her arms protectively about Camilla.

'Kate' held up his hand for silence but they refused to heed him. Doctor Tisch's face had gone a deep suffused red, as though he was going to have a fit. "No bloodshed," he spluttered, "no bloodshed. Herr Slinger I appeal to you!"

The McKay released the Prince and stepped from behind him with his chin stuck out. "Look here," he said firmly, "you can't get away with murder on the high seas in these days. Even if you butcher the lot of us, the truth will out, and if your own people don't give you away there are too many hands in the crew for one of them not to split on you. If you think you can make off safely because you've got this ship, you're mistaken. Within a week half the navies in the world will be after you."

"If you think that I could not kill her and get away with it you are wrong, my gallant Captain." The fair man suddenly leaned forward across his desk. "The Duchess, with her well-known love of excitement, has been sufficiently ill-advised to finance Doktor Herman Tisch's expedition for the rediscovery of the lost continent of Atlantis and become a member of it. You would not know it, of course, but the papers in London and New York are already full of wild statements regarding this unusual cruise. I have seen to that. Now the essential portion of the exploration is to be carried out by a series of descents into the ocean depths in Doctor Tisch's bathysphere. The public has been well informed, by my agents via the press, as to the very grave risk attaching to such courageous descents to the ocean bottom. Should some unfortunate *accident* occur to the bathysphere when the Duchess is in it no one will be the least surprised The newspapers will run it as a great story for a week and preach delightful sermons about this beautiful and wealthy young woman who so courageously gave her life in the interests of science. After that there will be silence and no one outside this room would ever have cause for the least suspicion that the Duchess had been murdered."

"You, I imagine, have taken steps to become her heir?" Count Axel suggested quietly.

"Exactly. You are a man of intelligence, Count."

"What!" barked the McKay. "You mean to send her below with a time bomb in that damned thing. God man! You're English! You couldn't do it!"

"I kill," shouted Vladimir lurching to his feet again. "I stamp out this so low swine."

The McKay, Axel and Doctor Tisch flung themselves upon him and forced him back before the gunmen could intervene. A storm of horrified protest rose from the others.

"I won't go," screamed Camilla, "I won't! I won't!"

"Silence!" 'Kate' brought his fist down with a crash on the desk. "If you were not so excitable and would listen instead of interrupting you would have heard, by this time, my true intention."

A sudden hush fell among them. The terrifying picture which had been conjured up in all their minds, and made more real by the stony unsmiling determination with which their captor spoke of it in his level cultured, voice had chilled their hearts and frayed all their nerves almost to panic but now, although they could not guess his meaning, something in the tone of his last words seemed to hold a glimmer of hope for Camilla.

"You are far better looking than I had anticipated," he said gazing at her thoughtfully. "However, that is beside the point. I kill without scruple when it is necessary—but never wantonly—so if you had been old and toothless I would still have had no objection to your living out your natural span— provided of course that you do exactly as I tell you. It is essential for my purpose that, as far as your friends in New York and London are concerned, you should die within a week."

Count Axel released his breath with a sharp sigh and spoke again. "You mean that the Duchess is only to die *officially*?"

"Yes."

A murmur of intense relief ran round among them as the man behind the desk went on.

"She will die in fact only if she refuses to do as she is told and, in such a case you can scream your heads off but, believe me, I'll send her down in the bathysphere and see to it that

82

she never comes up again. What's more I'll send the lot of you with her but, if she signs certain papers in accordance with my directions no one will have anything to fear."

"You mean her will?" asked Axel.

"Yes, that and a letter to her New York lawyer which she must write herself."

"Then you're planning to rob her of her entire fortune," exclaimed Sally heatedly.

"Why take two bites at a cherry," he replied evenly. "Do I appear to you like the ordinary gangster who risks a long term in Sing Sing for the sake of a few thousand dollars. However many fools may sneer at it there is some benefit to be derived from a decent education." He fingered his 'old school tie' with grim unsmiling humour.

"But what's to become of her if you take *all* her money?" Sally asked bitterly. "She—she'll starve."

He shrugged his broad shoulders. "Quite a lot of people are starving already through no fault of their own. She has been remarkably fortunate to have had the enjoyment of so much money for so long, and I see no reason at all why she should actually die of hunger. She is doubly lucky in having been blessed with good looks as well as money. I can't take those from her—at least I could—but I have no intention of doing that, so let her utilise them to provide for her future as other women have to."

"See here," Nicky remarked, "that means you'll have to land us all some place sometime, and it's not going to be so funny for you when the police have heard this story."

"You underrate my intelligence, I fear," 'Kate' sat back and brought the tips of his square blunt practical fingers together. "Let me outline for you my intentions regarding this interesting cruise. In a few minutes the Duchess will sign her last will and testament and the letter which I require. I shall take these documents ashore and register them through the ordinary post to New York to-morrow, or rather this morning. That is the last you will see of me. The cruise will then proceed as previously arranged under Doctor Tisch's guidance. My men however, will remain on board to assist Captain Ardow in his management of the crew and to make quite certain that none of you communicate by wireless or other means with the authorities on shore or passing vessels. The search for Atlantis will develop entirely as planned. Numerous descents will be made in the bathysphere and my friend Slinger will transmit carefully edited reports of each descent over the radio for the use of the press in both hemispheres. On the seventh day from now, by which time the documents will be in the possession of the Duchess's lawyers, an unfortunate 'accident' will occur—at least Slinger will wireless a report of it so that the world will learn from the headlines of its newspapers that the beautiful Duchess and her friends, with the exception of Miss Hart, have lost their lives a mile deep in the ocean—and of course her executors will meet to deal with the instructions in her will. This ship will then return to Horta. Slinger will land and hurry to New York in order to give a personal account of the tragedy and convince the lawyers beyond question that the report is genuine. Further he will state that Miss Hart is so upset by the occurrence that rather than face countless interviews with the press she has decided to be landed at an unknown destination and travel incognito until the public interest in the tragedy has died down.

"Captain Ardow then has his instructions. Having landed Slinger the ship will proceed on a delightful three weeks' cruise to the Falkland Islands. You will all be landed there with a supply of stores sufficient to keep you from starvation. Turning north again the ship will land my men at a small South American port whence they will travel by various means to rejoin me in New York. Captain Ardow will then dispose of this ship at a secret destination. I have never visited the Falklands and I fear that you will find the small uninhabited island upon which we intend to land you a somewhat inhospitable place, but in due course you will doubtless manage to make your way back to civilisation. By that time however, an ample period will have elapsed for the Duchess's executors to deal with the instructions in her will and, having suitably rewarded my companions, I shall have had an opportunity of distributing her wealth beyond all trace through various intricate channels. Your adventures will probably make a great story for the newspapers in a year or two's time and by then, of course, I shall have disappeared for good and all so that even the underworld of New York will not have the faintest idea as to my whereabouts—any complaints, eh?"

The McKay's face looked grimmer, greyer, and more lined than ever. He knew those barren rock islands that lie to the northward of the Falkland group. It would be no joke to be marooned on one of those with a couple of women. Ships only passed at rare intervals, a year might well elapse before they could attract attention to themselves or build a boat sufficiently seaworthy to carry them across those rough cold seas to one of the larger, inhabited, islands.

Count Axel was seeking for faults in the plan which their round-skulled sprucely dressed captor had outlined but he could find no reason why it should not be carried to completion. The utilisation of the public's interest in Camilla's doings to facilitate his coup was a devilishly ingenious piece of business. Countless newspaper readers in both hemispheres had been following the glamorous career of the beautiful millionairess ever since she came of age. They had glowed to the accounts of her romance with Solento-Ragina, devoured the columns of print upon her wedding, almost indecently lapped up the details of her trousseau and her honeymoon, then of her divorce. There had been rumours since of her marrying again, alternating with articles on her choice of underclothes and hats. Now, Oxford Kate had made her front page news again with the story of this expedition and at the same time made the world Atlantis and bathysphere conscious. Her adventurous nature would be stressed and the dangers of the bathysphere diving grossly exaggerated. During the next week, 20,000,000 people would read Slinger's accounts of their hazardous descents into the deep and then the blow would fall. The news of the accident would be flashed to every city in the world within ten minutes of its first being sent out, and why should it occur to anyone for a second to doubt the truth of it when the ground had been so well prepared. Slinger's personal testimony when he arrived in New York a few days later would set the final seal upon it. Count Axel took off his mental hat to Mr. Kate while hoping profoundly that he might yet devise a way to outwit him.

Nicky stood up and faced the desk, his Greek god features distorted to a mask of fury:

"Two years you say before we'll get back to civilisation. To hell with that! I've got important contracts I can't afford to miss—besides what'll my public do without my pictures? You can't know who I am."

"I know quite well who you are," 'Kate's' hard passionless stare met the indignant eyes of the crooner, "and if I have any insolence from you young man, I'll get Captain Ardow to put you on a ten hour job a day shovelling coal in the stokehold."

Nicky's mouth twisted venomously but he wilted where he stood and flung himself down on the settee again, as 'Kate' turned to Slinger:

"Have you got that draft letter for the Duchess?"

"Here it is, Chief."

"Thanks." He stood up. "Now Duchess, will you please come and sit here."

Camilla shrunk back against Sally. "No, no," she muttered, shaking her head. "No."

"Let me try and persuade you."

"It's no use," she stuttered, "I can't, I oh—" she broke off suddenly and burst into tears.

"Come. Surely you do not mean to compel me to take extreme measures?" There was a harshness now in 'Kate's' tone which made them all think again those horrifying thoughts which had come to them when they first believed that he meant to kill her. By giving ample opportunity for that fear to sink well into their consciousness while expatiating upon the ease with which he could do it and get away, he had very skilfully prepared his ground; for now, by comparison the loss, even of her entire fortune, seemed only a minor matter and Sally voiced all their feelings when she patted Camilla's hands and said:

"Go on, darling. Do as he says. This is an awful business but if you sign the papers at least we'll all remain alive."

That's the ticket, thought the McKay. While there's life there's hope.

"Would you—would you really, Sally?" Camilla asked tearfully.

"I would darling—I certainly would if I were you," and so, owing to 'Kate's' careful manipulation of the sequence of events Camilla sat down with far less fuss than might have been expected to sign away her fortune.

"This is the letter to your family lawyer whom you call Simon John," 'Kate' said placing a typed sheet of paper in front of her. "In so many words it says that in view of the fact that you are setting out to-day on this expedition, and intend personally to share with others in your party the risk of making numerous descents in the bathysphere, you feel that it is only right to set your affairs in order just in case any unforeseen misfortune should overtake you. There's a little joke about that showing that you think it extremely unlikely. Then you go on to say that you are enclosing a new will embodying your final wishes over which you've been thinking a lot and that the principal alteration in it is owing to your dissatisfaction with the way in which the Hart Institute funds are administered. You add that as it has been drawn up by Mr. Slinger, who did a certain amount of legal work for you in Paris and who of course they know has been handling your personal affairs for the last few months, you feel sure that they will find it all in order. Then there's another little joke about the old man's golf average, and you send your love to that little dog Skip of his you used to be so fond of. It's a nice chatty letter couched as you would write it in ordinary colloquialisms. Now please copy it out in your own hand on this blank piece of headed paper."

Camilla dabbed her eyes with her handkerchief, then took the pen he handed her and commenced to write in a round childish scrawl.

Doctor Tisch suddenly stood up. For some moments past he had been torn between fear and indignation. There was to be no bloodshed after all, it seemed, which was a great weight off his conscience, but what about the other part of the bargain which he had made in order to save his expedition? Surely this criminal could not mean to cheat him after he had made this tremendous coup possible by his complaisance.

"I wish to speak with you," he shot out at 'Kate'.

"All right—go ahead."

"With you alone."

"Sorry. I've no time to give you," Kate replied curtly.

"But how, if you send me to the Falkland Isles, can I make my great exploration?"

"You'll have a week. You must do your best in that."

"A week—a week! What is a week after so many years of waiting," cried the Doctor indignantly. "Come please I must speak with you alone."

"Anything you have to say you can say quite well here, but you will be wasting your breath anyway so if I were you I should say nothing. You might regret it afterwards."

The little Doctor's face went a shade deeper purple but after a second he plumped himself down in his chair again. He was caught. He saw that clearly now. They had no intention of carrying out their bargain with him and if he claimed it as a right they would still refuse, while he would have to suffer the ignominy of exposing himself as having been in league with these crooks to bring Camilla to her present pass which, so far at least, had been spared him.

"There!" cried Camilla throwing down her pen and staring angrily at Kate.

"Thanks," he picked up the letter and read it through carefully. "That's all right. Now Slinger, the will."

Slinger produced a bulky document from an attaché case and handed it across.

"You're sure it's all in order?" Kate's glance fixed him for a second.

"Certain, Chief. I've vetted it to the last detail and believe me it's a gem for plausibility. That was a great idea of yours having that codicil added. Just the sort of thing Camilla would do to her will the day after she'd made it."

'Kate' did not reply and they all waited in silence for a good ten minutes while he examined each clause in the lengthy document.

At last he looked up and addressed them again: "As you heard Slinger say this will has been drawn up with very great care and forethought. A young man who is in the office of the Duchess's lawyer was persuaded to give certain information to an associate of mine. Having been employed clerically on the Duchess's last will, made after her divorce, the particulars he supplied have enabled us to draft this new will on very similar lines. Miss Hart, as you may know, is her only near relative but all those distant connections who were beneficiaries under the old will retain their interest under this, for similar amounts so far as my informant could remember. Any slight variations are unlikely to cause comment since, the Duchess, not having the original before her when she presumably gave Slinger his instructions, would probably not remember all the amounts previously stated. The same remarks apply with regard to legacies to old family servants and present employees. All these have been allowed to stand and the faithful Slinger's name added for a substantial but not spectacular honorarium, which however, he will unfortunately be compelled to forfeit through not having been in the Duchess's service for three years—a nice touch that. In the matter of the various charities we have again adhered as closely as possible to the Duchess's intentions, the only considerable alteration being that, instead of the residue of her estate, which of course comprises the great bulk of her fortune, going to the Hart Institute, it will pass to the St. Protea Bible and Tract Society. For your information I may add that the Saint Protea Bible and Tract Society has been in existence for some years and its activities are quite beyond reproach. It has been built up at considerable cost and with much care for just such an occasion as this, but it will cease to function a few weeks after this extremely handsome bequest has been paid into its account, because of course, I am the Saint Protea Bible and Tract Society myself."

"Oh God," murmured Sally, "you've certainly thought of everything."

He favoured her for a second with the bleak smile which never lit his eyes. "I hope so—now Duchess will you sign here."

Camilla took up the pen and scrawled her signature.

"Now witnesses," Kate glanced round. "Will you oblige us, Captain McKay?"

"Not me!" rapped out the McKay. "I'll see you to blazes first."

"An unnecessary rudeness, Captain. It seems that vinegar has mingled with the salt which makes the old sea dog so crusty eh? But I have a liking for brave men and you're a V.C. they tell me so I'll excuse you. Doctor *you* will not refuse I know."

Doctor Tisch rose to his feet without a murmur. He saw no reason why he should suffer the ignominy of having the part he had played exposed now, to no purpose.

When the Doctor had signed his name 'Kate' looked round again and his glance fell on Sally.

"It's no good asking me," she said firmly.

"I had no intention of doing so," he replied tartly. "You cannot witness this will because you are a beneficiary under it. Which brings me to a further point that I must mention. The Duchess' fortune is so very large that I felt I could afford to be generous. Despite my remarks a little time ago it was not my intention to leave her entirely penniless and, as she could hardly inherit a sum under her own will, it occurred to me that if I increased the amount of fifty thousand, which you were down for, to one hundred thousand dollars, it would enable you to make some provision for her when you return from your official 'travels'. They may be a little long I fear as you are accompanying the others to the Falklands but it was for that reason your name alone of the party is not to appear among those of the dead. Captain Ardow will you sign as the second witness please."

As Captain Ardow took the pen Camilla looked at the man who was robbing her of her fortune in such a calm business-like manner, with new interest.

"Well, I must say that was decent of you," she exclaimed in some surprise.

"No. That one of you at least should officially escape the 'accident' gives additional plausibility to the whole scheme. However, I am happy to be able to arrange it in this way from an inherent dislike for seeing a woman of my own class on her uppers—engendered by this rag, I suppose." Once more he fingered the "old school tie", then picked up the will and gave a final look round him.

"Slinger, Captain Ardow, men, you will come on deck with me to receive your final instructions. Ladies and gentlemen, all things considered you have given me very little trouble—far less than I anticipated—I am grateful to you. Good-night!"

As his compact broad shouldered figure was hidden from view by the little crowd of his associates who hurried from the lounge after him Sally suddenly sat back and gave way to shrieks of hysterical laughter.

"I see nothing to laugh at," said the McKay grimly.

"Don't you—oh don't you?" Sally rocked helplessly from side to side. "Wouldn't you laugh if you'd just been left a hundred thousand dollars?"

CHAPTER IX

CAPTIVES IN CONFERENCE

I T was a silent and gloomy party which met some hours later for luncheon. Camilla and her friends had all been roused from their sleep at a little after three that morning; sustained nearly two hours of tense emotion in which fear, anger, and distress had been uppermost, while Oxford Kate unfolded his intentions to them; then crept miserably back to their beds round about five. They had slept late therefore, with the exception of the McKay who had freshened himself up by ten minutes noisy splashing in the swimming pool and lain for an hour baking what he was pleased to term "the imperial carcass" a shade more golden brown.

While the stewards were present there was a natural disinclination to discuss the situation, so conversation became strained to such an absurdly forced degree that after a few fatuous remarks about the excellence of the weather all further attempts were abandoned and Camilla told the steward to switch on the radio.

Slinger's chair remained empty, so it looked as if their principal gaoler did not intend to inflict his presence on them, but meant to take his meals in future with his confederate, the bleak-faced taciturn Captain Ardow. That at least was a relief, particularly to Count Axel and the McKay to both of whom it had occurred that if he put in an appearance they would have their work cut out in preventing Prince Vladimir from murdering him. Moreover, his absence enabled them to break into a free discussion of their plight immediately coffee had been served and the two stewards left the dining room.

"Well," said Camilla acidly, "how do all my champions feel this morning?"

"I am ashamed quite," declared Vladimir sadly. "One fellow I broke only with the smashing fist. Then I was sprung upon too much."

"Not you, my dear," Camilla laid her hand gently upon his. "I was enquiring after all these other *heroes*. A pretty picture they made last night."

91

"Yes, yes," Vladimir nodded quickly. "We are five men. If all of us had broken one of these bandits where would they be now perhaps. After, we would have together minced up the other three—for they are eight only."

"My dear Prince, you seem to have forgotten 'Oxford Kate' himself—and Slinger—*and* Captain Ardow—*and his crew*," the McKay protested sarcastically. "Personally I consider you were thunderin' lucky not to get a bullet in you when you started in on those toughs."

"You've said it," agreed Nicky with unusual cordiality.

"Still, I think Camilla's right. The five of you together might have put up some sort of show," remarked Sally coldly.

"M'dear, we weren't together," the McKay muttered irritably. "Each of us was woken and fetched from our cabins by a couple of gunmen. If we had all cut up rough as the Prince did—separately—it's pretty certain that the five of us wouldn't be sitting here now."

Count Axel nodded. "That is so. We had no chance then, or later, and, however unpleasant the situation is in which we find ourselves, we must at least give it to this man 'Kate' that the whole coup was admirably organised."

"If you are throwing bouquets you might as well hand one to Slinger," the McKay remarked.

"That rat!" exclaimed Sally angrily.

"Yes. He must have arranged this little picnic by cable before we started out from Madeira."

"Before that," declared Axel. "As you have remarked yourself, Captain Ardow and his crew are also in this thing. Slinger may be a very clever person but it is hardly likely that he could have bribed them all during our brief voyage. Moreover sea Captains are usually honourable men. The presence of this taciturn Russian, who turns out to be a willing accomplice of these crooks as well as commander of this ship, can hardly be chance alone."

"But they could have had no idea that I meant to make this trip until it was arranged in Madeira," Camilla protested. "I didn't even know myself."

The McKay smiled grimly. "Have you ever seen a trick merchant pass a card? You think you're choosing from the pack but all the same you take the one he intends you to. Well, that's what happened to you."

"You mean they guessed I'd fall for this expedition."

"That's it. You were jollied into it. Pretty skilfully I admit because Slinger was clever enough not to appear interested at the time. But that's about what happened."

There was a general murmur of assent, then, Count Axel, whose lazy glance had been fixed on the Doctor's face, sat forward suddenly.

"I think that Herr Doctor Tisch could elucidate the point for us—if he cared to do so."

The little German started guiltily then shook his round bristling head in quick denial. "It is not so! I know nothing. Only that I go to meet Herr Farquason at Madeira. Then I receive his radio and become desperate till the *Gnädige Hertzogin* agrees to save my great exploration."

"I see," said the Count silkily. "So you became desperate Doctor, when you learned that Farquason had failed you. Are you quite certain that you did not receive that information and become desperate, *before you left Paris?*"

"You impute—what?" the Doctor bluffed angrily, getting to his feet.

In Count Axel's view "Oxford Kate" was so obviously the dominant personality in the whole affair and his campaign had been worked out in such careful detail that both Slinger and Captain Ardow must have received their instructions from him long before the ship arrived at Madeira. It seemed to follow therefore that the Doctor must also have had at least some suspicion, if not guilty knowledge of their intentions.

"I impute nothing," he said bowing slightly. "I was only thinking that had my surmise been correct, and had you chanced to run into our friend Slinger, who must also have been in Paris at that time—it would explain quite a lot of things."

Little beads of perspiration broke out on the Doctor's forehead. He was not a good liar and he had never anticipated being placed in his present awkward situation. Slinger had led him to suppose that once they reached the Azores Camilla's party would be removed from the ship and he would be allowed to proceed untroubled, except for some slight pangs of conscience, upon his expedition. Now he found himself not only tricked but left suspended with a foot in either camp and, all his inclinations being towards the present company rather than the crooks, he was desperately anxious that his criminal complaisance should not be discovered.

He stuttered awkwardly for a moment under the battery

of eyes rivetted upon his face then, like a flash of light, he saw that this latest misfortune to his ill-fated enterprise could at least be utilised to counter Axel's shrewd innuendoes.

"The *Herr* Count imputes that I, for bringing you here, am in some way responsible," he blurted. "But I haf no interest except in my life work to find Atlantis. Explain please *Herr* Count how I shall accomplish *that* if I am to be taken with you as a prisoner to the distant Falkland Islands?"

Count Axel's suspicions of the Doctor's complicity were not entirely set at rest by this potent argument, but he had no answer to it so he replied even more suavely, "My dear Doctor, as I have said, I impute nothing. I voiced only an ingenious theory and as a practising scientist you will know how often theories are entirely wrong."

"*Danke schon Herr* Count." The Doctor thought it best to accept this half apology with as good a grace as he could put upon it, and sat down.

"Where are these Falkland Islands anyway?" Nicky enquired.

"In the South Atlantic off the coast of Patagonia," volunteered the McKay.

"The hell they are!" said Nicky.

"Yes. It either snows or rains there ten months in every year, and only the two large ones are inhabited." At the sight of Nicky's face, the McKay could not resist adding, with a chuckle: "The rest, on one of which they mean to land us, are nothing but barren rocks sticking up out of the sea to the north-west of the group."

"I see nothing to laugh at," Camilla cut in sharply.

"Neither do I really," he apologised.

"Do you think they'll let us take the servants?"

"What, your maid and Nicky's man? Yes, certain to. 'Kate' wouldn't allow them to get back to civilisation before us, in case they blow the gaff."

"Well that is some comfort."

"Perhaps. I hope you've both treated them decently for your own sakes. Otherwise they may not choose to continue as servants, without pay, once they find themselves on those barren rocks."

"Oh stop it," Sally abruptly stubbed out a half smoked cigarette. "Aren't we in a bad enough mess without your trying to depress us further."

"Sorry m'dear," the McKay apologised again, "but when

I'm in a nasty hole I always try and face up to the blackest aspect of the case. Things may not turn out so badly but it would be silly to start off by deluding ourselves."

"God we're in a hole all right!" Nicky hit the table viciously. "I wish to hell I'd never heard of this damn place Atlantis!"

The others ignored his outburst and the McKay went on: "What happened to the servants last night—by the way?"

"My fellow Bimber was locked in his cabin," Nicky muttered.

"Oscar—my telephonist also," volunteered the Doctor.

Camilla nodded. "My maid was locked in too. Oh, this is awful!"

"Yes, you're hit worst in this," Nicky said with sudden sympathy. It's going to be hell's own trip for all of us as far as I can see, and I just hate to think how long we may be parked on that filthy rock before we can get back to land, but when we do hit New York again you'll have lost every cent of your fortune. God! Just to think of that great fair-haired brute getting away with all that money!"

"There is just a chance the lawyers may not act on that faked will," said Sally.

"Why?" shot out the McKay.

"Oh, I don't know. I've just a hunch that way—that's all."

"The whole scheme seemed pretty watertight to me."

"Perhaps, but Camilla feels the same as I do. Don't you, Camilla?"

Camilla nodded. "Yes, I was talking to Sally about it in my cabin before lunch and we both feel that there may be a slip in it somewhere. You see old Simon John, our lawyer, has known us since we were children and that letter I was made to write was very clever but it wasn't *quite* in my usual style, so he may refuse to act until he gets some confirmation."

"Besides," Sally added, "the bulk of the estate was to go to the Hart Institute. That's for pensions, and libraries, and sanitoriums, for the workpeople in the factories from which the family made all their money. This sudden cutting out of that to leave it to a Bible Society instead is such a drastic sort of change that it is almost certain to make someone suspect that something queer's been going on."

The McKay shrugged. "Granted all that m'dear I hardly see how Camilla's lawyer could get a stay of execution of the will—even if he does suspect that there's been dirty work afoot. You see the publicity which will be given to the announcement of her death will be so enormous that no one will dream of questioning it. That's what's so monstrous clever. Her relatives, however remote they are, will be certain to call for the immediate production of her will in the hope of receiving large legacies. The executors will be bound to publish its contents and the representative of this fake Bible Society will arrive to claim the dough. The lawyers and the Hart Institute people, who'll naturally be mad as hatters, may enter a caveat against its execution but, immediately it comes into court, what proof have they got that it's not genuine. Camilla signed the bally thing and what's more she wrote the letter that accompanied it in her own fair hand. Whatever he may feel about it personally her lawyer would never dare to suppress such a vital piece of evidence. All the relatives and other beneficiaries will be backing the Bible Society of course to get their whack, and as far as the judge is concerned Camilla will be dead and that document the last expression of her wishes. What possible grounds will he have for refusing to let the share out take place. Get me?"

Count Axel nodded. "I think Captain you have given us an admirable forecast of just what is likely to happen. That very able rogue who has engineered this conspiracy is doubtless expecting some difficulty with the Duchess's lawyers and particularly with the trustees of the Hart Institute, who would be certain to contest the will even if it were genuine, providing they thought that there was the faintest chance of upsetting it and retaining such a tremendous benefaction as would be theirs under the earlier document. It is for this reason, doubtless, that all the old legacies have been allowed to stand and our charming Sally allotted the sum of one hundred thousand dollars. All dust for the Judge's eyes when the validity of the will is questioned. He will have to uphold it—there is no serious reason why he should do otherwise—but surely, instead of speculating as to whether he will or no, which is almost a foregone conclusion, would it not be better if we employed ourselves by endeavouring to devise some means of upsetting the enemy's apple cart before the will ever comes before a Judge at all."

"*Brava! Brava!*" Prince Vladimir sat back and clapped his hands. "The first speaking of sanity which has been made to-day. We attack eh!—For our so beautiful Duchess we will wipe off these bandits every one.''

Nicky regarded him dubiously. ''You've never been in the States, Prince—have you?''

''No, there I do not dwell.''

''Well, there's nothing wrong with the States as far as ordinary citizens are concerned. They live their lives and don't have to worry overmuch, but I was thinking of the lower East Side, and the bad belt in Chicago—particularly. You don't happen to know anything about them?''

''No—but bandits I understand. My uncle, Count Zirminie, was what you call Lord Captain de Police Provincal in my zone authorative last year. In the hillocks lurk bandits who make the workers on our lands pay too dear. We make a meeting with other friends and we take luncheons together. We toast the bandits, we toast ourselves, we toast everybody. Then we go out a moppings up to do. There are no more bandits when we remit ourselves to dine. Next day there is a funeral service, those of us who have come back from our celebration place flowers upon the graves. So is it done. I know all about bandits.''

Nicky sat back and raised his blue eyes to heaven. ''Tell him the truth someone for the Lord's sake—I can't.''

''It's like this Prince,'' the McKay sat forward. ''The people we are up against now are very different. There is every reason to believe them to be excellent shots and they are armed with the latest weapons—even machine guns as I saw for myself this morning. To endeavour to attack them therefore would be sheer suicide. They would shoot you without a second thought, so you had better put the idea right out of your head.''

''They are not then bandits,'' said the Prince, ''but what you call gangster such as I have seen in film plays but thought only to be a story for cocks and bulls.''

''That's it—that's right,'' a soothing murmur ran round and the Prince ten.porarily relapsed into silence.

''To get back,'' said Count Axel, ''the only chance which I can see of defeating these people's plans is by getting a message through to the authorities.''

''I agree,'' the McKay smiled grimly, ''but how?''

''Wireless,'' suggested Sally.

''Not a hope m'dear. You heard what Captain Ardow said last night after his Chief had left us. The bridge, the boat deck abaft the bridge, and the deck within twenty yards of the wireless house has been placed out of bounds for all passengers. Any of us overstepping those limits is not to be challenged—but shot on sight. While I was sunbathing this morning I took a dekko over the situation myself. Two of the gunmen were on the bridge and another two posted on the wireless house, the other four relieve them watch and watch about. They've even roped off the ladders and approaches to the limits set. Believe me 'Oxford Kate' is taking no chances of our getting near that wireless."

"We have a week to work in," announced Count Axel.

"True, but unfortunately we're miles from the track of transatlantic shipping. We may raise a stray cargo ship in the next few days. If so some of us must keep the gunmen occupied while others signal. If we can get a message through to New York they'll send out a destroyer to relieve us and the whole of Mr. Kate's pretty little scheme will be blown sky high—but that's about our only hope."

"Couldn't we bribe one of the stewards to get a message through to the wireless man," suggested Sally.

"There's no harm in trying, but the odds are he wouldn't send it. Captain Ardow is sure to have picked his men for this job and the wireless operator is a key man in the whole performance. It is he who had to send the fake message about the accident to the bathysphere and all our deaths remember, so he is certain to be standing in for a big fat cheque when it's all over. If we could reach him we might counter-bribe him with a higher sum but these people we are up against have foreseen that possibility and posted a couple of gunmen on him to keep him clear of all temptations."

"Well, couldn't we bribe the gunmen first then?" Sally persisted.

"Yes m'dear if you can get near them—and they'll listen to you—which I doubt. Don't you see that this whole thing's been worked out like a chess problem. We are up against a succession of cul-de-sacs whichever way we turn. It is because ideas like yours have been anticipated that the gunmen have been ordered to shoot us on sight if we approach nearer to them than twenty yards. How the thunderin' blazes can you try and bribe a man if you can't get within talking distance of him without forcing him to disobey his orders under the eyes of his bosses on the bridge or getting yourself shot. That wireless house has been ringed like a bullseye with concentric circles governed by the three great factors of, discipline, fear, and self interest. We haven't got an earthly chance of getting anywhere near it so you had better count that possibility out."

Sally made a face. "We're in a worse jam than I thought then!"

"Why, were you counting on getting a message through?"

"Yes—within a week."

"Why within a week? We'll have much more chance when Slinger's left us and we're running down to the Falklands. The gunmen may have got slack and bored with their job by then. They'll enjoy sitting up on deck in the sunshine for a bit, but later on they'll probably get fed up with doing nothing and we may be able to make friends with them or catch them off their guard."

"The Falklands," groaned Nicky. "Aw hell! Just think of all those pictures I'm contracted to make. It'll about break me I reckon."

"And it's winter in the southern hemisphere," added Camilla miserably. "Just picture us shivering on that barren rock the McKay says they mean to take us to, without any proper clothes."

Count Axel gave a heavy sigh. "I have always enjoyed cooking as an art but I am, I expect, the only one among you who understands it even moderately so I suppose I shall have to become cook. As a daily task I do not find it the least attractive."

"You'll be lucky if there's anything to cook after we've consumed the stores they intend to leave us," said the McKay bitterly. He did not mean to add to their depression but the remark slipped out and it was only a very moderate expression of the situation which he was visualising. He saw the seven of them and the two servants encamped upon a stony ledge a few yards clear of the spray from the thundering surf. A single lean-to tent had been erected against the cliff face and the edges of its canvas sides weighted down with huge stones in the hope of preventing the whole flimsy structure being lifted bodily into the sea by the bitter ice-cold unceasing gale that screamed and blustered. No fire was possible, for that appalling wind scattered the twigs, gathered with so much difficulty from the infrequent crevices, even before they could become glowing embers. The inmates were crouching, blue with cold, in an indistinguishable huddle of arms and legs against the rock wall in the most sheltered corner of the tent. Only so could they keep the ill-nourished flame of life still flickering in their emaciated bodies. In his mind's eye the McKay regarded that dirty unkempt heap of human flesh again and decided that the bodies only numbered eight. One of them must have died from exposure the day before and, facing such severe privations unsheltered from the elements it was reasonable to suppose that when the grey dawn came to light those semi-arctic seas another would be found dead to-morrow. He jerked his thoughts back and stared at Sally.

"We've simply got to get a message through in a week," she said firmly.

"Why? I don't see that," he argued. "We've got a month before they land us on the Falklands. That's the danger spot—the thing I really dread. If we can't do something before then we are going to be up against the sort of trouble that you have no conception of; but if we wait till Slinger has cleared out we shall still have three clear weeks and the gangsters will be getting slack about their job. That's the time to have a cut at outwitting these birds—in about ten days from now."

"But my dear don't you see," Sally insisted, "for this first week before the faked accident is reported, we are safe. No one is going to try and harm us—but after that—heaven knows. The real trouble is going to start the moment Camilla's death is reported. I've told you that I'm dead certain the faked will's going to be contested. Then, if it fails to go through that devil who was here last night will come back again. What he'll do, I don't pretend to say, but he'll be so mad that he'll probably shoot the lot of us or send us down to our deaths cooped up in the bathysphere. I'm certain he'll come back—certain—and that's why we've absolutely got to get a message through and have him arrested within the week."

"You seem very positive that there is going to be a hitch about the will."

"I am. Camilla don't you agree with me?"

"Yes, darling. I feel sure that old Simon John will contest it as it stands."

"Very well then," the McKay glanced round the ring of anxious faces. "What have we got to worry about? Surely you see that the acceptance or rejection of this will is the crux of the whole affair. If the judge once grants a stay of execution the enemies' entire plan of campaign breaks down. What would be the sense in shanghaing us to the Falkland Islands then.? They will have gone to a very great deal of trouble and expense for nothing so they certainly won't go to any more, because even if they sent us to the Mountains of the Moon they would be no nearer touching one penny of Camilla's fortune.''

"But we'll still be prisoners so that devil will come chasing back here," Sally insisted.

"Why should he? What's he got to gain. I suppose you think that having failed to pull off his big coup he'll try some lesser roguery. Force Camilla to sign him a whacking great cheque or threaten to kill her unless her friends pay up a seven figure ransom. But he can't m'dear because you see he will have spiked his own guns by having already caused her death to be announced. Her bankers will stop her account immediately they receive the report of it. They always do when anyone dies and even cheques already out are waste paper. Further payments from the estate can only be made by the executors and who could be fool enough to put up any ransom money for a woman that the whole world believes to be dead. No, if his big scheme fails he has sunk himself as far as attempting any other dirty work is concerned. We'll see no more of him and probably be put ashore at some little fishing village in the Azores while Captain Ardow and his cut-throats sail off into the blue.''

"His big scheme will not fail," announced Count Axel calmly. "The Judge may grant a stay of execution but this blackguard Kate has definitely anticipated that. You seem to have entirely forgotten the trump card which he has up his sleeve. Three days after the Duchess's death has been announced her man of business, Rene P. Slinger, will arrive in New York with an eye-witness account of the poor lady's death and, moreover, be in a position to give his personal testimony of the validity of the will as the man who actually drafted it. The Judge may hold the matter up until Slinger's arrival, but once he has heard *his* evidence he will not hesitate for one second to give a verdict in favour of the crooks.''

"Well Count you've certainly put your finger on the vital spot," said Nicky. "Sally and Camilla both seem convinced

101

that the will *will* be contested so if Slinger fails to arrive in New York it means the breakdown of the whole infernal business. It's up to us to deal with him so that he's in no fit condition ever to leave this ship."

Then, for the first time in their acquaintance Prince Vladimar Renescu regarded Nicky with a certain grudging admiration.

CHAPTER X

DAVY JONES'S LOCKER

I T was one thing to decide that the treacherous Mr. Slinger should not be allowed to proceed to New York but quite another to determine the method by which he should be compelled to remain in the ship against his will.

Prince Vladimir felt that this was an admirable opportunity for him to prove his devotion to his so beautiful Duchess and asked that the affair should be left entirely in his hands.

He obviously referred to his hands in the literal sense and the 'affair' as Slinger's neck, so Count Axel quickly demurred from the suggestion and the McKay hastened to back him up by pointing out that, even if Slinger were the biggest rogue unhung, murder was still murder, and they would certainly swing for it themselves if they did him in.

To imprison him seemed the obvious solution but how to do that when they were prisoners themselves—within the limits of their cabins, the lounge, dining room and fore-deck while he was their principal gaoler—they did not see.

The idea of rigging some booby trap which should maim him sufficiently to prevent him leaving the ship, but not kill him, was touched upon; yet that seemed such a distasteful piece of work that no one displayed the least keenness to take on the arrangement of it.

The problem of enforcing Slinger's detention was a knotty one, and although, realising it to be their one real hope of saving Camilla from being fleeced of her fortune, they discussed it in a desultory fashion for nearly two hours, they could devise no satisfactory plan. However, as the McKay remarked at the break up of the conference when the stewards reappeared to serve tea, "We've got seven days—six now rather before our friend is due to depart, and one can do a lot of thinking in that time."

He was right. They did little else but think in the hours that followed, singly or in couples; pessimistically giving each other the benefit of their gloomy and anxious forebodings aloud, or brooding over their inability to do anything about their intolerable situation in silence.

They were still thinking when Slinger appeared in the doorway of the lounge on the stroke of ten o'clock with a couple of gunmen behind him.

"You dirty double-crossing crook," Nicky shot at him.

Slinger, looking more like a benign bald-headed vulture than ever, smiled amiably.

"That stuff won't get you anywhere so you may as well cut it out. Now off you go to bed—all of you."

An angry murmur of protest went up, but he waved it aside.

"It's early I know, but we're instituting a ten o'clock curfew for passengers on board this ship just in case any of you feel tempted to start anything one night. That order, like all our other precautions is instituted for your own protection. Now drink up your drinks and get below."

Ten minutes later they had further leisure to think—in solitude, each of them having been locked into their cabins, and they were at it again as soon as they woke up the following morning.

Separately or in batches they went up on deck to reconnoitre the enemy's position; found all the approaches to the bridge and wireless house roped off and strictly guarded as on the previous day; stared morosely for a few moments at the gunmen who were on duty and then resumed their silent, unhappy speculations.

No one except the McKay felt any inclination to use the swimming pool despite the brilliant sunshine and when he appeared in his bathing robe, Sally remarked;

"Well, you're a nice sympathetic friend. Quite happy to enjoy yourself as usual eh! While the rest of us are racking our brains to try and think of some way out of this ghastly mess we're in."

"The old brain's had an overdose of thinking in the last twenty-four hours m'dear," he replied quietly. "So we're going to turn our attention to the imperial carcass for a bit instead."

"You've given up hope already then?"

"Not a bit of it. I never give up hope about anything, even that you might fall in love with me one day, and that's as unlikely as our getting out of this tangle with flying colours." He slipped off his robe and stood, just five foot seven inches of bronze muscular body in a pair of dark blue trunks, poised ready to dive into the water.

Sally's heart missed a beat. He had never said anything quite so nice to her before. Their troubles faded almost magically out of her mind. The sunshine seemed brighter and life full of pleasant possibilities once more, but before she had a chance to reply he had somersaulted into the water, swum round the pool beneath its surface, and come up puffing like a grampus as he shook the water from his eyes and crisp sandy grey hair.

"Don't sit there like a broody hen you young idiot," he admonished her. "Get your clothes off and come in for a swim."

After all, why not, thought Sally. So she went down to her cabin and donned a backless bathing suit which displayed her figure to perfection, then joined him in the water.

Prince Vladimir cast a disapproving eye upon them now and again as he restlessly paced the deck near the pool. He was not a young man of great intelligence, perhaps, but the heart of a lion beat with splendid regularity under his great breast bone and he was utterly disgusted to find himself in the company of men who possessed so little courage. In Nicky he felt "damp feet" as he called it, could be forgiven, for after all Nicky was a "cad" and one did not expect bravery from such people; but that Count Axel should sit placidly smoking right up in the bows of the ship, whole skinned yet unashamed, and the English Captain disport himself with senseless laughter while they were all held prisoners, filled him with disgust and contempt for both of them.

Even when Doctor Tisch appeared to tell them that the bathysphere had been sent down for a trial descent the announcement only roused them from their despondency for a moment. In their extreme preoccupation with the knowledge that, unless they could devise some way to outwit their captors, they were all to be shipped off to a desert island on the borders of the southern iceberg zone, where they would suffer months of acute distress, if not death—from exposure—they had forgotten all about Atlantis. With the exception of the McKay they had not even noticed consciously that the ship had left its anchorage off Horta in the previous night and now lay in the open sea, with the land only showing as a distant smudge on the horizon.

Upon being reminded of the object which had brought them all on board their reaction was only an added fury that any enterprise so speculative should have lured them into this damnable trap, and they soon relapsed into their squirrel-like mental revolutions upon the now sickening subject of their uncertain future.

After his swim the McKay joined Count Axel up in the bows of the vessel. "Well," he enquired with a smile, "did sleep bring you inspiration?"

The Count shrugged. "No, I confess myself at my wit's end. There are ways of course in which we could prevent Slinger leaving us in five days' time. Mussolini's for example which was used to prevent communist leaders from addressing public meetings when Italy very nearly went Red after the war—a pint of castor oil or its equivalent—that would lay him out for two or three days at least, but we couldn't put it into practice as long as he is accompanied by a couple of these gunmen each time he visits us. Have you had any ideas?"

"Not a ghost of a one," lied the McKay.

"Then it seems that we shall have to face a situation which I do not care to dwell upon. Think of these poor young women on the rock where we are to be left stranded. The hideous discomfort, the piercing cold of those southern regions. We may be there for a year before we are picked up by a passing vessel or can get away. I have few possessions but I would give them all to be assured that I am only dreaming of this colossal frame up."

"Yes, we're in it up to the neck," the McKay agreed bitterly. He had had no brilliant brainwave for their salvation, only a simple almost automatic idea, for one of his training, which might, as an outside chance lead to their rescue. Having little faith in it himself he did not even consider it worth mentioning and entirely shared the Count's extreme anxiety.

"The others don't know what they're in for yet," he added thoughtfully, "so best keep it from them till they have to face it for themselves. It would be no kindness to the women to cause them suffering in anticipation as to what we're likely to be up against this time next month; and I blamed myself afterwards for saying as much as I did when we had our conference yesterday. Unless we can detain Slinger I don't think there's the least chance of that will being set aside—do you? This bloke 'Kate's' been a damn sight too clever for the lot of us."

"Yes, he must have worked everything out to the last detail, and if we move against Slinger or these gunmen we would just be asking to be shot. The whole affair must have been planned months back, that's why I hinted that the Doctor was in it, yesterday. What do you make of him?"

"Oh, he's not a bad little cuss. Absolutely potty on this Atlantis business of course, but he's a genuine scientist all right. I looked up his record in the ship's library so I hardly think your theory about his being in with all these crooks can be right."

Count Axel smiled lazily. "It is just because he is so potty —a monomaniac almost, one might say—about what he terms his life work of the rediscovery of the lost continent that I believe him to be involved. Such expeditions as this are very costly you know and it is not easy to find anyone with sufficient money to finance them. Most capitalists who could afford to do so are hard-headed business men requiring a definite return for such an outlay. The uncertainty of actually securing gold from the venture would bar it out except in the case of a limited few. Farquason was such a one. A man of great vision who knew how to apply his dreams to modern commercial undertakings, and when he had made big money he was willing to apply that to the realisation of dreams which might bring no financial reward.

"Unfortunately he dreamed once too often. He will come back again of course, such men always do, but in the meantime he's had a nasty set-back and had to leave the Doctor in the lurch. Honestly I believe that Slinger or his Chief heard of the Doctor's project in Paris and the plight in which Farquason had left him, then tempted him to bring this ship down to Madeira by a promise that if he kept his eyes and mouth shut they would enable him to continue with this work in which he is so passionately interested.

"If you are right we should be well advised to exclude him from our councils."

"Certainly. Except in the case of some plan which necessitates an open united attack I think it would be wise if we all kept our own counsel for the moment." Count Axel also had the germ of a scheme already in his mind which was too vague for him to wish to share until he had had further time to deliberate upon it.

"However," he added blandly, "I believe the Doctor to be more sinned against than sinning. He could not possibly have suspected their intention of shipping us, and him, down to the Falklands. Consequently he is probably almost as much at his wit's end as we are now and would do anything he possibly could to help us. You see if my theory is right they've tricked him too and he would commit murder rather than be robbed of his great chance to rediscover Atlantis."

"You really do believe in Atlantis then? Surely if the Doctor is in with Slinger's gang that adds enormously to the supposition that it's only a myth and that they've utilised the old story to bait in an exceedingly clever job."

"No, my dear Captain. There you are wrong. That is just where these people have been so diabolically cunning. The Doctor *is* in dead earnest regarding his Atlantis theory so they made use of his fanatical conviction about it to induce Camilla and her friends to come on board this ship. Believe me, so certain am I that the Doctor is right, that if I had a million, and we had some unquestionable manner in which we could prove our bet, I would wager you nine-tenths of it that the land once trodden by living Atlanteans now lies beneath our feet."

"You know where we are then?"

"Yes. I was so perturbed by what had taken place that I hardly realised the ship had left Horta until we had been under steam for the best part of an hour but I looked out of my porthole then and saw from the stars that we were moving East South East. Unless I am completely astray, that smudge of land which we can still see to the north-west now must be the south-east point of Pico Island."

"That's it," agreed the McKay. "I took a look at the stars myself immediately the ship got under weigh and I'm able to verify the outline of Pico because, although it's years ago now, I've sailed before in these waters. You heard that the bathysphere had been sent down to the bottom?"

"Yes, they are reeling it in now. It took one hour and forty-four minutes going down. 5,168 feet the Doctor told me. I can hardly contain my impatience to learn if it reaches the surface again intact. So much depends on that."

"Getting on for nine-hundred fathoms, eh? The pressure must be something tremendous at that depth. Do you mean to chance going down there if the test has proved satisfactory?"

"Certainly. I would not forego the possibility of being among the first to behold these remains which have been under water for over eleven thousand years for anything in the world—not even to be free of this ghastly threat of being marooned on the Falkland Islands afterwards."

The McKay shrugged his square shoulders. "Well, each man has his particular kind of fun, but I *can't* see how you really believe in this old wives' tale. How *could* such tremendous destruction have taken place in one upheaval? It isn't reasonable."

"My dear Captain, the site of Atlantis is the very centre of an earthquake region. The nearest coast to it is that of Portugal and it was there that the greatest earthquake of modern times occurred. In Lisbon on the first of November 1775 the sound of thunder was heard underground and immediately afterwards a violent shock threw down the greater part of the city. *In six minutes 60,000 persons perished*. The entire harbour, built of solid marble, sank down with hundreds of people on it and not one of their bodies ever floated to the surface. A score of great vessels were instantaneously engulfed and disappeared with all their crews as though they had never existed. No trace of them has ever been found since and the water in the place where the fine quay once stood is now five-hundred feet deep."

"That's terrible enough I grant you, but it was a local calamity."

"How about the frightful eruptions which devastated the island of Sumbawa, east of Java, in 1815 then? The sound of the explosion was heard for nearly a thousand miles and, in one province, out of a population of 12,000, only 26 people escaped with their lives. Whirlwinds carried up men, horses and cattle into the air, tore up the largest trees by the roots and covered the whole sea with ashes and floating timber. The darkness in daytime was as profound as the blackest night and the area covered by the convulsion was 1,000 *English miles in circumference*. I tell you the accounts of the Flood in our Bible and the Mexicans' sacred book—the Popul Vuh —which are almost identical, are not myths at all but actual records of an historical occurrence; and every indication of the locality in which it took place points to Atlantis. Take the island of Dominica in the Leeward group of the West Indies,—the nearest land to the south-west of where the lost continent is believed to have been. That too is full of hot springs and in 1880 there was an eruption there of such magnitude that it rained *mud* in the streets of Roseau, miles from the centre of the disturbance, and simultaneously there was a cloudburst out of which great gouts of water came streaming from the sky. To read the description of it is to picture an exact replica, upon a minor scale, of the Flood described in Genesis where on the same day all the fountains of the great deep were broken up, and the windows of heaven were opened . . ."

"All right Count—all right. That's quite enough!" The McKay put up his hands in mock surrender. "I only wish to God that they were sending us to Dominica instead of to the Falklands. It's a charming climate and I had a friend there once—but that's another story."

Count Axel smiled. "Well, believe me or not I am absolutely convinced that Atlantis once existed and that we are now floating above the site it occupied. We may find nothing. Thousands of tons of ashes and volcanic larva may have buried its great buildings before they sank. The ocean bed changes and shifts through submarine eruptions from time to time but if the Atlanteans had pyramids as large and solid as those of Egypt or Mexico the remains of such mighty structures can hardly have disappeared like the flimsy hutments of a native village or even Lisbon's docks, so there is at least a fair chance of our finding them. In any case the search will serve to distract my mind from the damnable fate which appears to have been allotted to us for our very near future."

"You're right, and the descents will help to take Camilla's thoughts off this devilish business of losing all her money too, I hope. However, I prefer to relieve my anxieties by an occasional swim with Sally."

By half-past twelve, after a submergence of nearly three and a half hours, during nearly the whole of which period it had been travelling either down or up at the rate of a hundred feet every two minutes, the bathysphere reached the surface again.

To Doctor Tisch's overwhelming joy it had withstood the gigantic pressure at 5,000 feet and showed no trace of the strain which must have been placed upon it. Round, solid, its fuzed quartz portholes projecting from its sides like a row of stumpy cannons, uncracked, unscarred, it appeared above the waterline exactly as it had been sent down. As soon as

110

its weighty door had been lifted off a rapid survey of its interior revealed that all was well, and no more water had collected in its sump than was to be expected from the condensation natural during three and a half hour's submergence.

Frantic with excitement the Doctor came forward to report his news; and his enthusiasm was so infectious that it galvanised the despondent prisoners into some display of interest.

He said that he was going down at once since he could suffer not a moment's delay in making the first trip to the ocean bottom in this area that had so long held his imagination. That it was over 800 fathoms down and nearly twice the depth that any human being had ever been before troubled him not at all. If any of the others wished to accompany him Slinger had no objection to their doing so, he said; but they must make up their minds and be quick about it.

Camilla jumped up without the slightest hesitation. Her previous experience of the marvels to be seen on a deep sea dive had whetted her appetite for more. Count Axel stepped quickly to her side.

"Come on Sally—why don't you," Camilla cried. "It's so utterly thrilling to see all the wonderful things down there that one just forgets to be frightened the second the ball's beneath the surface."

"All right," Sally stood up a little slowly. "I'll come."

Vladimir shrugged his broad shoulders. "If we are to stand twiddling our toes instead of combating our distressers we can do it as well under sea, so I join you."

"What about you, Nicky?" Camilla glanced at the slim handsome young man who was wearing again his startling sky blue flannel suit.

"No thanks." Nicky shook his head. "If we're going to start playing games again just as though we had no cause to worry ourselves sick I'd rather take on the McKay at deck tennis—if he still doesn't care for the idea of going down."

"I'm your man Nicky," replied the McKay promptly. "Let's go and see all these folk safely locked into their padded cell, then we'll amuse ourselves by chucking bits of rope at each other—it's less dangerous."

"Come please," said the Doctor impatiently.

Ten minutes later the two girls, Axel, Vladimir, the Doctor and his little seedy-looking telephonist Oscar were inside the bathysphere and the bolts which secured the heavy door were being hammered home.

111

The McKay and Nicky had been allowed aft by the gunmen for the purpose of seeing the others off, and now they were leaning side by side over the rail. No one else was near them and under cover of the din Nicky said suddenly:

"Look here. I'm worried stiff over this hold up. What d'you think the chances are of that bird Kate slipping up over the will?"

"Not a hope in hell," replied the McKay tersely. He was not feeling too civil at the moment having just failed in an attempt to disuade Sally from going down in the bathysphere.

"Wish to God we could figure out some way of fixing Slinger," Nicky went on meditatively.

"So do I, but as long as he always moves round with those two toughs in tow how the deuce can we get at him?"

"We've darn well got to start something before the week's out. I got all the dope I could about these Falklands from a book in the ship's library last night and it sounds just one hell of a place to me."

"It is," agreed the McKay. "Still I'd rather sit on the rocks there for six months than go down in that bathysphere."

"Would you? By jingo I wouldn't. The risk isn't all that great."

"I mean go down in it regularly as the Doctor, Axel, and Camilla propose to do. I wouldn't jib at a single trip if I thought it would get us out of the clutches of these toughs. But sooner or later there's going to be a hitch somewhere; it will bust or they won't be able to get it up and I'd rather be smoking dried seaweed in the Falklands than in it when that happens."

"Well—there she goes." Nicky waved his hand as the great crane rattled and the bathysphere sank under the surface. "What about that game of deck tennis?"

The McKay grinned. "Right-ho! m'lad, such simple sports are infinitely preferable to an old man like me."

Inside the sphere, Sally clenched her hands and held her breath for ten seconds as the circular chamber slid under water. Staring upwards through one of the portholes she caught a glimpse of the surface from below. It looked infinitely calmer seen thus than from above where the wavelets chopped and splashed even on this calm day—just a quilted canopy of palish green dappled by constantly shifting patches of bright sunshine—then they slid downwards halting

112

for the first tie to be made, attaching the hose containing the electric wires to the cables, at fifty feet.

The silence seemed uncanny. Somehow she had expected to hear the constant rippling and splashing of the waves down there but there was not a sound. Strange as she felt it to be, too, the water did not seem to be wet any more. It was just as though she was staring into a solid block of pale greeny blue glass. Not a ripple or refraction gave the faintest suggestion of moisture and it was diamond clear instead of cloudy as she had imagined it to be.

Suddenly a three foot barracuda, that devil of the shallows, for whose attacks on bathers sharks are so often blamed, swam into the orbit of her vision. He paused for a moment to stare at the bathysphere and not the faintest movement except the slow champing of his horrid hinged jaws showed that he was alive instead of frozen into a great block of transparent, light greeny-blue ice. One flick of his tail and he was gone, yet no tremor of the water that he thrust from him with such vigour disturbed the glassy blankness in his wake.

Just as the bathysphere moved again two green moray eels slid by, then they passed a cloud of sea snails and a big jelly. As Camilla had done before her Sally forgot her fears and sat, her eyes rivetted on the window, enthralled by this ever changing panorama of life and colour.

The red and orange had faded from the light. Only a palish tinge of yellow now suggested the sunshine above the surface and the green was already being displaced by the vivid brilliant blue. After their third stop, at 450 feet no colour remained but the unearthly bluish radiance which filled them all with a strange feeling of vitality and lent their senses abnormal powers of vivid perception.

The Doctor adjusted the oxygen flow a trifle, to exactly six litres a minute, a litre per head for each person in the bathysphere. The weedy telephonist muttered into his instrument keeping in constant touch with his opposite number above in the ship.

As they descended a constant procession of living creatures seemed to be sailing upward before the windows; prawns, squids, clouds of fry, jellies, strings of syphonophores, shrimps, sea snails and beautifully coloured fish of every size and variety.

Gradually the intense blue light darkened to violet, then a

deep navy blue, blue black, and black only tinged with grey. Fish, jellies and squids carrying their own illuminations made the portholes like the eye of a kaleidoscope at the end of which were constantly shifting dots of many colours. At 1,200 feet the Doctor switched on the searchlight. Its powerful beam cut an arc of weak yellow light through the dark waters and at its extremity there seemed to be a turquoise coloured cap. A scimitar mouth was outlined in the very centre of the beam, it remained there absolutely immobile, as though it was only a painted plaster cast, showing as little reaction to the sudden blinding light as if it had no consciousness of it.

When the bathysphere hung steady at 1,850 feet for one of the ties to be attached above, a school of Rainbow Gars came swimming by. They were small slim fish no more than four inches from nose to tail with long snapper-like jaws. Their elongated heads were a brilliant scarlet, behind the gills their bodies turned to a bright blue which merged through a suggestion of green into clear yellow at the tail. No cloud of brilliant hued butterflies fluttering through a tropical forest could have been more beautiful.

At 2,050 feet the Doctor switched out the light. "We enter now," he said, "the region where it is forever night."

Not the faintest suspicion of greyness now lightened the appalling blackness of the waters. It was night indeed, but night such as they had never known. They felt that never again would the darkness of the upper world be real darkness as they understood it now. This was the utter solid blackness of the pit; that final blotting out of the life rays without which every plant and tree and animal and human must surely die.

"Put on the light—put on the light," cried Camilla suddenly, and for a second, before the Doctor found the switch, the fear which vibrated in her voice stirred a responsive chord in the emotions of them all, for they were now in one of those inexplicable patches, quite blank of life, so no glimmer from any luminous fish came to bring them reassurance. Land life cannot live below high water mark; or the shore life of seaweeds, shell fish, and rock dwellers, below the limit of the water covered slopes where the sun's light still penetrates; but living things, and those the strangest to us in all creation, still grew, and generated and fought and died by the million all about them and, when they dropped still further and passed the 2,200 level a fantastic variety of fresh wonders held their gaze.

The path of the searchlight had now lost its yellow tone and become a luminous grey; the cap of turquoise colour at its extremity seemed brighter and nearer in, yet they judged that they could see by its concentrated power of 3,000 watts a good sixty feet from the portholes. Outside its edge a variety of coloured lights moved constantly while hatchet fish, anglers, and fearsome looking squids with waving tentacles, pulsed slowly through the path of the electric rays.

As they were passing 2,500 feet a queer lightless brute, the colour of dead, water-soaked flesh, toothless and with high vertical fins on its hinder part but only a round knob for a tail, came into view.

"This inhabitant of deep seas Dr. William Beebe has named the Palid Sailfin," announced Doctor Tisch.

At 2,800 feet a monster passed. Twenty-five feet in length at least, oval in shape, monochrome in colour, and lacking both eyes and fins, a strange beast, unnamed, unknown to science. Some species of whale perhaps since nature has provided the whale with the amazing faculty of changing the chemical consistency of its blood which enables it to resist the gigantic pressures of great depths and, although a mammal, become capable, as has been proved, of diving a distance of a mile below the surface.

A moment later the sphere was halted for its next tie and the searchlight came to rest on an unbelievably gorgeous creature. It was an almost round fish with high continuous vertical fins, a big eye and a medium mouth. Its skin was brownish but along the sides of the body ran five fantastically beautiful lines of light, one equatorial and the others curved two above and two below. Each line was composed of a series of large, pale yellow lights and every one of these was surrounded by a circle of very small but intensely purple photophores. It turned and showed a narrow profile like a turbot, then swam away.

"Schön—schön," murmured the Doctor. "That beauty Doctor Beebe has named the Fivelined Constellation Fish."

At 3,200 feet the path cut by the searchlight had changed again. The turquoise cap had come right down to the very windows of the sphere yet they could still see distinctly for a considerable distance by its bright blue light. Along each side of the sharply marked beam appeared a broad border of rich velvety dark blue and outside this an indescribable blackness, which could almost be felt, made straining eyes as useless as total blindness.

"Lower than this no human has ever been," Doctor Tisch announced with satisfaction yet just a touch of awe. "William Beebe has only reached 3,028 feet. He is the pioneer who has made this journey possible for us and others who will come after. Later, perhaps, men will gather from the ocean beds fortunes of great size. Cortez brought home to Spain the wealth of Mexico. Pizzaro also brought back for his country the riches of Peru, but these names are not to us as the name of Christopher Columbus who was the first discoverer of the New World. When many years have gone the name of William Beebe will receive much honour and retain it for such time as our civilisation shall last. He also has opened up a New World for mankind. The pressure here is more than half a ton on each square inch of bathysphere but our instruments show all is as it should be. Where Beebe led we have follow satisfactorily—now we ourselves pass on. Oscar we are ready to go lower again."

The little telephonist muttered into his mouthpiece. The bathysphere sank further into the depths.

Suddenly the Prince leaned forward in his seat behind Camilla and kissed her on the curve of the neck.

"Vladimir!" she exclaimed with a start.

He chuckled. "Am I Columbus—no. Am I Beebe —no, but I am the first to make kissings with the so beautiful lady I love at such deeps under sea."

Camilla preened herself a little. "You are a dear," she murmured, "but you shouldn't you know. Just look at those marvellous lights."

Irregular formations of every hue were playing in the dark areas outside the beam and Doctor Tisch cut it off. For a further 800 feet they remained in the tense black darkness watching the fascinating display which now lit the windows. Angler fish came and went each with one to five lanterns bobbing from long rod-like fins upon their heads and sides. Stylophthalmas passed with luminous eyes on stalks one third as long as their entire bodies. Once Sally started back with a little cry of fright as some unknown organism collided with the port through which she was watching and burst like a firework into a thousand sparks, but immediately afterwards her entire attention was distracted by a single large dull green light as big as a cricket ball which went slowly past.

At 4,000 feet the Doctor switched on the light again and they saw their first great octupus, a parrot beaked creature with huge unwinking eyes and waving tentacles more than twenty feet in length. Instantly Tisch snapped out the light.

"He will not see us without lights," he remarked with unnatural calm. "Specimens of such size might be a danger if they believe our sphere to be some dead organism."

For a moment Count Axel's vivid imagination conjured up the picture of a giant octupus wrapping its tentacles round the bathysphere and, by its added weight making it impossible for the machinery of the crane ever to draw them up again, but second thought reassured him. When the creature found the steel ball too solid for its beak and quite inedible it would drop off and he knew from conversations with the Doctor that the cable could withstand twenty times the bathysphere's submerged weight. Nothing but the terrific jerk of flinging the crane into reverse when the sphere was running out at full speed, which it was never allowed to do, could possibly snap it, so they were safe enough unless attacked by some monster of undreamed of size.

When they had slipped down another few hundred feet the light was put on once more and nothing more terrifying appeared than a large eel with a couple of its slim transparent ghost-like larvae. Then at 4,800 feet the extremity of the light beam seemed to dim and they realised with a sudden tightening of their muscles that some gigantic fish was passing. Unlit, the colour of dead water-soaked flesh, like the Palid Sailfin it glided by, its shape unguessed since the searchlight showed no more of it than a rapid glimpse of its side, which appeared like the hull of some great battleship.

It seemed a Brontesaurus of the deep and the Doctor craned forward eagerly to watch it but his hands began to tremble with even greater excitement as he saw what followed in its wake. A school of strange roundheaded fishes with forefins which curved outward like clutching hands. They swam with malevolent carnivorous rapidity after the monster fish evidently in chase. There was something strangely horrifying in the sight of those sinister creatures never before looked upon by man, hunting their prey in a world of utter, forever unbroken silence, through the eternal night of the great deep.

It made the humans in the bathysphere realise more than anything else had done how completely cut off they were from that gay world of flowers and trees and sunshine

117

thousands of feet above. They were staggered at their own temerity and momentarily appalled at the thought that they had dared to invade this vast kingdom of the unknown, far greater than all the land surfaces of the earth together, with no more promise of security than the single thin thread of cable, stretching now to nearly a mile in length, from which they dangled.

Their thoughts were so occupied that they hardly noticed their descent of the last fifty fathoms. A sudden unexpected jar caused them to start from their seats in panic, but the Doctor's voice reassured them.

"We have made bottom—5,180 feet!"

They stared out through the fuzed quartz windows hoping to see something although they hardly knew what. Not temples and palaces of course but perhaps a great section of wall or part of a pyramid and they were vaguely disappointed when they saw that the strong beam of blue light revealed nothing except a barrel shaped fish and part of a mushroom like jelly with a trailing yellow skirt.

The bathysphere had landed on a gentle slope and so was tilted at an angle throwing the beam slightly up. The Doctor moved the lighting apparatus so that the long turquoise finger moved down towards the ground. Then they saw that they had landed on barren calcareous rock. There were no long waving fronds of seaweed, sea anemones, sponges or crustaceans to be seen. No trace at all of any undersea vegetation, for the multiform life of the beaches ceases entirely at a far lesser depth than that to which they had come being, like all vegetation dependent for existence on the light which filters down to it from the sun.

"The bottom is of volcanic rock as I expected," muttered the Doctor. "We will now proceed further. Oscar, tell them we ascend to five-thousand feet and then to move forward the ship one quarter mile."

"Why go up so high?" asked Camilla. "We couldn't possibly see the bottom from there. Can't they tow us along about six feet up?"

"A necessary precaution *Gnädige Hertzogin*. If we came suddenly to a submerged cliff face as the ships drags our sphere they would not have time to lift us over it owing to the length of the cable by which we hang. The sphere would crash against it and windows perhaps smash. This way our search will take much longer, but it is safer."

They were already rising and, after what seemed a long wait, felt the sphere begin to move gently forward through the ever changing constellations of coloured lights. It veered round to a new angle through the pressure on its big fixed rudder which ensured it travelling with its windows to the front, so that they could see what was ahead, whenever it made any lateral movement. They knew from the direction in which it had turned that they were being drawn over the downward slope of the rocky platform below and when, a few moments later, they were lowered again they landed upon a completely different type of bottom at 5,230 feet.

A mist of tiny white particles rose like a cloud when the sphere came to rest as softly as though upon a bed of down and, as it cleared, the beam showed the reason. They were now in an undersea valley bottom into which the currents of the ocean floor had carried millions upon millions of shells, octopus beaks and teeth of long dead fish. They lay there white and even like a snowy carpet as far as the light beam carried the vision of the watchers in the sphere.

"So! Here you see chalk deposits in formation," remarked the Doctor and he swivelled the searchlight from side to side, but the shell carpet was unbroken by any huge monolith rounded by countless years of passing currents such as he had hoped to find.

Suddenly a big squid inside the beam gave a violent jerk with all his tentacles and flicked away. At the same moment every light outside the searchlight's path vanished and that frightening empty blackness supervened. The beam was broken by a large round knob and, as they realised what it was, they were utterly overcome by shock and amazement. A human face was staring in at them through the window.

CHAPTER XI

THE EMPIRE OF PERPETUAL NIGHT

"UP!" shouted the Doctor, "up!" and a second after Oscar had spoken the one word "Emergency" into his mouthpiece the cable tightened jerking them away from the sea floor.

"Oh God! what was it," cried Camilla.

"The Devil—the Devil himself!" exclaimed Vladimir making the sign of the Cross.

Sally put her hand before her eyes. "That face!" she said. "That face! I've never seen anything more awful!"

Count Axel sighed. "Yes, I have only once looked upon a grimmer thing and that was the head of a man who had had his face burned to the bone when I was studying medicine many years ago, but, after all, whatever it was it could not have harmed us in this little steel fortress of ours so I think it a great pity that we did not remain down there to examine it more closely."

The others shook their heads. They were in entire sympathy with Doctor Tisch who, scientist as he was, had been so repelled by that incredibly evil countenance that he had given way to the overwhelmingly powerful impulse to escape from its baleful gaze without a second's delay. Now, he told Oscar to report all well and ask for them to be brought up in the usual stages; otherwise there would have been no time for the people on deck to coil down the hose containing the electric wires as it came in, and, as they slashed the ties, it would have slid down in a tangled coil while the cable was wound on to the drums.

"I haf heard of such things," the Doctor said huskily as he mopped the perspiration from his broad forehead with a big silk handkerchief. "But I did not believe. It was one such as we saw before who hunted after the big fish."

"Did you see its hands?" asked Sally with a shudder. "Ugh, they were horrible."

"And its teeth," said Camilla shakily. "That vicious receding jaw full of pointed fangs, I could almost feel them

120

snapping into me. I wanted to scream but I was too terrified. What was it, a special sort of fish or an unknown type of human which has adapted itself to living under water?"

"It was a fish from the waist down and it had a thick scaly brownish tail," Sally announced—"I saw it."

"So did I," agreed Axel, "but it was a mammal, didn't you notice its breasts? They were round and full as though moulded from a perfectly proportioned cup, and the only beautiful thing about it. The head seemed to me like that of a monkey."

"Yes, in a way. It had the same receding forehead but a monkey's teeth don't protrude like that, and this thing seemed to possess some horrible intelligence. Despite that flattened nose with the gaping nostrils it was more like the face of some unutterably depraved human."

"Undoubtedly it was a species which took to the water in the early stages of mammalian evolution," remarked the Doctor who had now recovered from that unreasoning fear which had gripped them all, sufficiently to be thrilled by their discovery.

"If you had told me of this thing I would have said 'Go and tell it to the mariners' " declared Vladimir. "But by Crikey I was here and saw it with my own look."

In the hour and three-quarters which it took them to ascend to the surface, lights came and went, a hundred varieties of sea creatures swam through the beam or later became visible by natural light in the upper levels, yet the party could think and talk of nothing but this ferocious race of fish men who lived and hunted a mile below the waterline unknown and undreamed of by modern science.

The McKay and Nicky were allowed aft again to meet their friends when the bathysphere had been hoisted on to its steel supports, and Sally, who was first out of the sphere ran up the ladder towards them. Her eyes were bright with excitement and her cheeks flaming.

"We've seen a Mermaid!" she panted breathlessly.

Nicky smiled, a tolerant but disbelieving smile. The McKay's blue eyes twinkled.

"Garn!" he said with frank derision.

"But we have I tell you—honestly," Sally insisted.

"And she had long golden hair done up in plaits tied with blue ribbon, eh?" he smiled sarcastically.

Sally shook her head. "No, it was beastly—the most

revolting thing I've ever seen. It had a round head like a cannon ball and a short thick neck; hardly any shoulders, but two short arms which from the elbows down seemed to be only skin and bone. It had proper hands with long clutching skinny fingers and sharp nails like claws. The fingers were webbed I think, but I'm not certain about that. I only saw it for a second. Then it had little round upstanding breasts just like a well developed girl of sixteen. From the stomach down, though, it was a fish and all thick scaley tail."

"Pity you didn't bring her up to meet us," Nicky suggested still obviously disbelieving Sally's story.

"You would jolly soon have asked us to send her back again if we had. Her face—well you'd never believe that anything so hideous could ever have been created. She had hardly any nose, just two holes instead of nostrils, a receding head and jaw with two rows of sharp teeth that stuck out a couple of inches beyond her bared gums. Her eyes were the worst though, they were round and unblinking and full of sheer vicious murder."

"Had she any hair?" the McKay asked. He spoke quite seriously now and a queer look had come into his eyes. "Fair straight bristly stuff almost like the quills on a young porcupine."

"That's right—that's what it was like exactly but—" Sally paused and stared at him. "How in the world did you guess?"

"By Jove! Jefferson wasn't pulling my leg after all," the McKay exclaimed softly.

The others had arrived on deck and the gunmen now insisted on shepherding them all forward to the lounge, so Sally had to stifle her impatience to hear the McKay's explanation.

"Goodness I'm hungry," Camilla cried as the gunmen left them, "D'you realise people that it's getting on for five o'clock and we've had no lunch."

"I thought of that," Nicky told her, "and asked them to start preparing something for you when you were about half way up."

"Nicky—you're a thoughtful darling," she cooed taking his arm as they walked down the companion-way. "You shall sit next to me while we eat. I suppose you fed ages ago yourself?"

"Yes, the McKay gave me a first class licking at deck tennis

122

and then we lunched as usual. It's amazing how agile the old boy is; I'm a pretty fit man—have to be for my job—but he can knock spots off me where hopping round's concerned."

"He's not so old my dear, only forty something, and look at the life he's led with the battles and bad weather he's been through. It's that and his grey hair which give him such a dried-up appearance, but he laughs as much as anybody and his 'imperial carcass' as he calls it is beautifully lean and muscular—I noticed it when he was swimming the other day."

Over their meal they talked again of the sub-human monster. It was the one enthralling topic which stood out from all the other weird and unusual sights which they had seen on their dive and the discussion of it even took their thoughts for the time being, from the fact that they were still prisoners, sentenced to exile upon a barren frozen rock.

The moment they had finished Sally cornered the McKay and carried him off to a quiet corner of the foredeck.

"Now Nelson Andy McKay," she said, "you're going to tell me just what you know about these extraordinary creatures."

"Well," he smiled, "it's like this. When I was on leave in England I used to be very fond of running down to Brighton for the week end. D'you know it—no, I see you don't. Brighton's a fine place, a few days there in the winter makes you feel twice your own man and then a bit more. I'd like to take you down for a couple of nights at the Magnificent—I—er beg your pardon. I suppose I shouldn't have said that."

"You certainly should not unless your intentions are honourable." Sally chuckled to cover her momentary confusion and added: "I'm a nice girl and don't go away with young men for the week-end."

"Pity—sorry I mean," murmured the McKay. "Anyhow, thank you for the young man part. However I'm a reasonably respectable person myself really and usually stay at the Royal Albion. That place has atmosphere and they always greet me as though I were their long lost son, besides Harry Preston who runs it is a great personality and has the biggest heart of——"

"Now, now," Sally interrupted, "I've heard of him even in the States—who hasn't? Let's get back to the Mermaid."

"Oh! Ah! the Mermaid. Well there is—or was—a fish

and oyster shop just round the corner from the front, in West Street, and for years, up to about nineteen-twenty-nine, if I remember, they had a strange looking brute in a glass case always on show in the window. I often used to go and look at it on different leaves and it was only about three feet long but exactly like this monster that you say you've seen to-day."

"The thing we saw was only about four feet from head to tail as far as I could judge, not more than four foot six at the outside. But how amazing that they should have caught one. Were the people in the shop able to tell you anything about it?"

"Not much. It was said to have been caught in African waters and brought home by an old sea captain about a hundred years ago. When I last went to look at it a waiter in the restaurant told me that it had been sold to some doctor who has a private museum of curiosities—at Arundel I think—and it's probably there now. Of course I always looked on it as a fake, a baby seal perhaps that had been tampered with—they are round headed you know, or perhaps the forepart of a monkey grafted on to a fish's tail. But the strange thing is that I did once meet a man who said he'd seen another like it."

"Really!" Sally exclaimed, "tell me, do."

"He was a chap called Jefferson, a Captain who was transferring from the West African Regiment to the West Indian Regiment after a spot of leave in England.

"When he was ordered to report for duty to his new headquarters in Jamaica, he had the sense to apply for one of these liaison trips whereby soldiers become the guests of the Navy. It's a chance for each side to swop ideas and talk a bit of shop you know, so as to have some sort of line on each other's functions and work together better in the event of war. Anyhow he was allotted to the hooker that I was taking out to the West India station and a very amusing fellow he proved to be. We were exchanging yarns one night when the talk turned to Loch Ness Monsters, and sea serpents and the like so I told him about this queer fish I'd seen at Brighton. He was mighty interested in that and told me at once that he felt certain it couldn't be a fake because he's seen its twin in Africa—on the West Coast. It seems that he was miles from his base with a shooting party fairly near the coast and one day he went down to the shore—I've forgotten why now—and there he stumbled across one of these Mermaid things exactly the same in every particular as the one I had described. It was dead, of course, and must have been washed up in a storm. It was half rotten and stinking like blazes under the African sun when he found it but, despite that, he said that he would have given anything to have been able to take it back with him. As he tried to pick it up it fell to pieces in his hands and he was five days march from any place where he could have got a big jar of spirits to preserve the bits in so he just had to leave them there."

"Why did you think he was pulling your leg though?" Sally asked.

The McKay closed one eye in a gentle wink. "Jefferson was a decent enough fellow but he had a peculiar sense of humour and I had a sort of feeling at the time that he had invented his little story just to persuade me that the Brighton fish was not a fake after all."

"What had he got to gain by doing that?"

"The chance that I might start airing a serious belief in Mermaids to my brother officers. He was the sort of man who would have got a lot of quiet fun out of seeing me do that and I wasn't having any. Still it seems as if he must have been telling the truth and that the Brighton beast was a genuine fish. I remember too how definitely we agreed that both these things were the most vicious looking brutes we'd ever seen."

They remained together until cocktail time while Sally recounted, in what she felt to be totally inadequate words, her impressions of the marvellous things she had seen on her first dive. The others too had been busy discussing their experiences, comparing notes upon the wonders that they had glimpsed and persuading Nicky to accompany them on the next descent; for, having come to the conclusion that, evil as the fishmen appeared they could not possibly harm them in the bathysphere, they were all going down again the following day.

When they met for dinner however, the topic of the wonder world that lay beneath their keel had been temporarily exhausted and the knowledge that they were still prisoners having again come uppermost in their hands, it irked and fretted them into stilted conversation punctuated by awkward silences.

"Well," Camilla said the moment the stewards had left them. "We were all pretty nervy yesterday, which was

125

hardly to be wondered at after the shock we got in the early morning, and I think this undersea trip has at least helped to steady us up a bit, but time's passing. It's Monday evening now and on Saturday the balloon's due to go up—we've only five days left. Has anybody had any brain waves as to how we can turn the tables on these crooks?''

A gloomy silence was the only result of her enquiry.

"We've got to do something before the week is out," Sally announced after a moment.

"You tell me what and I'll do it m'dear," the McKay said quite seriously. "The only thing I can think of is signalling a passing ship."

"Admirable, my dear Captain," smiled Count Axel, "but, as you know the Azores lie about four hundred miles to the south of the great shipping track between North Europe and New York, and we are at least seventy from Punta Delgada, the capital of these islands, where the smaller shipping calls."

"True, O Count," agreed the McKay, "and although I've been keeping my weather eye on the horizon, as they say in the story books, I've raised nothing but a smudge of smoke and a couple of local fishing boats in these last two days."

"The sea's so damn big," complained Nicky as one who has discovered a profound truth, "people don't realise just how vast it is until they get stuck on it in some place like this."

"Oh, think of something do," Sally implored glancing round. "I simply couldn't sleep a wink last night for thinking what that man Kate may do to us when he gets back."

"He *won't* come back m'dear," the McKay tried to comfort her. "We went into all that yesterday. If the will goes through he'll collect the cash and if it doesn't he's got nothing to gain by returning here, so try to put that out of your mind."

"He won't get the cash because I'm certain there'll be a hitch, and directly he learns of that through the clerk they've bribed in Simon John's office he *will come back* I tell you," Sally persisted. "He'll be so livid that he'll kill the lot of us I shouldn't be surprised."

"Well m'dear, it's no good anticipating things like that. We must just try to think of some way to get the better of these scoundrels before they send us to the Falklands."

For about three minutes nobody spoke at all. Then Camilla broke the silence by exclaiming sharply: "Have none of you men any brains?"

Nicky tentatively resurrected his first idea: "We've got to get Slinger somehow in the next five days and prevent him from quitting this ship."

"But how?" Camilla shot at him angrily. "That's what I want to know?"

A miserable wrangle ensued during which wild schemes were produced by both Vladimir and Nicky only to be torn to shreds by the cold logic of Count Axel, whom in retaliation they accused of lack of endeavour to help by putting up any suggestions himself. The McKay sat all through it, placidly smoking his after-dinner cigar and watching their faces from under his beetling grey eyebrows; unable to give his support to the hot-headed proposals of the younger men or rescue the Count by putting up some new proposition. He had squeezed his wits until he was half stupid with bumping up against the succession of cul-de-sacs in which Kate's perfectly planned coup had left them and had not the ghost of a new idea to offer.

Their anxiety had shortened all their tempers to such an extent that they were being openly rude to each other without having advanced one step nearer to a practical solution of their problem when Slinger arrived with his two attendant gunmen.

He rubbed his knobbly hands together and smiled round at them. "Well, I hope you've all had a nice day. I've been able to turn in a report of real first class interest over the ether of your dive in the bathysphere."

"Oh, go to hell!" said Nicky rudely.

"No, only to bed when I've seen you all safely locked up for the night," beamed Slinger. "But the account of the Mermaid was great—just the stuff to catch public interest. Camilla and her party will be front page news all over the world to-morrow. We couldn't have had a finer story for our purpose if I'd thought it up myself."

"What the devil d'you want to go and tell him about that for," the McKay snapped turning suddenly on Doctor Tisch.

The little man spread out his hands and was about to reply when Slinger answered for him.

"That's the price the Doctor has to pay for being allowed to go down in his ball, so you mustn't blame him for it. No

127

stories no diving—that's the order, and if he didn't care to play I'd just have to fake the reports. Now drink up your drinks and off you go to bed."

They knew from the previous night that nothing was to be gained by argument so with sullen faces they did as they were told.

Tuesday dawned bright and clear again. At nine o'clock the party gathered at the stern of the ship and the McKay duly saw them off. Despite the desperate plight they were in these excursions under water seemed to hold such a fascination for them that once any member of the party had been down nothing short of an immediate prospect of escape would have tempted them to forego a repetition of the experience. Camilla had persuaded Nicky into going with them now but Sally failed in her attempt to make the McKay change his mind.

"Besides," he had told her, "even if I wanted to I wouldn't. Someone must stay on deck to keep a look out in case a passing ship does come near enough for us to flag her, and I'm probably the only one among you who can semaphore," so he had to spend the best part of the day on his own.

When the bathysphere had reached bottom it was hauled up again for two hundred feet and trawled by the ship a quarter of a mile to the south-eastward, then let down again. In that manner they cruised for nearly three hours but covered no great distance. Each halt with the raising and lowering of the sphere occupied about ten minutes since they remained for a couple of minutes at the bottom every time they settled on it. The McKay estimated the ship's total movement to be roughly four miles. At two o'clock they asked to be drawn up to the surface, and by four were safely on board again.

"Any luck?" asked the McKay as Sally scrambled up the ladder.

She shook her head and they walked forward together without waiting for the silent, watchful gunmen to give them any order.

"It was just as wonderful as ever," she said. "Every sort of beautiful thing that you can imagine and more. That brilliant blue light too, that I've told you about, that one sees going down and coming up between 100 and 800 feet, gives ten times the kick that one can get out of a couple of absinthe cocktails, but we didn't find any traces of Atlantis.

The sea floor is nearly all hard volcanic rock except for the valley of white shells that we landed on yesterday, and a nasty patch of oozy mud that we struck on our last two dips."

"Any Mermaids to-day?" the McKay enquired.

"Yes, they seem to frequent that valley of shells, we didn't see one anywhere else. I think it was the shock of having a living thing like that come and stare in at the window which scared us all so yesterday. They are very horrible, of course, but I wasn't a bit frightened of them to-day. They became rather a nuisance though and so many of them came crowding round the ports at one time we couldn't see anything else so the Doctor had to drive them off."

"And how the devil did he do that may it please your Majesty—make a rude face at them?"

"No, stupid. The bathysphere is a wonderful piece of work you know and there are electric rods on hinges in its outer surface that can be made to stick out like the spines on a sea urchin when the current is turned on from inside."

"I see, same principle as a diver's electric knife that they tackle sharks and conger eels with?"

"That's it. You can't stab fish with these but anything that touches them get a nasty shock. They were fitted originally in case some giant squid tried to wrap its tentacles round the sphere and made it difficult to pull up.'

"How did the Mermen take this unusual treatment?"

"They simply hated it. If they had been above water and had voices I'm certain that they would have been absolutely screaming with rage. One was knocked right out and the others swam off with his body. That shows that they are not quite brute beasts or like other fish otherwise they would have eaten him I think."

"They'll eat you all right if anything goes wrong with that sphere, but I wouldn't mind having a cut at that meself."

"Nelson!—Andy!—McKay!"

"Did you see any more curiosities?"

"The biggest squid the Doctor's seen so far. An awful brute, its tentacles must have been at least forty feet long—but nothing really new. Oh, except that the Mermen have horses."

"Now come on," he smiled at her quizzically. "You must save that for the marines!"

"Well, not horses exactly, but they ride on other fish. At least that's what we imagine. On three separate occasions

129

we saw one of them go by in the distance with its body lying along the top of a thing rather like a small shark and their claws dug into the back of its neck. They may have just been attacking it to kill and eat, of course, but it didn't look like that. They don't swim very fast themselves you see and these fish they perch on just stream through the water like a flash."

"They say wonders will never cease—so I'll take your word for it. Now what about a swim before the cocktails come round?"

"Love to," said Sally. "I missed my dip this morning."

"Right, skip to it m'dear, and I'll meet you at the pool in five minutes."

At dinner that night it was Nicky who kept the conversation going. He had fallen utterly and completely for this new world which his trip in the bathysphere had opened up to him. Towards the end of the meal he had talked himself almost into a state of artistic inspiration and suddenly announced a marvellous idea which had just entered his mind. Here was ideal material for a new super-film. A spot of drama in the bathysphere perhaps, then all the underwater stuff with squids and scenes of the Mermen. One of the Mermaids would have to be lovely, of course, a swan among the ducks, actually she'd be a star with a first class voice so that she could come up to the surface and sing opposite him, just as they'd done in the old stories about their luring sailors to their deaths. It could all be filmed by back projection except the above water level scenes, and those of the interior of the bathysphere could be shot in the studio easily enough against the background of a half sphere made of wood.

Everybody thought it was a fine idea until the McKay remarked that Nicky would have plenty of time to practice crooning his theme song to the Mermaid—in the Falklands.

An angry silence ensued after this piece of acidity and, when coffee had been served they commenced their gloomy speculations once again.

The McKay was asked if he had seen any shipping during the day, and he replied abruptly.

"You would have heard about it before this if I had—I didn't set eyes on a masthead and I'm beginning to doubt if anything will ever come near enough to us in these unfrequented waters to be any good."

"Oh dear, oh dear," Sally looked across at him despairingly. "What are we going to do—we can't just sit still and let things take their course."

"'Fraid there's no alternative m'dear until these gunmen get fed up with their job and slacken off. There's no sign of that yet though. A better disciplined set of men I've never seen. I tried to speak to one this afternoon but he just quietly pointed his pistol at me and he would have used it too, I believe, if I hadn't stopped."

"Oh, they're well disciplined I admit," Camilla conceded. "Quiet as mice although they're always close at hand. It's extraordinary how polite they are too in stepping aside and that sort of thing when we go aft to the bathysphere, despite the fact they never open their mouths. They're nothing like I've always pictured gangsters and hoodlums to be at all."

"They are not like ordinary gangsters," said Count Axel with conviction. "But neither is their Chief like any ordinary boss racketeer."

Nicky nodded. "If he cleans up on Camilla's packet he'll be the biggest shot since Al Capone was put behind the bars."

"He won't—but he'll come back," Sally insisted, "and we've just *got* to think of some way to save ourselves before he turns up."

The now sickening subject was miserably debated again but by the time Slinger arrived with his guards to see them to bed they had only become exceedingly irritable without having produced a single new idea.

On Wednesday all of them except the McKay went down again in the bathysphere at nine o'clock, taking with them a picnic luncheon. The ship covered about six miles in a new direction with continual stops to haul them up 200 feet before proceeding and then lowering them to the bottom again; it was nearly six o'clock when they returned to the surface but, despite the usual excitement which always seemed to possess them for an hour or two after each dive, they had nothing startling to report.

Several new varieties of deep sea creatures had appeared in the beam and they had seen more Mermen apparently riding their swift fish horses to unknown destinations, but the bottom they had traversed was all bare volcanic rock with the exception of two new shell strewn valleys, and there was nothing to indicate the presence of the lost city for which they were searching.

131

"D'you know you've been cooped up in that thing for close on nine hours," the McKay asked Sally as they went in for their belated evening swim.

"Really," she replied casually. "It doesn't seem as though we had been down half that time to me. Every second of it is so vitally interesting, I even forgot to eat more than one of the sandwiches we took down so I'm just dying for dinner now."

"But isn't there a most appalling fug—I wonder you haven't all got splitting headaches in spite of the oxygen that keeps you from passing out."

"No, it's amazing really. The air in the sphere was as fresh when we came out of it just now, as when we climbed in at nine o'clock. The Doctor allows one litre of oxygen per person per minute to escape from the tanks and that seems to do the trick."

"How about the temperature though—isn't it darn near freezing?"

"Not inside. It drops about six degrees in the first two-thousand feet, but after that you don't get the benefit of the sun anyhow and it doesn't alter so quickly, two degrees in the next thousand and only one degree for the last two-thousand to the bottom if I remember right. It was never lower than sixty-six degrees to-day, the Doctor said so as we were coming up, although outside it's ever so much colder and if you touch the walls of the sphere they feel like ice."

After dinner the McKay was asked if he had sighted any ships during the day and he informed his fellow prisoners that at about two o'clock a fishing boat had tried to come alongside—probably in the hope of selling some of its catch.

"I've had this all packed up ever since Sunday," he added producing a flat tobacco tin from his pocket. "It contains a full report of our situation and a request for immediate assistance addressed to the Chief of Police in the Azores, also a fair sized bank note to ensure its delivery and a promise of more substantial reward to follow if help is secured for us without delay. I meant to chuck it down to one of the fishermen if such a chance occurred but unfortunately Captain Ardow was on the bridge and he ordered this little craft to sheer off, through his megaphone before it was anywhere near the distance I could throw the tin."

Sally was cheered a little to think that although he had said nothing of this idea he was exercising his wits to plan

132

such measures which might yet lead to their release but she started in on her old cry that Kate would return with diabolical intent in a few days time and that they had simply *got* to do something definite before he put in an appearance.

"Yes," Camilla sighed, "do you realise that four whole days have gone and we haven't thought of a single practical idea between us. In three days now my death will be announced and then we shall be really up against it. Oh, what *are* we going to do?"

CHAPTER XII

COUNT AXEL WINS A TRICK

THE nightly gloom would have descended on them all again had not the McKay made a determined stand against it. He was utterly sick of the topic of their captivity and these endless discussions as to whether the faked will would be successfully contested and whether or no Oxford Kate would return to perpetrate some new villainy. They had, he felt, exhausted every possible avenue of speculation and now their only chance lay in waiting, with as much patience as they could muster, for some opportunity such as he had only missed by a narrow margin when the fishing boat had endeavoured to come alongside that afternoon.

Despite the fact that their uncertain future was dominating all their thoughts once more, he insisted on discussing the search for Atlantis which was now actually in progress.

Doctor Tisch rose readily enough to the bait and, after a few moments, Count Axel, guessing the McKay's purpose, loyally came to his assistance. In a quarter of an hour the others too found themselves examining the contour chart, plotted by the Doctor, of the ocean bottom from the dives they had already made, and listening to him with a revival of keenness as he poured out a mass of geological information.

He maintained that the sea floor was exactly as he had expected to find it and that he was not in the least discouraged by their lack of immediate success in locating the Atlantean city. In the cataclysm it might well have slipped laterally with the whole surface of the land a mile or so one way or another just as it had sunk downward at least a mile below its original level, but wherever it was all the buildings would have slid in the same direction and if they could sight one they would find all the others piled up as a great mass of monoliths and boulders in that immediate area.

"What proof have you got geologically that the sea bed here was ever dry land at all?" the McKay enquired.

The Doctor placed his stubby forefinger on an irregular patch of lightish blue in the centre of his map of the North

Atlantic. The Azores were well inside it and it ran down towards the northern coastline of Brazil:

"Here," he said, "is the Dolphin ridge. The whole of that must once haf been land. All geologists are agreed on that. The inequalities of its surface—mountains—valleys—could not haf been made by deposit of sediment or submarine elevation according to the known laws. They could only haf been carved by agencies acting *above* the water level—rain—rivers and so on."

The McKay studied the contour chart based on the bathysphere's dives again. "There don't seem to be many mountains and valleys here," he said.

"That *Herr Kapitan*, is local only. Here we are, as I anticipated, above a rolling plain."

"In that case surely there's an easier method for you to conduct your search than by bobbing up and down in the bathysphere every quarter of a mile. The range of vision from that thing must be very limited. You might be within fifty yards of a great group of stones and never suspect their existence. In fact you might criss-cross this area every day for months without actually landing on the place you're looking for. There is an electric sounding machine fitted in this ship—why in the world don't you make use of it?"

"How does that work?" asked Sally.

"Eh!" he glanced across at her. "Oh! a compression hammer released by electricity strikes on the ship's bottom and the echo, thrown back from the sea floor, is picked up by a microphone, amplified and recorded. The longer the echo takes to come back the deeper the water is in that place."

The Doctor nodded. "But tell me please how that would help us. To know the depths is of little use—we shall only discover by actual sight."

"Listen," the McKay leaned forward. "These electric sounding machines are pretty accurate you know. They'll give you your depth to within half a fathom every time and the sea bottom we're over seems to be rather like a succession of gentle sloping downs; anyhow there's nothing jagged about it. Now you're hunting for a group of great stones twenty or thirty feet high at least—if not a hundred. All right then, if we sail up and down working the electric depth recorder as frequently as possible and it suddenly starts to show sharp variations that ought to be the place you want. You stop the

135

ship at once and down you go in your sphere—see what I mean?"

"Himmel, yes! Why did I not think," the Doctor cried with his fat face beaming. "I thank you *Herr Kapitan*. That will be far quicker than our dives every quarter mile. To-morrow we will try——"

"Time please ladies and gentlemen—time," called Slinger with sardonic humour, suddenly appearing in the doorway with his men. And thus ended another day.

By seven o'clock next morning the fanatically eager little Doctor was up and dressed, and the moment he was let out of his cabin he sought Captain Ardow. The taciturn Russian made no difficulties and agreed with cold courtesy to his using the electric depth recorder. For four and a half hours the Doctor sat over it as the ship steamed at his request, round and round an outward spiral in a series of ever increasing circles. Depths from 850 to 902 fathoms were recorded, but the upward or downward curve of the graph never showed any sudden alteration. It was obvious that they were sailing round and round above the slopes of a rolling plain. Then at 11.30, more than seven miles south of the point from which they had started, the soundings suddenly became erratic. 901—893—900—890—888—897—. After which the echo did not reach the microphone clearly since the instrument only registered uneven scratches. The Doctor left it at the run to stop the ship proceeding further.

A quarter of an hour afterwards the bathysphere went under water, only the cautious McKay remaining, of his party, in the ship.

At 1.32 they had reached bottom and a message came up that they wished to rise 200 feet and then be towed a quarter of a mile towards the east, the drift of the ship having carried them to the west, despite the efforts of the officer on the bridge to keep, as nearly as possible, on the spot at which they had halted.

The McKay was just finishing lunch when the movement had been executed and, as he came on deck again, he wrinkled up his nose and sniffed a little. The sky was still serenely blue but somehow he didn't like it. There was an uncanny stillness in the air. Without the least hesitation he turned aft and, stepping over the rope barriers at the risk of being shot, addressed the two gunmen who were standing by the wireless house:

136

"Captain McKay presents his compliments to Captain Ardow and says he had better haul the bathysphere up at once because we're in for dirty weather."

The men stared at him for a moment but, in a clear firm voice he repeated his message then turned his back and walked away to show that he had no hostile intentions, upon which one of them went off to find the Russian.

No reply came back, but the clanking of the great crane, very shortly after, informed the McKay that his advice had been accepted. He glanced at his wrist watch, the time was 1.45 p.m., then again at the sky. It was still perfectly clear but he did not like the uncanny hush that had fallen.

At 2.15 a small black cloud appeared on the horizon. The McKay studied it with grim foreboding. By 2.30 the whole sky in that quarter had become dark and threatening. There was still an hour to go before the bathysphere was due to reach the surface so the McKay again risked a bullet by telling the gunmen that, orders or no orders, he meant to go aft and take charge in the hope of expediting its arrival.

One of the men held him up with a pistol but the other went off to find Slinger and a few moments later returned with his consent to the McKay being allowed aft to superintend operations.

Having reached the scene of action he took the deck telephone from the man who was in communication with the bathysphere and shouted down it:

"Below there?"

"Yes," Oscar's voice came up over the line clear and untroubled from 3,000 feet beneath him.

"Captain McKay presents his compliments to Doctor Tisch. There's bad weather ahead. Tell the Doctor we mean to reel you up at top speed and that he's to inform the ladies they have no need to be alarmed if they get a bit of a bumping— got that?"

"*Jawohl, Herr Kapitan,*" came the rather scared acknowledgement.

"Right. Now we'll have no time to coil the telephone hose down so it may kink and cause the wires to break. If you are cut off you'll know that's what has happened so sit tight and don't worry."

"*Jawohl, Herr Kapitan,*" Oscar replied in an even fainter voice and, despite the McKay's injunctions not to worry, if Oscar could have seen the great black clouds which now

137

obscured the sun he would have been very worried indeed. The bathysphere was not built to be hurled about in a violent storm or the cable intended to take the strain of spasmodic jerks from a ship pitching and tossing in heavy seas.

The McKay thrust the instrument back into the operator's hands and began to snap out orders. At first the seamen regarded him with hostile surprise as an interfering civilian, but they very soon understood that they were dealing with a man who knew his business. The crane began to reel in the cable at its utmost speed, a man with a sharp knife was set to slash the ties holding the rubber hose to it as they flashed past, and the hose itself was hauled on board coil after coil in wild confusion by all the hands that could be mustered. It wreathed and knotted in great loops and festoons despite their efforts to control it but the McKay felt that it mattered little if the wires it contained were broken in consequence. His one concern was to get the sphere up before it became impossible to land the party.

The sea began to heave in a long rolling swell, the sinister moaning of a distant fast travelling wind reached them; great heavy single drops of rain hit the deck with a sharp crack then, at ten minutes to three, the storm burst with the bathysphere still 1,500 feet under water.

The crew may have been the riff-raff of the seven seas who had accepted quadruple wages to shut their eyes to any irregularities which might occur on this unusual voyage, but they were sailors by profession and understood the brother-hood of the seas. That lifelong enemy of them all—the ocean —had risen against them. There was a job of work to be done and though the rain sheeted down in cataracts soaking them to the skin they stuck to it without a thought of question-ing their unofficial orders. The McKay stood there short and square and grim at the after rail but cloaked in all the natural authority which came from years of command at sea and, to his occasional shouts there came back a cheerful "Ay, ay, Sir!" as they jumped to do his bidding.

The ship was pitching heavily and every few moments a wave hit the stern with a loud thump, sending clouds of spray over the streaming men as they fought and struggled with the seemingly endless hose pipe. For one moment the McKay considered sending a message to Captain Ardow asking that the vessel should be headed due west to bring them under the lee of Pico Island but any movement of the ship would mean added strain upon the cable, so he did not dare to risk it.

The wind increased to half a gale, moaning through the rigging. The McKay cocked an anxious eye at the masthead to judge their degree of pitch and was not comforted by what he saw. Captain Ardow had the ship just under way and head on to the storm but the waves were breaking over the bow and each time their main bulk surged below the hull the stern lifted right out of the water. The bathysphere was up to 500 feet, but the McKay knew that the strain on the cable must be appalling. It might snap at any moment. He sprang up a ladder into the control room of the crane house.

"We'll have to play her like a fish," he told the engineer. "Steady now—watch for my signals," then he clung to the doorway—peering out through the sheeting rain to judge the lift of the ship and raising or lowering his arm in accordance with it.

As the stern was buoyed up on each successive wave crest the bathysphere cable was allowed to run out fifty to one hundred feet, then as the strain slackened it was checked and, when they sank into the trough, reeled in with the utmost rapidity.

For close on half an hour the crane man played the bathysphere under the McKay's directions like a salmon trout while the ship rode through the storm, but at last they got it to the surface and now the most difficult part of their task began. They had to land the sphere on its steel supports without staving it in against the girders.

The risk entailed in this proceeding was so considerable that the McKay was almost inclined to leave the sphere dangling fifty feet under water, despite the awful buffeting that its inmates must be receiving, but he had no idea how long their oxygen supply would hold out. The storm might well continue to increase in violence and not blow itself out for forty-eight hours. It was certain now that it would not abate that day and if he left them there they might all be dead by morning.

In consequence he called for volunteers to man a boat. Half a dozen of the crew stepped forward and he went over the side with them.

Another half hour elapsed. Hampered by their cork jackets, their fingers numbed and slippery from the driving rain they tossed up and down beside the bathysphere striving to attach the rope guys to the steel eyelets, but at last the job was accomplished. Battered and breathless they scrambled back on to the deck then came the tense moment when the crane and winches were brought into play.

The McKay stood with his left arm round a stanchion and his right raised in the air. He waited for a big wave to break and then, as the ship sank into the trough, gave the signal. The bathysphere was lifted almost entirely out of the water, the winches clanked, the ropes pulled taut and drew it suddenly towards the stern of the ship. There was a loud clang on the girders and when the ship rose again it had been landed.

The whole platform was awash waist high every other moment but the McKay and two other men were lowered to it with ropes round their bodies and succeeded in getting undone the bolts which held the sphere door in place, and ten minutes later the diving party had been hauled to safety.

They were a pitiable sight, bruised, ill, terrified. Count Axel alone among them was able to climb the ladder to the deck; the rest had to be carried up bodily. Vladimir was unconscious, having hit his head against the steel wall of the sphere when thrown violently sideways by a heavy wave. Nicky's face was chalk white and the Doctor's a bilious green. Oscar had fainted and both the girls were trembling and retching in desperate bouts of sea-sickness.

The sailors carried them to their cabins. Camilla's maid put her mistress and Sally to bed while Slinger sent the stewards to look after the others. Count Axel attended to a nasty cut on his face, changed into dry clothes and then staggered up the heaving companion-way to the lounge. He found the McKay there already changed, busy mixing himself a badly needed whisky.

"Drink?" said the McKay gruffly.

"Thank you Captain, that was an exceedingly unpleasant business."

"That's putting it mildly—you're darn lucky to be alive in my opinion."

"You're right, and we owe our lives to you so Slinger tells me. I can only hope for some opportunity to repay you."

The McKay shrugged. "Don't thank me—thank the men. Whatever the risk to themselves they never hesitated for a second to obey my orders. It is a pity though that you should have got off lightly. You deserve to be below retching up your heart with the women."

"Really Captain!" Count Axel raised his eyebrows. "Isn't that a little ungenerous. May one enquire in what way I, particularly, have incurred your displeasure?"

"Well—you encouraged them to go under in that blasted ball from the beginning—didn't you?"

"Yes, I did. I was anxious that none of my friends should miss such a remarkable experience. You would, I think, feel the same if you had been down yourself and knew the strange beauty which lies beneath our feet. I was wrong to persuade the others perhaps but it had not occurred to me that we might be caught so suddenly in a storm. Surely that was rather an exceptional occurrence and one usually has ample warning when bad weather is approaching?"

"True," the McKay admitted a little reluctantly, "you might do a full season's diving and not get caught again like that, but I've been scared of these descents from the first. Something else may happen. Say one of the windows was cracked against a jutting rock as you are lowered to the bottom. You'd all be dead in ten seconds."

Count Axel smiled as he drained his whisky. "Such a misfortune is most unlikely. Anyhow I shall not let to-day's unpleasant experience prevent me from going down again immediately the weather clears."

"By the time that happens we may all be on our way to the Falklands," said the McKay gloomily.

"True. For the moment I had forgotten our more serious trouble. I should be terribly distressed though if we are shanghaied before we can go down again, because I am certain now that we are about to succeed in proving the Atlantis theory."

"You did find something on this last dive then?"

"Yes—not much. We were down for so little time. Our first landing was useless owing to the fact that the ship had drifted from its original position, but we tried moving a quarter of a mile to the east and found ourselves on the fringe of a group of enormous stones. They had been rounded by the centuries of friction from the currents on the ocean floor but they were quite unlike any natural formation. We only saw them for a moment and then we were pulled up. We asked the reason over the telephone and were told 'Captain Ardow's orders.' Having no knowledge of the approaching storm we were very annoyed, and puzzled. Then we got your message. The trouble began about half an hour afterwards and by the time we were up to five-hundred feet that infernal ball was being tossed about like a crazy thing. The telephonist was being violently ill already and one by one the others followed suit. Sally was the last to give way except for Vladimir and he, poor fellow, knocked himself out when the cable was slackened too suddenly and the sphere nearly turned turtle."

"Well, I'm glad I was out of that party," the McKay remarked grimly; "but if you're right and you have actually found remains of the Atlantean city, I still don't see how the Doctor's going to prove it. Any hieroglyphics which may have been on these stones will have been erased by the currents long ago."

"Above the sea floor yes, but remember that they are half buried in solid lava and, just as the lava from Vesuvius covered and preserved the contents of the houses in Pompeii so that by scraping it away even wall paintings, and the most fragile ornaments have been recovered—so it should be here."

"Perhaps, but it is impossible for you to carry on any excavations while you are cooped up in the bathysphere, and equally impossible for you to get outside it."

"The bathysphere will do our excavating for us," smiled the Count. "Rough and ready excavating I admit, so unfortunately there is little likelihood of our getting any but broken remains to the surface. However, it is a very remarkable piece of mechanism, and in its undercarriage it contains an electric drill capable of boring holes in the larva wherever we want them. Another attachment will insert dynamite charges in the holes then we shall be drawn up a few hundred feet and explode them."

"I see. After that I suppose the sphere will go down again and collect the bits with its claws and shovels so that you can bring them up with you and sort out your catch at your leisure."

"Exactly."

The McKay nodded. "Well, I certainly take off my hat to the little Doctor for having thought it all out so thoroughly. But I doubt if you will be able to go down to-morrow."

The ship had covered about fifteen knots and was now coming under the lea of Pico island but she still rolled and shuddered each time the great waves buffetted her beam and clouds of spray mingled with the rain that lashed her decks.

That evening Count Axel and the McKay dined alone. The others were far too ill to join them and Vladimir, they feared,

142

had sustained slight concussion. He had received the blow on his head while endeavouring to hold Camilla steady and, sick as she was, she sent hour by hour to enquire after him.

When Slinger arrived on his nightly visit to enforce the curfew he smiled at the McKay.

"Great stuff to-day, Captain. The show you put up getting in the bathysphere enables me to give the waiting world a real thrill to-morrow."

The McKay only grunted.

"EX NAVAL CAPTAIN, ZEEBRUGGE V.C. SAVES MILLIONAIRE DUCHESS AND HER PARTY." Slinger went on with an amiable grin. "That's the headline twenty million people will be goggling over at their breakfast tables. I've radioed a great description of your epic battle with the elements and started a rumour that the lovely Duchess is thinking of marrying her brave rescuer. I'm beginning to think I ought to have been a journalist and not a lawyer after all."

"You're a bloody crook!" said the McKay sullenly.

"So it seems," agreed the imperturbable Slinger. "I am that greatest of all tragedies. A gifted and conscientious professional man who has failed to make an honest living. Now drink up and think *that* over between the sheets."

On the Friday conditions were slightly better but, although the storm had blown itself out, the sky was still leaden and high seas put any descent in the bathysphere out of the question. The ship still rolled and pitched with a beastly lurching motion and every rivet in it strained when an unusually large wave lifted its screw out of the water.

The Doctor spent the morning with four members of the crew straightening out the fantastic tangle in which the last half mile of communication hose had had to be abandoned on the previous day. Then, when it had been coiled down again, although the bathysphere platform was still awash, he was helped into his ball so that he might test the telephone and lighting wires. To his intense relief their inch thick rubber coating had saved them and, when he came for'ard to lunch, he was able to state that they still carried the current to their instruments.

For want of something better to do, apparently, Count Axel offered to lend his assistance in straightening up the contents of the sphere and getting it all in order so that they could descend again without delay when the sea was calmer,

Slinger's permission was obtained for the Count to go aft and so, when the meal was over, he disappeared for the afternoon with the Doctor.

Nicky had put in an appearance for lunch and although his bout of sea sickness seemed to have done him little harm he was peevish and irritable. His mind was obsessed once more with the question of whether he would get back to Hollywood 'this year—next year—now—or never' and the cherry stones on his plate having declared 'Never' he had gone off in a fit of black depression to mope alone in a corner of the lounge. The McKay sought out Camilla's maid and sent a message by her to the two girls.

"Captain McKay presents his compliments to the ladies and if they are capable of getting up they will feel far better out in the air on deck."

This resulted in both Sally and Camilla staggering up the hatchway about an hour later and, having selected a corner sheltered from the wind, the McKay soon had them tucked up warm and comfortable in a couple of deck chairs.

Both of them looked pale and shaky. They had not been actually sick since the previous afternoon but their experience had been extremely frightening and the bout had been a bad one while it lasted. They were now more sorry for themselves than really ill and the salt air soon got a little colour back into their cheeks once the McKay's chatter had taken their thoughts off their condition.

He did not attempt to reproach them, as he had Count Axel for being fools to go down in the sphere at all, but fussed over them without ostentation, in a nice comforting sort of way which caused Camilla to say that she had never quite appreciated what a frightfully nice person he was until that moment, and made Sally somewhat secretly thrilled to have him like her. She almost regarded him as her personal property now and preened herself that Camilla should see him in such a good light when he laid himself out to entertain them.

He was recounting an episode of his earlier years when he had tried, and failed miserably, to get off with an extremely good looking young woman in Malta. Then, having the horrifying experience of meeting her at dinner two nights later and learning that she was his Admiral's wife just out from England.

"Was she a sport or did she tell?" asked Sally.

144

The McKay's eyes twinkled. "She never told—then, *or* about the fun we had together later."

"You wicked old man!"

"No, m'dear it was the Admiral who was old—in that case."

"Ship!" Camilla exclaimed suddenly.

The McKay had been sitting on a small stool at their feet with his back to the sea. He jumped up and stared at the long low craft that had just come into view round the corner of the deck house.

"She's an oil tanker," he cried, "driven out of her course by the storm last night I expect. Where the devil are the others."

He dived through the door of the lounge and saw Nicky poring gloomily over a scribbled sheet of figures which showed roughly what his broken contracts were going to cost him.

"Hi!" he called "Ship—only a quarter of a mile away on our port beam. Come on m'lad and keep your eye on the gunmen by the wireless house while I flag her."

Nicky needed no second bidding. He rammed his sheet of calculations in his pocket and tumbled out on deck.

"Let me know the moment you see them coming," cried the McKay and he produced a couple of large white handkerchiefs that he had kept ready on him for the purpose of signalling.

Sally and Camilla had already cast aside their rugs and were watching the long barge like craft with its single funnel at the stern. Now they glanced anxiously at the bridge fearing that the McKay would be spotted at any moment.

He had ensconced himself in an angle made by the deck house which was not visible from above however, and was waving the two handkerchiefs at the full extent of his arms in an endeavour to attract the attention of the people on the tanker.

Nicky had hardly installed himself beside the rope barrier and endeavoured to assume his most innocent expression when Slinger came dashing out of the deck house.

"In you go," he shouted. "*And* the rest—where are they?"

Slinger, for once, was not accompanied by any of the gunmen so Nicky stood his ground hoping to give the McKay another few moments.

"Get inside," cried Slinger. "Get inside d'you hear me."

At the sound of raised voices Sally and Camilla appeared and the former stared at Slinger with well assumed surprise.

"What's all the excitement about!" she enquired innocently.

"Get inside," repeated Slinger savagely. "See that damn ship—think I'm going to give you any chance to signal it —where's the McKay got to?"

The McKay was just round the corner waving his arms frantically up and down but Slinger did not wait for an answer. His arm shot out and caught Nicky on the shoulder giving him a violent shove towards the entrance of the lounge.

Nicky thought again of the total figure on that horrible piece of paper in his pocket and decided to risk it. He lashed out with sudden vicious savagery and caught Slinger full on his beak-like nose.

"Well done," cried Camilla. "Oh well done, Nicky darling."

Her encouragement was all he needed to get him really going and he began to hit out right and left. For a moment Slinger was blinded by tears and could see nothing, then he too began to drive and hammer, while he bellowed with all his might for assistance.

Neither of the two were trained boxers or had ever struck a blow in anger since they had left their schools so their scrap was more humorous than dangerous except for the first solid punch that Nicky had landed.

A moment later two of Slinger's men came running up with drawn pistols. Nicky now felt that discretion was far the better part of valour and holding his hands above his head backed into the deck house.

Meanwhile, Captain Ardow and two more men had hurried round from the starboard side and surprised the McKay in his violent endeavours to flag the tanker with his handkerchiefs. He too felt that a day was a day and thrusting one of them into his pocket began to blow his nose violently with the other.

"Inside please, Captain," snapped the Russian with a stony glare. "Else you will catch something more dangerous than influenza."

"Certainly," said the McKay laconically, "but so will you, Captain, unless you see reason before you're much older."

"Get in—also stay in until further order," Captain Ardow

146

waved his gun with a significant gesture and so the McKay joined the others in the lounge.

"Any luck?" asked Sally.

"No m'dear," he shook his head. "The tanker probably only had a cabin boy on the bridge. In any case they never saw me."

"You should have seen me hit him," said Nicky excitedly. "I got him—didn't I Camilla—right on the nose."

"Yes darling," she cooed. "You were a perfect hero. I shall never forget the way you stood up to him—never."

Certainly nobody was allowed to forget Nicky's bravery in the hours that followed. Much as he disliked Prince Vladimir he could not resist paying the invalid a visit to give him a personal description of how he had hit Slinger—"right on the nose"—and of course Count Axel and the Doctor were treated to every detail of the scrap when they returned from getting the bathysphere in order for its next descent.

After dinner that night this one abortive attempt to secure assistance was the sole topic of conversation and they only came down to earth when Sally said irritably:

"Oh, Nicky was splendid we all agree but that doesn't alter the fact that we are in just as hopeless a mess as ever, and—this is our last night here—to-morrow's Saturday."

The McKay glanced at Camilla. "I suppose if we *could* arrange something you'd be prepared to pay pretty handsomely for it?"

She nodded. "Yes, Sally suggested that the other day There's a quarter of a million dollars for anyone who'll see us landed safe in a United States port."

"All right—I doubt if anything will come of it but I'll have a talk with Slinger. There's just a chance that he might be prepared to double cross his boss for a whacking great sum like that."

"We'll leave you to it then." Sally stood up. "There's more likelihood of his listening if he finds you on your own and the sight of Nicky is pretty certain to infuriate him."

The others followed her example and when Slinger arrived at ten o'clock the McKay was the sole occupant of the lounge.

A big strip of plaster decorated the lawyer's beak testifying to Nicky's prowess, and he displayed none of his usual good humour.

"Down you go," he said abruptly.

The McKay glanced towards the two gunmen who remained standing quietly in the doorway, then at Slinger.

"Can I talk to you alone for a minute?"

"No," said Slinger, "go below."

"I'm unarmed as you can see and you can keep me covered if you wish—but I've got to talk to you."

"Get—below!"

"All right," the McKay shrugged, "if you won't send your friends away I'll talk to all three of you. This game you're playing looks pretty profitable I know, but if that faked will fails to be upheld in the courts you won't get a penny piece and, what's more, sooner or later the police will run you down and you'll all get a long stretch in jail for this hold up."

"Get below," Slinger repeated.

"I'm going—when I've said my say," announced the McKay doggedly. "Now the Duchess knows that her lawyers will contest that will and if you go off to New York to-morrow you'll find a policeman on the quay to arrest you."

Slinger's eyes narrowed. "How can you possibly know that?"

"Never you mind. Trying to semaphore with a couple of handkerchiefs isn't the only way of communicating with passing shipping."

"Have you been up to something?"

The McKay met Slinger's angry glance with a cold stare. "D'you think I'd tell you if I had—but I wasn't born yesterday and you can't keep a man who's spent his life at sea in a ship indefinitely, against his will."

"Well—what have you got to say."

"Send your friends away and I'll tell you."

Slinger shook his head.

"All right then. If the three of you will come in with us and arrange for our party to be landed at any port which possesses a United States or British Consul the Duchess will guarantee you the sum of two hundred and fifty thousand dollars cash, and no questions asked or action to be taken. That's a hell of a lot of money—what about it?"

The barest flicker of a smile touched Slinger's lips. If they were offering a quarter of a million dollars for their freedom they could have very little hope of gaining it by any other means. Obviously this talk of the will being seriously contested and communications with other ships which would assure his arrest on landing was pure bluff.

148

He hardly hesitated a second before dismissing the offer from his mind but even before he spoke one of the gunmen tapped him on the arm.

"Send him below Boss—or Captain Ardow'll be wantin' ter know just what's been keepin' you all this time."

Slinger jerked his head in the direction of the companion-way. "Forget it," he said, "and no more attempts to signal ships. I shan't be so lenient next time. Down to your cabin now."

The McKay saw the futility of endeavouring to prolong the discussion. Slinger had been set to watch them but Captain Ardow had been set to watch Slinger and probably one or more of the gunmen were completely loyal to Kate and watching both Slinger and the Captain in his interest, on top of which the whole lot of them were keeping the wireless men, officers and crew under their observation. Mentally, the McKay was compelled to salute that some-time scholar at one of England's leading public schools who had organised the whole business, and physically, he took himself off to bed.

In the morning a long rolling swell, aftermath of the storm, still made bathysphere diving impossible, but the sky had lightened and the weather was warmer. The McKay and Sally bathed in the pool. Vladimir was on deck again, hand-some and romantic looking with a white bandage round his dark curly head. For Nicky the night's sleep had only served to reinforce his opinion that he was in truth a hero and Camilla's chosen champion. He had no doubt whatso-ever that if only they could get out of the clutches of this gang she would marry him to-morrow. He was the only person who had actually struck a blow for her and the episode grew in his mind to gigantic proportions. "Well, I hit him anyhow—right on the nose," was the remark which he made to various members of the party at least a dozen times during the morning.

The sea had eased at least sufficiently for them to steam out into the open and by the employment of the electric sounding machine locate the site of the lost city by mid-day. The sun came out and there seemed no reason now why it should not stay out for several consecutive days. By half past two the swell was no more than an undulation of the glassy surface and the Doctor announced his intention of going down. He was however in some difficulty because Oscar, his telephonist, had gone on strike. That seedy youth had not yet recovered from his experience of two days before and had definitely stated that nothing would ever induce him to go down in the bathysphere again.

Doctor Tisch called for a volunteer among the passengers to take Oscar's place and looked confidently towards Count Axel, but the Count said that willingly as he would have done so, he was the victim of a wicked migraine and, to his great disappointment, was not well enough to go down at all that day. Upon which Nicky, who was suffering from a bravery complex at the moment, promptly said that he would take Oscar's place.

Vladimir, not to be outdone, declared his intention of accompanying them but the two girls said that although they might go down again later, their last experience was too recent for them to care about another trip at the moment. The McKay refrained from reminding them that since it was Saturday this was probably their last chance of ever going on another dive and settled himself to entertain them. Count Axel, holding his forehead with his hand, went down to his cabin just as the bathysphere party departed aft.

It was sunset before the sphere was hauled in again and even so it had been less than an hour at the bottom. Nicky and Vladimir hurried forward to report the Doctor's operations. They had landed in the outer fringe of the great stones again, some of which they judged to be eighty feet in height, bored three holes at the base of one, inserted charges, been drawn up 400 feet, and then exploded them. After which they had descended again for the sphere's undercarriage to collect as much of the débris as it could carry and the Doctor was sorting the contents of the dredge at the moment.

"Well, it's some comfort to think none of you will have any further opportunity of risking your necks in that darned thing," the McKay remarked, "we'll be sailing for Horta I expect this evening."

"Oh, this is hellish!" exclaimed Sally hitting the arm of her chair with a small clenched fist. "The whole week's gone and we've done nothing. Isn't there any way we can save ourselves from that devil Kate?"

The McKay shrugged. "M'dear I told you what happened when I tried to scare Slinger and then bribe him last night. Even if he were willing he couldn't help us. The whole crowd are watching each other like cats and they've got us cold at the moment. Try and be patient. I think our chance may come before we reach the Falklands."

"We'll never reach the Falklands," said Sally with conviction. "When Kate learns——"

She never completed her sentence for at that moment Doctor Tisch came bursting into the lounge.

"Look," he cried and the pudgy hand he held out was quivering with excitement. It held a triangular piece of stone, one side of which showed a smooth dull cloudy reddish surface. "Look please," he repeated. "I haf polished a little —soon I will polish again and it will become clear and bright. This stone is faced with pure red copper—orichalcum. Atlantis is found again—found I tell you. To-morrow—next week I will bring up silver and gold."

They stared at this first certain symbol which honestly justified the Doctor's theories. Copper facings did not grow on rocks at the sea bottom, no one could contest that. Some long dead human must have worked this metal found 5,000 feet under the sea. It was an incontestable proof that the great stones beneath them were truly the remains of a mighty building erected by an ancient race. Further dives might bring the most staggering discoveries; not only gold and gems but perhaps the data of arts and sciences unknown to even the modern world as yet.

Slinger, accompanied by his gunmen, had stepped through the doorway unobserved by the little group gathered round the excited Doctor. Suddenly he spoke:

"I'm sorry. It's real hard lines now the Doctor's proved his fairy story to be true after all, but this time to-morrow you'll all be the best part of two hundred miles from here."

They swung round on him and the Doctor stuttered: "You cannot—you cannot. Think please what this discovery means for science—and for the whole world. There is gold also— much gold. Take that if you like—but my exploration must go on.

Slinger shook his head. "I'm sorry but our plans are made and I couldn't upset them if you promised me a million. I radioed the announcement about the bathysphere having burst at four o'clock this afternoon and ten minutes later every wireless station in the world will have known of the Duchess's death and that of her whole party except Sally."

"Please—please," moaned the Doctor. "Think what this means for science."

"Come on, Slinger," urged the McKay. "Now the Doctor has proved his point you might give him a chance. You know we are completely helpless against your men. If we had thought there was any chance of upsetting your apple cart we should have started something long before this. What's it matter giving him a few days anyhow before running us down to the Falklands."

"It's no good," said Slinger firmly. "I've got to catch the weekly boat from Horta to-morrow morning, so as to see things through in New York. We are sailing right now."

Count Axel's head appeared above the banisters of the companion-way. His headache had apparently disappeared. He smiled his lazy indolent smile.

"I'm afraid you're mistaken Slinger. This ship is not sailing anywhere for some considerable time."

He gave a quick glance at his watch, grabbed the banisters with both hands, and shouted:

"Hang on everybody and be ready for the shock."

Nobody but the McKay heeded his warning and for thirty seconds there was a tense silence as they tried to grasp his meaning.

Then the deck seemed to rise up and hit them, the whole ship shuddered violently and, as they were flung off their feet a deafening explosion shattered the silence like the crack of a twelve inch gun.

CHAPTER XIII

THE MC KAY MAKES A GRAND SLAM

THE first to recover was one of Slinger's gunmen who fell sprawling in the doorway. Quick as a cat he rolled over on his stomach, fired a warning shot through the skylight before the reverberation of the explosion had died away, and bellowed:

"Put 'em up all of you—Put 'em up or I'll drill you!"

The McKay was still standing and, as he raised his arms under the threat of the pistol, he whipped round on Count Axel:

"God man! Have you holed the ship?"

A confused shouting and the sound of people clattering down ladders came from outside on the deck.

Slinger staggered to his feet and glared in the same direction. "What the hell have you been up to—what have you done eh?"

"I don't quite know yet," the Count admitted, lifting his hands to the level of his head. "We were a little anxious that you should not leave us so I took steps to ensure that the ship would be quite unable to proceed to Horta."

"Damn you, what have you done?" snarled Slinger.

The Count smiled with considerable enjoyment. "I've had no chance to investigate the extent of the damage but I stole half a dozen of the good Doctor's depth charges when I was helping him in the bathysphere yesterday and, this afternoon, I inserted them in the machinery. Unfortunately, I know very little about engines but I trust you will find that the propeller shaft is beyond repair."

"Hell!" exclaimed Slinger turning to the doorway. "Here Bozo, keep these people covered and let them have it if they play any monkey tricks." Then he dashed below to find out what had happened.

The ship had steadied, the whole party were on their feet again but Bozo and his companion held them motionless under the muzzles of their guns.

Suddenly the McKay began to hum with quiet enjoyment:

"What shall we do with a drunken sailor?
What shall we do with a drunken sailor?
Put him in a boat until he's sober.
Early—in the—morn—ing."

Sally giggled and joined in the chorus.

"Hi! Hi! up she rises
Hi! Hi! up she rises
Hi! Hi! up—she—rises
Early—in the—morn—ing."

Nicky stared angrily at the gunmen. "I wish to God you birds would go away so we could have a drink."

"Keep 'em up," said Bozo, without the shadow of a smile.

The clamour outside had died down and a silence fell which became monotonous. Camilla broke it by turning the battery of her limpid blue eyes on Axel and saying softly:

"I always knew you had brains, Count. I think you're simply marvellous."

He gave his elegant little bow. "Madame, it is a half measure only, but I hope that it will serve our purpose for the moment."

"Why the deuce did you go and say that it was you who'd done it?" asked the McKay.

"My dear Captain, they were bound to know that one of us was responsible and, if I had not admitted it, they would probably have suspected you."

"Oh—ay! Very decent of you," the McKay nodded his appreciation. "I only hope they won't bear you too much of a grudge. It was a thunderin' good idea."

"Well—anyway I hit him—didn't I? Right on the nose," Nicky muttered in an endeavour to recapture some of his fast vanishing glory.

"My arms," sighed Camilla. "They'll drop off if I'm not allowed to lower them soon."

"Better keep 'em up, sister," the muscular looking thug who answered to the name of Bozo advised her seriously, "or it's you who'll be dropping."

To their relief Slinger came panting back up the companion-way a moment later.

"It would serve you damn well right if I had you put in irons," he snapped at Axel. "Anyhow I'm not trusting any of you an inch after this. My two men will keep you company from now on and none of you are to move out of the lounge until you go down to dinner. You can put your hands down now."

"Aren't we to be allowed to change?" asked Camilla. "We're late to-night as it is."

"No you'll dine as you are and be locked in your cabins immediately afterwards." With a worried frown Slinger stamped angrily away to find Captain Ardow.

"Well—that's that," said the McKay, moving over to a wheeled tray which one of the stewards had brought in just before the explosion. Two of the bottles on it had fallen over but all were corked and only one glass had been smashed. "Anyone like a drink?"

"Thank you—I would," Sally replied as she flopped down on a settee.

"Nicky darling, will you do things for us," Camilla said sweetly as she took the opposite corner to Sally.

Under cover of the rattle made by the ice in Nicky's cocktail shaker the McKay remarked to Count Axel: "It was a darn fine idea, but why by all that's holy didn't you tell us what you meant to do—we might have jumped the gunmen if we'd had a little warning."

The Count shook his head. "That would have been dangerous and useless. For one thing I did not know that these two would be here and even if the four of us had succeeded in gaining possession of their weapons there are so many more of them outside. They have a machine gun in the wireless house and another on the bridge. What could be easier than for them to push the machine guns through the skylight and massacre us all."

"True," the McKay agreed taking the glass of froth topped mixture that Nicky offered him, "but we might have held Slinger and these two birds as hostages."

"I doubt if that would have had much effect. No one of them is more than a cog in Oxford Kate's machine. I have prevented the ship from leaving this area and Slinger from reaching Horta by to-morrow morning so I am content—for the moment."

"Yes, it was a good show and you're mighty lucky to have escaped being put in irons in my opinion."

Count Axel smiled. "I agree, I had to take that risk, but I considered this creation of delay worth it."

The cocktails had passed round. Bozo and his friend had settled themselves in chairs, each guarding one of the deck entrances. The McKay glanced from one to another of them. "You chaps care for anything," he asked affably.

Bozo replied for both of them. "We'll help ourselves if we feel like a shot, but we got plenty of liquor aft an' the orders about our being dumb to your crowd stand—so you'd best forget us."

To ignore their presence was easier suggested than carried out so conversation among Camilla's party became a little halting, but, when dinner had been announced, and the guards had accompanied them below, they saw that if they were to be driven to their cabins immediately afterwards their only chance to discuss the possible effect of this new development on their own situation was between the soup and the savoury —even if it necessitated being overheard by Bozo and his friend.

Doctor Tisch was entirely one minded on the matter; full of praise for Count Axel and in a high good humour. What ever might follow he felt that the wrecking of the engine had ensured him at least one, if not more opportunities to explore the sunken capital of Atlantis.

The McKay agreed, and stated that since he had seen the crew casting out kedge anchors from the deck house windows while they were drinking their cocktails it was reasonably certain that the ship would remain in much the same position considering that the evening had produced an almost glassy sea but, he added, "Things won't be half so funny if it begins to blow. A ship that lacks power is like a man who's lost the use of his legs. Neither can either fight or run, they've just got to take what's coming to them. If a sea gets up we're going to roll like blazes, so make up your minds to that, and although the chances are against it, we might quite well be piled up on the rocks of Pico."

"Can't they keep the rudder straight," asked Sally ingenuously.

He stared at her from beneath his bushy eyebrows. "A rudder m'dear can't steer a gig unless there's pressure against it by the boat being forced through the water. We'll be just like a cork in a whirlpool if a storm does get up but fortunately there is little likelihood of that."

"I wish you wrong," declared Vladimir. "If the weather remits a storm we take ourselves to the boats. The sand of Pico is hospitable to our nearness. Then, this conspiracy of bandits is wrecked by crikey and we put our thumbs to our eyebrows."

"That possibility did occur to me," announced Count Axel modestly.

"How long do you think it will take to repair the engines?" Camilla asked.

The McKay shrugged. "It's difficult to say since we don't know the extent of the damage, but if the Count is right and he has wrecked the propeller shaft it's not a question of days but complete refitting in dry dock. As a first move, if that's happened, they've probably wireless Punta Delgarda for a tender to tow us in. There wouldn't be one at a little place like Horta."

"Then Slinger will be able to leave the ship after all to-morrow." Nicky's voice held grievous disappointment.

"Yes, but he'll have missed his boat for New York so he is stuck in the Azores for another week, and that, I take it was the Count's principal object.'"

"True," the Count bowed, "that, I think we agreed, was our most immediate necessity."

"But it won't prevent Kate coming out to us," said Sally miserably.

"How?" asked the McKay. "How can he, even if he wants to, and I've never seen any reason why he should."

"We were all reported dead this afternoon. Fifty people will have been on the long distance to Camilla's lawyers by this time pressing for particulars of her will. Kate will get wise to it somehow things aren't going to run as smoothly as he thinks for him. Then he'll come back here just as fast as he can. That's the sort of man he is."

"But what are you afraid he is going to do if he does?"

"Heaven knows," Sally dug viciously into her biscuit ice, "I don't—but I've a feeling that he'll make things horribly unpleasant for us all."

"Leastways," Vladimir commented. "If this defence you sit upon so forcibly is made by our so beautiful Duchess's lawyer why should we sad ourselves. For a week more her fortune is reserved and in that space Nicky our probation shall accept to give Slinger a blue-eye."

"You missed it," said Nicky, "but the others saw. I hit him, didn't I—right on the nose."

"How unfortunate," remarked the Prince with a flash of his white teeth, "that I was lying still in my cabin this time. Otherwise that poor Slinger's thick ears would now be standing out on the backside of his head."

Bozo, sitting by the doorway of the dining room coughed. It was not that he had the least interest in Slinger's ears, in fact the conversation was almost unintelligible to him, but he did want his own dinner, and knew that he would not get it as long as the people at the table talked stupid nonsense instead of eating up their food.

The reminder of his presence, and that of his friend at the far end of the apartment stilled conversation and five minutes after coffee had been served he was able to stand up, cough again, and see his charges to their cabins. Vladimir taking the Kummel bottle with him as he said, "To be a safe guarding against revisiting pains in the old knob."

As they went below the McKay got next to Sally and murmured under his breath, "Don't worry m'dear. Unless Captain Ardow's mad he'll have to get us towed to safe anchorage by a tender. When it comes alongside I'll chuck them my tin box with the letter to the Police. Then we'll have Mr Slinger cornered and your friend Kate too if he turns up in time for the party."

Sally wished him a loud good-night but gave his hand a grateful squeeze as she turned with new cheerfulness towards her cabin.

Slinger had far more cause for worry than his prisoners that evening. He knew that his chief would not take at all a good view of this new situation and would call upon him to answer for not having kept his charges more closely under guard. Over dinner with Captain Ardow he aired his anxiety and the Russian was neither comforting or helpful.

It seemed that despite his lack of knowledge of machinery Count Axel had succeeded in completely disabling the ship without injuring any member of the crew. A reconstruction of his sabotage showed that he must have managed to reach the after hold without being spotted while pretending to be ill in his cabin that afternoon; stacked his dynamite round the propeller shaft, waited until the bathysphere had been hauled up in case the force of the explosion wrecked the crane on the deck above; then lighted a time fuse and gone forward. The engine room remained unharmed and, as the hold was empty the explosion was not sufficiently confined to blow a hole in the bottom of the vessel, but the propeller shaft was cracked and twisted so that they were now completely at the mercy of the ocean. Captain Ardow explained with brief and bitter feeling that only the kedge anchors that he had thrown out prevented the ship being washed up on the shores of Pico or drifting, completely helpless, down to the South Pole.

Slinger declared that he did not give a cuss what happened to the ship. The all important thing was that he should reach New York at the earliest possible moment.

"So," said Captain Ardow. "Well, I have already wire-lessed Punta Delgarda for a tender."

"The devil you have," exclaimed Slinger. "That's a mighty risky thing to have done. The radio about the Duchess's death only went out this afternoon and we made no request for assistance then. It was not suggested that there had been an accident in the ship but stated clearly that the bathysphere had suddenly caved in under the immense pressure a mile below the water. Don't you see that the news of a second big calamity in the space of a few hours may make people suspect that there's something fishy going on."

Ardow shrugged. "There was no alternative. The ship must be towed to safe anchorage otherwise we perhaps become a wreck. Later the tender can run you in to Horta."

"How long d'you think she'll take to reach us?"

"It is an unusual call upon the resources of so small a port so it is unlikely that they will be ready to leave before midnight. Then it is from a nine to twelve hour trip."

"She may be here any time from nine o'clock on then, but that's too late for me to catch the Horta boat. Even if the tender left you to run me in I'd not get there before midday. God! How livid Kate's going to be when he hears about this mess. It means a week's delay and he's depending on my personal testimony to quash any suggestion of contesting that will."

"When the tender has towed me to a safe anchorage you can return by her to Punta Delgarda," Ardow suggested. "There you might catch a cargo boat calling before it proceeds to an American port, and perhaps save yourself a day or two."

"Yes, that's an idea, but what are you going to do? It's

impossible now for you to run these people down to the Falklands as planned."

"My engineer has not yet reported the full extent of the damage. It may be that we shall have to go into dry dock before we can fit a new shaft. If not so bad and repairs are possible we shall lie up and wait delivery of new pieces from the States, refit ourselves and proceed south."

Slinger angrily stubbed out his cigarette and stood up. "We're in a fine mess either way as far as I can see. I think the best thing would be for Kate to charter a new hooker, have it handed over to you and your crew in Horta or Punta Delgarda then you could collect the passengers and guards off this one and abandon it. The cash doesn't matter if only we can carry the big deal through, but Kate must decide himself, of course."

"Yes. Kate will decide. I have already reported in our code to him and anticipate a wireless at any time. I have said too that the accident makes it impossible for you to catch the Horta boat—so also he will direct if you are to wait or try Punta Delgarda."

"Nice of you to let him know before I had a chance to think things over," remarked Slinger sarcastically. "If you want me I'll be on deck."

The night was peaceful and starlit. The only sound was the gentle lapping of the water against the vessel's sides. She was rolling very slightly having no cruising speed to steady her, but Slinger was used to that from their frequent dead stops in the last week to operate the bathysphere. His nose was still a little sore and uncomfortable from the blow Nicky had landed on it the day before and as he paced up and down chewing the butt of his cigar he brooded unhappily upon the unpleasant possibilities of Kate's cold hard rage when he heard of the way in which his carefully laid plans had been temporarily but very seriously disorganized.

Slinger was still brooding, an hour later, when Captain Ardow sent to tell him that a message had been received. They decoded it together in the chart room and it ran:

"Allow no one from tender on board. Keep passengers below. Order tender to tow you to safe anchorage south of Pico and leave you there. Slinger to remain on board. Leaving midnight by amphibian to join you.

K."

Slinger's hand trembled slightly. "So he's coming to take charge himself, eh? Well, I wish to God I was safely through to-morrow. He'll create merry hell for all of us the moment he sets foot on board the ship."

"He has pluck," said Captain Ardow. "To fly two thousand miles of water from New York to the Azores is a thing for which I would not care."

"Oh, he's got pluck enough for ten," Slinger replied abruptly. "But he retains a first class pilot and that amphibian of his is specially built to cover long distances. Good-night, I'm off to bed."

He was awake and about again early next morning. At seven o'clock he invaded Captain Ardow's cabin and asked anxiously, "Look here what are we going to do with the passengers all day. It's vital that they shouldn't get any message to the people on the tender when she turns up."

The Russian yawned sleepily. "Kate has said keep them below. Do so then. Let them remain locked in their cabins."

"That's all right maybe but the trick they played us yesterday has made me nervy. The tender will have to come pretty close alongside, won't it?"

"Yes."

"How close?"

"So near that they can throw a line by which we shall pull up their hawser."

"Exactly," Slinger nodded. "Then what's to prevent Count Axel or one of the others throwing something out to them from a cabin porthole. A promise of a big reward for help or a message to the Punta Delgarda police. They could weight it with coins or any old thing so that it doesn't flutter down to the water."

"You must prevent them then."

"But how? We can keep them all together under Bozo's eye in the dining saloon while the tender is alongside, but one of the men might chance a bullet and chuck something out of the port before the guards could stop him. The tender's deck should be just about that level so there will be plenty of temptation if they do think of trying something of that sort."

Captain Ardow scratched the bristly stubble on his unshaven chin while the two men regarded each other thoughtfully for a moment, then he said slowly. "Why not send them all down in the bathysphere."

161

"Damn it! You took that straight off my tongue," Slinger exclaimed, "and it's a great idea. I'll go and have them knocked up now so that they're safe under water before there's any likelihood of the tender putting in an appearance."

Orders were issued through the stewards and by 8.15 Camilla's party were assembled in a sullen group to learn Slinger's latest decision.

"You don't get me going down in that infernal thing," the McKay growled angrily. "I've never been yet and I'm not going now."

"You are," said Slinger firmly. "And if you won't go quietly my men will tie you up and push you inside it head first—so you can take your choice."

The McKay's weather beaten reddish face went a good three shades deeper in colour and his eyes began to pop below the beetling brows. Sally thought he almost looked as if he was about to burst and quickly placed a restraining hand on his arm.

"Please," she whispered, her grey eyes frightened and pleading, "please don't make a scene—I implore you not to."

"All right, m'dear," he grumbled touched by her concern. "But I'd love to have a cut at 'em."

"Perhaps, but you'd only get shot if you did," Slinger said evenly, "so you'll be wiser to keep your temper and do as you're told."

"I—I don't want to go," Camilla stammered. "It may turn rough again."

"The weather is all set fair. It is unlikely that we shall be caught in so, twice," Vladimir sought to comfort her.

"And Atlantis is to be seen beneath us," chipped in the Doctor cheerfully. "For the ship can have drifted little in this glassy sea."

That certainly was a thought of sufficient interest to intrigue most members of the party in spite of their first reluctance to go on this enforced descent, so without further protest they followed Slinger aft.

The McKay guessed the reason for Slinger's decision to order them all into the sphere and he was furious at it; for he knew that with the ship in its crippled condition Captain Ardow would have been compelled to wireless for assistance and had counted on being able to get his letter to the tender even

162

if he had to go overboard and swim with it. However, he endeavoured to console himself with the thought that there were many fresh possibilities to talk over since the explosion; in the bathysphere they would at least be clear of their guards and so able to do so freely.

The same thought had occurred to Count Axel, but both were disappointed. Slinger announced that he had no intention of giving them the whole day to plot fresh trouble for him and in consequence Bozo had agreed to go down as a check on any scheming.

One by one they climbed into the sphere. The McKay was last and before he entered it he gave a long look at the sky. It was serene and cloudless but there was no unnatural stillness and as far as he could judge they had no need whatever to fear an unexpected return of bad weather. Actually he was not really afraid. He had often made trips in submarines without the least anxiety and the bathysphere had now been proved capable of withstanding pressure equally well even at the great depths to which it descended. He had only refused before from a natural caution and the feeling that some time or other the sphere would meet with a totally unexpected accident. However, it might well go down a hundred times before that happened and therefore the probabilities were all against this proving its unlucky day.

"Nelson Andy McKay, where are you," called Sally from inside the big ball in sudden fear that he had remained outside with the intention of endeavouring to smash up Slinger after all.

"Coming m'dear," he sang out with reassuring cheerfulness and began to wriggle through the small circular opening. The door was clamped on and at 8.45 the bathysphere went under water.

Slinger joined Captain Ardow on the bridge to wait for the tender to turn up and, at the same time, he began to keep a nervous eye on the sky towards the west to sight the approach of Oxford Kate's big plane.

They had their breakfast sent up to the chart room and discussed Kate's possible reactions on his arrival, in a desultory, gloomy sort of way. Both knew that Mr Kate was capable of being not only extremely unpleasant but definitely dangerous when his plans had gone awry. The Russian spoke little except to impress upon Slinger that the prisoners had not been committed to his care so that the lawyer

163

was alone responsible and should be prepared for all the blame
—which he would undoubtedly receive.

Ten o'clock came—eleven, and eleven-thirty. The bathysphere party had reached bottom and although they could not
be towed in any direction, owing to the disablement of the
ship, they had already asked once to be pulled up 300 feet,
and then let down again, so obviously they had struck some
portion of the sunken city and begun blasting operations without delay. At eleven-forty a wisp of smoke was reported by
the look out on the eastward horizon then, two minutes later
Captain Ardow himself drew Slinger's attention to a speck in
the sky to the west north westward; there could be little doubt
that it was Kate's plane and, after circling overhead the big
amphibian swooped down, cut the calm surface of the water,
churning it into creamy foam, and came to rest fifty yards
from the ship.

Ardow had already given orders for a boat to be lowered
and stood by the rail ready to receive his Chief. Slinger
hovered near him, nervous and unhappy. He knew that his
fears had not been without reason the moment Kate's head
appeared over the side.

The plane being enclosed, the broad shouldered elegant
Mr Kate had no need of airmen's helmets or leather jackets.
He was wearing a light grey lounge suit to-day and an
experiment in violet shirting with socks to match. The 'old
school tie' still adorned his neck but the face above it was
as smooth and hard as the prow of a battleship.

Captain Ardow instinctively touched the peak of his
uniform cap and Slinger, forcing a pale smile to his lips,
murmured, "Well Chief—how's everything?"

Kate's cold eyes held him for a second. It was not his
way to discuss business before the crew and he only asked
quietly, "Where are the passengers?"

"On the sea floor in the bathysphere. I thought it best to
get them out of the way as we're expecting the tender from
Punta Delgarda any moment. That's her you can see coming
up in the distance. Slinger pointed to the smoke stack, now
grown larger, on the horizon.

"Right, we'll go up to the chart-room then." Without
another glance Kate led the way and the others followed.

As Slinger shut the door behind them his Chief swung
round upon him. "Now! What have you two been up to?"

"No responsibility for this rests on me," declared Ardow

boldly. "For me the crew to discipline. For Slinger the passengers to guard. That was the arrangement."

"Well, Slinger?" Kate's voice was quietly menacing.

"Damn it all I couldn't help it," Slinger began to bluster. "Count Axel—the Swede—you know, swung the lead yesterday. Pretended he was ill, pinched some dynamite from the Doctor's store, sneaked down into the hold while we thought he was in his cabin and blew the propeller shaft to blazes."

"You think it a sound thing to leave dangerous explosives in the hands of your prisoners eh?"

"Oh have a heart Chief, this stuff was intended for blasting operations under water."

"Under water!" sneered Kate with icy contempt. "Is that any reason to suppose that it would fail to explode in the air. The Count must be soft witted I think not to have blown the bridge up while he was at it and sent the two of you with half my men to Hell!"

"We didn't lose a man," pleaded Slinger. "Not even one of the engine room hands received a scratch, and we had the whole party cold within thirty seconds of the explosion."

"Why should *you* take credit for that. It was merely their own incompetence."

"But Chief there's never been any question of their escaping or securing help. The whole bunch are every bit as much under your thumb as they were this time last week."

"It's lucky for you they are, since I made this trip to see them. Ardow! get them pulled up at once."

The Russian gave an order down the bridge telephone. Slinger felt just a shade easier in his mind. The implication was that Kate had not flown two thousand miles specially to berate him for his carelessness but had a more important reason for his return. After a moment he ventured:

"Did the New York papers play up on the radios we sent?"

"Oh the Press haven't had such a break in a generation," the big square faced man in the grey suit stared moodily out of the chart-room window. He seemed to have forgotten Slinger's criminal negligence. "The papers last night had headlines inches deep about the Duchess's death. It's a great human interest story of course—this poor little rich girl and her bunch of lovers. The Atlantis story alone would have made the editors' hearts rejoice when this crank of a Doctor started discovering mermaids, but with the Duchess in it as well even the marriage of King Karloff has been crowded out. But the innocent looking little devil tricked me and by God she's going to sweat for it. You just watch her eyes start out of her head when I tell her how."

"Tricked," exclaimed Slinger. He almost added, "You," but caught himself in time. "Why, are they contesting that will then—seriously?"

"Yes—it's my fault—mine entirely. The only slip I've ever made I think and it's hard that it should occur in my biggest coup. It never occurred to me to get a specimen of her signature so that I could verify it when she signed the will. She had the wit to alter it apparently and only half an hour before I got your radio I learned from our pigeon in the lawyer's office that they had suspected the genuineness of the document the moment they received it. Immediately her death was reported of course the rat began to stink a mile away. That's how he got on to what she had done."

"What—what do you intend to do, Chief?" Slinger hazarded.

Kate was still staring out of the window, his thoughts apparently far away. He fingered his 'old school tie' meditatively and replied in a voice lacking all emotion:

"Teach her just what it costs to try and be too clever, as I will teach you not to be quite so careless—later on."

There was a horrid silence which continued for several moments, neither Slinger nor Ardow cared to break it. Then a red-faced sailor flung open the chart-room door and thrust his head inside.

"Warship coming up on our port quarter, Captain," he reported, and slammed the door again.

Instantly the three men in the chart-room were startled into activity. Captain Ardow grabbed his glasses, but Kate was the first to tumble outside. They stared in the direction where the smudge of smoke had first appeared on the horizon half an hour before. It was not the tender that they had expected but a long low trim destroyer cleaving the water dead towards them at thirty knots.

Even without glasses they could see that she flew the White Ensign and she was approaching at such speed that in another moment they could see the faces of the men on her decks.

"Hell!" muttered Kate, "I thought the U.S.N. might send a ship out to investigate, what with your radio for a tender and the lawyer's questioning the will all within a few hours of the Duchess's death being reported—but they couldn't have got here under three days and even if they'd sent a plane it wouldn't have started till this morning. But how have the British rumbled us? This can't be coincidence."

"We can neither fight nor run," said Ardow, "and if we *were* under steam that thing could catch us in ten minutes. Look there's another smoke stack about three degrees to the left. That's the tender I expect."

"Never mind the tender," Kate snapped. "Stop that bathysphere coming up. I don't want the party here if we've got to face an enquiry."

"They'll not be anywhere near the surface yet," demurred Slinger.

"You heard me. Do as I tell you. Then get the men together. Ardow have a boat got out on the starboard side. The destroyer can't have been near enough to have seen my plane when it came down and it's concealed now by the bulk of the ship. The gun squad are to be sent off to her without a second's delay. We'll remain for the moment and attempt to bluff things out. Say the sphere caught in the rocks on the bottom when it burst and that's why we can't get it up. With the passengers and guards clear of the ship there'll be nothing suspicious to give us away even if they search it from stem to stern. Sally Hart will have to have been in the bathysphere too, when it burst, after all, so she'll lose her hundred thousand if we do succeed in forcing our version of the will through the courts. Her heirs will get it instead but I can't help that. It's her unlucky day. Immediately the two of you have got the men away you'll receive the visitors. I'm only a curious idler who was staying in the Azores and flew out this morning to see the scene of the tragedy."

Slinger shouted hoarsely down the bridge telephone for the bathysphere to be halted on its upward journey, then shot down the inside ladder to get the men, while Ardow dashed aft to order out a boat.

With what seemed incredible swiftness now the destroyer leapt towards them. It made a graceful curve and came to rest about two hundred yards to port. The shrill pipe of a whistle sounded and, by the time Slinger came panting up the ladder again to report that the gunmen were safely in the boat, the blue jackets had begun to lower a whaler with swift efficiency from the destroyer's side.

"By Jove, they're smart, aren't they—and just to think

that I might be commanding that if I'd gone to Dartmouth as the Governor wanted." Kate spoke with a whole-hearted admiration which left Slinger in open-mouthed amazement then, as Ardow appeared, he snapped. "Down you go—both of you. There's nothing to be scared of. You've got a water-tight story and it should be easy to pull the wool over the officers' eyes."

He stepped out on to the port side of the low bridge where he would be able both to see and hear what passed at the interview, while Slinger and Ardow hurried down to the deck. A ladder was lowered and then they stood waiting with nervous impatience to learn the meaning of this visitation.

The destroyer's boat was gently fended off and a Naval Officer came up the ladder followed by a dozen men all armed with short rifles. He carefully dusted his coat, saluted the quarter deck, and took in Captain Ardow with a glance that was almost as steely as Kate's.

"You are the Captain of this ship," he asked.

"Yes, Captain Ardow at your service," the Russian replied.

"You have a Captain McKay sailing as one of your passengers?"

"We had until this terrible tragedy. You will have heard I——"

"You *have* I said," the Naval Officer repeated icily, "and you will send this message to him. 'Lieutenant Commander Landon Macy presents his compliments to Captain McKay and would be grateful for a word with him at once.' "

"But that is impossible," Ardow protested. "Did you not hear over the wireless last night——"

"Yes, I heard," Landon Macy interrupted grimly, "but the game's up my man. Captain McKay was too smart for you. He's been morsing with his cabin light each night in the hope that some ship would pick up his signals. Last night he was successful although he got no reply because he kept on sending out a warning that his signals should not be acknowledged in case you tumbled to what was happening. The whole story was relayed to Gib and we were wirelessed to pick you up, so you'll send my message at once."

Slinger had gone deadly white. "We—we can't," he stammered. "The accident did happen and the bathysphere's stuck on the bottom with them dead in it."

The Naval Officer swung round on him. "They're no more dead than I am, but I suppose you sent them down in it to get them out of the way. You'll get that bathysphere up, blast you, and be quick about it or I'll know the reason why.''

Kate had been listening on the low bridge above. His hands began to tremble with fury when he realised that the McKay had outwitted him and that his entire scheme had been blown to smithereens. Now he slipped down a ladder and ran swiftly aft.

Landon Macy caught sight of him out of the tail of his eye. "Who's that?" he snapped.

"A—a visitor," Slinger stuttered uncertainly.

"Visitor be damned!" exclaimed Landon Macy swinging round to a Petty Officer. "Stevens keep a couple of men and arrest these two. The rest of you follow me." Then drawing his revolver, he dashed after Kate.

Kate reached the open sided crane house thirty seconds in advance. White hot with rage he had determined that the skilful manoeuvres of Camilla and the McKay to outwit him should cost the whole party their lives.

The machinery was silent. The bathysphere dangling, halted on its upward journey in accordance with his last instructions. A group of seamen lounged idly by, waiting for fresh orders. Kate pushed his way past them and leapt into the crane house, thrusting the engineer aside.

For a second he stared at the machinery then he seized the big lever and pulled it right over. The cable began to run out at lightning speed. "That's done it," he thought. "When the cable comes to an end it will snap off the drum or if they reach bottom first the bloody thing will be smashed up on the rocks."

"Shove up your hands!" yelled Landon Macy, bursting in through the port door.

Kate threw him one swift contemptuous glance, then in a flash he had bounded out of the starboard entrance on to the deck.

Landon Macy followed. His pistol cracked. Kate lurched wildly just as he reached the ship's rail then recovered and leapt over into the sea.

The blue jackets, their rifles at the ready, dived through the maze of winches, hose coils, and cable drums which crowded the stern of the vessel, following their officer as he ran towards the ship's side.

Kate's head had already appeared above water and he was

swimming strongly towards his amphibian. They raised their rifles to take aim.

Suddenly a machine gun began to stutter from the plane. A hail of bullets spattered the machinery and the deck. One sailor fell, hit in the stomach—another in the legs. The rest dashed for cover.

Crouching behind the winches two of them took pot shots at Kate but he dived again and the bullets missed him. Two more machine guns were brought into play by his men. Three streams of bullets now thudded, zipped, whined, as they sprayed the deck and ricochetted from the machinery. The sailors were compelled to keep behind their cover and under such terrific fire dared not peer out to risk another shot.

Landon Macy, back behind the crane house was rapidly semaphoring his ship, to tell them of the hidden plane.

His Commander had heard the shooting and ordered out another boat with reinforcements. Now, he stood gripping the bridge rail with a little group of officers and men behind him all taking in Landon Macy's signals. None of them had yet seen the plane which lay concealed behind Doctor Tisch's ship but immediately they realised what was happening orders were given for an anti-aircraft gun to be prepared for action immediately the plane left the water.

Kate was being hauled aboard at the very moment the order was given. The engines of the plane burst into a roar. With hardly a second's delay it began to move swiftly over the smooth water while its machine guns still kept up a heavy fusillade to cover its retreat.

By the time the canvas gun-covers had been removed the amphibian had already circled into the wind and risen in the air.

With frantic haste the gun's crew loaded up and sighted their weapon. The plane had climbed five hundred feet.

Suddenly it swerved, losing height a little. Then shot up at so sharp an angle that it seemed certain it must stall and come crashing down tail first into the water; but Kate's pilot was an ace and knew his business. The pompom gave a series of staccato cracks, but the livid flame of the shell bursts surrounded by their fleecy clouds of grey smoke were three hundred feet beneath him.

The attempts to bring down the plane continued. The Commander of the destroyer, a little man, not unlike the McKay in his general appearance, got redder and redder in the face as Kate's amphibian rose higher in the air, successfully avoiding the successive bursts of shell fire from the anti-aircraft gun by constant dives, twists, and changes of direction.

Landon Macy and his men stood gaping skywards on the scarred after deck among Doctor Tisch's machinery, praying for a hit which would bring down the plane, but after a few moments the gun on the destroyer ceased fire. The amphibian was now only a black spot in the bright blue sky disappearing swiftly to the westward.

As the men moved to pick up the wounded, Landon Macy suddenly thought of the bathysphere again. He ran to the crane house. The engineer was lying hunched at the foot of the starboard ladder, blood dripped slowly from his shattered head into a great pool on the deck. He had been caught in the first burst of machine gun fire and was quite dead. The other members of the crew had dived below to safety.

The Lieutenant Commander sprang up the ladder. The big lever was still turned right over to 'full out' where Kate had jammed it. The cable was sizzling through the steel blocks above it at a terrific speed. They would have been on fire with the heat caused by the friction if they had been wood. The great drums were whirling round like the wheels of a locomotive as the cable left them, the whole machinery hummed and vibrated like a powerful dynamo at full beat. Landon Macy gave the roaring machinery one anxious glance then grabbed the lever. As he jerked it back to stop the bathysphere crashing on the bottom its gears grated harshly— then it slid into reverse.

CHAPTER XIV

THE LAST DIVE

O N the day after Kate's seizure of the ship the McKay, almost as a matter of routine, had played with his gold pencil and a piece of paper for half an hour until he had drafted a brief message stating the situation without one unnecessary word. It began: "S.O.S. Do not acknowledge. Relay to Admiralty." Then followed a concise account of Kate's conspiracy.

That night, and each night since he had morsed the report by means of the light switch in his cabin at least a dozen times between ten o'clock and dawn; taking his sleep in three hour stretches. He had felt convinced that providing his little game was not stopped through one of the people on the bridge spotting the reflection of his flashes in the water, the message would certainly be picked up sooner or later, and help arrive; although he had no great hopes of getting it through until they crossed the great shipping belts on the way south to the Falklands.

When he scrambled into the bathysphere at 8.45 on the morning after the explosion therefore, he had not the least idea that his signals had been picked up the night before and that the Admiralty had ordered a destroyer to be detached from a flotilla which was proceeding to the Bermudas, for their rescue.

Sally insisted that since this was his first dive he should be given one of the canvas chairs nearest the portholes and, to get him settled in it, needed considerable manipulation owing to his having been last through the door. The bathysphere had been designed to hold eight persons and it was now full to capacity. Camilla, Sally, Axel, Vladimir, Nicky, Dr. Tisch, the McKay and the gunman Bozo made up the party. Sally, the McKay and the Doctor, who controlled the search-light, had the better seats, Camilla, between two of her lovers, Axel and Vladimir, sat behind them, while Nicky as volunteer telephonist, with Bozo, who made a point of having his back against a wall, occupied places by the door.

As the sphere went under the McKay was not particularly intrigued. Three aurelia jellies drifted by and a big shoal of arrow worms then, at their first halt they saw a Puppy Shark about two feet in length with a Pilot fish beneath it. A hundred feet lower the strange exhilaration of that unearthly blue light had begun to get hold of him a little and he leaned forward to peer at a big Snapper which goggled in at him, pressing its face close to the window. A moment later a whole battalion, several hundreds strong, of great blue Parrot fishes came into view swimming almost vertically downwards and through them, in a horizontal direction passed a division comprising thousands of smooth silvery Sardines. The effect of this warp and woof as the two different coloured schools passed through each other was indescribably lovely. Similar sights had often been seen by the others since they occurred several times on every dive, but it was new to the McKay and he admitted to himself that the small element of risk involved in a single trip, now that the bathysphere's resistance had been proved, was worth it.

He was peering out of the porthole with his face so close to the fuzed quartz at 500 feet that his breath condensed upon it and he pulled out his handkerchief to wipe away the moisture.

"Good God!" he exclaimed, "what's happened?" He knew quite well that the handkerchief was a bright scarlet silk bandana patterned in green. Now it appeared dead black and the design had vanished.

The Doctor gave his throaty chuckle. "The red rays of the sun no longer penetrate to here *Herr Kapitan*. I was surprised myself when I first beheld this strange phenomenon, although I knew it to be so from accounts of deep sea diving."

At 800 feet the deep blue light remained but everything had taken on a ghostly form. Strange shadowy shapes flickered past and as the sphere descended further many of them began to show luminosity. When they came to rest at 1,600, five fishes swam past with blotches on them which glistened like tinfoil in the grey blue darkness then some unseen organism spat out a rocket like burst of luminous fluid.

At 2,000 feet the Doctor put on the light for a few moments and a shoal of brilliant silver fish were caught in it turning like a flight of birds. Later they saw a creature with two large reddish lights in front and a constellation of smaller ones, all pale blue, then a great Squid with light organs encircling its eye, but the teeming life changed so constantly as the

173

sphere was lowered that they caught little more than a glimpse of individual specimens and had no time to examine one tenth of all the marvels that passed the windows.

The Doctor judged that the day before they had been on the western fringe of the Atlantean city and he feared now that the drift of the ship might have carried them away from the area of its remains, but when they reached bottom at 10.40 he found to his joy that they were apparently well inside its limits. A line of tall rounded stones equal in circumference but uneven in height, rising quite near them from the ocean bed, definitely suggested a row of truncated columns.

By means of operating the claws in its undercarriage the Doctor turned the sphere gently and a solid surface, reaching up into the darkness like a great blank wall, came into view. For a moment he swivelled the light up and down but the beam could not reach its top and any ornamentations which it might once have had the waters had long since erased into a uniform smoothness.

As the sphere turned further the beam lit up an irregular pile of stones. All their corners and edges were rounded but they still suggested square and oblong blocks of masonry. Opposite the row of columns came a blank space where little was visible except the shadowy outline of more great monoliths in the distance; then a long smooth slope running upwards from the sea bottom at an angle of about thirty degrees and quite different in appearance from it. A dull irridescent sparkle which showed as the searchlight moved across its polished surface made it seem likely that it was a vast slab of granite. The columns appeared again and they had completed the circle.

"We are much handicapped," remarked the Doctor, "that the ship above can no longer move us as directed. I haf wished to make a tour of at least an hour before deciding the better place for excavation but we must drill here or not at all—so let us be busy."

With Count Axel's help the drilling machine was set in motion at the base of the nearest column, which was quite near them. Inside the sphere they could not hear the faintest murmur as it bored into the solidified lava and the indicator on a small dial near the door was the only means of knowing when it had completed the first hole. A charge of explosive was inserted down a tube by an automatic loader, with an electric wire attached which could be reeled out as the bathysphere was drawn up, then the drill was set to work upon another boring.

All the time these operations were in progress fish came and went beyond the windows, flitting like ghostly shadows in and out of the bright beam. A sabre-toothed Viper fish snapped its wicked jaws within a few inches of Sally's face, but on touching the fuzed quartz, whipped off again, startled perhaps by this invisible barrier. The shrimps at this depth were big fellows eight to ten inches in length. They appeared to be bright scarlet with jet black eyes whereas, at about 1,500 feet the McKay had noticed that they were only pale pink and near the surface a transparent white. Seven black jellies came bobbing along in an uneven row and then a large umbrella-like pink one with luminous spots at the base of each of its threadlike tentacles. Nearly every creature seemed to possess its own lighting apparatus, some having a coppery or silvery irridescence over their whole bodies, others luminous teeth, or portholes in their sides; only the Palid Sailfins and Eels showed no illumination. For an hour, that ghostly shadow dance, lit by displays of ever changing coloured fireworks, went on without a second's interruption, then the Doctor reported the first borings to be completed and Nicky asked Oscar, who had taken over the deck end of the telephone, to have the sphere pulled up 300 feet.

As they ascended the McKay noticed that they were not going up quite straight but at an angle and, for a second, he feared that the sphere would be dashed against the solid wall upon their right.

His mouth set tight as he waited for instant oblivion to overwhelm them. He had just time to think grimly that this was the sort of unexpected calamity which he had visualised, when the wall top came into view six feet away and they passed clear above it. The whole episode was over so quickly that the others had failed even to realise the danger and the narrowness of their escape.

The wires connected with the charges in the bore holes had reeled out automatically as they rose and when they halted the Doctor put his hand on the lever to explode them.

"It's no good I'm afraid." The McKay shook his head. "We only remained stationary on the bottom because the drill and the claws held us. The ship is drifting to eastward slightly, and as she is not under power they won't be able to tow us back to the place we've mined."

The Doctor grunted with disappointment. "I will explode the charges all the same," he said after a moment. "We may see the effect perhaps when we descend again even if we cannot collect the débris."

No faintest sound came to indicate that the explosion had taken place when the Doctor pressed the lever of the detonator but, just after, the bathysphere lifted slightly as the water was forced upwards, then settled till the cable took its weight again with a very gentle jerk. Nicky requested that they should be lowered and six minutes later they came to rest on the bottom.

They turned the bathysphere on its own axis and could not recognise any of the stone masses as those which they had seen before. A faint cloudiness at one point, seen in the extreme end of the searchlight's beam, indicated the probable direction of their previous position, as the explosion would have pulverised some of the stone and lava into fine dust, but they were too far off to glimpse the row of columns.

Further mining operations were obviously useless so it was decided to rise thirty feet and then drift with the ship. For the next twenty-five minutes they moved very slowly to the westward passing through two huge pillars and then across a comparatively open space, at one side of which great blocks and hummocks were vaguely discernible in the distance.

The McKay estimated that they were drifting at about 200 yards an hour and he explained that in addition to the kedge anchors, which Captain Ardow had thrown out, the bathysphere was acting as a super kedge which assisted in slowing up the ship's movement. Even at this low speed their position must have altered at least a mile and a half since the Doctor and Nicky had found the Atlantean remains the previous afternoon—if they had been shifting steadily in one direction. The wind had changed twice however so the probability was that they were still within a mile of the spot over which the ship had been when Count Axel staged his explosion, but it was possible of course that the ruins of the sunken city covered a much greater area.

A large headed rat-tailed macrourid a foot in length and with at least six lights had paused to peer in at the window when, without warning, the sphere suddenly began to rise.

"Oh, what's happening?" cried Camilla in a frightened voice. "I do *pray* that there's not another storm approaching. Ask Nicky—ask why they are pulling us up."

Nicky asked, paused for a moment, then said with a start "Ah—what's that?"

"Tell us. I'd much rather know the worst," Camilla urged him.

"It's the worst all right," he muttered. "Oscar says that Kate's just come on board and wants to see us."

"Oh heavens!" exclaimed Sally, "I knew this would happen. What *are* we going to do?"

"Steady m'dear," the McKay took her hand and pressed it, "Kate won't try and eat you. Besides the tender should be alongside by now and we'll—" He broke off suddenly as he remembered the Bozo was within six feet of him, placed there by Slinger for the special purpose of reporting any further measures against their captors which they might be indiscreet enough to discuss in his hearing.

"How can the tender help? Its crew won't be armed and it would be hours before they could get us assistance. Whereas Kate's there—already—up on deck—waiting for us." Sally burst out excitedly.

"But what are you so scared he's going to do to you m'dear?"

"Oh, I don't know—I don't know. But he's found out about that will and he'll be furious. You know that horrid cold merciless stare of his."

"I've got much more to fear than you darling," Camilla gulped and suddenly burst into tears.

Vladimir did not know how to contain himself any longer. The sight of his so beautiful Duchess weeping in a fit of uncontrollable terror from fear of this bully Kate was too much for him. Bozo was seated immediately in his rear. With a sudden totally unexpected movement he swung round and smashed his great fist into the gunman's face.

Bozo's head was jerked backward and hit the steel side of the bathysphere a terrific crack. His gun slipped from his fingers before he knew what had hit him and he slid down to the floor unconscious, black blood streaming from his broken nose.

The Prince grabbed the automatic and laughed with boyish glee. "Now," he declared waving the weapon dangerously in challenge to the world, "who shall lay a touch upon my pet-lamb. Camilla my so loved remit your fears I beg. Anyone who speaks unpleasantness to you so beautiful I will shoot, yes instantly—just as I would a dirty dog."

"For God's sake be careful with that thing!" cried the McKay.

"Have no troubles my nice Captain. With firearms I am an intimate, and in shooting I crack like a double dab."

"Well I congratulate you Prince," said Count Axel. "That was a courageous piece of business and admirably executed. This man's pistol may come in handy if the fears of the Duchess and Sally are justified, but I do hope you won't use it except in the last extremity. Remember there will be at least a dozen like it against you and a couple of machine guns as well."

"I don't see that you've done much good anyhow," remarked Nicky gloomily. "It will only infuriate them when they find that you've knocked out one of their men, and we've no means of getting rid of the body even if he were dead. The moment he fails to come out of the sphere and they find him unconscious they'll cover us with their rods and take that one off you."

"My poor Nicky you are made jealous," the Prince laughed again, "because I also can now say 'I hit him—didn't I—right on the nose.'"

The incident at least had the effect of stopping Camilla's tears and she clung to Vladimir's free arm while she stared out of the porthole; no longer even registering the great lemon yellow Finger Squid they were passing on their way up, but endeavouring to persuade herself that her brave young Roumanian would protect her from Kate's wrath when they reached the surface.

Sally sat silent, clutching the McKay's hand in both of hers and trying to still her fears, while he, Count Axel and the Doctor considered the new position. Although they did not voice their thoughts all three had come to the conclusion that, courageous as Vladimir's action had been, considering that he might well have received a bullet in the back, his bravado would be of little use to them when the bathysphere was hoisted on to its supports. The McKay placed his chief hope in obtaining help through the people on the tender, but he was not acutely worried by Kate's arrival since he could not convince himself that there was any real reason why Kate should have any cause to put them through the mill.

Count Axel was dreading that Vladimir's rashness might precipitate a general massacre and had determined to keep within clutching distance of him directly they left the sphere;

in order that he might prevent the Prince using the weapon he had secured unless it came to the unlikely point of their lives being actually threatened.

"Sally," said Camilla in a low voice.

"Yes, darling?"

"Don't you think we ought to tell them—now."

"I don't see that it matters dear. When we discussed it we agreed that their knowing would not make the least difference to our chances of escape. But tell them if you like."

"Well," Camilla hesitated. "This is why Sally and I are so frightened. When Kate forced me to sign that will he didn't know that——"

She got no further. They had risen about 800 feet and only just moved on after one of the regulation halts for a tie to be removed. Now, quite unexpectedly, they stopped again.

For a moment they sat silent, expecting their steady upward progress to be resumed, but nothing happened. The ball continued to hang motionless.

"Ask what is the matter," said the Doctor. He had a faint but uncomfortable thought that the crane machinery might have jammed.

"What's happened? Anything wrong?" enquired Nicky into the telephone.

Oscar's voice came back in reply: "Orders from the bridge that we are to let you remain suspended where you are *mein Herr*."

Nicky informed the others and, as they pondered silently on this change of plan, he turned back to the instrument. "Let's have it Oscar—what's the big idea?"

"Wait," said Oscar. Then, after a pause of quite two minutes, he spoke again in a guttural whisper: "A warship has arrived. It is British and they have lowered a boat."

"Good man!" said Nicky, "keep me posted if you can." With a beaming face he swung round and passed on the news.

"By Jove! Then my signals were picked up after all." The McKay suddenly burst into song.

> "What shall we do with a drunken sailor?
> What shall we do with a drunken sailor?
> Shave his chin with a rusty razor
> Early—in—the——"

179

"Stop!" shouted Sally, among a chorus of excited enquiries. "What signals?"

"Why," he announced with modest pleasure, "I've been morsing from my cabin with the light switch every night since Kate first seized the yacht. Someone was bound to spot the flashes from the porthole sometime—but I didn't hope for much until we crossed the shipping belts on our way South."

"O! you hero!" Sally's big grey eyes were damp with relief and joyful emotion. "You never told us a thing about it—you've saved us after all!"

"By Crikey!" Vladimir slapped the McKay on the shoulder enthusiastically. "You are a black horse and no mess up!"

"What's that," Nicky asked eagerly at the telephone. Then he turned again: "Oscar says that a Naval Officer and a party of men have just come on board."

The McKay winked at Sally. "Aren't you glad that scoundrel Kate came back now? He's arrived just in time to meet the Navy."

Count Axel gave a low delighted chuckle. "It has been an amazing experience and we are no worse after all. Now that the world knows of the hold-up the Duchess's fortune is safe, and while Kate has spent thousands in organising his coup, we have been quietly carrying on our diving just as we planned. All his schemes have gone for nothing while *we* have actually found Atlantis!"

"The exploration—you will not stop now *Gnädige Hertzogin*—but permit it to go on," the Doctor asked anxiously.

"Of course, Doctor—of course." Camilla gave him a gracious smile. "We will refit as soon as we possibly can and then you shall carry on for just as long as you like."

He seized her hand and kissed it, while the McKay broke into song once more:

> "Hi! Hi! up she rises
> Hi! Hi! up she rises
> Hi! Hi! up—she——"

Suddenly the sphere began to move again. Not up—but down. They stared at each other questioningly. To find themselves sinking when they expected to be drawn up at any moment by their rescuers was startling enough but what followed held them silent with a quake of fear.

180

Instead of being gently lowered at the usual speed of two minutes to a hundred feet, the ball was gathering speed as it went down. Fish, squids, prawns, jellies, sea-snails and shoals of arrow worms began to flash past the windows at an alarming speed.

"Quick Nicky!" yelled the McKay. "Order them to slow us up—what's that madman on the crane up to?" The appalling thought had flashed into his mind that the under-carriage of the sphere contained a load of dynamite and a couple of dozen fulminite of mercury detonators. If they hit bottom at this pace they would all be blown to hell.

"Stop us!" shouted Nicky into the telephone. "Stop us, damn you or we'll crash for sure!"

No reply came from the other end, and so it seemed that Oscar had left the instrument. Then he heard a ragged fusillade of distant shots.

"Something's wrong," he gasped, "they're shooting at each other up there."

About sixteen minutes had elapsed since the bathysphere had started, without warning, on its upward journey. It had risen some eight hundred feet but now, despite the resistance of the water, its weight and that of the eight people in it, caused fish and squids to slither past its rounded sides as it hurtled unchecked at full speed towards the bottom.

Fortunately Sally and Camilla were not aware of the acute danger due to the dynamite stored in its base, and anticipated no more than that it would hit the sea floor with a horrid bump. They were much more concerned in wondering what was going on above.

"Try again Nicky—try again," Camilla cried anxiously. "Ask what's happening up on deck."

"I am," bawled Nicky, "can't you hear me—but the swine refuses to answer," and it was true that he had never ceased to demand or plead for information from his instrument which was now so sinisterly dumb.

The McKay judged that they had dropped at least 700 feet. He knew that the crash must come at any second and then the horrible blackout. It would be almost instantaneous anyway; yet time is an illusion, happy days pass before their full joy is even remotely realised, one can only savour something of them afterwards in retrospect; and anxious hours drag by while the minute hand of the clock crawls like a snail circling the dial. Who can say, when a man blows his brains out, that the pause between his finger pressing the trigger and the moment when he is really dead may not seem to him like a month of shattering overwhelming agony in which tissue is torn from tissue with unendurable successive and separate spasms of torture as the bullet crashes through his skull. He put his arm round Sally's shoulders then closed his eyes and waited.

Suddenly there was a terrific jolt, they were lifted from their seats for a second, then flung together in a tangled heap.

The bathysphere had been completely arrested in its rapid descent, and hovered uncertainly for a moment. When they recovered from the shock they realised that the searchlight had gone out.

Nicky screamed down the telephone. He screamed and blasphemed in vain. He knew that the line was already dead.

Camilla clung to Vladimir. He had his two great arms locked round her in a defiant, protective embrace.

The Doctor scrambled to his feet and produced a hand torch. He flashed it at the window, the sphere was sinking again, but more slowly now, it had not had time to gather pace.

After what seemed to be an eternity but was actually no more than a minute they came to rest on the bottom with a gentle bump.

The blue beam from the Doctor's torch, focused on a porthole, penetrated the inky blackness no more than a foot, but into it there swam a new snake-like creature from above. Dead black, no more than three inches thick, and seemingly endless, it passed through the beam in graceful looping curves.

The McKay stared at it with sudden horror. He knew that it was no living thing but the cable coiling down from above as it sank in great festoons about them. It had snapped, and they were trapped there, 900 fathoms down, where no human hand could ever bring them aid.

CHAPTER XV

DEATH HOVERS IN THE DARKNESS

THE Doctor knew too what that thin curving line of falling cable meant. Someone in the ship above had jammed the lever into reverse when the bathysphere was running out at a speed far greater than had ever been intended. The violence of the check had proved too great a strain. It had snapped somewhere in its mile of length above their heads. There was nothing to be done—nothing. He switched out his torch.

The black, utterly impenetrable, darkness closed down upon them as if they had suddenly been struck blind. Then a glimmer of greyness showed the ports and, as their eyes recovered from the change, they saw once more that eternal devil dance of ghostly shapes in the dull luminosity carried by the strange creatures of the deep.

Each one of the seven conscious persons in the sphere now guessed what had happened and each was so appalled that none of them could speak. Subconsciously they understood that they had been caught—trapped beyond any possible hope of escape—in this small circular steel chamber nine hundred fathoms down; but for a little their brains refused to take it in —could not admit it—and rebelled against the terrible thought that they had been severed completely from all the life that they had previously known—with utter unalterable finality.

A horrible unnatural silence lasted for almost two minutes, each of which seemed like the passing of many days. Stark ungovernable fear held them in its grip like a physical paralysis then Count Axel relaxed a little and sighed heavily.

He had always hoped that when death came to him he would be able to meet it with a bow. He was not afraid of death because he had unshakable faith in the survival of his Kama. He had enjoyed his present life but his principal regret to leave it would be that he must pass that strange barrier which blots out all but the vaguest intuitive memories of earlier experiences before a soul is born again. Now, he was not so certain that he would be able to greet death as he had always planned. It was one thing to die by a bullet, drowning, a street accident perhaps, or even after a long and painful illness during which such fortitude as he could muster had been displayed; but quite another to sit there cramped and hopeless waiting for his companions to show the first signs of madness and eventually to die a screaming maniac, fighting for the last breath of air.

"We're going to die!" said Sally at last, in a whisper that held a terrible conviction, and then again, her voice rising to a shriller note, "We're going to die!"

"Steady m'dear," the McKay's arm was still round her shoulders and he pressed her nearer. He would have given anything in the world had he been safe and possessed it then to be able to think of some words to comfort her, but his tongue was dry in his mouth and there was no shred of hope that he could offer.

"I'm not going to die! I won't! I won't! Help! Help! Help!" screamed Nicky down his useless telephone.

Vladimir released Camilla from his embrace, turned and struck out twice into the darkness behind him. He barked the knuckles of his right fist badly on the ice cold steel of the sphere but the left caught Nicky behind the ear. Suddenly his frantic gibbering ceased. He choked and slid down on to the body of the still unconscious gunman.

"Oh what have you done!" moaned Camilla.

"I could not wait by and see such behaving in your presence." The Prince excused himself soberly then he added in a meditative way with no trace of laughter in his tone. "Often I have wished to kick that Nicky in his so colourful pants but never did I foresee this kicking with so little happiness to myself."

"Oh Vladimir—Vladimir," Camilla suddenly reached up in the darkness and put her arms round his neck. "Can't you do something—please, please—get us out of this."

"Ah my so beautiful," his deep vibrant voice held a soft caressing note. "If it were my life only—it would not be much to give but—but—what can I do?"

"We're going to die," said Sally again in that toneless whisper and the McKay felt her tremble as she leaned against him. He was still searching his mind desperately for one ray of hope when Vladimir exclaimed:

"The dynamite! All that we have let us drill into the rocks. The explosion beneath our bottoms may drive us sky high!"

"Absurd," grunted the McKay. "The electric wires

snapped with the cable, so we can't work the drill or explode the charges, and anyhow I doubt if there's enough H.E. in Chatham to blow this ball up through five-thousand feet of water. Besides, even if one *could* perform such a miracle we'd only sink again immediately.

"*Gnädige Hertzogin, Fraulein* Sally. *Herrshaft,*" the German addressed them with his usual formality. "I make my apologies now to all. I haf trusted in the cable being able to withstand any strain and haf been proved in error. That was a miscalculation for which I too shall pay with my life since there is no help for us. One tank of oxygen will last forty-five minutes for eight people—an hour perhaps if we use it sparingly. There are twelve tanks but we have been down four hours and have used five and a half tanks already. The remaining six and a half tanks will keep alive the eight persons here six and a half hours only."

"As a warship has come to our assistance—they may try to hook us up with their end of the cable," muttered the McKay yet even as he spoke he realised the absurdity of the suggestion. If sufficient cable still remained attached to the drums for the broken end to reach the bottom the ship was still drifting and, since they had no means of communication, the chances were a thousand to one against the people above lowering the cable over the exact spot where the bathysphere had come to rest. Besides it would be the supreme irony of all if such an attempt succeeded. They were sealed and riveted into the sphere and had a great hook been dangling before the windows at that moment they would have been completely powerless to reach and attach it.

The Doctor shook his head. "All the ships in the world might be above but they could not help us in any way. We can do nothing—nothing but wait until death comes."

"You are wrong, Doctor," said Count Axel quietly. "A little manipulation of your instruments and we should barely live out another minute. Surely that would be more merciful to us all."

The horrid silence came again as each debated with themselves if they should choose slow or instant death but it was was broken by Camilla almost immediately.

"No, no," she cried, shuddering in Vladimir's embrace. "No! I can't bear to die!"

"I had already thought of the *Herr Count's* suggestion," announced the Doctor heavily.

"Sally m'dear," questioned the McKay, "it's a rotten business I know—but what about it?"

"We're going to die," repeated Sally with rising hysteria. "We're going to *die*! We're going to *die*!"

He pressed her hand and let his head sway from side to side a little with the intensity of his frustration.

"Please," he murmured, "now or later?"

She did not reply and the sudden impression reached him that she was going off her head with shock and fear already. Camilla's terrified outbursts were more normal than this dreadful repetition of the one hopeless phrase. He shook her roughly.

"Sally d'you hear me—did you hear what I said?"

"What is it?" she asked vaguely and then, as though waking from a dream: "Oh God! What are we going to do?"

"Listen m'dear," he said gently, "we're trapped here. The cable's snapped—get that? And there's no way out. We haven't a hope in Hades so it's a choice if we hang on for about six hours—then suffocate, or if we take it now—standing up as it were—since the Doctor can black us out in about a minute."

"I don't care," her voice was dull—apathetic. "We're going to die—that's what it is. We're going to die and we just can't do anything to stop it."

A groan came up from the darkness in their rear. At first they thought it to be Nicky, but it was Bozo coming round. Axel and Vladimir fumbled about until they could haul him into a sitting position. The Doctor flashed his torch to help them, but when they had propped him up his head sagged forward and he apparently passed out again.

Then Nicky, who had come to as his body was lifted from on top of the gunman's sniffed, choked on a sob and muttered. "Undo the door—can't you. Let's take a sporting chance that the air bubble from this thing carries us to the surface."

They could not see the Doctor's eloquent shrug but he spoke a moment later. "The door has been riveted down from the outside, we could not open it even if our lives depended on it and we were in the air above. Here, even if we had the power to do so, which we have not, the in-rush of water would compress the air to a bubble no larger than a football and crush us flat."

Camilla was crying quietly on Vladimir's broad chest. "I

don't want to die," she sobbed, "I don't want to—something may happen—it must."

Nothing could happen. Count Axel on her other side, the Doctor, Vladimir, the McKay all knew that.

"Who's snatched my rod?" A gruff voice came from by the doorway. It was Bozo whose wits were slowly returning to him. "Put on the light damn you—the boss'll grill you all for this when we get back on deck."

"I'm afraid there's been an accident," Count Axel told him quietly. "Your friends were careless in reversing the crane after they had let us come down with a rush."

"Is—that—so? Playin' a joke on me eh—I'll learn them plenty when we hit the surface."

"I only wish you might have the opportunity, but unfortunately the cable's broken and we're on the bottom here—stuck."

"The hell we are!" Bozo lurched drunkenly to his feet, hit his head on the roof of the sphere and swore profanely—then bellowed: "Where's that lousy Doctor. Come on—get busy. You've got to get us up."

"I—I wish with all my heart I could," Doctor Tisch stammered, "but the *Herr Count* is quite correct. The cable has broken and we are at rest on the sea bottom—I can do nothing and no help can reach us here."

"Hi! quit bluffin' Doctor." Bozo's voice had suddenly gone scared. "That's not straight—is it?"

"I speak quite truthfully," the Doctor assured him. "We face death. There is no alternative. At most we shall all be dead in seven hours."

"An' you've let me in fer this—have you? All right! I'll mince you first a piece if I've got to die like a rat in a trap."

The gunman threw his heavy body in the direction from which the Doctor's voice had come. Camilla and Sally clutched nervously at the McKay. This fighting in the pitchy blackness distracted their thoughts for a moment yet added to the macabre horror of their situation.

The Doctor grunted as Bozo landed on him, but he still held his torch and switched it on. Vladimir gripped the big gunman by the scruff of the neck and with his tremendous strength hauled him off as if he were only a puppy. Then flung him to the floor.

"Rat is what you are," declared the Prince contemptuously. "Open your face again and I will beat you to a pulping."

187

Bozo squirmed into a sitting position and sat there hunched, staring with wide eyes into the terrifying darkness. He would have taken on the Prince for a tussle in free air but the appalling finality of the calamity was just beginning to penetrate his dull brain. They were to die then—all of them —like rats in a trap and there was nothing they could do about it—nothing at all. A sort of terrified coma gripped him as, for the first time in his animal existence, he began to visualise certain death in the agony of suffocation.

No one spoke then for a little and the silence was only broken by Camilla's sobbing. She tried to stop but she could not. The great fear seemed to be there right inside her somewhere in the pit of her stomach reaching up and dragging at her very heart.

"It's true you know—we're going to die," Sally murmured again almost as if talking to herself.

"Everyone's got to die some time," said the McKay soberly, "we're only anticipating the natural course of things a bit m'dear—that's all."

Camilla heard them and shuddered. Everyone had to die some time of course but she had never paused to face the thought that death must come one day to herself; and here it was hovering over her, in that fearful darkness that could be felt, and seemed to press with the gentlest persistence on her skin. She had taken such a harmless joy in all the flattery and adulation, the handsome lovers and the lovely clothes. Perhaps she might have done more good if she had spent less time amusing herself, but a special department of the Hart estate gave away enormous sums each month in response to genuine appeals for charity which had been properly investigated, and she had never harmed anyone wilfully in all her life. Both she and Sally had been brought up very quietly, hardly allowed to see anyone or go out into the world at all, until they were twenty-one, in order to protect the young heiress from fortune hunters. They were only twenty-three now and so had had barely two years of glorious freedom.

It was unfair—unjust to be cut off like this when life was only starting, Camilla felt, and impotent rage momentarily conquered her fear. Never again to admire her own beauty in the dressing table-glass while the maid did her hair. Never again to be able to display her supple rounded limbs, while sunbathing, to the admiration of all beholders. No more laughter, no more flirtations, no more joyous passionate love-

188

making, but darkness—death—and decay. She thought of her exquisite, so carefully tended body, wasted, useless, rotting there, turned to a mass of putrescent stinking carrion, and sobbed afresh.

Aeons of time seemed to drift by while they sat huddled together motionless, their brains racing madly towards the borderland of insanity, or steeped almost to numbness now in blank despair.

The McKay glanced at the luminous dial of his wrist watch and announced: "It's ten past one. We've been down here just on an hour."

Nickey laughed, unnaturally, shrilly: "It's cocktail time—cocktail time up there," and they knew him to be on the verge of a breakdown.

"I've got a flask of brandy," the McKay offered. "I never go on any sort of risky business without one—here, have a pull at it if you like." As he reached behind him in the darkness to hand over the flask he hoped that a good stiff peg might hold Nicky together for a little longer. He was dreading more than anything the time which must inevitably come when someone's nerve would snap.

"Thanks," Nicky grabbed the flask gratefully and held it to his mouth.

"You poor dear," Sally turned her head which was resting on the McKay's shoulder. She spoke normally again now. "How right you were in trying to dissuade us from coming on these dives. You always foresaw that one of them would end in a tragedy. What rotten luck for you that just this one time you're with us should be the time the cable breaks."

He shrugged. "It can't be helped m'dear. I'm lucky, considering what I've been through, to reach the age I have—and anyhow I've had a lot of fun. It's yourself, and Camilla, and Vladimir and Nicky who're hardest hit. You're all young people who had a right to expect many happy years ahead."

"You're a dear," she murmured and snuggled closer to him.

Another hour drifted by while the lights of the luminous fishes came and went with monotonous regularity outside the ports. Inside the sphere they sat cramped yet motionless sunk in a hopeless apathy.

"I wonder," said Count Axel meditatively, after he had

asked, and been told, the time, "I wonder how long will elapse before they find our bodies here?"

"From now till doomsday," replied the McKay briefly.

"Oh no, my dear Captain, you are quite wrong. I should say fifty years at the utmost and it is possible that our human remains may be brought to the surface long before that."

"Why should you think so?"

"Remember that before our unfortunate descent to-day the Doctor had already proved his theory to be correct. Slinger, Ardow, the telephonist Oscar, who has had a most fortunate escape by the way, and doubtless all the members of the crew, know that the remains of the Atlantean capital do really lie beneath them. This great discovery is now the property of the whole world; other, greater, bathyspheres with stronger cables will be built and new expeditions will find ready financial backing since that is always forthcoming when there are definite prospects of finding gold. Then the advance of science is so rapid these days, that every ruin in these waters will be mapped and examined. They are bound to discover this rusty ball before they are done and it would not surprise me at all to learn—if I could see into the future—that before twenty years are past the sphere will be a greatly prized exhibit in some museum and our bodies buried with considerable honour in——"

"Stop!" cried Camilla wildly. "Stop! How can you!"

"I am sorry Madame," he apologised turning his head to smile in the darkness. "I had hoped to distract your thoughts a little."

"Don't, please," she begged. "It's bad enough as things are but to hear you calmly speculating on what may happen to our corpses will drive me out of my mind. Besides——"

"Besides what, Madame?" he prompted her.

"I've just remembered," her voice went tremulous again. "The Doctor warned us when we first went down that we should not talk too much, because the more we did the more—the more oxygen we used up."

"I know, I hoped that you had forgotten that, because it had just occurred to me again. I was really trying to reduce our supply and, automatically, the time we still have to wait."

"Camilla's right!" snapped Nicky, "Camilla's right! For God's sake shut up."

"I will," agreed the Count—"since it is her wish."

The silence was longer this time, so long that they almost

190

seemed to have been asleep and suffering in some fantastic nightmare when the Doctor spoke:

"Nine out of our twelve tanks are used now."

"Would it not be better if we made an end then?" Count Axel suggested again.

"No," cried Nicky promptly. "That's suicide and I won't have it. It may surprise you to know it but I'm religious in a kind of way. I don't mind telling you now it—it can't get any further but all that dope about my being an American and graduate of a swell college is sheer huey. I'm only half American through my mother and my father was North country English. I was born in a London slum. I ran away from home to better myself and I did by golly—but they were a religious pair and deep down in me their teaching stuck. We'll all have to go before the Judge's seat when the last trumpet sounds and that scares me more than the thought of death—I'll not add suicide to all the lying and cheating I've had to do to get up to where I got."

"You're right, Boss—you said a mouthful," Bozo came out of his coma and unexpectedly backed Nicky up. "My folks was religious too—and what I've got to answer for's enough. Yes, Sir, I'm with you all the time."

The McKay would have clung to his life like a limpet had there been the remotest hope of retaining it but, since they had to die, he preferred the Count's way out to the horror of madness and torture of suffocation. He too possessed deep religious convictions although he was not given to talking of them but the Doctor expressed his belief exactly when he said:

"I am no atheist. In fact I was educated for the Lutheran Church, ordained, and practised as a Minister until I was twenty-eight. Only my intense interest in archaeology and an offer of employment on an expedition to Assyria tempted me to resign from the Ministry; but I haf always believed that God's mercy has no limitations. I am unorthodox perhaps but I cannot think He would withhold his pardon from anyone who shortened their life by an hour or two when in such a hopeless predicament as ourselves.

Camilla settled it. She began to scream and beg them frantically not to do anything—yet.

Vladimir declared jumpily that he would shoot anyone who attempted to go against Camilla's wishes, and they settled down again to wait for death in grim silence.

The atmosphere was so tense that they could almost feel

191

each other thinking. Sally had not spoken for a long time now and a shivering fit took possession of her. The McKay felt her slim body trembling beneath his arm and once more he racked his brains for some way to comfort her.

"Look here," he said, suddenly, "I'm no story teller but oxygen or no oxygen I'm going to tell you a story m'dear. It's the only one I can think of at the moment because my old brain's gone woolly, and you'll have heard it years ago but if you'll listen a bit maybe it will give you something to think about."

The others turned towards him in the darkness and he began:

"Once upon a time there were three sisters, or rather two of them were sisters and the other was a step-sister if I remember. Anyhow two of them were much older than the other one and they were both very ugly, and lazy and bad tempered, while the youngest was a beautiful young girl like you."

Sally stopped shivering. Just those four first words: "Once upon a time," had caught her back from that maze of dread speculations; yet she was not listening to him as he went on; she was thinking of one thing only now. The full realisation that she loved him with all her heart and soul, had just come upon her. He might be nearly twice her age and grey haired, but he had all a young man's virility and in his heart lay youth tempered by a great gentleness. That his concern for her was so great that he could put aside the thought of his own approaching end in an endeavour to distract her, like a little child, with a fairy story, touched her more deeply than any experience she had ever known. She lowered her head against his chest and burst into a violent storm of tears.

"What is it then. What is it Sally m'dear?" he asked tenderly as he stroked her hair. "Listen to the story I'm telling you and try and forget everything else. Now these three sisters lived——"

"The fish!" exclaimed the Doctor suddenly. "What is the matter with the fish?"

They all roused and stared out of the portholes. Something unusual was obviously happening outside. The lights had ceased to dance, every single one of them was streaming now in one direction, back from the open space, perhaps upon the western verge of the Atlantean city, where the bathysphere had fallen, towards the shelter of the ruins.

For a moment the prisoners in the bathysphere watched in wonder. Lights of every size and colour streaked by. There could be no doubt whatever that these creatures of the deep were fleeing in terror of their lives, just like animals before a forest fire, and the danger they feared was coming up out of the deeper waters to the westward.

The numbers of lights increased. The things outside dashed themselves against the fuzed quartz windows in their frantic panic to escape. They seemed to burst, scattering clouds of luminous food and multitudes of coloured stars. The press became so great that, for the first time since the electric wires had broken, the group in the sphere could see each other's faces faintly illuminated in the unearthly radiance caused by this multitude of terrified creatures.

Then the lights dimmed, and the cataract of racing flashes ceased, yet a number of bright blotches hovered at the portholes bobbing feebly up and down as though their owners were caught in the crush and could not escape.

The Doctor switched on his torch and by it they saw that a solid writhing mass of fish and squids and prawns were now jammed up against the windows. Not an inch of water showed and the surface of each port was covered completely by wriggling tentacles and fins. Suddenly the bathysphere began to move.

"Gott in Himmel!" exclaimed the Doctor. "What now!"

Slowly but surely the sphere moved sideways and was drawn along the surface of the ocean bed surrounded by the press of captive fish. The party sat tight and held their breath, utterly bewildered by this extraordinary phenomenon. They were dragged about a hundred yards, as far as they could judge, then the sphere tilted gently and fell over sideways.

Sally screamed—Camilla fainted—the others clutched wildly at each other as they were flung sprawling against the side of the sphere which held the searchlight and had now become it bottom. Yet there was no violent shock as they turned over. The sphere seemed to be sinking as though it had fallen over a cliff, and the second they had sorted themselves out the Doctor flashed his torch on the ports.

Nothing was to be seen. Only the mass of writhing creatures still pressed against the windows. For nearly fifteen minutes the feeling that they were sinking, first gently, then quite fast, then gently again, continued while they strove to revive Camilla and examined the damage which had been done.

Fortunately the tanks were safe and still functioning, only the now useless lighting apparatus had been smashed. Camilla came round and went off again. Sally and Nicky were babbling half hysterically while the rest were wrought up to an almost unendurable pitch of excitement, although they were too staggered even to hazard an opinion as to what was going on outside.

Suddenly they knew that they had ceased moving yet their downward motion had been checked so gently that it was almost as though they were attached to the cable and only halting for one of the hose ties to be put on. There was a pause of about two minutes then, whatever held them pressed in the mass of fish, began to haul them in a fresh direction.

They started to bump a little and the Doctor cast anxious eyes on the tanks where the spotlight of the torch showed them tilted at an angle. The sphere rolled over again, but not very much this time, only sufficient to make it necessary for them to change the place where they were crouching to a few feet nearer the door. The jolting ceased and they were sinking once more—still further into the abyss.

"What the thunderin' blazes *is* happening," growled the McKay. It was the first coherent remark which emerged from the almost perpetual cries of fear and astonishment following their upset.

"We have been swallowed with these many fish," said Vladimir. "We are now as that poor Joshua in the belly of a whale."

"I do not think so," the Doctor shook his head. "We know little yet about life in the great deeps but it is quite unreasonable to suppose the existence of any such gigantic species. A swallow large enough to pass the bathysphere as part of a single gulp would need a submarine monster as great as a two-thousand ton ship—I do not believe it possible."

"Besides," Count Axel added, "we were dragged along the sea floor, sank several hundred feet, were dragged again, and are now sinking once more. Our movements would be quite different if we were in the stomach of some undreamed of Leviathan."

As he ceased speaking they came to rest as gently as before. There was another pause then, for the third time the sphere was dragged sideways. They had to move again. The door was now almost at the bottom of the sphere, the ports were tilted upward at an angle in the slope of what was now the

194

ceiling. For ten minutes the sphere moved forward, jerkily at times, while they lay or crouched among the broken canvas chairs and débris in its bottom.

It halted again and remained quite still. Then the blotches of light at the portholes began to move more freely. The Doctor lifted the beam of his torch from the cylinders to the ports and they saw that the pressure upon the great shoal of living creatures outside had been released. They were no longer jammed tight, but a seething mass leaping and thrashing in the water. After a moment bubbles appeared then foam and a little wavelet splashed against the fuzed quartz. The fish slid downwards and disappeared. A water line now showed in the top sections of the ports then sank jerkily until that too was gone.

The Doctor stumbled to his feet and held his big torch close to one of the windows, the others craned their necks, standing on the broken chairs, to peer out over his shoulders.

Outside it was pitch dark and the beam did not carry to any roof above them, but in front and a little higher than the level of the sphere they could just make out a wall that had a flat even surface and seemed like the side of a stone quay. All about them were a solid mass of squirming fish and squids of every colour and variety which stretched right up to the wall and on either side of them as far as they could see. The bathysphere was half buried in them right up to the lower edges of its ports which were now almost at the top of the sphere.

"Where in heaven's name are we?" gasped Nicky.

"I don't know and I don't care!" exclaimed the McKay with sudden excitement, "but there's air outside—air. Come on! We've got to get out of here."

Count Axel sighed, then he said slowly, "I'm afraid you've forgotten my friend that we are bolted in. Our two ton door is screwed down from outside. Escape is quite impossible and our oxygen will only last us just over another hour."

CHAPTER XVI

TRAPPED IN THE SPHÈRE

COUNT AXEL'S sober statement brought them crashing down from wild heights of excitement to a new level of despair. It was true. They were still sealed in the sphere and any attempt to break out of it must prove as hopeless as if they had been locked into the strongest vault under the Bank of England.

For a moment they were frozen into silence then Nisky cried: "Look—look! There's something moving on that wall out there!"

As they stared a bulky greyish mass appeared out of the darkness and they saw they were right in supposing the wall to form a quay, for the mass came forward and it was recognisable as a solid block of countless human figures.

"Saved by Crikey!" exclaimed Vladimir. "Camilla! We are saved I say!"

She had come out of her faint again and, picking her up bodily, he held her so that she could see out of the port. A fresh wave of tremulous hope surged through the others. If these were human beings they would surely find some way to unscrew the door bolts of the sphere and let its occupants out.

But how could they be? In breathless silence Camilla and her friends pressed their faces to the windows and watched the advancing mob. They appeared human, yet they moved in darkness. No trace of light except the beam of the Doctor's torch and the luminosity of the creatures packed tight about the sphere, showed in this great undersea cavern; and the newcomers carried neither flares nor torches. Moreover, they wore no clothes or ornaments; everyone of them was stark naked and their bodies were an unhealthy greyish white.

"They're not human," whispered Sally. "And they are horrible—horrible."

The McKay felt too that there was something utterly repulsive about that crowd of nude leperous looking bodies huddled

196

on the quay, but he was not so ready to exclude them from the human race. They were a small people, the tallest among the males being only about five feet in height, but they certainly were not monkeys and each of them held a long spearlike weapon in his hand. Their bodies were hairless except for the pale, lank, almost white hair which grew sparsely on their narrow skulls. Their faces were curiously uniform with large parroty, wide nostrilled noses, heavy lidded, almost colourless eyes, large mouths filled with white even gleaming teeth, and weak underhung jaws, yet they had nothing of that savage vicious look which had characterised the faces of the Mermen.

No leader appeared to control or direct their movements. They pressed forward, then sideways, all together, like a herd which scents danger or fresh pasture, in a wind. One of them slipped and fell from the quayside into the mass of fish. A great squid reached out a tentacle and curled it, snake-like, round his neck.

The others made no attempt to help him but stood there gibbering and twitching their heads from side to side, as though they knew what had happened without glancing down, but were only concerned with acute anxiety for themselves.

The one who had fallen fought and struggled, striving to break the grasp of the tentacle with one stubby claw-like hand and stabbing frantically with his long sharp spear, but the squid reached up three more tentacles and, wrapping them round his arms and torso, dragged him down.

It was all over in a moment, almost before Nicky had time to gasp: "Why don't they help him?" and Sally moaned.

Upon the quayside the great mob had steadied. The front rank threw themselves upon their knees, the others pressed up behind them leaning across their shoulders then, as though upon a common impulse rather than at any word of command, they all began to stab downward with their spears, striking again and again at the heaving fish below. The torrent of blows was so fast and regular that nothing could live under it; the long spears reached right down to the bottom of the harbour and soon even the tentacles of the squids had ceased to wave, for every creature within six feet of the quay was dead—stabbed through and through a dozen times.

Suddenly, like a herd once more, the whole mob leapt from

the quay wall into the slippery sea of carcasses and attacked the still living creatures further out with the same rhythmic stabbing. A spear struck the bathysphere, another and another. The party inside it could not hear the clang of the blows upon the metal but they realised then, that this strange race of half men was blind.

As the mob advanced, wading waist high in the slimy shoal of dead sea creatures, a small fat woman with enormous hanging breasts stumbled head first against the bathysphere. She opened her mouth in what appeared to be a scream and, almost instantly the mouths of all the others opened too then, as one man, they turned and fled. Floundering, slipping, thrusting each other aside they fought their way back to the quayside, and scrambled on to it. There they turned again and crouched in a great huddle, their spears upraised, staring blindly out towards the sphere.

"We'll get no help from them," declared the McKay bitterly. "They're wild things and blind I think. Anyhow they wouldn't know a rivet from a cocoanut."

"Is there *no* way we can get out ourselves," Sally asked with sudden desperation.

"None I fear, *Fraulein*," declared the Doctor gently. "The door is rivetted down and the bottom—well, that is impossible."

"What's that!" snapped the McKay. "Is there an entrance in the bottom?"

"No entrance *Herr Kapitan* but the bottom of the sphere is not solid as the sides. It has four layers of steel plates with supports between which will resist equal pressure. Each can be unscrewed in turn to enable us to get at the machinery which operates the claws, the dredges, and the drill."

"Why the hell didn't you tell us that before?" the McKay blazed out at him.

"I never thought to see the bathysphere upon its side which alone makes such exit possible," protested the Doctor, "and, since our arrival here, our every moment has been taken by watching these strange people; besides it would take two men a whole day's hard work to remove enough of the machinery to get out that way and we have oxygen to last us now an hour and a half only."

"Reduce the oxygen supply to half. Show a light on the bottom, and give me a screw driver," ordered the McKay.

"It is useless, *Herr Kapitan*," the Doctor's voice was

198

apathetic. "If we had six and a half hours oxygen as when we were first cut off it might be done. But now—no. You will tear your fingers for nothing. The hundreds of screws and joints to be——"

"Do as I tell you—I'm taking charge here now." The McKay pulled another torch from his pocket and thrust it into Sally's hand. "Take that. I brought it on the off chance the lights might fail. The more light we have now the better."

The Doctor shrugged. "I have a dozen torches here in case of need but this attempt is useless. We shall be dead before——"

"Stop talking, damn you. It uses oxygen and every ounce of that is precious now. Issue four torches and keep the rest in reserve. Everyone's to remain silent till we're out. Nicky! Axel! Bozo! you're to remain in the back of the sphere, away from its bottom. You two girls hold the torches—give you something to think about. Vladimir, you're the strong man come and help move the plates as we get them up. Doctor, how many screw drivers have you got in your chest?"

"One large—one small."

"Good, give me the large one then—thanks. Use the other yourself. You know the machinery. Silence now—get busy."

They obeyed him without questioning his commands. He stripped off his coat, flung it down to kneel on and began to attack the screws in the sphere's wooden floor.

In five minutes they had torn away the central floor boards but it took ten to remove the first layer of steel plates which was immediately beneath and only then did the McKay realise that the Doctor had real reason for his pessimism. They were faced with literally hundreds of small girders and slender rods all criss-crossed and mixed up with wheels. It looked a sheer impossibility to get them out under two hours at least and there were two more similar barriers to cross before they could reach the outer air.

The Doctor had already produced his whole set of tools and spread them out on the underside of the sphere. With these and frantic fingers they attacked the jungle of steel mechanism.

After twenty minutes the McKay was streaming with sweat and the Doctor blowing like a grampus. The air was already beginning to get thick and stuffy owing to the reduced supply of oxygen.

"Axel! Nicky! take over," ordered the McKay when half an hour had passed and he sank back panting against the side of the sphere.

Nicky was quick and efficient at the job, but Axel's beautiful slim hands had never been created for such work. When he had watched the Count for two minutes the McKay called out, "Bozo—did you ever run a car?"

"Sure boss—I've known the inside of a flivver since I was ten."

"Take over from Count Axel then."

The big gunman shambled forward and flung himself eagerly upon the floor, but his hands were large and clumsy. He was painfully slow at unscrewing the complicated joints.

"Let me have a go," whispered Camilla. "I'm good at screws. Meccano was my favourite nursery game."

"Good girl! Take over from Bozo then." The McKay wiped the dripping perspiration from his face.

Camilla proved a real asset. Her quick fingers slid in and out among the rods and Vladimir, just behind her, had all his work cut out to hand her spanners and pass the pieces she and Nicky freed into the back of the sphere where they were making a dump.

The whole of the work had to be carried out under the greatest difficulties. The sphere was only built to accommodate eight persons—the number in it at the present time—and each was supposed to sit in an allotted space which gave little play for movement. Its bulging sides allowed no additional freedom as these concave surfaces held all the instruments, the searchlight, the oxygen tanks, the fans, the trays of calcium chloride for absorbing moisture, and the even more important ones with soda lime in them for removing the poisonous excess of carbon dioxide from the air.

Now that the sphere lay on its side the broken chairs occupied valuable floor space despite the fact that Vladimir had smashed their slender wooden frames to matchwood to reduce their bulk. The members of the party who, in turn, were fighting so desperately to get at the mechanism under the floor had to be given elbow room as they knelt at their work. The torch-holders bent in cramped attitudes, shining the lights over their shoulders. Behind, the rest crouched or stood in strained positions, helpless but frantically anxious to glimpse what progress was being made.

Each time the workers were changed it necessitated their reliefs forcing their way through a crush that resembled a small section of the Black Hole of Calcutta. As the floor plates and pieces of machinery were passed back the press became even greater for, while the workers were unable to get more than their heads and their hands into the space which they had cleared, the awkward spiky dump of steel in the back of the sphere continued to occupy more room nearly every moment.

It took an hour to clear the first space between the quadruple floors, of machinery. Then the McKay and Doctor Tisch attacked the second lining of steel plates.

Their fingers were no longer as supple as when they started, and their hands were bruised and torn. The air was stale and foul so that they panted and gasped as they twisted and jerked at the screws. In consequence it took them nearly twenty minutes to get up the second floor.

Another mass of levers now barred their passage. Not so many but larger this time and more difficult to get at. In addition there was a square steel box in the centre of their path. It contained the dynamite and, immediately the lid was off, the slabs were passed carefully back. The Doctor and the McKay got the box out but when they had done so they both had to give up, and lay gasping for breath on the floor.

At the McKay's order Sally and Vladimir tried their hands while Count Axel passed the freed material to the dump. Sally was nothing like as quick as Camilla and Vladimir was tempted into trying his strength instead of skill. He wrenched out two small rods with the assistance of a spanner, but the third only bent and caused them more trouble than they had experienced with half a dozen others put together, so the McKay put Camilla and Nicky on again, since they had done so well before.

Their partnership was not so successful this time. Nicky stuck to it gamely and did yeoman service but Camilla was so overcome now by the heavy atmosphere that she could hardly move her hands. The Doctor too seemed pretty done as he lolled uncomfortably, almost comatose, against the side of the sphere.

The McKay pushed Camilla aside and took her place. As

he did so he called out to ask the time and, when Count Axel gave it to him, ordered the supply of oxygen to be reduced again by half. It seemed impossible that they could carry on at all with only a quarter of the normal allowance but he knew now for certain that they would never be able to free themselves in the three hours which was all that a half ration allowed them.

Count Axel, who felt his uselessness acutely, had secured another torch and, standing on tiptoe, took a look out of one of the ports. "These people," he said slowly, with laboured breath, "are eating the fish raw—now."

"Silence," snapped the McKay angrily. He knew how infinitely precious every ounce of oxygen must be. As matters stood at present there seemed little enough chance of the supply holding out. Sally, lighting him at his work, felt too exhausted to be more than faintly disgusted at the mental picture which came into her mind that showed the host of blind grey ghouls greedily devouring the freshly killed fish.

Nicky's brain conjured up a memory of some shots from an Eskimo film—Mala the Magnificent—in which the native actors had fed, with gluttonous delight on handfuls of warm blubber torn from the body of a captured seal; but his fingers never paused in their frantic efforts to loosen the joints of the machinery.

Time passed. The air became thin and rarified. It was as difficult to draw sufficient into their lungs as if they had been locked up for hours in the dry heat of the hottest room in a Turkish bath. Camilla said nothing but she had an awful feeling that instead of being about to faint again she was really dying now. She tried desperately hard to keep herself upright but her body suddenly went limp and she fell forward in a crumpled heap. Vladimir saw her and motioned to Bozo to take his place then, as the gunman crawled painfully forward, he lifted Camilla tenderly in his arms, kissed her gently on the cheek, and propped her up against the side of the sphere next to the oxygen tanks where she would reap the benefit of more than her fair share of their precious supply.

After two hours and a half they had cleared the second lot of machinery and begun on the third floor, but the air had become positively stifling. Their breath came in quick short pants and an examination of the oxygen tanks showed that even with the reduced supply they had only three quarters

202

of an hour to go. Another hour and they would certainly all be dead.

"We've got to get out—we've got to!" wheezed the McKay, "Come on Doctor—your turn now."

The Doctor roused himself, wiped the sweat from his face and rolled over, then set to work again with a sudden spurt of energy. Nicky, whom he had just relieved, managed to reach the back of the sphere and then collapsed.

The McKay felt his fingers grow numb and clumsy. He hated the idea of giving up but knew that he *must* have another spell of rest, otherwise he would be delaying progress. He muttered to Bozo who took his place. The gunman's thick blunt hands were trembling and the sight of his slowness almost drove the McKay to a frenzy, but he worked doggedly at the job and his tools never slipped.

By the time they'd got the third floor up Count Axel knew from a quick glance at his watch that their limit of life was now reduced to a quarter of an hour. Without reference to the McKay he turned the oxygen valve a fraction lower— even another two minutes might mean the difference between safety and death, but if he could have seen the work still to be done from where he crouched behind the others, he would not have bothered.

A fresh barrier confronted them. Great reels of electric wires for exploding detonators from several hundred feet above the ocean bed—masses of springs and interlocking levers. The Doctor groaned but he and Bozo laboured on.

Their heads ached appallingly, their eyes seemed about to burst from their sockets, their tongues were swollen to almost double their normal size and filled their mouths so that they had to keep them wide open as they fought for the last breaths of oxygen.

Sally's torch slipped from her hand, smashed on the steel floor and went out. Then she slid to her knees and fell backwards. Bozo was the next to go. He had never fully recovered from the blow which Vladimir had given him eight hours before, soon after the cable had snapped, and now he just toppled over sideways like a shot rabbit.

Vladimir reached backwards and shook the Count out of his semi torpor, then he pulled Bozo away from the mass of levers that still faced them and took his place. Axel crawled over the prostrate bodies and lit the workers with his torch.

The next to go was the doctor. He had succeeded in freeing

one of the big reels of wire so that they could actually see the last floor now, beyond which was the life-giving air. With a great effort he lifted the reel and, turning, placed it on Sally's chest, then without a murmur he fell forward senseless across her legs. The McKay picked up the spanner he had dropped.

It was now a nightmare scene. Enfeebled almost to fainting point from lack of air, the McKay and Vladimir still struggled with the many struts; Count Axel held the torch; while behind, five limp unconscious bodies lay huddled in grotesque and horrible disarray.

About eighteen inches square of the last floor was clear but the McKay knew now that he had failed. A dozen jutting rods had still to be removed before the smallest of them could force their way through the gap, and they were so weak that the floor itself would take another hour's work to get up. The oxygen was all but finished and death hovered waiting, in the shadows of the sphere to touch them on the shoulder.

He no longer had the strength for rapid action but he turned and whispered painfully:

"Count—dynamite—on your—knees." He knew that what he was going to do was the most desperate hazard— they might all be blown to fragments, but what did that matter. Still there was a fraction less chance of the dynamite exploding through concussion if it were removed from contact with the surface of the sphere.

As Count Axel exerted all his remaining strength to lift the box the McKay laid his hand on Vladimir's arm. "Give me —your—gun."

With slow fumbling fingers Vladimir pulled it from his pocket and passed it over.

The McKay took it and, as Count Axel focused the light again, he lifted it. The weapon seemed to weigh a ton, but he brought it up to a line where two of the bottom plates in the last floor were jointed—and fired.

In the confined space of the air-tight sphere the succession of explosions sounded as though a whole munition works was blowing up. For a second the McKay thought that, as he had feared, the shock of the vibration had set off the detonators. The automatic had dropped from his hand. The crash seemed to have burst his ear-drums. Vladimir was gasping out something but he could no longer hear.

He swayed feebly, peering through the little cloud of

204

smoke that obscured the remaining machinery. Count Axel's arm was resting on his shoulder, still holding the torch. No hoped-for hole showed in the plates, only an irregular round dent on the joint that he had aimed at. It seemed now that their last hope had gone.

As the McKay crouched there, the echoes of the shots still reverberating in his ears, his head singing and whirling, his eyes suffused with blood, Vladimir picked up a heavy lever—the last that they had removed. Gripping it with both hands he lurched forward, his strength gone but his great weight behind the stabbing blow with which he jabbed the dented surface.

The bullets from the automatic had sprung the plates a trifle and Vladimir's last desperate effort completed the work. They only parted the sixteenth of an inch but an insistent hissing came like the sound of angels' music and they knew that the air was coming through.

For over an hour the McKay, Vladimir and Count Axel lay utterly exhausted and semi comatose, then they began to revive and one by one resuscitated the others. The air was still stifling hot, oppressive, and lifeless but it was just breathable, so they got to work again on the bottom of the sphere.

They took their time now; an hour and a quarter elapsed before they cleared the machinery and had removed sufficient plates in the last floor to crawl through.

The bottom of the sphere was tilted towards the harbour floor but, to their surprise, it was completely clear of fish. Hardly a trace remained of that mass of creatures which had flooded the whole space between the quayside and the sphere six hours before. The surface was just awash with a few inches of clear water.

Through the portholes they examined the quay. The great mob of greyish-white half-men were still there—all seated now on their haunches, peering blindly out of their almost colourless eyes in the direction of the bathysphere.

"I do not like the look of these people," said the Doctor heavily.

The McKay shrugged. "I'm afraid we've got to chance what they think of us. We can't stay here."

"How long is it since we left the ship now?" asked Camilla.

After glancing at his watch Count Axel replied: "We went down at 8.45, Madame. It is now 11.30 at night, so it is nearly fifteen hours and we survived nine of those hours on

our remaining oxygen after we were cut off." Before returning the watch to his pocket he methodically wound it up.

"Really?" Camilla's voice conveyed surprise and she
added despondently, "It seems as though it was at least a
week."

"I am a fasting man," declared Vladimir, "and would eat
any old kipper that these so loathsome people can provide."

Sally sighed. "Need we go yet? There is our picnic
lunch still that we've never had time even to think of eating.
I'm so dead beat that I could drop. Can't we sleep here
through the night?"

"Sorry m'dear," the McKay laid his hand gently on her
arm, "I'm afraid we can't. Heaven alone knows what really
happened to us but, as I see it, the sphere got caught in some
sort of trawl and was dragged among these people's catch
through a succession of locks which prevent this place being
flooded. Anyhow, at any moment some flood gate may open
and disgorge another haul. The crowd on the quay are
probably sitting waiting for their next meal to arrive. If we
remain here we may get caught in the sphere again—only
next time, owing to the hole we've made in it—we'll all be
drowned for certain."

"The McKay is right," urged Count Axel, "and right too
in his theory about the manner of our arrival here. Do you
remember how gently we came to rest each time we sank to
a lower level. We were probably falling down some deep,
narrow shafts in which the catch of fish was packed so tightly
together that those under us acted like a feather bed as we
approached the bottom. Our briefer sideways movements
were perhaps when we were being dragged through tunnels
which form the actual locks beyond each of which the pressure
of water above lessens."

"These people look so revolting," demurred Camilla. "It
seems absurd in the face of what we've gone through—but
somehow I'd much rather stay in the old sphere a bit longer."

"We daren't risk it," the McKay insisted. "We'd have
to abandon ship in any case in a few hours when our food and
drink runs out, even if there were no danger of being
engulfed by another mass of fish. I don't want to be unkind
but just imagine that *is* going to happen in above five minutes'
time and that as the water gushes up through the opening
we've made, an octopus reaches in one of his tentacles to get
you."

"You brute! aren't things bad enough?" murmured Sally.

"No, honestly—however doubtful the future looks it will be a better bet once we're out of this and up on the wharf."

The Doctor nodded. "The *Herr Kapitan* speaks sense *Fraulein* and although these people are primitive beyond belief they may prove hospitable. One thing is certain—they will be more frightened of us than we of them."

Sally looked at Camilla, who nodded faintly. "All right," she said, "do as you wish," and so the matter was agreed.

A hasty meal was made, to keep up their strength, of half the picnic lunch. The remaining torches were distributed and every tool or item which might possibly be of use later, apportioned out amongst them.

The McKay still had the automatic; four bullets remained in it and he reloaded to capacity from Bozo's only spare clip, so that he had eight in the magazine and one in the chamber with a last reload of a further three in his pocket.

He picked up a three-foot steel bar with a big joint at its end from the dump at the back of the sphere as an additional weapon. The others, including the girls, armed themselves with suitable pieces of the machinery which had been removed from the bottom of the sphere in such desperate haste.

"Ready?" asked the McKay.

A murmur of assent went up.

"All right then," he grinned for the first time since he had left the ship; "it's just on midnight and a very appropriate hour to step ashore in an unknown land like this. Come on, help me through the hole some of you."

Legs foremost they pushed him through and his feet splashed into the shallow water. Immediately he was standing upright they passed through his pistol, torch and steel bar. He thrust the latter through his braces like an awkward blunt sword, and began at once to take closer stock of his surroundings.

The torch showed him that they were in a lofty cavern—the roof was just visible. The wall opposite the quay reached sheer up to it—the extremities on either hand he could not see; he turned the beam on the quay.

It was of solid, well-built, even masonry and, above it, he saw at once that, whether they were blind or not, some sense had warned the half-men that he had left the sphere. Everyone of the grey-white mob had risen and was staring at him with pale, blank, apparently sightless eyes.

"Hello there!" he called, waving the hand that held the torch in greeting, and holding his pistol ready with the other.

The response was instantaneous. Countless shrill voices broke into piercing cries, a thousand arms lifted—and a thousand stones were hurled in the direction of the sphere.

CHAPTER XVII

THE KINGDOM OF THE DAMNED

IF those hundreds of nude grey-white figures on the quayside had been able to see the thing at which they aimed their missiles the McKay would never have survived that moment. It was too late for him to attempt wriggling back through the bottom of the sphere. He could only slip to his knees beside the under-carriage and fling his arms above his head.

The stones, so wildly thrown by the blind sub-humans, came whizzing down for fifty feet all round him. Half a hundred clanged on the bathysphere and, for a moment, it rang under them like some huge gong. The shallow water about it was churned to splashing wavelets as the missiles clattered on the harbour floor but the McKay, partly protected by the under-carriage, was only hit by half a dozen.

One large one landed on his elbow and gave him momentary but exquisite pain, another caught him on the thigh. The rest were smaller and bounded off his body like a series of half-spent blows.

Immediately the hail of stones had ceased he sprang to his feet and, before the submen had time to follow up their assault, thrust his head and arms inside the sphere.

"Haul me in—quick!" he cried.

Willing hands grabbed at his shoulders and he wriggled violently. An irregular shower of stones began to fall again, but after a moment's tussle, he was pulled into safety.

"By Jove! That was a narrow squeak," he panted as soon as he could speak. "If those brutes weren't blind they would have pounded me to pulp."

"My dear—are you hurt?" Sally put her arm round his shoulders anxiously. The din from the stones ringing on the sphere was so great now its bottom was open that she had to shout to make herself heard.

"They got me on the elbow and the thigh, but it's nothing much," he shouted back. "Now listen—all of you. We've proved them hostile so we've got to make a plan of attack."

The clamour lessened. Evidently some sense told the sub-men that their unseen enemy had escaped.

"Oh, can't we stay here," Camilla pleaded, "anyhow for a bit."

"No, that's impossible. We'll only be trapped or driven out eventually by starvation. We've got to establish ourselves on that quay, somehow, and as soon as possible."

Nicky was holding a torch to one of the portholes and peering out; "There seem to be such hundreds of them," he said in a low scared voice.

"Yes," the McKay agreed. "Their numbers are difficult to estimate with no more light than the beam of a torch—but they're packed so tightly that I should think there must be fully a thousand on the quay. What are they doing now?"

"Crouching again in a great huddle just as they were before you went outside. They're gibbering like mad too—as if they were scared to death—you can hear them if you listen."

As Nicky ceased speaking the party inside the sphere all heard the shrill excited twittering which came from the quay. It sounded like a flock of frightened birds.

"They have much fear of us I am certain," the Doctor announced, "if only they could see that we would be friends."

"Well, unfortunately they can't," the McKay spoke abruptly, "and we're not going to have much chance to show them we mean no harm if they're going to pelt us each time we put our heads outside the sphere."

"Ach, fear!" sighed the Doctor, "fear without reason—that is the cause of half the misery in the world. We are afraid of them because they are so numerous. They are afraid of us because they cannot see and believe us to be some dreadful monster which has become entangled in their catch. Therefore we must fight and maim each other—it is horrible!"

Count Axel nodded. "Yes—it's sad. But it's their lives or ours and, although they outnumber us by a hundred to one, we, at least, have dynamite."

"Get it out, Count," ordered the McKay, "and the detonators. We must try to fix up some bombs to make a really telling demonstration."

The two of them set to work with the Doctor. The others could not help, except by holding lights, as they had no knowledge of explosives but, after half an hour a dozen large grenades had been manufactured encased in various portions of the now useless instruments which they stripped from the walls of the sphere.

"The next thing is to protect ourselves—" The McKay flashed his torch round. "What have we got here that might be useful?"

"We can use the canvas chair-seats as head covers," suggested Axel, "and the bottom boards could be converted into rough shields perhaps."

"Good for you, Count—let's get to it."

Soon they were all busy. The girls had no needles or thread but they twisted and tied the squares of canvas, as well as they could, into conical helmets which would serve to shield their heads a little from the stones since, with the exception of Bozo, who had refused to be parted from his dark felt, they had all gone down without their hats.

Sally invented a special model, which met with much approval, by utilising some broad strips of canvas which had formed the chair arms, as chin straps. These served to bandage the cheeks as well as to keep the rough helmets on their heads.

The men worked at the bottom boards, using the wire which was on the detonator reels instead of leather, to make an armlet for each. The boards were only about eight inches wide but, when the left forearm was slipped through the wire loop, they formed long narrow shields, which would at least protect the users' faces.

"Now," said the McKay, when all was done, "this is the order of our going. You'll slip me out quietly and I'll have another shot at parleying with these people—although I don't think for a moment that it will be any good. Any more stone throwing and I'm chucking a few of these bombs up on to the quay. The moment you hear them explode—out you come. Get that?"

They muttered agreement and he went on: "The men will be the first to follow me—old business of women and children last—with the exception of Vladimir who's to stay behind and help the girls out in case they get a fit of nerves at the last moment. You've *all got to come*—whether you like it or not because we can't afford to waste explosives, and this first time we'll have the value of surprise. They can never have come up against such things before—so it's our one big chance to establish ourselves on that quay. See what I mean?"

Further murmurs conveyed their understanding.

"Right then. Now, once we are all out of the sphere we've got to adopt a definite formation and stick to it. We shall form three ranks. Count Axel and myself will be in front. Behind us the second rank will march four abreast. Sally and Camilla in the centre with Nicky and Doctor Tisch on either flank. Our third and last rank will consist of Bozo and Vladimir walking behind the two girls. I've placed them in the rear-guard on purpose because they are the strong men of the party and it is essential that our biggest strength should be concentrated to protect our backs. Are you ready now?"

"Yes," said Camilla in a whisper, "we're ready."

Then, just over an hour after he'd made his first appearance the McKay again crawled through the hole.

The great herd still crouched on the quay, peering into the darkness with their blank pale eyes. As the McKay's feet splashed into the few inches of water there was a rustle among them and they all stood up.

"Hello there?" he shouted, but the shrill cries broke out again and their arms lifted.

He was prepared this time and slipped behind the sphere. It formed good cover and not one of the shower of stones touched him. Then, as it slackened he came round the sphere's side and lobbed a bomb right over the quay wall into the midst of the nude grey-white figures. After it he flung a second, then two more which he took from his pockets. As the fourth sailed into the air the first exploded. There was a stab of flame among the densely packed mass, then a shattering crash which reverberated through the whole vast cavern.

The McKay never saw what happened for he had dodged back behind the sphere to avoid the continuous rain of stones. Three more crashing explosions followed and he knew that his home-made grenades had not let him down. The stones ceased clanging on the sphere. He peered out. The quay was empty but for four little heaps of whitish-grey writhing figures who twittered now in a pain-racked falsetto. Axel and Nicky were already outside the sphere. Bozo was coming through the hole. The rest soon followed and fell in as he had ordered, the two girls together in the middle. The McKay only paused to see that they were properly placed in formation then he yelled:

"Come on now," and splashed through the water at a run towards the quay.

He and Axel carried two bombs apiece, the other men one

212

each, but there was no need to use them. Except for the little piles of dead and stricken creatures the great deep quay ran back into the darkness as desolate as though no multitude had ever occupied it.

"Give me a leg up now," the McKay cried to Count Axel as they reached the slimy eight foot wall. The Count obeyed and the McKay scrambled over the edge on to a flat surface. He paused to flash his torch round. No walls were visible—only the dripping roof above, and nothing stirred in the deep shadows ahead. He turned to help Count Axel up.

"So far so good," murmured the Count. "You keep a look out and I'll give a hand to the others."

The McKay swung round to face the darkness again. In his left hand just beyond the edge of his wooden shield he held his torch, in the other a bomb ready for any emergency. The revolver was thrust into the top of his trousers and the steel lever through his braces. For a couple of minutes he stood there—feet firmly planted, legs wide apart, his ears keen to catch the patter of bare feet on the rocky floor, his eyes intent and watchful.

"We're all here now," Count Axel reported softly. Somehow, in this tense darkness, none of them felt like speaking above a whisper and the McKay's reply was only just audible.

"All right—form up as before and follow me."

He gave them a moment to fall into their ranks then, with Count Axel beside him he advanced warily.

Apart from the treble whimpering of the wounded submen no sound stirred the stillness. This strange new world was one of silence and eternal darkness.

The McKay walked on, the others followed. All of them advanced with slow, instinctively cautious, steps; fearing that the enemy might spring out on them from behind some hidden corner at any moment, and all the time the beams of their torches flickered hither and thither, stabbing the blackness with eight shafts of light—yet finding nothing.

They passed within twenty feet of one of the heaps of grey-white creatures. Sally felt physically sick as she glimpsed the leprous limbs splashed with blood and the naked torsos twisted so unnaturally, but Doctor Tisch had her firmly by the arm. One of the group, temporarily knocked out by the explosion but otherwise apparently unharmed was crawling in their direction. The Doctor's torch lit his face—stupid, bestial, repulsive; the high nostrils in his parrot-beaked nose distended and quivered, his heavy eyelids flickered down over his pale eyes as though, despite his blindness, he knew and feared the light. In a second he turned and scuttled away without a sound.

A nauseating smell arose from the heap of corpses. The McKay had been among men who had met sudden death from high explosives before and he knew that it was not the smell of entrails or spilled blood, nor had there been time for the carcasses to putrefy. This was like the revolting stench of bad fish and came, he guessed as much from the still living as the dead, when he remembered Nicky's description of how these people had gorged themselves on their catch while it was still raw.

After advancing two hundred yards he halted. His torch had just picked out a blank wall straight ahead of him. He went a little nearer to examine it. The wall rose sheer to the high ceiling and stretched, as far as he could see, unbroken on either side.

"We'll turn right," he muttered, "anyhow this will serve to protect our backs if we are attacked."

They followed him, keeping their formation, but treading with a little more confidence now that one of their flanks was secured from surprise. The curve of the wall was hardly perceptible in the pitch blackness, but after a few moments it brought them back to the edge of the quayside and appeared to continue round the curve of the harbour without a break.

"This will be the opposite end to where the bathysphere came in," said the McKay. "It looks as if the cavern is an oval shape cut lengthwise by the quay. We'd better about turn and try the other way."

"Oh, I'm so tired!" Camilla leaned heavily on Nicky who was her flank guard, "I can hardly walk another step!"

"That goes fer me too sister," Bozo mumbled, "I'm not meself somehow since your boy-friend put me to sleep." His thick skull had saved the back of his head from being split open when Vladimir had smashed it against the steel side of the sphere, but ever since he regained consciousness he had been suffering from a worse headache than he had ever experienced after a bout of drunkenness on illegal hooch, and now he felt that, instead of a head he carried the bathysphere —rolling from side to side on his thick neck.

214

Sally stretched out a hand and touched the McKay on the arm. "Can't we stay here and sleep a little," she pleaded. "We're safe from drowning in the sphere now and anyway—what's the use of going on?"

"Sure. What's the use?" agreed Nicky who had also been knocked out temporarily that day and was feeling utterly done in after his spate of terrified energy in helping to remove the machinery from the bottom of the sphere. "What do you hope to find if we go on—the Ritz-Carlton Grill Room round the corner or a handy Lyons?—For God's sake let's call it a day."

"I was hoping to find a cave with a narrow entrance where we'd be reasonably safe for the time being," said the McKay slowly. "What do you think Count?"

"I am for remaining here," Count Axel replied at once. "If we were fresher I would say 'push on' but half our party, at least, are unfit to proceed any further. It might even be necessary to carry them later and that would be a terrible handicap if we were attacked. Our present position is not so bad. We are in a triangle of which the wall forms one side and the quay another, so we have only one of three sides to defend. Let us remain here for a few hours until we are rested."

The McKay nodded. "All right then—we'll park down for the night."

His decision was an unutterable relief to the party. Camilla, Sally and Nicky were already sitting on the rocky floor, gratefully seizing the opportunity for even a short rest, while the stronger members of the group sagged as they stood, dumb now—their energies at the lowest ebb from their terrible experiences in the last fifteen hours.

No rocks or boulders were available for them to form a barrier across their exposed front, so for a moment, the McKay considered the possibility of erecting trip-wires fifty feet out in the darkness to give them warning of any hostile approach. He had the necessary material, salved from the bottom of the sphere, but there was nothing to which wires could be attached on that even floor and improvising supports meant fetching more gear from the abandoned bathysphere. The business would involve at least two hours hard work for the whole party so he had to give up the idea and they all sank down, unprotected at the extremity of the quay wall where they stood.

The McKay arranged that he and Axel should take the first watch and that Vladimir and the Doctor should relieve them after two hours had passed. He did not dare to make the spells of duty longer in case he and Axel dropped off into a doze. They were both feeling the strain and fatigue of the nightmare sequence of events as much as the others and only refrained from showing it in the same degree because the one had reserves of mental strength to draw upon and the other the life-long habit of responsibility.

Vladimir tried to make the two girls as comfortable as possible. He sat between them with his back against the wall and, placing an arm round each of their shoulders drew their heads down on to his broad chest. The other men curled up on either side of them, so weary that they hardly noticed the hard discomfort of the unyielding rock. Only the McKay and Count Axel remained, some feet in front of the group, side by side, still wide awake and watchful.

For a moment or two the six huddled figures by the wall endeavoured, in a groping way, to straighten out in their minds the extraordinary series of happenings which had brought them to their present situation. It was now one-thirty in the morning—eight and a half hours since the sphere had been carried into this undersea cavern, and in all that time their thoughts had been concentrated on immediate emergencies. They had not had one moment to speculate on their utterly miraculous escape from death or any explanation for the existence of this hidden world in which they found themselves. Now, their brains were so clouded with fatigue that they could not attempt to grapple with the problem and almost instantly surrendered to a heavy, death-like sleep.

The McKay and Count Axel, out in front, dared not relax and began to devise means to keep themselves alert. Fortunately a breakdown of the electricity supply from the ship when the bathysphere was on the bottom, was a normal possibility which the Doctor had foreseen, so the dozen torches which he had stowed in the ball against such an emergency were all new and large in size; but now, light was infinitely precious. In this grim underworld there could be no dawn to hope for and once the batteries ran out they would be completely at the mercy of anything which might steal upon them in the darkness. The McKay suggested that, to economise their light he and Axel should only use one flash every half minute—alternately. The necessity for regular switching on and off would help to keep them wakeful and, for the same reason it would be best to talk.

The Count agreed and, for what seemed an eternity they spoke in whispers, advancing every sort of fantastic theory to account for the nightmare place in which they had arrived, or speculating on the origin of the great herd of creatures who inhabited this subterranean domain. Even Count Axel was not bold enough to face the future squarely yet and he had formed a half belief that this was death. They had been so near the end when fighting to escape from the sphere that it seemed almost more reasonable to suppose that they had all died then—or even earlier, when the oxygen had given out without, perhaps, their being aware of it—than to credit the actual existence of their present surroundings.

The McKay's practical mind revolted equally from any attempt to foresee their future. It was unknown—unknowable. Obviously they were cut off completely and forever from the world above. This was no prison from which one could plan escape, no seeming impasse out of which wits and bravery might still find a way. When their torches failed they would be encompassed about with blackest darkness, and when they had consumed the last of their meagre supplies hunger and thirst would come upon them. Death must surely follow—either at the hands of those abominable submen or from weakness and exhaustion. Yet the "will to live" is so strongly developed in the human consciousness that it never occurred to him not to play out the game of life to the very last trick.

At two-thirty he moved over to waken the reliefs and shook the Doctor into semi-consciousness, but when he saw Vladimir —his head fallen forward between those of the two girls—he knew that, to rouse the Prince, he must rouse them too so, instead, he shook Nicky by the shoulder.

Nicky started up and shuddered as though in the grip of some frightful dream but the McKay reassured him. Then he gave instructions about economising the light of the torches —told Doctor Tisch to wake him promptly at four-thirty, so that he could witness the changing of the guard—then he curled up on the hard floor at Sally's feet. Count Axel dropped beside him.

The Doctor and Nicky sat out in front now, the small pile of bombs between them, staring nervously ahead into the pitchy blackness of the great cavern.

217

Their two-hour sleep had refreshed them but they still felt slow and groggy from their previous expenditure of nervous energy. They agreed, as the McKay and Count Axel had done, that to talk was the best way of preventing themselves dropping off to sleep, but they had little to say to each other.

Nicky's contribution to the conversation consisted almost entirely of periodic exclamations—"Where the devil *are* we, Doctor?—Oh, God, I'm tired!—Doctor, what the hell *are* we going to do?" which he repeated at brief intervals.

The Doctor had not even the shadow of a theory to advance and could only mutter gutturally. "I haf no idea—no idea at all. Of our future I can guess nothing and for the present we can only obey the *Herr Kapitan's* orders."

It was almost at the end of their watch when they heard the muted patter of naked feet. The Doctor instantly flashed on his torch while Nicky sprang up and roused the others.

The McKay was wide awake at once: "Prepare for action" he said in a sharp whisper.

For a moment the other, newly awakened, members of the party could not get a grip of their surroundings. Automatically they stumbled to their feet, picked up their weapons, and adjusted the board shields over their left forearms. Then the pattering footsteps and the horrible smell of rotten fish which the advancing herd carried with them brought full realisation of past events and their present peril.

"It's—it's not a nightmare then?" Sally choked. "We're really here— Oh, this is——"

"Silence!" the McKay cut her short. "If they can't scent us they'll believe we're still in the sphere. Quick Doctor— put out that torch."

They waited then, their blood throbbing again at full pulse through their arteries—tense and expectant—anticipating that the attack might open at any moment as they listened to that soft padding of innumerable footsteps in the darkness.

The sound ceased. The great cavern became silent as death. They could hear their own laboured breathing and judged tha the unseen horde had halted somewhere in the centre and the far end of the big oval rock-roofed chamber.

Nothing happened. Camilla began to tremble. Sally put out a protective hand to her although little tremors of fear were running through her own body. The men were grouped round them, nervously fingering their weapons, ready instantly, at the McKay's order to press the buttons of their torches.

Suddenly there came a noise like thunder—a dull heavy rumbling in the far distance. It continued for some minutes yet seemed to grow no louder. Then it stopped abruptly.

The McKay shifted his weight from one foot to the other Then this new silence was broken by the chirping and mutter ing of the herd out there in the darkness.

The thunder rolled again—this time much nearer. The unseen roof and walls of the cavern vibrated and quivered under the repercussion from the blows of some unknown force. The very air was tremulous.

Nicky cowered back against the wall. Camilla endeavoured to gulp down sobs engendered by the extremity of fear which seemed to grip her physically below the breasts. Sally was half fainting. The two leaned on each other for support or else their legs would have given way beneath them. The rest held their ground, white-faced and with protruding eyes which strained in vain to see one inch ahead in that impenetrable blackness.

Time passed. Not one of the little group could attempt to assess its duration but at last the thunder ceased again and now the shrill note of the submen's chatter had risen to a fiendish clamour.

Vladimir felt his dark hair clinging damp about his temples. The Doctor's soft collar was a wet rag round his neck. Every-one of the eight humans was sweating or shivering as they stood there—black night all about them—listening to those ghoulish cries.

A new note suddenly drowned the screeching. The thunder had turned to the roar and hiss of tossing water. A blur of silvery light appeared low down at the far end of the harbour. With horrifying suddenness it increased in size and leapt towards them.

Next second the foremost wave, released by some great subterranean floodgate, slapped against the wall—curved upwards scintillating with a million flashing lights and descended, drenching the little party on the quay with great splashes from the backwash.

Below them now, on their left under the quayside, they could see the furious churning of the waters as they seethed and foamed, lit dully by the lights of another great haul of deep sea creatures thrashing and leaping in a frantic effort to escape.

The luminosity from the harbour now lit a fair portion of the cavern with a dim ghostly light. Its roof and furthest walls were not visible, but the herd could be seen in a leprous mass, tightly packed together yet constantly moving like some vast blotchy writhing animal. Its nearest fringe was no more than fifty yards from the McKay but obviously they had no knowledge of his presence.

"Steady," he said in a low voice. "Steady now, they've come down here for the fish—not for us."

"It's close on twelve hours since they had their last feed," muttered Count Axel.

Again they waited, relieved a little, but still acutely anxious. It was almost certain that the submen would spread out along the quay and find them crouching there against the wall at its furthest extremity.

Sally was just behind the McKay. He could hear her breath coming in quick short gasps. Occasionally she choked in an endeavour to steady herself. Suddenly she screamed.

Her scream was so wild that it echoed right round the lofty chamber. Something soft had touched her shoe. For an instant she had thought it was Doctor Tisch's foot, but the thing had stayed there and, before she had time to move, twined round her ankle like the gentle caress of some slim fingerless hand. Now its grip tightened and it began to pull.

Instantly the semi-darkness was shattered. The torches flashed out—cutting great swathes through the greyish gloom —dazzling and bewildering.

Vladimir saw the 'thing' first and, dropping his weapon grabbed her round the shoulders. Another second and the others had seen it too. An octopus had reached its long tentacle up from the waters that seethed three feet below upon their left and, passing it in front of Doctor Tisch, had her by the leg. The fleshy pointed arm with its long row of suckers was taut with the brute's effort to drag her off the quayside into the harbour.

They had no knives with which to sever the tentacle so they slashed at it with their steel levers while Vladimir exerted all his strength to prevent Sally being wrenched from his embrace. The McKay jerked Bozo's automatic from his trousers top, focused the curved beak and enormous soulless eye of the octopus in the beam of his torch, then fired down into it.

A fountain of black liquid spouted into the air but still the creature kept its hold on Sally's ankle and reached up another waving tentacle which searched blindly for her companions. Sally screamed and screamed. Terrified, heart-rending cries came shrilling from her wide open mouth and Nicky, as he flashed his torch on her face noticed, quite consciously, despite his own terror, that one of her back teeth had been crowned with gold.

The McKay fired again and again—and yet again. At last the tentacle loosened its grip; the others threshed the water furiously for a moment and the octopus sank from sight hidden under the mass of fish.

Sally went limp in Vladimir's arms, then slid to the floor like a half-empty sack as he released her, for the submen, warned of their presence by her screams, were now surging towards them.

As the McKay switched round from shooting the octopus he saw the great grey-white herd all facing in his direction. The front ranks wavered, pressing back in fear, but the hundreds behind thrust them forward with shrill cries and clamour.

The nearest were no more than ten yards away and held their long spears blindly before them. A shower of heavy stones came hurtling down, thrown from the back of the mob which was still hidden in the darkness.

"Bombs!" yelled the McKay. "Axel, keep yours—the rest of you—let 'em have it!"

They hurled their canisters while Camilla crouched above the unconscious Sally.

The nearest submen began to stab with a jerky motion of their spears but the light of the torches seemed to disconcert them, for they shielded their faces with their free hands, and jabbed indiscriminately at the empty air. Knocking a couple aside, the McKay lashed out with his lever felling a fat fleshy creature who goggled at him blindly.

As he swiped at another he prayed for the explosion of the bombs. In another minute his little party must be crushed up against the wall or forced off the quay into the water by the relentless pressure of the herd.

Suddenly one of the grenades went off. The crash seemed to shake the roof. Then another and another followed. The

221

submen dropped their spears and broke in wild confusion, screeching vilely.

The McKay had already decided that, if their chance did come, they must take it immediately to get out of this dangerous corner and not let themselves be trapped again in any similar situation.

He gave one swift glance behind him to assure himself that his party was all together—paused for a second as he saw Sally unconscious on the floor, but started forward as Vladimir dragged her up and slung her bodily across his shoulder.

"Quick—keep your formation and follow me!" The McKay exclaimed then, as the fourth bomb exploded, he led the party back in the direction from which they had come nearly five hours before, sticking close beside the wall.

The cavern was now like a scene from hell conjured up by the vivid brush of some early Flemish painter. A broad swathe of silvery-grey luminosity, given off by the big haul of fish and squids, rose above the whole length of the harbour, fading into darkness about ten feet up. As the party of humans advanced along the blank wall which curved in a great arc round the inland side of the quay the herd were thrown up in silhouette against the silvery grey mist. Screeching with terror little knots of them ran blindly from side to side, slipping and falling in the blood of their wounded or blundering into the piles of corpses which marked the places where the bombs had fallen.

The party advanced to near the spot where they had first struck the wall after they left the sphere, when Sally began to whimper. They halted a moment for Vladimir to set her down and the McKay forced a sip of brandy, from his flask, between her lips.

"Think you can walk m'dear?" he asked urgently.

Sally stared with terrified eyes at the nightmare figures moving in the silvery haze. "Oh God!" she gulped. "If we're caught I—I believe they'll eat us."

"We'll be dead before that," Nicky's voice quavered.

"Can you walk Sally?" repeated the McKay. "We've got to make an effort now."

"Yes," she shuddered, "I'll manage somehow."

Camilla and Doctor Tisch took her arms, Vladimir dropped to the rear, and they hurriedly set off again in their original formation. Instead of fleeing as they had the night before,

222

the submen were concentrating now at the far end of the chamber, and a scatter of rocks and stones began to fall.

They were wildly aimed and most of them pitched among their own gibbering wounded, but a few clopped against the wall and one caught Nicky on the shoulder.

"Up shields!" ordered the McKay, as he continued to press forward, then, when they had advanced another hundred yards he saw a lofty break in the wall beyond the place where the herd were massed together.

"That's the way they come," he whispered to Axel. "God knows where it leads but we've got to chance that and get through it somehow. I had hoped that the bombs would clear this place altogether."

"You forget the fish," Count Axel whispered back. "Last night they had full stomachs when you attacked them, but now they are empty and they will not leave this place until they have secured their food."

The stones were flying faster now, clicking and rattling as they bounded from the flat rock floor. A dozen had already thudded on the shields which the party held over their heads and faces.

Within fifty feet of the enemy the McKay halted. The big arch showed quite distinctly now, lit by the unearthly glow thrown up from the harbour. Between it and him a solid jamb of the naked sub-race, males and females, were pressed— jostling each other as they threw their stones—a hundred deep, barring the passage.

"Clear me that entrance Count," said the McKay, "use both your bombs."

Count Axel lobbed one carefully into the centre of the crowd and threw the other high with all his strength, so that it landed just short of the archway.

"This is sheer murder," murmured the Doctor in a horror-stricken voice.

"D'you think I like it?" snapped the McKay.

They waited then, clustered together, their shields held up to protect them from the still-falling stones which continued to clatter all about them.

A blinding flash lit the cavern for a second. Again the whole place vibrated with the crash. Another followed two seconds afterwards. Once more there came those piercing screams of agony and the frantic gibbering as the herd parted, stampeding in great batches. One group, distraught with

223

terror, rushed straight off the quayside into the harbour, another blindly collided with the wall only ten feet from where the McKay was crouching.

"Come on now," he called, "stick together and follow me!" Then at a quick trot he headed for the archway.

The submen seemed to know of their approach by the flashing of the torches, and with animal courage, turned to attack their tormentors.

For five minutes the little party of humans fought their way forward, striking out ruthlessly with their steel levers.

The filthy stench of rotten fish was so nauseating now they were right among the herd that they were nearly overcome by it.

They were terribly handicapped by the semi-darkness, as the beams of their torches only lit the thing upon which they were focused for the moment, and everything outside the rays was hidden from them.

Tripping and stumbling over dead bodies and writhing wounded they literally hacked their way through the mass of short, naked, stinking, grey-white people until, at last, the McKay reached the entrance of the lofty arch.

It was black and empty. In it he turned to assure himself that the rest had got through. The others were close upon his heels. Vladimir and Bozo were beating off the submen in a desperate rear-guard action.

"Come on," he called. "We've got the legs of them, and a clear run before us." Then he plunged into the tunnel.

The others followed, breaking clear of the mob almost immediately. Yet, as they ran, they knew that they were pursued, for even the echo of their own flying feet did not entirely drown the soft padding of those countless others and the shrill birdlike voices of the submen twittered angrily in their ears.

Count Axel lit the way, his torch focused to the front but downwards, so that they should not rush headlong over some precipice hidden in the velvet blackness. Once or twice the McKay flashed his light up to the roof or walls. The tunnel was about twenty feet in height, and, apparently hewn out of the solid rock.

After a few moments they outdistanced their pursuers. The cries and patter had died down behind them. They eased their pace and dropped into a steady loping trot.

The tunnel ended abruptly and, almost before they had

realised it, they were traversing a level open space which sloped downwards. The roof was visible, but no walls until. two hundred yards further on they ran slap into one. Turning left they sped along it, hoping to find a break in its smooth surface but, before they did so that stealthy padding of the now silent mob upon their heels, could be heard again.

Unseen by the humans the submen streamed into the chamber, cutting diagonally across it and now it was evident that they were not totally blind, for they began to cast stones in the direction of the torches.

The McKay turned to face the new attack but, as the first shower of stones descended, Nicky cried: "Here—this way! There's another tunnel."

"Keep in your ranks," called the McKay and, thrusting past Nicky, with Axel at his side, he led the way down it.

The second tunnel was much longer than the first and after a half a mile they had outdistanced the short-legged submen again. They slowed up then into a quick walk, all breathing heavily.

At last the second tunnel ended in another high-roofed chamber but the eyes of the whole party were instantly rivetted on one spot in it, low down towards their right. A pale cloud of luminous silver light broke the curtain of pitchy blackness. Like children who have ventured into the dark cellars below some old house, they instinctively ran towards it.

The light came from a round pool about fifty feet in diameter, edged by a broken stone wall just knee high. The water was oily and showed not a ripple, the luminosity came from pieces of dead fish, transparent scales and spiky fins that were floating in a silvery scum upon its surface.

At first they thought the pool to be another of those strange subterranean harbours like that from which they had come, but suddenly the waters broke.

An utterly hideous and rapacious face stared up at them. It was a Merman, such as they had seen on their later dives but larger, and the fair quill-like hair not only stood out backwards from its narrow skull but also sprouted from its fanged receding jaw in a jagged beard.

They drew back in repulsion as others, females of the species rose silently beside it, staring at them with beady unblinking eyes.

"If I could spare the bullets I'd put some into them,"

muttered the McKay. "But every one I've got is worth its weight in emeralds. Come on—we'll choose another place to rest in before we go any further."

After exploring for a little while they found two fresh tunnels about fifty yards apart, but owing to their visit to the pool they were now no longer quite certain of their direction, so chose the entrance of the largest and sat down in it for a breather.

"How are you all feeling?" asked the McKay anxiously. "Anyone get hurt in our last scrap?"

"My calf is cut by a stone," complained the Doctor, "but that is now of no consequence. What matters is that I have a pain in my stomach from hunger."

The McKay considered for a moment. The herd had evidently given up the chase or taken a wrong turning among this labyrinth of chambers and tunnels. It seemed that they might just as well consume such food as they had left now. What object was there in saving it until later. In another twelve hours they must find a new source of supply or the game was up—and the sooner it was over, the better then. Since breakfast on the ship—yes, twenty-two hours ago— although it felt like a separate life-time, they had had only one scratch meal to support them. He ordered out the remainder of their provender.

An utter silence filled the great black spaces. Only the sound of their munching broke the heavy stillness.

In ten minutes they had finished up all that was left of their picnic lunch and were temporarily rested. The weaker members of the party had had four hours sleep before the fight in the harbour and, in spite of her horrible experience with the octopus, the freer feeling of the great tunnels made Sally a little less nervy, while Camilla's tendency towards hysteria had played itself out, so that she squatted beside Vladimir now, sunk in a natural silence.

"We'll move on I think," said the McKay, but as he was about to rise Count Axel held out a restraining hand.

"A cigarette first please. I have some still since we were not allowed to smoke in the bathysphere. After all why should we hurry, as we have no idea where we wish to go. Our only clear objective is to avoid those filthy fish-eating creatures."

"Just as you like," the McKay sat down again. He remembered that he had some cigarettes too—one would be very welcome. Most of the others had small supplies and soon they were all lighting up.

"This was a good idea," said the McKay softly as he offered Axel a light. "Restore the old morale eh? You're a cool hand Count and I take off my hat to you."

The Count shrugged. "It is only the outcome of a life-long habit of procrastination," he replied, "no more." But in his mind he knew that the reason lay far deeper and could not be easily explained. He had decided definitely now that they had all died in the bathysphere. Slinger—Ardow—the immaculate but unscrupulous Mr. Kate—were all so infinitely far removed from this new existence.

That the party had remained together was quite explicable. From people who believed that they understood at least the fringe of such things he had heard that in a railway accident those who met sudden death could not quite realise at first that they were really dead, and spoke to the rescuers who removed their bodies, hoping they would hear. Yet they found no response—only from those who had died with them and, for a little while, they were earthbound with those dead companions. Then in due course they became accustomed to the new plane they occupied and drifted apart from their fellow dead—impelled by an omnipotent guidance towards the sphere reserved for their new activities.

It seemed to the Count that this dark underworld must be that in which the ancients had believed so universally; a sort of Purgatory where he would suffer in proportion to his sins but, as surely as the sun would rise again upon the upper earth to-morrow, the vital essence of himself would remain unharmed. Why therefore should they hurry anywhere.

His cigarette was only two thirds smoked when that stealthy patter of naked feet reached his ears again. The others had heard it too. As the McKay sprang up they all scrambled to their feet. The sound seemed to come down the tunnel in the entrance of which they were sitting.

"Form up!" rapped out the McKay, "we'll take the smaller tunnel," and at a trot again he led them to the other opening in the wall fifty yards further on.

Their sense of direction had deceived them in the darkness but they realised it too late. As they reached the second tunnel the submen came streaming out of it right on to them.

"About turn," the McKay bellowed as he emptied the

227

remaining contents of his pistol into the foremost wave, hoping to stem the attack, but the host trampled down their slain and pressed forward without the slightest check.

Next moment the humans were fighting for their lives, hacking and hewing desperately at the purblind faces which surrounded them, while the filthy stench, drawn into their nostrils with every breath, made them want to vomit.

Perhaps the McKay's formation saved them then, for they closed in back to back with the two girls wedged in the middle, yet striking out over the men's shoulders wherever the need for help was greatest.

With Vladimir leading now they retreated like a square of infantry, fighting every inch of the way, until they were in the entrance of the cave where they had had their last meal. Then, at the McKay's order the group turned as on a pivot. He and Count Axel struck down the blind creatures that barred their path and led the way along the tunnel into temporary safety.

The party broke for a moment but re-gathered when they caught the McKay's shout that they must run, and after a hundred yards their longer legs had already carried them clear of the clamouring herd.

A shower of stones followed them down the tunnel but that curved a little, and they slackened to a gentler pace, trotting down hill for a quarter of a mile.

It was only when they broke into a walk and Vladimir cried "Where's Bozo?—he is with us no more," that they halted dead in their tracks.

Vladimir was right. The gunman had vanished, felled by a stone on the head perhaps—he must have dropped without a sound as they fled.

"We must go back," announced the McKay without hesitation. "We can't leave him in the hands of these brutes— they'll tear him limb from limb."

The party turned. In two minutes they had covered the distance back to the entrance to the tunnel. It was empty, but in the great cavern an extraordinary and horrifying scene was in progress.

The luminous mist which rose above the pool lower down the slope showed hundreds of the squat grey figures gathered about it. At one point a compact little company carried a dark shape as ants would carry a dead grasshopper. It was Bozo, and before any move could be made to stop them they

228

threw him, with one heave, head foremost, to the bearded monster and his horrible companions in the oily pool.

Camilla, who felt that she had passed beyond all terror, bit into her knuckles and whimpered pitifully with a fresh access of fear.

Sally closed her eyes and leaned limply against the wall. "Oh heaven! Then that's what will happen when they catch us!" she whispered half fainting with horror.

"He was unconscious," said the McKay softly, "or dead perhaps. We should have seen him struggling otherwise."

Count Axel did not speak. It was fitting he thought, that the simplest among them should pass on first. Bozo had paid, no doubt, for the crimes he had committed purely as a means of livelihood. A low mentality, seduced in youth to easy living by carrying out the orders of his criminal superiors without thought of their consequences to other people. Axel judged his own sins and those of his friends to be of a more subtle kind, and such as the human law could take no ready hold upon. Some power had it seemed, decreed that *they* must suffer further agonies before they had worked off the debts they had accumulated in the life they had just left and be granted rebirth into a more pleasant existence.

The herd had now fallen face downwards in a densely packed circle round the pool. Grovelling, with arms outstretched, they beat their foreheads on the rocky floor, and twittered without cessation, as they made obeisance to the swirling waters into which Bozo's body had disappeared.

"Dagon!" exclaimed the Doctor suddenly.

"What?" asked Nickey unsteadily.

"They worship Dagon," answered the Doctor, "or Ea, if you prefer that name. The oldest god of all. It is a sight I never dreamed of witnessing. He was the Sea-god. The fish with a man's head who came up out of the great waters and spewed up the earth at the very beginning of time. India and Chaldea both retained traces of this cult. *Himmel!* that I should see it practised is past belief."

"Let's get away from here." Even the McKay's voice was a shade jerky now.

They turned then and ran, retracing their steps on the downward road through the tunnel which they had already partly traversed.

After covering half a mile they came out in another, smaller,

229

cavern. It had only one other exit, as far as they could see, so they took that and proceeded into the unknown.

The ground sloped upward now and they felt intensely weary but under the McKay's leadership they stumbled on. This passage was narrower and seemed endless but after they had been marching for twenty minutes Count Axel broke the silence.

"Am I imagining it or is it lighter here?" He switched out his torch and they halted for a minute, then agreed that the impenetrable blackness had given way to a greyish murk.

"Another chamber ahead with some more of those revolting fishmen in a pool I expect," said the McKay gloomily but, as they advanced again the greyness lightened and took on a warmer yellowish tinge.

They could see each other without the aid of their torches for the first time in many hours. Each thought how tattered and dishevelled the others looked and that their strained, anxious faces had aged ten years in a night.

For a few more moments they plodded on through the half-light until they came round a bend and saw the exit of the tunnel, an arch, brightly lit by what appeared to be golden sunshine.

With cries of surprise, hope, and wonder they ran the last hundred yards, then halted, grouped together in the archway, utterly amazed at what they saw.

It was a cavern, larger and loftier than any which they had yet entered; roughly oval in shape and brightly lit through all its length by a ribbon of steady unflickering golden light which ran round its roof; but the sight which held them spellbound was the luxuriant vegetation covering almost the whole of its floor space.

Only a narrow shelf of bare rock ran round the walls of the vast hall, then came a deep ditch—fifteen feet wide, filled with clear water. On the far side of this moat rose a waist-high cactus hedge whose needle-like spines made it an almost impassable barrier. Above the level of that thick prickly fence flowering shrubs and fruit trees grew in wonderful profusion while beyond, a grove of forty foot palm trees towered up, all but hiding a square pillar of rock which supported the centre of the lofty ceiling.

A heavy silence brooded over the sunlit scene which added to its unreality. No breath of wind stirred the leaves or palm fronds and no rustle in the undergrowth betrayed the presence of any animal life, yet the whole fairyland of verdure made the air balmy with the sweet perfume of its flowers and grasses.

The McKay stood staring across the narrow strip of water no longer trusting his eyesight, until exclamations from other members of the party assured him that they too could see this enclosed woodland paradise.

Dazed and bewildered they moved forward along the narrow shelf of rock outside the water-filled channel, seeking a bridge over it, but they made the whole circuit of the place without finding the least variation in the ditch or any break in the thick spiky hedge of cactus which grew like a low wall on its far side.

This orchard jungle was an island, secreted behind strong natural defences and there seemed to be no way in which it could be entered.

The party paused again about fifty yards from the tunnel entrance, opposite a climbing growth of wistaria heavy with blossom, which rose above the thorny hedge.

"We've damn well got to get in there somehow," exclaimed the McKay.

Suddenly, as though in answer to his speech, the tendrils of the wistaria parted and a man stood there, framed in flowers and greenery, eyeing them with extreme curiosity across the low cactus wall. He was as tall as Vladimir, beautifully proportioned, and as handsome as Nicky but his features had the firmness of middle age and he was olive-skinned. The graceful folds of a white linen garment edged with purple hung from his shoulders. His expression was serene and kindly. He smiled at them and said:

"Good morning."

CHAPTER XVIII

THE GARDEN OF THE GODS

"NOW," said Sally, "I *know* we're dead. I've suspected it for a long time but it's nice that we should still be together, isn't it?"

Count Axel nodded. "We all died together in the sphere—quite painlessly. There is no other explanation for . . . all this!"

"You are mistaken I think." A gentle humour twitched the lips of the man beyond the cactus hedge. "You do not look at all dead to me."

The McKay's eyes were popping out of his head. With a rudeness quite contrary to his nature he ignored the stranger and addressed the others. "He's speaking English. I heard him—can you hear him too?"

The man on the island seemed to be more amused than ever. "I speak in English because I heard you use that language," he said, "but, if you prefer it I can talk with you in any one of the five tongues which are most commonly used in the modern world and I know enough of several others to get about without difficulty."

"To get about?" exclaimed Nicky. "Just listen now—he's talking as though he might set off at any moment on an autumn cruise!"

"My surprise at this meeting is almost equal to your own," remarked the man, "as there is no record of any human from the upper world having penetrated here before—but not quite so great, for we at least had knowledge of your upper world whereas you were naturally ignorant of this. My name is Nahou and I am, what you would call, an Atlantean."

Count Axel stepped forward to the brink of the water-filled ditch with a belated effort to show some courtesy. "Sir," he said gravely, "if my belief that we are dead is right you are surely the subject of a gentle God. If I am wrong you are a civilised and cultured man. In either case I beg your pity and protection for myself and my friends. We have suffered much on our journey here. Our endurance is almost at an end, and we shall surely become the prey of evil things unless you grant us sanctuary in your island Paradise."

The Atlantean eyed him with equal gravity and spoke again with the same gentleness. "Humans in such a desperate situation would have my sympathy in any case but your words, Sir, show you to be one of the elect—a twice-born—and for your sake, if no other, I make your party welcome here. Yet your request for sanctuary raises a problem which we have never had to face before. You will, I fear, find some difficulty in crossing our broad ditch."

"We can swim," said the McKay abruptly. "Our real trouble's going to be when we have to try to scale that beastly cactus hedge."

"All problems solve themselves with a little thought," declared Nahou easily. "I will fetch bedding to cast over the needle-thorns; then, if you can swim, I will haul you up one by one." He turned away and the greenery closed behind him.

"By Crikey!" exclaimed Vladimir, "I am either drunk or should be locked in a cushioned cell."

"We all feel a bit that way I think," agreed the McKay "but we've just got to hang on to ourselves and see what happens next."

Camilla laughed—quite naturally. "We're neither," she said obscurely. "This is only a very vivid dream. We'll wake up in our beds to-morrow in the hotel in Madeira. Doctor Tisch and his expedition to find Atlantis have never happened really."

"Forgive me, *Gnädige Hertzogin*," protested the Doctor who was just behind her, "but I am quite real—also this cut in the calf of my leg which hurts greatly."

Nahou returned and with him came a girl. "This is Lulluma," he introduced her as he began to pile a great bundle of finely woven linen, which he carried, on to the cactus wall. "The others are away and so may not be disturbed to welcome you."

They did not seek to probe the meaning of his last words because all their eyes were riveted on the girl. A head and a half shorter than Nahou, she too was dark, with smooth neatly parted hair which ended abruptly in a mass of thick curls on the nape of her neck, but her face bore not the slightest resemblance to the man's in racial characteristics. He was a pure Mediterranean type, or might even have been

233

a fair-skinned Berber from North Africa. She had all the dark loveliness of a Celtic woman, but there was an added squareness and stockiness about her build which, together with the proud directness of her gaze, suggested a dash of the courageous aristocratic Norman blood. Her forehead was very broad, her head perhaps a trifle large for her short, beautifully rounded, body. Her eyes were very big and limpid, her skin clear and soft with the lustre of perfect health. Her lips were full, smiling, and moistly red.

Count Axel was long past his first youth and had known many women but now, on the instant he saw Lulluma, he knew that she was a being apart. It was not only her bodily loveliness but the very spirit of eternal youth and sparkling merriment which she seemed to carry with her as she moved. She might grow old in body but to her dying day she would retain a courageous gaiety despite every attempt of fate to break it down. Yet the laughter in her eyes as she gazed with surprise and pleasure on the strangers was not all of her. Count Axel guessed rightly that she was born under the sign of Scorpio and therefore thought deeply, kept her own secrets well and, under the beautiful gay mask could be intensely serious and practical; turning her hand when necessity arose to any business just as easily as she could spend hours of idleness guzzling more good things to eat and drink, than were strictly good for her, between bursts of infectious laughter.

She was wearing red, the colour of the Scorpions, which set off her warm dark beauty in such a way that it was impossible to look at her and not feel a new vitality pulse through one's own body.

"Come now—the rest lies with you," declared Nahou when he had arranged the bedding across the prickly hedge. "We will help you over."

"Vladimir—you will go first, then you can give the girls a hand in landing," ordered the McKay who was still nominally in command of the party. "Nicky, you go after the girls—then the Doctor and Count Axel. I will come last."

The Prince plunged into the narrow canal. His feet could not touch bottom and its sides were sheer so he would have found it impossible to gain a foothold on the island if Nahou had not reached down, gripped his wrist, and hauled him up. Sally pinned up her skirts and swam the fifteen feet of water, then the three on the opposite shore pulled her over the hedge

234

into safety. Camilla followed her example, then the rest of the party splashed into the channel one by one and, in a quarter of an hour had entered—by this prosaic and most undignified manner—into Paradise.

The McKay introduced each member of his party by name and gave a short, very garbled, version of how they came to be there, then Nahou and Lulluma led them towards the centre of the vegetation where the palm trees rose towards the cavern's roof. The island was hardly a garden in the strict sense of the word for it lacked paths and borders, but the thick jungle-like growth which hid its interior from external view gave way, after a few yards, to a variegated orchard in which the trees were set wide apart, giving light and air to great clumps of flowers or little single coloured blossoms that starred the grass beside their footsteps.

"I'm afraid things are not looking quite their best just now," Nahou apologised, apparently quite unnecessarily, as he led them forward. "If you had visited us a fortnight earlier you would have found the Styglomenes in full bloom."

Lulluma gave a deep chuckle. It was like gurgling water bubbling from a secret well that held the source of all the world's merriment. "And if you had come a fortnight later," she said seriously, "the Prathatontecs would have been out for you to see!"

"You are a wicked child Lulluma," Nahou smiled, throwing his arm carelessly round her shoulders, "You mock at everything for your amusement." His voice was gentle, caressing, yet it was not the tone of a lover, only that of one who had an infinite capacity for understanding and companionship.

"Dear fool," she laughed, "how can they care for the beauty of our blossoms now. They are wet and tired and hungry. When they have rested and are more themselves we will show them everything and also satisfy our burning curiosity about them."

A vista opened showing a fairy-like scene. A little temple, no more than eighteen feet high, but built of pure gold, stood out against the background of the palm grove. Before it lay an open swimming pool, some thirty feet in length, its sides faced with deep blue lapis lazuli, a flight of white marble steps led down into it at the nearest end. At its far extremity, a dozen yards in front of the temple, a big satyr's head faced them and, from its mouth a cascade of sparkling water constantly refreshed the pool.

235

As they advanced the newcomers saw that on either side of the pool, but some way back from it, there stood two rows of low one-storied buildings.

"We have not beds enough," said Nahou suddenly, "and we dare not wake those who are away."

"No matter," Lulluma replied quickly, "we have pillows in plenty. They can sleep naked on the grass while I dry their clothes in the earthshine."

"They do not understand nakedness, as we do who are so old in time that we have come to appreciate the wisdom of reverting to the customs of simple savages in some things," Nahou said seriously. "You have not travelled as much as I and therefore know less of the habits of our guests."

Lulluma threw a lightning glance at the bedraggled party. "How strange," she said, "but never mind. You will soon learn the joy of being free from such stuffy clothes and your skins will be the better for it. In the meantime you can keep your bodies covered with linen if you wish?"

"What do they mean?" Camilla whispered to Sally. "I've sunbathed since I was a kid."

They had reached the swimming pool and as she spoke Nahou turned; "Is it your desire first to eat or sleep," he asked.

"For myself I am hungry please," replied Doctor Tisch without hesitation.

The others agreed. Utterly weary as they were they all felt an overwhelming craving to learn more of this secret island before they gave themselves to sleep.

"Very well then. Please be seated here while Lulluma and I prepare food for you." Nahou waved his hand towards the even grass which bordered the marble surround of the pool and added, "I ask only that you refrain from examining the buildings where we live. Our companions are away and it would be dangerous to wake them before they arise of their own free will."

"We would not dream of abusing your hospitality," Count Axel assured him, and the two beautiful beings walked leisurely away from them.

"This party's got me beat entirely," admitted the McKay when their hosts were out of earshot. "Are we dead or drunk or dreaming? That's what I'd like to know."

Sally leaned against his shoulders; "Does it matter my dear? This place is infinitely more lovely than any dream could be.

236

I feel just as though I'd come home again after a long, long journey. You heard what that wonderful girl said about our taking off our clothes? Well, I don't mind a little bit. I wish that God had been a bit kinder about my ankles, but I'm not ashamed of my body."

"What's the matter with your ankles?" asked the McKay loyally. "To hear you talk anyone would imagine that your legs had no shape to them at all. They may not be as slim as Camilla's but they're sensible and the bits where they crease behind your knees are devilish attractive. I was looking at them just now."

"Nelson—Andy—McKay! I *don't* keep my ankles behind my knees but I think you're a darling," sighed Sally as she spread herself out luxuriously on the warm grass.

They all removed their drenched outer garments and sat there silently, almost stupefied with fatigue; gratefully drinking in the warmth of what Lulluma had termed the earth-shine, which streamed upon them in sun-like radiance from the broad band of golden light running right round the roof of the high cavern above the island's protective water channel.

Presently Nahou returned, carrying a big bowl of red metal which Doctor Tisch recognised as orichalcum. Having set it down he took from it first a smaller bowl containing a variety of fresh fruit, then another which held flat round wheaten wafers and, lastly a stack of thin gold plates. As he handed round the latter he tapped the big bowl with his finger. "This is for your pips and rinds and scraps. It is our habit here to consume all waste matter with fire immediately."

Lulluma then appeared with a large oval dish which had a number of compartments. In its centre there was some sort of meat, already cut into joints and round this were heaped half a dozen kinds of vegetables, some cooked and others raw like the ingredients of a salad.

"I hope you will like this," she said anxiously. "It is the loin of a small animal which you would call a buck, I think. We breed them in captivity and it is the only kind of meat we have in our island."

The Doctor beamed. "It smells most tempting *Fraulein*—but if you have only one kind of meat do you not get very tired of it?"

She shook her head. "We eat it only occasionally—when we feel like a change from fish and fruit. I give it to you

237

to-day because your bodies have need of such nourishment. Fortunately some was killed about a week ago."

"You have fish here then?" asked the McKay.

"Yes, a dozen kinds which we breed in the lake behind the temple. Eat now, or your food will grow cold."

Camilla and Nicky exchanged an awkward glance. No knives or spoons or forks had been provided, but Count Axel put out his hand at once and took a small joint of the roast meat in his fingers, just as if he had never seen table implements in his life.

As the others followed his example Nahou smiled; "I know what you are thinking. 'How strange that a people who eat their meals from gold should pick up cooked food in their bare hands.' But our life here has been reduced to the essence of simplicity. Gold is unbreakable, does not tarnish and conveys no metallic taint to food; also plates and dishes are essential—but not so knives and forks. The use of them would only mean unnecessary labour and we have no slaves to do our work for us."

Lulluma squatted down on her heels before them as they ate. Only her admirable manners restrained her curiosity about the visitors. She was longing desperately to question them about themselves but all she said was; "Do you like the flavour of the meat?"

Count Axel threw a bone into the metal bowl and turned to her with a bow as he took another piece. "It is excellent, and your cooking does you honour. You are right too about it being like buck—we should call this venison—and it is regarded as something of a luxury in the countries from which we come."

"It has a pleasant flavour," agreed Nahou, "but we have no opportunity to compare it with other meats. That is as well perhaps otherwise we might have become—as you—a people whose staple diet is meat, and that is not healthy. Animal flesh has certain properties which are of the greatest value when taken with discretion, but eaten frequently and in too large quantities meat coarsens the body and leads to many of the internal complaints which are so prevalent among the white races of the upper world." He too was eagerly awaiting the time when he could hear the story of his guest's journey, but for the moment confined himself to polite conversation.

Lulluma looked at Count Axel again: "When you have

slept," she said, "you must tell me all about the upper world. I know it only slightly and there is so much that I want to hear."

"You know it?" he exclaimed, "and Nahou knows it?—but how? I confess that I am completely mystified."

She smiled. "I will tell you—that and many other things —all in good time."

Nahou removed the meat dish and as they started tasting the fruits, some of which were similar to varieties they knew and others totally different, Lulluma fetched some round goblets made of the halves of cocoanut shells, highly polished and mounted on gold stems.

"Now that you have eaten you must drink," she said, and poured out for each of them in turn from a golden jug.

It was an opaque greeny-yellow liquid and, as her guests tasted it, they realised that it was some sort of fruit juice—diluted with water, sweet flavoured yet with a refreshing tang which cleansed the palate.

Sally guessed it to be a mixture of limes and grenadillas but there was some other taste in it which eluded her completely.

When they had had all the fruit they needed Nahou went into one of the low buildings and brought back another set of cups. Tiny ones this time, and with them he produced a big flask.

"This is a cordial which will aid your digestion," he told them as he handed round the cups. "It is rather strong so you would do well to sip it slowly."

Camilla sipped and choked immediately. The sticky dark-green fluid was not unlike Chartreuse. It was flavoured with flowers and herbs and was highly alcoholic. The fiery spirit sent a warm glow right through her body as it went down.

While Nicky thumped her on the back the McKay sniffed at his tiny cup suspiciously then, having tasted its contents with extreme caution, he suddenly looked up.

"Thank God you've got liquor on the island. Well, here's how!" Next moment he tossed off the cordial, sat with compressed lips and starting eyes for a second, then let out a long drawn sigh of extreme contentment.

"A-a-a-a-h! By Jove—I needed that!"

"Will you have some more?" Nahou proffered the flask but the McKay shook his head.

"Not now thanks. I'll come again another day if I may. That's the stuff to give 'em with a vengeance."

Now that they had eaten their fatigue returned and they all felt terribly drowsy. Nahou glanced at Lulluma and she nodded; then he said: "If you are willing I propose to send you into a dreamless sleep. You have suffered much in your journey here I know and if I do not it may be that hauntings of your recent past will trouble your unconscious minds."

They showed their acquiescence by a series of sleepy nods, except for the McKay, who did not care for the idea of giving up his free will to anybody, but he remained silent.

"Look now at this gold plate," Nahou continued, holding it before him so that the light shone full upon it. They obeyed—except for the McKay who kept his eyes focused on Nahou's knees a few inches lower down, while he wondered if he had not been a bit of an idiot to refuse another go of that excellent liquor. Lulluma rose and stood behind Nahou where he sat, cross-legged on the ground, placing her left hand on his head. Then the two Atlanteans concentrated, willing their guests to sleep.

"Won't we get rheumatism sleeping in these damp things?" Camilla asked drowsily, but no one replied to her. A great silence seemed to have descended on the garden again, broken only by the continuous splashing of the water which gushed from the satyr's head into the pool.

One by one the strangers in Paradise closed their eyes. The light reflected by the golden plate seemed to have obscured everything else and about them spread only a gentle golden radiance. They sank back on to the grass and fell into a dreamless sleep.

The McKay alone remained conscious but he wished to sleep too. Politeness restrained him from saying that he preferred to do so in his own way without any assistance but, seeing the others slumbering he turned over and curled himself up.

Lulluma removed her hand from Nahou's head. "They won't wake for a long time," she said in her own tongue. "They look revolting now don't they? but when they wake they will have lost some of the horrid lines on their faces and after a bath some of them may not be quite so awful to look at. We had better take off those strange damp clothes they wear."

Nahou rose to his feet and followed her silently. With gentle care the two Atlanteans began systematically to strip

240

their guests, then to arrange them one by one, as they were denuded of their clothing, in more comfortable attitudes with pillows under their heads. Suddenly Lulluma began to titter. Only the McKay and Doctor Tisch remained to be dealt with and they had just pulled off the latter's woollen pants.

She held them aloft so that Nahou might also appreciate this strange covering worn by beings from the upper world. He began to laugh too and soon both of them became utterly convulsed and helpless. They were no longer a middle-aged man and grown woman, dominated by the restraint and responsibility which affects most adults, but a pair of beautiful children enjoying an absurd stupendous joke. Lulluma laughed until the tears ran from her lovely eyes down her delicately coloured cheeks, and Nahou began to cough— holding his sides in pain because he had been so shaken by his merriment.

They sat down on the ground and leaned against each other—a little exhausted now but still giving way to new fits of uncontrollable mirth as Lulluma explored the intricacies of Doctor Tisch's long nether garments.

At last they recovered sufficiently to stand up again, then Lulluma regarded the Doctor's round protuberant stomach with a surprised stare.

"He's very fat, isn't he?" she said solemnly.

Nahou nodded. "Yes, but we will teach him to breathe properly and that will soon reduce his body to normal. Providing of course that Menes permits them to remain here."

"But he couldn't do otherwise," protested Lulluma quickly. "The poor things would all die in the darkness if we forced them to leave the island—and why should they not stay? —we have food enough for all."

"True. We shall have to concentrate our yellow rays on them while they sleep though, and also strengthen that aura about ourselves when we have finished touching them—for they have probably got every sort of horrible disease. Come —help me with the little man who has such a strange red face." Nahou turned towards the McKay.

He had removed his own coat and Lulluma was only just beginning to unbutton his trousers when he stirred, grunted, and sat up.

"What the thunderin' blazes—" he began, grabbing at his trousers in outraged modesty. He saw Lulluma bending over him with an amused smile, and then—behind her rounded

241

shoulder—he caught sight of the stark naked bodies of his six friends as they lay sleeping in the sun.

He shut his eyes tightly for a moment then opened them again. Lulluma was still smiling at him.

"Good God!" he ejaculated, "it's still there—I thought it was a dream but you're real apparently. Anyhow whatever you are you're not undressing me!"

"Please," Lulluma pleaded gently. "Why shouldn't I. You don't seem to be deformed at all and you would be so much more comfortable."

He shook his head firmly. "Very nice of you m'dear and I'm sure you don't mean any harm, but although I'm *not* deformed I'd rather not."

"You did not look at the gold plate as I suggested," Nahou accused him mildly, "or else you would have been in a deep refreshing slumber."

"No," the McKay confessed, "I didn't. I'm most awfully grateful for all you're doing for us but I prefer my own way of going to sleep."

Nahou shrugged his shoulders lightly. "That must be as you wish. No one person ever compels another here. We only help and guide each other where we can, and even in that we use the very greatest discretion in case the other person were offended—for then we should surely die of shame. You have accepted food and drink because you were hungry and thirsty—why then do you refuse my offer to throw you into a healing sleep which will refresh your whole body, now when you are so tired?"

The McKay considered for a moment then he glanced apologetically at the beautiful girl kneeling by his side. "If you don't mind going for a stroll Miss—er—Lulluma I think I'd like to avail myself of Mr Nahou's kind offer after all. It seems a sensible suggestion but I'm an old fashioned sort of cuss and with you—er—looking on you know——"

Lulluma felt an intense desire to giggle again. This little man was funnier even than the one they called the Doctor but from her childhood she had been trained to suppress any emotion which might give pain to other people. With a grave smile she stood up.

"Certainly I will leave you if you wish. Forgive me please that I should appear so ignorant of your customs—but I have had so little opportunity to travel yet."

With a friendly wave of her hand she left them and, gathering up the soiled dishes disappeared behind the nearest block of buildings.

The McKay waited until she vanished then he turned back to Nahou and said slowly; "This travelling business—is it true that you and she have both been in the upper world among ordinary human beings?"

Nahou nodded. "Yes, Lulluma is young yet but I and my companions have visited your country and other centres of modern civilisation many times."

"Ah!" the McKay's eyes brightened. "I felt certain that must be so. It's the only possible explanation of you being able to speak such darn good English. There's a way out of this place somehow then. A long tunnel which leads up under the sea and comes up in the Azores eh? By Jove! we're not sunk yet—we'll get back after all!"

Nahou regarded him a little sadly. "Did you learn much of the tradition which still exists about Atlantis before you came on this expedition?" he asked slowly.

"Enough to write a book," declared the McKay. "No offence of course—but I'm fed to the teeth with the whole darned business."

"Then you will know that the earlier Atlanteans were credited with powers which the ignorant term 'Magic'?"

"O-ah! Sons of the God going in unto the daughters of men, Nephilim, and all that sort of thing—hence the Flood. Yes, I know all about that but what's it got to do with this secret entrance to the place by which we can get home?"

"We still retain certain of those powers," said Nahou gently, "and they enable us to travel *in the spirit*, but none of my race have ever left this island in our physical bodies for over eleven thousand years. I am afraid my friend that you must put out of your mind once and for all any hope of being able to return."

CHAPTER XIX

COUNT AXEL TREADS THE FIELDS
OF ASPODEL

COUNT AXEL was the first to wake. All his friends were still sleeping soundly on either side of him but Lulluma was sitting near by busily stitching at some form of garment.

His first impression was of her serene untroubled smile and that she was no creation of his sub-conscious imagination but warm flesh and blood; his next, that he had grown a beard. As he passed his hand over his face he felt it—a stubby growth on his lips and chin.

"How do you feel now?" she asked, laying aside her work and standing up.

He took a long breath and sighed contentedly. "If I were on my death bed I believe that the sight of you would be enough to raise me from it—but I never awoke feeling less like death than I do at the moment."

"That is as it should be—you have slept well, nearly a week."

"A week! surely that is impossible?"

"Almost a week" she assured him "and you look terribly dirty. Come with me and you shall have a bath."

Axel took the hand that she held out to pull him to his feet. Then he noticed that he and his friends had been stripped during their sleep; but the girl beside him did not seem the least embarrassed by his nakedness and he could not help murmuring as he surveyed the others; "Don't they look funny without their clothes?"

Lulluma chuckled. "The fat doctor is a very queer shape. The tall dark man has a good body though also the fair one whom you call Nicky."

"Yes" he agreed, as he studied his friends with complete detachment, "Vladimir is a fine figure of a man and both the girls do credit to their race. Camilla is particularly lovely."

Lulluma jerked his hand with sudden petulance, "She is just passable—but she is nothing like as good-looking as I am!"

Count Axel had drawn her attention to Camilla's loveliness with deliberate intent. She had risen to the bait magnificently and he almost trembled with joy at this first real assurance that she was as vulnerable as any ordinary human girl. When he turned and looked into her eyes he meant every word as he said "You are right—in all my life I have never seen anyone quite so beautiful as you."

She shrugged her well-covered shoulders; "My mother carried out her ideas of my type quite well in me I think, but you may change your opinion when you see my companions. I would not change my nature with any of them but they are more beautiful. I am too short and lack the grace which they possess. Come now and wash."

He followed her to one of the blocks of buildings which faced each other across the pool, each of them had six curtained entrances. She pulled aside the hangings over one doorway and disclosed a large square room furnished with spartan simplicity. There was a couch against the far wall, a dressing-table to one side, above which was set a large metal mirror and against the other wall stood a single oblong coffer. In the middle of the floor was a low sunken bath.

"This is my room" announced Lulluma. "You are not afraid of me I hope like the little muscular man who nearly had a fit when he found that Nahou and I were about to remove his damp trousers."

Count Axel stood in the doorway, his hands on his hips and quite at his ease. "No" he replied, passing his fingers over his chin. "If you do wish to eat me I am yours to eat, but first I would prefer to remove this beard—if that is possible. It would be more comfortable for us both."

"Later on, if I find that I like you I might try" she said with delightful frankness, "but I would hardly care to touch you as you are. Look! Nahou has provided this sharp steel against your waking. In this vase you will find oil for lather and here is a linen towel. Water will enter the bath from the hot spring if you press down the Triton's head which decorates its end. After you have finished remove the spigot from the bottom and it will drain away. On the bed there I have put out a selection of men's garments. Since you are the first to wake you can choose which you like best. Now I will leave you to make yourself presentable."

As she turned to go he laid his hand gently on her arm to detain her. "Forgive me" he said "but, since neither of

us suffer from any shyness may I confess one thing to you?—
I have never found it altogether easy to wash my own back."

Lulluma looked at him for a moment and then she began
to laugh again "Well really" she declared "You are almost
civilised. Quite like one of us. I will bath you with pleasure
if you like?"

When Axel looked at himself in Lulluma's highly polished
metal mirror he saw that he was indeed a filthy sight, but after
some initial difficulty with Nahou's big hand-ground razor
he got the hang of it and soon his chin was as smooth as silk.
A good wash restored his face to its normal appearance and
then he studied himself again. He saw a long humorous
countenance smiling at him lazily and decided that his forty
odd years had not treated him too harshly. He felt no more
than thirty and the abnormally long sleep seemed to have
removed half a dozen years of deepening wrinkles from round
his eyes and mouth. With an impulsive gesture he swung
round to Lulluma.

"Well, how do I look now?"

She was sitting on her divan polishing her toe-nails and
she looked up with a start. "Why—you're quite good-
looking" her big eyes widened, "I thought you were almost
an old man and was only attracted by something about your
mind which your friends do not possess . . . before!"

As he turned on the water she stood up and added; "I
only consented to bath you out of courtesy you know—but
now I think it will be rather fun."

With a little wriggle of her shoulders she slipped off her
red dress and picked up the vase of oil. Then amid splashings
and laughter she scrubbed him so vigorously that he had to
cry for mercy.

He chose a green tunic and when she had helped him to
adjust it they went outside together. The others were still
sound asleep so she offered to show him the island and they
strolled off side by side.

In the grove of palm trees behind the temple there was
another group of buildings. A wide kitchen, a small laundry,
and a row of workshops for metallurgy, dyeing, weaving, and
distilling. All were quite deserted and showed no signs of
recent labour. The rows of golden plates and dishes were
arranged neatly in the kitchen racks, every tool and implement
in the shops occupied its special place; no trace of waste
material marred the scrupulous cleanness in any corner.

"You see, each of us make what we require for ourselves and nothing more" Lulluma explained "and when we wish to eat we gather whatever fresh fruit is in season from the trees or net a fish in the lake and cook it. All waste is consumed immediately after by the earthshine."

"How does that work?" he asked. "It seems to have all the properties of sunshine."

"It has" she assured him. "You doubtless know that the centre of the earth is molten and gives off gases which are exactly similar to those which shoot out in great flames from the sun. Long ages ago our people tapped that source of heat and light and then it was a comparatively simple matter to conduct it through certain minerals so that it should give a steady glow. The circular arrangement round the roof enables the trees and plants to benefit from it at every angle in the same degree so that they are never distorted in one direction. The result is similar to that produced by the movement of your sun."

"Forgive me, but there are so many things I want to ask you" he smiled down at her, "From the way you speak you are obviously familiar with our upper world?"

"There is little to do here" she answered enigmatically "except make love!"

"You find that pall at times?"

"No, never—because we do not abuse our zest for it. Once every year or two each of us has some tremendous affair which lasts a few months, then when we are satiated for the moment, we go away. Later the urge rises again and when we feel it really strongly we take our happiness with another."

"You speak of going away. What do you mean by that?"

"Two of us are always what you would call 'on duty' here. It was the turn of Nahou and myself when you arrived. The others spend most of the year in sleep. Sometimes we sleep for a month or more at a stretch, and during that time our spirit travels—as quickly as an ether wave. We have learned to direct it to the place where we wish to go. The eyes of our invisible bodies can observe your customs and our ears can hear your speech. That is how we have learned your languages and know quite a lot about you, but there are many things you do which puzzle us still."

Axel nodded. "That sounds amazing—but I understand it. In a rudimentary way the people of the upper world

247

practise thought transference at times or visit their friends in dreams, so that they are able to listen to their speech and see what they are doing. Such things with us are rare, haphazard and chancy though, whereas you must have developed these faculties to a fine art."

"We have had an unbroken civilisation for twenty-nine thousand years in which to do it" she said simply.

"Twenty-nine . . . thousand . . . years! That makes us seem to be still in the embryo stage then—but tell me more of what you do?"

"We remain here for a few days to renew our strength, then we set off again, and so life goes on until the love-urge is upon us once more; then, for a little while, we revel in what you would term a new honeymoon."

"I should have thought that your bodies would have wasted during those long periods of sleep."

"On the contrary. It is that which enables our tissues to restore themselves and rests the organs, so that we remain young and beautiful far longer than the people of your world above. Come now—I will show you what *you* would call our 'Kitchen Garden'."

She pushed her arm impulsively through his and led him out of the palm grove to the far side of the island.

Just as the flower garden behind the pool was different from any which Axel had ever seen before so this 'Kitchen-Garden' was quite unusual in its lay-out. It extended the whole breadth of the island between the ten-foot deep creeper-clad walls and covered about two acres of ground, but there were no large ugly patches of vegetables and it had been planned with the most skilful care.

Its design was rigidly formal and the intersecting paths were bordered by successive rows of different plants, each slightly higher than the one in front until the rearmost hedged in solid squares of cereals. On each side of the paved walks Axel noticed lines of low root-crops—types of radish, carrot, turnip and many others which he did not recognise. Further in there were lettuces, dwarf beans and peas, then potatoes, broccoli and cabbages until rows of tall artichokes and espaliered fruit trees fenced in the blocks of wheat, oats, barley and maize.

He would never have believed that any purely utilitarian garden could be made so beautiful, yet the long lines of contrasting greens were worthy of Le Notre and the restful colouring gave a peace to the eyes which no massed ranks of flowers could have conveyed.

Lulluma pointed to a low, square building at the far end. "That is where our roots and crops are stored—also it contains our wine-press and our mill. The wines of course have to be kept underground for many years before they are drinkable. Beyond is the enclosure where we pasture our herd of deer, and the fish-pond. Then at the extremity of the island is the jungle. Would you like to see those too?"

"Please" Axel moved forward beside her, "I wish to admire everything. Your domain is more enchanting than any fairy-land of which I have ever dreamed."

The vegetable garden ended in a metal fence almost entirely hidden by vines from which hung bunches of small unripe grapes. They passed through a gateway in it to a grassy, uncultivated wilderness. The island was slightly narrower here and a small stream, fed by some hidden spring meandered through the meadow to a lake fringed by tall reeds. As they walked forward a little herd of antelope, no more than twenty inches high, raised their heads to gaze at them with large liquid eyes, then scampered off to cover in the wall of greenness which kept the island secret and enclosed.

Beyond the lake another fence cut off the far segment of the island which was entirely covered by dense jungle. At first, when they entered it through another gate it seemed a solid mass of flowering creepers so inextricably interwoven that it was difficult to see the tree trunks on which they climbed. Splashes of blossom, yellow, pink, blue, and scarlet stood out against the massed green of the background and scented the air with the fragrance of a perfume-maker's laboratory.

Lulluma pulled aside a bunch of hanging tendrils and Axel followed her into a cool dark maze gently dappled by the earthshine which penetrated in speckled patches between the leaves above. Hardly discernible paths wound in and out among the massed bushes and clumps of flowering vines while here and there were more open spaces and recesses which invited rest on their mossy banks among the warm shadows.

"It is here" said Lulluma "that we often come to make love."

Axel felt his heart pounding beneath his ribs and his arm trembled as he put it round her shoulder, but a subtle instinct told him that she intended no invitation and that his only

249

hope lay in exercising the greatest restraint. This small warm pagan goddess was no primitive creature to be taken by rough assault. Something told him that in spite of her apparent youth she knew the game of love even better than he did and could only be caressed at her own pleasure. When that time came he felt that she would show her desire as naturally as she would hunger or thirst.

His blood was pounding heavily behind his temples and he knew that he must break the tension or else he might do something which he would ever afterwards regret, so he removed his arm and leaned against a tree trunk, then spoke unthinkingly of the first thing which came into his mind.

"This is like Eden—to make it complete you only need the Serpent!"

Instantly she sprang away from him with dark, fear-distended eyes.

"What is it? . . . I'm sorry! . . . please, what have I done?" he exclaimed, holding out his hands to her in quick supplication.

She shuddered and glanced over her shoulder fearfully. The jungle garden seemed very silent now as though every tree and vine were listening. Then she sighed and placed her hands in his.

"You should not have said that" she whispered, "Never —never speak of evil. It is almost our only rule but very strictly kept. The Ancient One has been barred out of here for countless centuries but he still waits, as he will wait until the end of time, for an invitation to enter in."

Her voice was so intensely earnest that he could find no adequate apology and only bowed his head as though guilty of having broken some fragile priceless treasure.

She lifted a hand to his cheek and stroked it gently, seeking now to comfort him; "You spoke only thoughtlessly and in jest I know but words have such terrible power. They vibrate on the ether long, long after our ears have ceased to hear them and evil forces focus, unseen, all about them. I am so afraid that what you have said may, in some awful way, mar the wonderful happiness I foresee for us—but that which has been spoken can never be recalled. All I can do now is to throw my vibrations about us both and trust that they may prove an effectual barrier.

In silence now they moved on again yet, after Lulluma's outburst she soon seemed to push the episode into the back of her mind and regain her spirits. A few moments later she put her finger to her lips to enjoin quietness before drawing him round a corner of the maze.

There, in a nook, a fully grown girl was sleeping at the foot of a stone pillar topped by a bust of the God Priapus. A garland hung from the age-old symbol by which Axel recognised the Deity. The girl wore only a light tunic of white linen edged with gold; her hair, a lustrous ash-blonde colour, contrasting also with Lulluma's in that she wore it long, covered her shoulders and fell below her delicately modelled breasts. She was extremely lovely, with the milk and rose complexion of Axel's own Nordic people and her limbs, scarcely veiled by the semi-transparent material of her dress were long and graceful. He could not remember ever seeing such a perfect example of her type.

"Well, what do you say now?" Lulluma asked with a mocking glance, "Would you not rather make love to her than to me? Speak truthfully—I shall not bear any ill-will. No man could hesitate at such a choice for she is far lovelier than I."

Axel shook his head and his tone carried conviction: "Many men might judge her to be more beautiful," he acknowledged. "But you have something which she lacks. Camilla is by no means perfect yet she might prove no mean rival to this girl, for the love of a man, whereas you are apart —infinitely rarer and more desirable. It is possible to meet such loveliness as hers on earth but yours only in the Garden of the Gods."

Lulluma accepted this praise but seemed only moderately pleased by it. She looked down on the sleeping girl and murmured: "I thought she was unique. I am intensely proud of her. She is Danöe—my daughter."

"What?" exclaimed Axel incredulously. "But that is impossible."

"Hush!" Lulluma drew him hurriedly back behind a screen of hanging creepers.

"But you?" Axel lowered his voice. "I don't understand —you can't be more than twenty yourself—or let's be lavish and say twenty-two."

"That is just it." Lulluma smiled enigmatically. "You do *not* understand. In this place we come normally to maturity in twenty years but after that the fact that we pass two-thirds of each year in sleep preserves our youth almost indefinitely. Presently you will see another of us—Laötzii, a woman of ninety, but to you she will appear to be only a little over forty."

"But you?" persisted Axel, "perhaps it is rude to ask but —how old are you?"

"I am young yet." Lulluma gave her deep gurgling chuckle. "Only forty-four next birthday."

Axel surveyed again the warm loveliness which glowed before him; "I would have wagered a fortune that you could not be more than twenty-three."

"It is these long periods of sleep," she repeated. "How old do you think Nahou is?"

"If one judges by appearances I should say fifty. His muscles are so supple. There is not a single thread of grey in that fine straight black hair of his—he *cannot* be more."

Lulluma laughed at his indignant tone. "He has lived over one hundred years. If I remember he is a hundred and four. He is my grandfather and, with the exception of Menes, the oldest man amongst us. . . . Also he is a most accomplished lover," she added naïvely.

"To what age do you live then?" Axel asked, ignoring her last remark.

"A hundred and thirty-eight to a hundred and forty-five. The last is a record I think."

"How many are there of you here—awake or asleep?"

"Twelve only. Six women and six men. That number was decided on within a few generations of the Flood and it has never been varied since except for brief periods when we are eleven or thirteen. A child is born to one of our women every twelve years and if the eldest of our community is not already dead, they die quite naturally within a few months of the birth because their time is done and they no longer wish to live. Semiramis is the oldest of our women now. She is about a hundred and forty and if she is not dead before she will die soon after my daughter Danöe bears her first child —which will be in about four years' time."

"You speak as if that was quite certain. Have you the power to control such things?"

She nodded. "With us the gift of life is at the discretion of the giver's will. Such power was only achieved after innumerable generations of conscious effort by every mother, but concentrated thought is the greatest force in the world. By it we can heal very serious injuries when they occur in

252

the mill or metallurgical workshop—although accidents are very rare with us."

"Yes—I understand that," said Axel thoughtfully. "In the upper world there are now many people who follow a religion which centres largely round faith-healing. They are not always successful in fighting disease but they have worked a lot of cures where the doctors have failed. That you should have developed a similar faculty to a more perfect degree is not so surprising but the control of childbirth by will is a much greater problem, or have you reached that degree of evolution whereby only one sex is necessary for the reproduction of the species?"

"Of course not, you dear fool!" Lulluma laughed as she opened the gate from the jungle to the meadow; "There was a lot of difficulty at first but our women had already progressed considerably in regulating the size of their families artificially even before the cataclysm. When they wholeheartedly desired to have a child it was considered a sin not to do so though, for only by intent can the most beautiful and balanced children be born.

"Then it was discovered that time and seasons played a great part in determining the child's appearance and character, so people began to choose the planets under which their children should be born in accordance with the type of baby they desired. As the ages passed women went even further and took it upon themselves to prepare with great seriousness for these important events. They spent many months visualizing the child they were to bear as a grown man or woman in its full beauty, and by strong thought processes they threw up barriers against the entry of deformed, ugly or evil-natured offspring into life. Eventually through cumulative hereditary effort, the woman's will became the dominant factor so that without the definite desire to become a mother it was impossible for her to bear a child."

Axel took her hand as they strolled slowly past the lake. "Is the fact that there are six women and six men amongst you just chance," he asked, "or do you determine sex as well?"

"Oh, that was all planned long ago—it was one of the first steps. Each of the six women here bears two children—a boy and a girl. Your people will reach that stage of development soon I expect."

"We are fairly near it now," Axel told her. "I don't know

very much about it but I believe it is a matter of the glands. Tell me, could you have more children if you wanted to?"

"I suppose so—but I've had my two. Danöe, the girl you saw, who is twenty, and Ciston, a boy of eight. Therefore I should never give my will to that again. It would be unutterably wrong."

For a moment they walked in silence then, as they passed through the vine-covered trellis into the vegetable garden, Axel said: "No one seems to be working here or in the shops. How is this place cultivated if ten out of twelve of you are asleep and the remaining two laze away the hours in the sunshine?"

"We do not laze," she said quickly. "The two of us who are here work for long hours tending our fruit trees, flowers and vegetables. It keeps us healthy and we need little sleep because we get so much at other times. Our only holidays are when two of us fall in love—*then* we are free to laze together for as long as we like. The arrival of your party is a tremendous event and that is why work has ceased in the last few days. Besides, in addition to the two months' labour each of us puts in to provide our necessities we all return for four fortnights in the year during which we sow and harvest our biannual crops. I enjoy those fortnights— just as I am enjoying all the strangeness of having you here —for it is then that we tell each other of our journeys into distant lands and at the end we have a festival!—a Feast of Love."

"But I thought you told me that you only had affairs every two years or so?"

"The serious ones—yes. Those which I was speaking of grow from flirtations during the period of harvest and generally end quite naturally at the Feast—but in them often lies the seed of deep attraction which leads to a more lasting attachment sometimes of months."

She suddenly caught sight of his face and began to laugh. "I believe you are shocked," she said. "I forgot that the ideas of your people are as ours were before the Flood!"

"I'm not shocked," he countered her teasing, "but it is all so strange. Most upper-world people could call you an immoral baggage, but after all it is quite natural to you and nothing," he added seriously, "which is natural can be immoral."

"Only anger and the giving of pain are immoral," declared

254

Lulluma firmly, "and, after all there are only six men here to choose from—I'm sure you've known at least a dozen women?"

"Quite," Axel went so far as to admit, "but don't let's go into that."

"Why not?" she asked curiously. "If we are going to spend a lot of time together it will give us some amusing and interesting subjects to discuss."

"I suppose there's no reason why we shouldn't but I was brought up in the tradition that one might kiss a lot—but never tell!"

"We are not jealous as your women are, so it could do no harm among us, and any confidences you make to me can never reach the upper world because none of you will ever be able to return."

He sighed happily and put his arm round her shoulders again. "That is not a distressing thought—in fact I am convinced that I have been waiting all my life for the moment when I should meet you in this garden."

Lulluma smiled up into his eyes and he caught his breath in wonder at her loveliness as she asked: "Would you be content to stay here making love a little—working regularly —talking a lot?"

"My dear," he said and put his hands behind his back. He felt that he was treading on sacred ground and must be careful not to make the smallest slip which might dash all the great hopes which had risen in him like an overpowering force since he had walked and talked with Lulluma in the Garden.

"My dear," he said again, "what more could one do if one had all the upper world to do it in and were a millionaire besides? There, one is beset with constant cares. If you possess no property you go hungry and if you own land or business interests life is one constant war to defend them from others who would take them from you. Here all causes of worry seem to have been eliminated. You have enough work to keep you healthy but no more and interests and food enough for all. What mortal who had eyes to see and understanding could ever wish to leave this Garden of the Gods?"

Lulluma stretched out her hand and put two cool fingers on his forehead. She seemed to listen for a moment and then she took her hand away and said: "It is strange but you are, I believe, one of us in spirit—I am glad! But your friends—some of them are as different from you as we are from the creatures of the depths. I fear they will make themselves miserable by always craving to get back."

"I had thought of that too," acknowledged Axel, and his face clouded. "I wonder if any of them have woken yet?"

"If so Nahou will look after them—or Rahossis."

"Who is Rahossis?"

"My mother. She returned from a journey two days ago. She is very beautiful and very gay—red-haired and statuesque —and in the full bloom of her beauty—you will imagine her to be about thirty-two—but really she has lived many more years than that. She is twelve years younger than Quet, the son of Nahou, who was my father, and twelve years older than Peramon who was the father of my first child Danöe."

They reached the palm grove and, walking through it, came round the miniature golden temple to find that only Nicky and Vladimir were still asleep. Camilla and Sally had disappeared while the McKay and Doctor Tisch, with only trousers on, sat side by side on the grass near the bathing pool. Their coats were now covering—or partially so—the middle portions of the bodies of their still sleeping friends.

As the McKay's glance fell on the Count, arm in arm with Lulluma and dressed only in a short airy green tunic he clutched the Doctor's arm and exclaimed in a horrified voice:

"Good God! Look at Axel—he's gone native."

The Doctor scratched his bristly head and laughed gutturally. He was still vaguely wondering where all this was going to end. It had not yet penetrated to his mind that those great stones he had discovered on the ocean bed were only the ghosts of a past Atlantis, whereas here, he was seated in the very heart of that long dead civilization which it had been his life's ambition to find.

"Well, how are you both feeling?" Axel asked as he came up. "I see you've both had a bath and a shave and are looking years younger already so your long sleep must have done you good."

"Oh, I'm feeling all right," the McKay agreed guardedly, "and Mr Nahou has been kindness itself although when I agreed to him putting me to sleep I didn't know it was to be for a week!"

Axel's lazy smile flitted across his face. "We should all be most distressed, I know," he said, "if that has caused you to miss any important engagements."

"Eh?—Oh!" the McKay's friendly grin appeared.

256

You've caught me out there, Count—but I find it a little difficult to get the hang of our new quarters and he wanted me to put on one of those fancy dress affairs you are wearing. Well, no offence, but I thought that *was* a trifle thick!''

"Thin you really mean," giggled Lulluma as she hung on Axel's arm, "but why have you covered up your friends and where are the two young girls you had with you?"

"The girls went off together with a fine strapping red-haired wench—lady, I beg your pardon—who said her name was Rahossis. As for us putting our coats over our friends—well, I mean . . . !'' The McKay shrugged eloquently.

"That was silly of you," Lulluma said gently. "We have covered you up each night. But in a health sleep such as you have undergone it is important that the gentle earthshine should play upon every portion of your bodies."

"You do have night here then," said Axel. "That is interesting because my only fear was that one might tire of perpetual day."

She nodded. "The earthshine is under our control and for ten hours out of every twenty-four we dim it, turning its principal energy into other channels. You saw all the little trenches in the vegetable garden—it pumps the water up which irrigates those and makes the fountains among the clumps of flowers play."

"I see," Axel murmured. "I wondered how you could find time to water everything, but that makes it unnecessary."

As he spoke a young boy came dashing out of one of the buildings. He raced across the grass and flung his arms round Lulluma.

"My darling," she cooed in her own tongue, stooping to embrace him. "So you are back at last—did you have a good journey?"

"Yes—yes," his dark eyes were bright with excitement. "I found a long lonely beach and examined all the shells, then a wooden boat came past with men in it and I went over the water to them. They caught fish out of the sea, and two days later they took it home. I followed, to find out where they lived but they had only dark dirty huts and no gardens— Poor people, I was so sorry for them I . . .''

He broke off suddenly to stare at the strangers. Lulluma translated what he had said then, as an afterthought, introduced him: "This is Ciston—the youngest amongst us."

Apparently he understood the drift of her last words for

257

he bowed gravely giving the Doctor, Axel and the McKay a friendly smile apiece.

The McKay grinned back and held out his hand. "Shake me'lad," he said. "You and I will make some boats to float on that pond together."

Ciston took the proffered hand though he could not understand what the stranger was saying, but Lulluma did and in that second, all thought of him as a weatherbeaten, truculent little man with absurd inhibitions passed from her. He could be gentle with a child and would make toy boats for the boy's amusement. Her heart warmed towards him and, to his intense embarrassment, she stooped and kissed him impulsively upon the neck.

"Now for your swim," she said quickly to Ciston, giving the McKay a moment to recover from her assault, and the boy bounded away like some young faun. His head was covered with dark thick close-cropped curls and his body was a golden brown. Axel thought of a young Sicilian fisher-boy as Ciston plunged fearlessly into the pool.

He swam with ease and grace and they were still watching him when Camilla and Sally appeared. Their corn-coloured hair now hung round their shoulders and both wore only Atlantean tunics. Camilla's was blue with a silver border and Sally's a dove-grey edged with something which looked like mother of pearl. Rahossis accompanied them. She was a good few inches taller than either of the cousins and a magnificent woman of Junoesque proportions. Her skin was very white and her hair Titian red—shorter than Lulluma's. It made a halo for her head and clustered all over it in a forest of auburn curls.

The McKay put his hand in front of his eyes as Sally approached in her almost transparent tunic and she flushed a bright lobster pink as she said abruptly: "Don't be a fool, Nelson—Andy—McKay, and get rid of those hideous trousers. When in Rome, you know . . ."

Then he removed his hand and she saw that he was laughing so she added defensively: "Don't you think this suits me?"

"Very becoming, me'dear," he chuckled, "very becoming. God forbid that I should ever prevent any Roman lady doing her duty."

"We're not Romans," said Camilla, who caught the last words as she preened herself in front of Axel, "we're

258

Atlanteans now—and we've got to stay like this for the rest of our lives."

Rahossis had drawn Lulluma aside. "Well," she said indulgently in Atlantean, "this is a fine piece of good fortune for you, my sweet—I'm so glad that you were here when they arrived."

"And for you, darling, too," replied Lulluma. "None of the five men will look at me now that they have seen you."

"Nonsense." Rahossis shrugged her fine shoulders. "The one they call the Count is kissing your little feet already in his mind. I can tell from the way he's watching you out of the corner of his eye. As for myself—I could take any of the others if I wished but I do not think I want to. They are such intensely stupid people. Those girls are like small children—why, your little boy, Ciston, is more entertaining to talk to and any one of the men would bore me in an hour. But if you wish to enjoy yourself lose no time about it."

"Why, darling?" asked Lulluma quickly.

"Because Menes has returned and he will exercise his sole right of re-calling all the others. There will be a council to-night for nothing like this has ever happened in our history before."

Lulluma shrugged. "What of it, dearest?"

"Our ancient law limits our number to twelve, and it may be thought that by allowing the strangers to remain we should bring about our own destruction. If so, Menes will order them to leave the island."

CHAPTER XX

MENES SPEAKS

IT was with a certain awe that the McKay's party watched the procession of Atlanteans going into their temple some six hours later.

The earthshine had just begun to dim and it was the first suggestion of 'night' which the strangers had experienced in this subterranean island. The flowers lost colour though much of their fragrance still perfumed the air; a vague mysterious twilight crept stealthily among the shrubs and trees, veiling them in a new secrecy, and a renewed sense of unreality troubled the newcomers, except Vladimir and Camilla, with fresh speculations as to whether they were alive or dead.

These two were occupied with happier thoughts for Vladimir had woken early that afternoon and, after his ablutions, taken Camilla for a walk through the meadow to the jungle. Tall, bronzed, handsome, his magnificent body set off in its full strength and beauty by the light Atlantean costume, he was as splendid a specimen of manhood as any of his hosts. In this new setting his qualities far outweighed those of either of his rivals, at least in Camilla's eyes and, moreover, it was to him she had turned in every crisis of their dark journey. They were here for the rest of their lives it seemed, and she knew in her heart that she had always liked him best, so in a passionate outburst she had confessed that she loved him and promised to marry him just as soon as he wished.

Their news had been received with enthusiastic congratulations by their friends but when the practical side of the matter was discussed and it was discovered that the Atlanteans never married, or at least had no sort of marriage ceremony, Camilla had become a little dubious about the matter.

It seemed to her conventional mind not quite right somehow just to go off into the wood as Lulluma suggested. That might be all very well for these lovely savages, and privately that was how Camilla thought of the Atlanteans, but it wasn't like being really married at all. In fact, looked at squarely there would be no permanent tie, only casual indulgence in what she had always been taught to regard as sin.

"Besides" as she said privately to Sally "If there's no service or anything I wouldn't really be his wife so what hold would I have over him if he starts to go after one of these Atlantean girls later on. I do love Vladimir terribly of course but they *are* such a frightfully good looking lot that I'm scared about losing him already. That's why I said 'yes', before one of them could snap him up, this afternoon."

Sally agreed about the extremely dangerous beauty of Lulluma and her friends but forbore to point out that if a man's pledge to a woman he said he loved was worth nothing when given to her alone, no amount of bells and rings and blessings was going to make it any more binding however many people heard him make it before an altar. She knew the way Camilla's mind worked and could only sympathise while being just a little bit amazed to see her cousin's complete change of attitude brought about by coming into collision with other women as beautiful as herself.

Fortunately however Doctor Tisch arrived on the scene and came to Camilla's rescue by reminding her that he had taken orders in his youth. His offer to perform the rites of the Lutheran church over the pair was accepted with grateful thanks and, since there could be no question of 'going away' after it, the time of the ceremony had been fixed to tally with the conclusion of the evening meal that night.

Nicky had been the last to waken, and bathed while Camilla and Vladimir were hugging each other in the jungle. He did not seem as cast down by the news of his rival's victory as might have been expected. Rahossis had taken care of him while Nahou was showing the Doctor and the McKay round the island. Since then he had not been able to take his eyes off her whenever she was in view, and he had already confessed to Sally that he had suffered an unrequited passion for Mae West before he left Hollywood, whom Rahossis undoubtedly resembled.

All of them now with the exception of the McKay, who declared a conservative preference for his trousers, were clad in the flimsy costumes usual among the small population of the island. The two girls did more than justice to the Atlantean tunics and the McKay, who had seen them many times in bathing suits or evening dress, admitted to himself that he had never seen them look more beautiful. That they were conscious of it was evident from the proud way in which they held themselves. Axel and Nicky, like Vladimir, seemed more handsome and virile from the simple change of costume. Even the stout Doctor who had succumbed to Lulluma's wiles, far from looking ridiculous appeared to take on a new dignity in his dark purple robe which he entirely lacked in his untidy checked lounge suit. The McKay was only saved from seeming quite out of place because he remained stripped to the waist and the rippling muscles of his fine torso had their own beauty.

They had met all the Atlanteans now, after the emergency waking which Menes had decreed and watched them in silence as they proceeded to their special conference.

Two by two they walked up the steps of the Temple, hand in hand. Menes and Semiramis first—both grey and white haired, yet upright elderly people, very gracious and benign in mien as befitted the rulers of such an advanced community.

Nahou followed them, leading a dark smooth-haired Russian looking woman called Tzarinska.

Next came Quet, who might well, the onlookers thought, have been called Montezuma, for he had the features and colouring of a Red Indian and the haughty aristocratic bearing suitable to a Mexican noble before the Spanish conquest. With him walked Laötzii. She looked to be a little over forty and possessed that curious beauty which is seen only in half castes resulting from the mixed union of a European and a Chinese.

Rahossis came after her and by her side a fair Greek-God-like young man called Peramon. He was better looking even than Nicky, although of the same type and, realising it Nicky was filled with a deep jealous rage which made his face turn almost chalk white.

Lulluma walked behind her mother escorted by a tall dark boy. His features made the spectators of the procession think of Ancient Egypt or Peru and they knew that he was named Karnoum.

Last of all came Danöe, splendid in her Nordic loveliness and by the hand she clasped her young brother Ciston—a true child of Italy or Spain.

Sally shivered slightly as the last two closed the golden doors of the temple behind them. Axel had learned only ten minutes before from Lulluma the reason for the council and passed it on to the rest. The knowledge that their fate

262

still lay in the balance had turned their gaiety into an anxious gravity.

"I wonder what they will decide," she murmured half to herself.

"It is death for us if they will not allow us to remain," said the Doctor.

"Is it?" enquired the McKay, bracing his shoulders. "It may be death for them! I've still got a couple of bombs left you know."

"You couldn't!" exclaimed Camilla "after they've been so kind."

"If you did I'd never speak to you again," declared Sally almost in the same breath.

"Well," he apologised, "God forbid that we should do them any harm but we'd be sunk for good if we had to leave this place—and if it comes to a choice of their lives or ours what's a chap to do?"

In the face of this potent argument they all fell silent except the Doctor, who announced: "Fear! that is the great curse of the world. If it were not for fear all the millions on the upper earth might dwell as happily as these people here. *They* are afraid that our presence might upset their well-ordered lives, and *we* are afraid to go out into the darkness. Ach! If only all men could cast out fear all should be saved."

For a few moments they remained staring at the closed doors of the temple, then Sally said suddenly:

"It's no good us standing here. I've got a feeling that it is going to be all right. Anyway they're far too gentle to turn us out summarily before we've had another meal. Let's do what we can to prepare supper for them and for ourselves when they have finished their pow-wow."

Her idea was accepted readily and the whole party trooped off to the kitchen. There, to their surprise they found many things already prepared. The Atlanteans had apparently busied themselves with arrangements immediately after their awakening.

There were four freshly caught fish, two of the little deer already skinned and gralloched and a quantity of newly gathered vegetables spread out on the tables.

Axel took charge, since he considered himself, with some justification a master of the culinary art. The girls understood enough simple cooking to follow his directions and the others took the necessary platters for the meal out into the garden.

263

In three quarters of an hour the gold plate was spread out below the temple steps for eighteen persons to banquet facing the swimming pool. Fruit, flowers, and the wheaten biscuits which served for bread, had been arranged; only the cooked dishes remained—nearly ready and gently simmering on the long stove which was automatically fed by heat directed from the earthshine.

The McKay was setting the golden goblets and the little liqueur cups opposite each place when the doors of the temple opened and the Atlanteans came out. He straightened immediately and, abandoning his task, confronted Menes.

"Well, Sir," he said abruptly "We'll be glad to know what decision you've arrived at."

The grey-haired Atlantean raised his hand in a gesture like a blessing; "The Gods are favourable" he answered gently. "You and your people may remain—we make you welcome!"

He did not specify if by 'The Gods' he meant the Council of the Atlanteans or Deities whom they had consulted, but the McKay did not bother his head about that. He gave his frank smile and said:

"That's very nice of you Sir. We are all more grateful than we will ever find words to express, I'm sure. Anyhow we'll give you no trouble and conform to your laws to the best of our ability. We'll work for our keep of course, most gladly, and lend a hand to keep the place just as shipshape and lovely as you've made it."

Menes laid his hand on the McKay's shoulder. His humanity urged him to accept the coming of these strangers now that a general sanction had been granted, although it was against his better judgement but, in his wisdom, he knew that time would inevitably unfold the true nature of the newcomers and if the need arose the Council of the Gods must meet again.

"I thank you my son," he said gravely. Then he smiled towards the array of gold plate. "It pleases me to see this earnest of your willingness which you have given us already."

"That's the least we could do Sir. The girls are busy cooking supper. You've only to say the word and it shall be served when you wish. We thought, with your permission, we'd wait on your people since they've been hard at it looking after us all day."

The fine old man shook his head. "A courteous thought, but one to which I cannot agree. Now that we have accepted you there are neither hosts nor guests amongst us. Each will

264

do his share and look first to the wants of his immediate neighbour, as is our custom here. Now, by all means, let us dine."

The Atlanteans invaded the kitchen into which Lulluma had already run, carrying the good news to Axel and the two girls. A quarter of an hour later they were all laughing and jesting as they sat on the grass before the temple steps, participating in the alfresco banquet.

By the time they had finished the earthshine had dimmed to its lowest limit and there was only just sufficient light for them to see comfortably. To read by it would not have been possible but they could still see each other's faces as they would have in the gentle starlight of an August night in that upper world so far above their heads. Behind the pool the gardens were filled with shadows and the large trees were now black shapes, rising from mysterious scented belts of darkness, yet the air remained warm and still.

The plates and dishes were removed and then Nahou produced fresh goblets and half a dozen flasks from which he poured a thick, dark-golden liquid.

"This is our wine for festivals" he said "I hope that you will find it compares favourably with those of the upper world. I am chief vintager and responsible for its keeping."

Doctor Tisch's eyes grew round with pleasure as he sipped it. "This is Rhine Wine" he declared "and the finest which I haf ever tasted although it has a something different flavour also. No Palatinate, even in the greatest years, could be so rich."

"More like Chateau Y'Quem I should have said" remarked the McKay with relish. "Chateau Y'Quem, my friend, with a dash of old sherry flavour to it."

"We call it *Nektar*" said Nahou with quiet satisfaction. "It has been known under that name from the beginning of time. It is made by allowing the grapes to hang on the vines until all their water has been absorbed by the earthshine. They become wrinkled then, like raisins, so that all their flavour and sweetness is condensed."

Vladimir gave a long-drawn happy sigh "A rose between two other thorns can smell as good" he misquoted solemnly. "This is not Hock, Y'Quem, or Sherry—it is Imperial Tokay and vintaged similarly."

He swung round then with a great laugh to Camilla and raised his goblet in the air. "Drink my sweet beautiful! for

265

God is gracious to his child Vladimir Renescu. Gracious indeed to give me wine, that I never thought to taste again, for my wedding's night. Drink! and later we will make great happiness together. Drink, all of you, I beg. Pledge us in this so magnificent Tokay."

Both his friends and the Atlanteans responded with the utmost heartiness. The former loved him for the brave simple soul they knew him to be and the people of the island were already attached to him more than to any of the other strangers, with the exception of Lulluma's preference for Axel, because his spontaneous gaiety fitted in so well with their own nature. Even Nicky raised a cheer, for now that Camilla was stripped of her millions she no longer held the glamour she had had for him and was no more than just a very pretty girl such as he had dallied with by the dozen in the past. Besides he was sitting next the auburn-haired Rahossis so Vladimir could have Camilla, and Sally into the bargain, as far as Nicky was concerned.

As the plaudits and good wishes ceased Nahou refilled the goblets and Menes held up his hand for silence.

"Dear children" he said "None of us have yet heard more than a garbled version of the manner in which our friends arrived here. To come down through the sea and then through the black lands of the fish-eaters must indeed have been a desperate venture. You are all on tenterhooks I know to hear particulars of this wonderful journey." He glanced at the McKay whom he had placed, quite naturally, as the leader of the party, "Will you not entertain us by an account of your great achievement?"

"Well, Sir" the McKay hesitated "I'd be only too pleased to tell you, but spinning a yarn about the adventure in which we've been involved is not my strong suit—Count Axel now is a born raconteur. He'd make a far better job of it than I should."

The Count was persuaded without any difficulty and, with Lulluma nestling against his shoulder, thrilled by his every word, he told their story from the day of Doctor Tisch's arrival in Madeira.

The Atlanteans listened absorbedly, refraining courteously from interruptions except when Menes asked for a point to be explained—much as a judge does who may already know the answer but wishes that a, possibly ignorant, jury may be further informed.

266

When the tale was done many questions were put to Axel and the Atlanteans regarded the newcomers with a new admiration now that they understood to the full their fortitude and courage in the perils they had shared. Then Axel bowed to Menes;

"We too, Sir, have an even greater curiosity—since you at least knew of our race, whereas we were totally ignorant of yours. Is it permitted that we ask some questions in our turn?"

Menes inclined his high polished beautifully proportioned forehead; "Ask, and you shall be answered my son."

"These fish-eaters, as you call them," Axel began. "Are they human or animal?"

"They are neither—and to explain them I must go back many centuries" Menes smiled. "Perhaps it would be best if I recounted to you something of Atlantean history and explain how it is that although our great race were almost annihilated by the cataclysm, we twelve descendants of it live now, a mile beneath the ocean, at the present day."

There were eager murmurs from Axel and his party and so the benign old man went on;

"The birth of our nation goes back into the mists of antiquity, further even than we can ever know. We can only say that we possess twenty-nine thousand years of recorded history. That is to say, our people had reached a sufficient degree of civilisation to hand down the story of their doings eighteen thousand years before the Flood, although of course in those early days they can have been little more than barbarians who elected chieftains, one of whom was strong enough to become paramount above the rest and keep the peace in order that progress towards true culture might begin.

"Those of you who believed in the legend which still lingers in the upper world of a great island, lying at one time in the centre of the North Atlantic, are correct. It was there that, for countless generations, safely secured from extermination by the savage hordes who populated the whole of the outer world through our surrounding seas, we advanced in all things to such a state that, apart from your mechanical inventions of the last hundred and fifty years, you can still show us nothing new.

"We domesticated many animals training them to our uses and, with patient care, converted the wild grasses into cereal crops. The larger portion of our island consisted of a great

267

plain which lay to the southward under almost constant sunshine and which was blessed with an unusual degree of fertility, so that there was abundant food for all and yet still room for wild forests in which our ancestors preserved every sort of game.

"To tell you one tenth of the marvels of that country in the days before the cataclysm would take a year. Let it suffice that our architecture was advanced far beyond anything which man has yet achieved; our system of supply regulated to a degree in which no man ever needed to go hungry but no troublesome surplus ever arose; and that the systems of law and morality which we evolved through so many centuries have never been equalled for their justice and toleration.

"The time came, alas! when evil powers filled our people with greed and sloth. They began to accumulate riches, which in themselves could bring them no more than they already had, and they were no longer content to work, even their easy hours, in the mines or fields.

"As with all other nations we had had in our midst from the beginning certain persons who practised what, for want of a better name, I will call the Black Art. At first they were comparatively harmless, dealing only in spells, love-tokens and minor witchcraft, but the time came when they began to concern themselves with what you call 'science' and that proved the most unholy alliance which has ever entered the world.

"To secure our precious metals we had mines in those days as deep, and even deeper than you have now. Some of them ran to eleven or twelve thousand feet below the surface of the earth, but we lacked your wonderful mechanical lifts which I have observed with interest on my spiritual journeys to the upper world. In consequence the shifts of miners could be relieved only in batches of a few hundred every day. They went down for a period of two weeks and on their return to the sunshine had to be hauled up those many thousand feet by hand.

"You can well imagine how loathed and dreaded this twice yearly period of duty in the mines became to our people—for none was exempted—not even the sons of the inherited as does always the eldest male here."

He paused for a moment and laid his hand on the shoulder of the gracious white-haired lady who sat next him.

"Semiramis, too, inherits her title from the great queens of those days, and when she dies, her daughter Tzarinska, will take the name instead, just as my dear son Nahou will be known as Menes after my death—of what was I speaking, though?"

"Of the miners," prompted Sally gently.

"Ah, yes. It was in this ever growing labour, as the mines grew deeper year by year, that the sorcerer-scientists saw their great chance to corrupt our people with their evil arts. They carried out many experiments in order to see if they could not succeed in creating life without the sanction of the Gods. 'Black' Magicians in your upper world have endeavoured to do the same and have, as you may know, at times been partially successful. Such creatures are incubated in large glass containers and are termed Homunculii. They have the rudimentary form of man yet lack that God-given flame which you call the Soul. Our masters of Evil succeeded in the dread mystery at last, thus introducing a new and hideous race upon the earth. Beasts which moved and talked and functioned just like men although, unlike the lowest forms of true animal, they had not the faintest spark of the divine nature in them."

"Those are the submen then" murmured the McKay.

Menes nodded. "Yes. You of course, only saw their descendants after nearly a thousand generations, for they had the power to breed like other species, although they come to maturity very rapidly and their lives are short. Their first ancestors were sent down into the mines and trained to hew and carry so that our forefathers might be relieved of that irksome but health-giving labour. Later they were driven to work in droves and the only Atlanteans who remained in the mines were experts who directed the operations and overseers who supervised the slave gangs." He sighed and paused; his audience waited patiently until he went on.

"The Gods move slowly but they miss nothing and when they found that man had usurped their privilege of giving life they were exceeding wrath. They gathered in their strength and might and power to discuss the evil which had been done by bringing brute beasts into the world, and they decided to destroy utterly our portion of the earth.

"Once they had made this decision they acted swiftly and in a single day and night of untold horror the greatest civilisation the world has ever known was blotted out. Thunderbolts streaked the air; the fountains of the deep gushed up, the floodgates of Heaven were opened, the rivers rose and overflowed their banks. Great winds carried men, houses, animals and trees like chaff before them through the torrential rain. The Palaces and Pyramids were shaken to their foundations and cracked as the earth shuddered beneath them. The earth sank into the ocean bed and vast tidal waves swept it from end to end. One, perhaps, out of every hundred thousand of our people escaped alive, the rest perished utterly —and after, the Empire of Atlantis became only a name— a legend which men speculate upon over their evening fires just as they would tell again an oft told fairy tale."

Menes sank into silence again, the horror of this colossal destruction of a mighty race, which he had conjured up and which they now knew to be true history, strong upon him.

It was only after what seemed a long while that Axel plucked up courage to ask: "Would you tell us, Sir, how your own ancestors managed to escape this terrible calamity?"

"Surely, my son" Menes' gentle smile lit his face once more. "You have traversed some portion of these big chambers and their connecting galleries. They were our mines. The chambers were concentration points where stores were kept and the slave gangs mustered. In certain of them Atlanteans resided permanently or almost so, for as I have said the Gods move slowly and a hundred years or more had elapsed between the introduction of the beast men and the great destruction.

"The earthshine had already been tapped to light the workings several thousand years before and this enabled the mine superintendents to live in some comfort. On this island site of ours there lived then an Atlantean named Petru. He had a house here with offices from which he administered his section of the mines—also, for our eternal blessing—a small garden.

"When the cataclysm came huge sections of the earth's crust were torn away and slid southward. All the upper galleries of the mines were, naturally, destroyed, but the lower workings remained unharmed and the sideways movement of the earth above sealed certain of the shafts, thus mercifully preventing these regions from being flooded."

"You are the descendants of Petru then?" the McKay enquired as Menes paused for a drink from his goblet.

"Partly, but not altogether. As Petru's employment kept

him underground for many months of the year his wife and sister lived here with him, also his family consisting of one son and three daughters. But, it chanced that when the calamity occurred they had several visitors. Petru's cousin was a learned priest named Zakar. All teaching whether civil or religious was given by the priests in those times and Zakar, who was a wise and upright man held a high appointment in the College of Mines. In order to give certain of his more advanced students practical instruction he had brought four of them to stay for a few days with his cousin Petru, so that when the chastisement of the Gods occurred there were twelve Atlanteans—men, women and children—imprisoned here.

"Petru's sister, and his three daughters when they grew up, bore children to Zakar's students and that is the fount from which we spring."

Axel nodded. "We saw many females among the brute race which of course accounts for its survival, when they were imprisoned, too."

"Yes. Females may not be as strong as males but their work on mechanical tasks in fields and mines is more consistent. Immediately it was discovered that these brute men could reproduce themselves the Black Scientists gave them their own women to labour with them. By so doing the complicated preparations and immense concentration of thought necessary to produce Homunculii in the laboratories were no longer required after a time. You tell me that these creatures are now blind. They were not so originally but many generations having lived in total darkness from birth to death they would naturally lose the faculty of sight by evolution."

"You've made it wonderfully clear so far Sir," said the McKay, "but what I don't understand is how *we* got here?"

"That I think I can explain" Menes answered. "From the earliest times it was necessary to bring air into the mines and my forefathers devised a very efficient system. You will be aware that water has, mainly, the same constituents as air and that the gills of a fish are only a cleverly constructed piece of mechanism which enables it to extract what you call oxygen from this medium. A gigantic shaft was made down which, when it was opened, many thousand tons of water would descend from the sea—distant only sixty miles from the Atlantean capital. This water was filtered through many layers of rock and mineral deposits then evaporated by

271

currents of the earthshine until the oxygen was extracted and renewed the air even in the deepest workings of our mines."

"But wasn't the whole plant smashed up in the earthquake?" asked Nicky.

"No, a large portion of the upper tunnel was shorn away but the essential part of this great filter—forty miles in extent —was ten thousand feet below the surface of the earth and so remained unimpaired. It works to this day, just as a mighty dam would still check the course of a river although the nation which had made it were long since dead. Your sphere was swept from the ocean bed and carried to these subterranean regions by the inrush of the waters."

"But they can't keep rushing in" objected the McKay "once this deep shaft was filled with water there would only be gentle percolation at the bottom and therefore very little downward current from the top."

Menes shook his head. "I fear you underestimate the wonderful scientific achievements of my ancestors. The shaft is comparatively narrow at the sea bed and when it is filled the pressure of the water, striking its bottom with tremendous force, sets a series of immense lever stones in motion which close its top. They are released in turn, every twelve hours, when the tunnel has emptied, by the action of the tide. The whole process is automatic therefore and operates without the aid of man."

"A truly wonderful arrangement." Axel commented, "but surely, without attention or replacement any such mechanism would have worn out by now?"

Menes smiled again and the slightly superior note in his voice was softened by its gentleness; "My son, you are but as little children striving in the dark compared with that great people who were swept away. The Pyramids of Egypt, which far surpass any monuments you have yet erected, are small by comparison with the great works which my nation undertook. They only represent a feeble effort made by a few survivors from the cataclysm to copy a state which it is not possible for your minds, as yet, to conceive. Those little pyramids have lasted for five thousand years, virtually unimpaired, and you still have no true knowledge of the reason for their building. In another ten thousand years they will still be there, neither man or nature—short of another vast upheaval—has power to destroy them. How then can you even suggest that similar works upon a far greater scale, operated by natural causes, the turning of the tides and the bi-diurnal releasing of cataracts greater than any waterfalls you know, should become worn out in the time which has elapsed since their installation."

For a moment they were silent all striving to adjust their minds to such a gigantic undertaking accomplished by the puny hands of man. Then the McKay said slowly:

"You'll forgive me Sir, but I'm still in the dark about how we arrived in the middle of a great haul of fish."

"That too I can explain," Menes turned towards him. "When the brute creatures had been created in large numbers it became something of a problem to feed them, for all supplies had to be transported to such a great depth in the mines. In order to save themselves this labour our ancestors conceived the idea of utilising the tunnel by which the water is conveyed to the filter beds giving us air, to trap large quantities of fish. You doubtless know that oil means death to all sea creatures, so gushers were conducted to points which formed a circle half a mile in diameter round the opening of the tunnel in the ocean bed. When the work was completed the inrush of the first waters at each tide forced up the oil from the lower earth, forming a circular wall of polluted water. The fish could not pass through it and so fled to the centre of the circle and, except for those who escaped by swimming upwards were caught in the current and drawn down through the narrow opening into harbours especially constructed to take the catch. It was your good fortune to be engulfed in such a haul when the main tunnel was nearly full and thus conveyed safely through the automatic locks, instead of being swept below in the first great spate of waters. If that had happened you would have been carried past the harbour entrance and dashed to pieces, or left submerged in the miles of underground cisterns which feed the filters. Have I now made the reason for your miraculous escape quite clear?"

The McKay smiled a little wryly. Man-planned construction on such a tremendous scale was at first a little difficult to grasp, but he recalled Doctor Tisch's statement that the artificial irrigation works of Moeris, in Egypt, were four hundred and fifty miles in circumference and three hundred and fifty feet deep. Yet the Egyptians were considered by these people as only decadent imitators of their race. He thought too of the underground railway systems which serve the teeming millions of the great modern capitals and had to

273

confess to himself that there was nothing at all impossible in a civilisation which had lasted eighteen thousand years before the Flood engineering this wonderful network of subterranean canals.

"Yes, I understand that Sir," he said at last, "and obviously it must be so. We couldn't have got here in any other manner but there's one point I'm not quite clear on yet. Granting the big air-filtering reservoirs and harbour, and the locks, were all safe thousands of feet under the ground, and that your ancestors had harnessed natural forces like the tides and oil-gushers to work the system so that it is still working—surely the earthquake jammed the whole caboodle at the upper end when Atlantis met its Waterloo?"

"You speak in riddles my son, but my mind, now attuned to yours, picks up your meaning. You are right of course. Over fifty miles of the tunnel leading to the original sea bed was shorn away, the oil-gushers—no longer checked—leaked into the ocean, polluting the water for a hundred miles around instead of spurting only for a few moments each half-day so that the currents could cleanse the area for fresh shoals of fish between catches. But Zakar saved us. Zakar took command and fought death in the darkness for the salvation of his people through forty days and forty nights of terror and confusion.

"By far the greater portion of our mines were flooded and destroyed. Only this comparatively small area was saved through the accidental blockage of shafts and channels. Whole legions of the brute creatures with their Atlantean overseers died almost immediately, others must have been imprisoned in galleries and chambers by falls of rock and compelled to surrender to death a few days later. Yet in the section which remained there were forty thousand of the beast slaves and Zakar had the power to direct their energies through his will.

"The earthshine had burst into a roaring volcano two miles from here, thus plunging this area into total darkness. Ten thousand slaves were burnt to death in the endeavour to restore it to its proper channels, but at last Zakar got it under control again. Then he drove his brute battalions to the task of capping the oil-gushers so that they would throw up their fountains only under pressure. Lastly he cleared the locks of fallen debris, blocked the new tunnel entrance on the ocean floor, drained out the water into now useless chambers, and reconstructed its opening on the original lines. When all was done no more than a few hundred slaves remained alive but their twice-daily supply of fish was assured to them and the twelve Atlanteans settled down to live on this site in Petru's house."

"By Jove, Zakar must have been a great fellow," murmured the McKay. "I wonder though that, knowing there was still land left up in the Azores he did not attempt to dig a tunnel up to them and get out safely after all?"

"He did attempt it, years later, in his old age, but you must remember that none of the survivors had any idea at first that some portion of our land remained above water. Spirit travel was almost unknown then, and nearly as rudimentary as it is with you to-day. Zakar was its first practical exponent. When he was very old he dreamed much and, had it not been for the respect in which he was held he would have been laughed at for his insistence that the Atlantean mountain tops still protruded above the ocean in the form of islands. The direction of each peak was known, of course, to a half point of the compass and one of the larger abandoned mine galleries ran towards the island which you call Pico. He explored it for some miles and then set the slave creatures who had bred and multiplied again after this lapse of fifty years, to the task of clearing the passage. Much of the work was done but Zakar was never able to lead his people out into the sunshine because he was killed by a fall of rock before his last great effort was completed."

"Why didn't the others carry on?" asked Sally.

"Because my child a great slab of stone barred the way and, with the death of Zakar we lost our power to control the slave creatures who might have moved it. He was a High Priest and what you would call a White Magician of the first order. Mass hypnosis may be known to you and is even practised by some people of the upper world upon a few dozen subjects at a time, but to dominate thousands so that they give their lives to your will requires very exceptional mental endowments. Zakar had those, and, unfortunately, believing that he still had many years to live, he had only just begun to train his successor. At his death the slaves turned hostile and revolted. The Atlanteans were forced to take refuge here. Between them they had just sufficient power to prevent the hordes entering this chamber, but that was all—and none of their descendants since, have ever left it."

"I see," the McKay nodded, "then that's the reason for your defences—the deep ditch and the cactus hedge?"

"Yes, at first there were attacks when the earthshine was dim at night so these barriers were erected. The slaves cannot swim so the fifteen foot canal became a trap for them and the thorn hedge made it impossible for them to land if they did succeed in floundering to the other side. Now they remain as an almost unnecessary precaution from surprise for it is thousands of years since the slaves made any attempt upon us. Like true animals they guzzle the two meals of fish a day which arrive, as far as they know by a natural process, and for the rest they breed and sleep without thought, governed only by their brute instincts."

Menes paused again and it seemed that the tale was done when Camilla spoke in her most persuasive voice: "Won't you tell us more about the making of this island?"

He smiled at her. "There is little more to tell my child. The debacle occurred on November the 1st, in your calendar, which is the new year with us. On that date the memory of the great destruction was perpetuated by those who escaped into the Upper World as the Feast of the Dead. Egyptians, Persians, Mexicans, Eskimoes, Celts, all kept that festival during the first days of November long after its origin had been forgotten. When the Christian Church rose to Power they encountered what they considered to be this pagan rite, both in Europe and America. Since they could not suppress it they gave a legal cloak to its celebration by calling it "All Saints Day". Yet, even then, they found that their converts gave more thought to the Dead than to the Saints, so strongly ingrained is custom in mankind. Very reluctantly, at last, they admitted "All Souls Day" to their calendar as well, making it the 2nd of November since, to go back on their previous decision of giving November 1st to the Saints, was hardly politic. So you see that those little cakes which are baked and eaten, or left for the spirits of the dead, in a million peasant homes on both sides of the Atlantic still are not offered on that one day in all the year by chance, but in unconscious awe on the anniversary of the most terrible calamity which has ever befallen mankind.

"Under the earth here, immediately the remaining Atlanteans found that they were cut off from the upper world, Zakar ordered the strictest supervision of all stores. Then, a few days later, when they realised that they were permanently entombed he directed that nothing should be consumed without a full examination as to its future usefulness. Petru's garden was enlarged to the full extent of the cavern, pips and fruit stones were saved, dried and planted in it, corn and vegetable roots were likewise husbanded. Since then many new varieties have been evolved but all our trees and plants are descendants of his original stock. The lake was dug and suitable species of fish bred in it; the first of course being taken from the subterranean harbour. Very gradually they were acclimatised to fresh water instead of salt to save the labour of carting tanks of sea water through the tunnels. That was accomplished before Zakar's death. The ancestors of our little herd of deer were originally kept in the mines because they were very sensitive to poisonous gases, so were stalled in new workings to give warning of such dangers. Later they were concentrated here and carefully tended by Zakar's orders. After his death the island was fenced about to protect our people from the rebellious slaves as I have told you. The number of its population was fixed and the sexes regulated, so that the number of men and women should be equal. Since then Atlantis has passed into that happy state where it no longer has any history to record."

"Happy state indeed," Doctor Tisch nodded solemnly, "for history is only a record of man's brutality and folly caused by fear. The murder of Kings—the butcheries inspired by religious fanaticism—or senseless slaughters to pile up more possessions or gold—all caused by fear. That is history. But tell please *mein Herr* how you have managed to regulate the sexes for it seems you have no marriage here and must be all one family."

"It was not difficult," Menes assured him. "Of the six women each bears two children only, generation by generation, a boy and a girl. Thus the original strains are perpetually intermingled at their most distant point of relationship—having regard to age."

"How then are you related to each other *mein Herr*?"

"Listen and I will tell you for these are the generations of Atlantis in our day."

"Semiramis is the eldest amongst us and to her uncle—now dead she bore a daughter, Tzarinska. Then twelve years later to me, her half-brother, she bore a son, Nahou.

"Tzarinska bore to me her uncle a daughter, Laotzii—then

277

twelve years later to her half-brother Nahou, she bore a son, Quet.

"Laötzii bore to her uncle Nahou a daughter, Rahossis—then twelve years later to her half-brother Quet, she bore a son, Peramon.

"Rahossis bore to her uncle Quet a daughter, Lulluma—then twelve years later to her half-brother Peramon she bore a son, Karnoum.

"Lulluma bore to her uncle Peramon a daughter, Danöe—then twelve years later to her half-brother Karnoum, she bore a son, Ciston."

The doctor inclined his bristly head in his formal little bow. "I thank you *mein Herr*, but tell me one thing more— You are one family, yet you defy the laws of heredity. No one of you bears any resemblance to another. You range in type from *Fraulein* Danöe who might be a maiden of East Prussia to young *Herr* Karnoum who appears to be of African descent or yourself who has the features of one of our Biblical patriarchs. How can this be?"

"Because, my son, we have passed into that stage of evolution where, although the physical is still necessary, the mental plays a much greater part in conception. We all spend two-thirds of our lives in spirit travel as you know—therefore our women study types in the upper world before they decide which they will bear. Then during many months they concentrate and their thoughts produce the colouring, every shade of which lies dormant in our bodies from past ancestors, and mould the form of the child that they desire. Semiramis was inspired to create Tzarinska by the sight of a Russian dancing girl. Tzarinska roamed further afield and produced a masterpiece for me in our dear Laötzii, from the study of a half-caste Chinese maiden who had been fathered by an Englishman in Hong-Kong. Thus are our features and forms determined and our women's greatest pride is to present to our island, in each of her children, a new and distinctive form of loveliness."

Doctor Tisch was about to speak again but Menes held up his hand: "May the Gods give you many days to ask all the questions you will, my son, and grant me time to answer them, but for to-night we have talked enough of serious things. There is a ceremony to be performed between two of you is there not? Nahou, my child, fill our cups that we may do honour to this custom of our brothers."

When they had drunk again they moved to the other end of the pool where, with the Atlantean's help, a temporary altar had been arranged before it was generally known that an adverse decision at the Council of the Gods might render it a terrible cynicism for those who were compelled to leave the island and go out to die.

Now all thought of that was past and Doctor Tisch took up his position before it. Camilla had asked the McKay to give her away and Vladimir chose Axel as his best man since the McKay, who found himself embarrassingly popular, was otherwise engaged. Sally was the only bridesmaid and Nicky, with all the Atlanteans made up the congregation.

Doctor Tisch gabbled the lines a little as it was many years since he had performed such a service and he was no longer quite word perfect, but Camilla did not notice that. She only felt a very real satisfaction as Vladimir slipped his signet ring over her finger.

Afterwards more toasts were drunk to the health and happiness of the newly married pair, then everybody wished them good night; the Atlanteans with unrestrained enthusiasm and good cheer, the others with a certain shyness. There could be no official "going away" for there was nowhere except Lulluma's quarters, which she had placed at their disposal, for them to go to but they retired there after a little time.

Thus, in the unusual surroundings of the dusk-laden flower scented garden, Camilla at last became the Princess Renescu and Vladimir got his heart's desire.

When they had departed the others resumed the feast. Rahossis danced for them and Karnoum sang. The wine circulated with more rapidity. An hour sped by and the scene had become Bacchanalian. Semiramis had crowned Doctor Tisch's bristly pate with a wreath of flowers. Nicky was lolling against Rahossis and telling that Junoesque lady that she was 'jus' the sweetest lil' thing'. Axel held Lulluma in the curve of his arm and was gazing down into her dark starry eyes as though he could never feast his gaze upon her long enough. Peramon had wandered off into the shadows with Laötzii. Menes sat enthroned in their centre, benignly smiling on them all—a jovial Zeus now rather than the Old Testament Patriarch to whom the doctor had likened him and, as Quet began to dance a wild Mexican reel he clapped with surprisingly youthful enthusiasm.

The McKay shot an anxious glance at Sally. "How about

it me'dear. The pace is getting a bit hot for respectable people like you and me isn't it?'' he said under his breath. "Like me to take you away?"

"I wish you would," she whispered quickly.

As they left the party nobody seemed particularly interested in their going. Quet was spinning like a teetotum. Tzarinska had joined in and was dancing opposite to him. The dusky skinned handsome Karnoum was letting Danöe's wonderful golden hair slide through his fingers while she gently caressed his cheek. The rest were gaily applauding the dancers.

"Phew!" Sally whistled when they were out of earshot. "It was getting pretty thick wasn't it. I'm not used to those sort of parties and I'm jolly glad you took me out of it."

"Do you want to go to bed—or to sleep rather on one of those mattresses they've laid out for us?" he asked.

"No, I'm not a bit tired. I was only frightened that at any minute one of them might come up and start mauling me about."

"They're a decent crowd really. They don't mean the least harm—it's just their natural way of living."

"I know, but it's not mine I'm afraid, and that's going to make things a bit difficult."

"Let's sit down under this tree," he suggested, "and decide what you're going to do with yourself."

"All right," she seated herself beside him and stared out into the darkness, "how do you mean though—decide what I'm going to do with myself?"

"Well, I mean!" he spread his hands out in rather a hopeless gesture. "You've got to face it sometimes me'dear—and sometime soon. If you want to go native there are plenty of good-looking chaps about and nobody's going to think any the worse of you for it."

"But I don't," Sally protested quickly. "I'm not like these girls here. They're awfully sweet but they're different. I should hate to be handed on from man to man and have romps between whiles with the others."

"The McKay shrugged his shoulders. "Well, I mean . . ." he repeated, "it's not in their nature to stick to any one woman for more than a couple of years from what I hear and you can hardly expect them to make you the Virgin Queen—besides you've never given me the impression that you're that sort of girl at all!"

280

"I'm not," declared Sally firmly. "I want one man whom I can love and stick to. I'm old-fashioned enough to want to be married like Camilla—for keeps."

"Well, Axel's a bit old for you, although he seems to have taken a new lease of life and is on the point of going off the deep end with Lulluma—how long that will last goodness knows! Still there's Nicky. Rahossis doesn't strike me as the sort of woman who'll want to have him playing around for long—she's got her eye on that dark bloke—Quet."

"Nicky!" echoed Sally contemptuously. "I wouldn't marry Nicky for ten million dollars."

"They wouldn't be much use to you if you did," the McKay commented unhelpfully. "That only leaves the Doctor and . . ."

"Yes—go on," she prompted "and . . .?"

"Why me! but I'm too old for you Sally."

"Oh you brute" she suddenly began to sob. "Haven't you any feelings at all. Have I just got to go down on my knees and ask you?"

"Sally!" his voice had fallen to an awed whisper. "I've been adoring the very sound of your foot-falls for weeks—but, well I never thought you could care a hoot for . . ."

"Oh stop talking you dear fool!" sobbed Sally "stop talking and take me in your arms."

CHAPTER XXI

THE COMING OF THE SERPENT

ON the following morning little dark-haired Ciston had the island to himself. None of his elders had thought of sleep before the small hours and it was the custom of the Atlanteans that no work, other than the necessary preparation of meals, should be done on the day after a Feast.

Like a slim golden-brown faun he ran on tiptoe from one grove to another until he had discovered the resting places of all his family and the newcomers whose arrival had amazed everyone so much. When he was older he too would be able to join in these revels at which the grown-ups laughed and sang far into the night but in the meantime he knew what he could do to please his beautiful mother and all these wonderful people who never seemed too busy to play with him and tell him stories.

He climbed on the kitchen table and took eighteen plates from the racks, picked a selection of fresh fruit, laid it out, and carried the plates one by one to the places where his elders slept, putting them carefully within easy reach. Then he got cups and, staggering round the island with a great jug of fruit juice, poured a draught into each. Lastly he gathered eighteen little bunches of flowers and laid them beside the fruit, after which good work he felt entitled to turn a couple of noiseless somersaults and dive into the pool for his morning swim, carefully refraining from his usual splashings in case he woke the sleepers.

It was not till after mid-day that his elders began to stir. Then they sat up drowsily, drank their fruit juice so thoughtfully provided by Ciston, nibbled the fruit, smelled the flowers, kissed their companions and made for the bathing pool. Soon there were a dozen of them laughing, shouting and plunging in the clear cool waters, or reclining on cushions along its marble sides.

Sally and the McKay declared their intention of being married that night upon which Menes decreed another Feast. Some of the Atlanteans did not at first see the reason for this, but Menes told them that as it was a custom in the upper world he desired to honour their new friends by its observance.

Quet laughed impishly and said: "If we adopted such a custom here it would bring us to starvation, for every day would be a feast day and no work would ever be done" but everyone welcomed Menes' gesture and made a fuss of the couple who were to play the principal parts in the ceremony.

Only dark-haired serious Tzarinska remarked privately to Rahossis that she thought it rather barbarous to make such a fuss about such a very normal thing and that it savoured somewhat of savage exhibitionism.

In the latter part of the afternoon most of them slept again but Semiramis invited Camilla and Sally to her apartment. She was a picturesque old lady with a fine head of silver hair and a high bridged Roman nose. The girls thought that she must have been extremely good-looking in her youth.

After some little courtesies she told Camilla that she fully appreciated the differences between the woman of the upper world and her own. She would have spoken the day before, she said, but one day was of small importance out of a lifetime, particularly as she understood that Camilla had been married before.

Then she proceeded to give them both the benefit of the cumulative experience of the women of her race and, by the time she had finished they were both convinced that she could have made the Professors of Psychology in Vienna and the British Medical Council look like first year students.

She had a deep throaty chuckle and a shrewd witty humour which saved her conversation from any resemblance to a lecture and the two girls listened with immense interest as pearls of wisdom regarding the handling of their menfolk rolled continuously from her tongue.

When she had done she kissed them both, made the sign of the Swastika on their foreheads, breasts, and thighs with a curiously scented oil from a tiny bottle, then bundled them out with instructions to rest until the evening.

Sally and Camilla were both a little silent as they walked away. The old lady had told them that their coming involved a readjustment in the population of the island, but that was a matter which would be settled when the Gods gave Menes enlightenment, as they surely would in due course. In the meantime she would perform a magical ceremony which would cause their unions to be sterile. Later they would not be robbed of their right to have children but they must be trained in the tremendous responsibility of the task, since in the years to come their stock would mingle with that of the Atlanteans.

That night there was another banquet. Afterwards Doctor Tisch married the McKay and Sally before their assembled friends, then the feast was resumed and Carnival reigned as King until the small hours of the morning.

The next day they slept late and lazed again but on the following morning the work of the island was resumed. Semiramis and Menes were exempted by their age and rank from all manual labour, also the two newly-married couples for the Atlanteans considered their honeymoons in the same light as when a real love affair occurred between two of their own people. All the others set about the varied tasks of tending their crops, laundering their tunics and tidying the pleasances.

The work was not heavy because it was so admirably organised through long centuries of custom and they sang, bandied jests, and laughed while they toiled. After the first meal in the morning they played games for a spell which necessitated the incorporation of certain exercises and holding the breath in a particular manner, to ensure their continued fitness. After the midday meal they slept for an hour or so, the rest of the day they worked until they gathered for the evening meal after which, in the scented dusk of the dimmed earthshine, they told stories or discussed the histories and religious beliefs of many nations.

Conversation was conducted principally in English in deference to the newcomers and most of the Atlanteans spoke it fluently. The younger ones understood enough to follow the talk and to contribute their share in broken accents.

Quet, alone, always spoke French—a language for which he had a passion, while Danöe and Karnoum often addressed each other in Spanish as they were practising that tongue together.

The new arrivals were called on to answer innumerable questions of a fantastically varied nature. Some showed an extreme astuteness or were on subjects of which the upper world party were completely ignorant, others were of such a childlike simplicity that they amazed the people who were questioned.

It transpired that in their spiritual journeys the Atlanteans witnessed many happenings, the true significance of which entirely escaped them. Nearly all of them had been horrified spectators of certain phases of the last great war, but it had taken them many months to discover exactly who was fighting whom and for what reason. They had no means of getting inside books or newspapers and could only read the printed page if it was spread out before them and if their knowledge of the language proved sufficient. In consequence they had constantly placed wrong constructions on past events from being unable to learn their context. Since broadcasting had been general however they were far better informed as they could listen in to any set which was functioning at their leisure.

Rather surprisingly their principal interest did not centre in world events or such problems as to why many people in the great industrial centres remained permanently unemployed, or in slum clearance, or needless mortality in childbirth. They accepted these as ills common throughout the centuries to a civilisation which they considered to be in a comparatively low state of evolution, and were far more inclined to follow the fate of individuals. For weeks on end, it seemed, they would watch the romance of a pair of young lovers in some obscure township, or a domestic drama in one of the luxurious homes of a modern capital. Such scenes from human destinies were their story books, their theatres, their talking pictures, and on their return to the island, so they said, it was their practice to recount the stages of these comedies or dramas which they had witnessed, in such detail that the others also felt they knew the protagonists in them, not only by name but by the minutest particulars of their daily lives and surroundings.

It was a slow method perhaps of satisfying that craving for stories common to all humanity, but the very details intensified the plots and the instalments followed each other from time to time like the longed for portions of a serial.

Every one in the island at the present time was on tenterhooks to know if a certain Esteban Manillo, who dwelt in a sleepy old-fashioned Spanish town would have secured the job he was after and be able to marry his Juanita, or if her loathsome step-father would throw her out of the house while Esteban was still penniless—and the latest moves in half a dozen other life dramas which various members of the community would be able to report upon after their next visit to the upper world.

285

Doctor Tisch spent most of his time happily discussing a thousand problems with Menes whom the McKay had christened the Admiral. The Doctor had also started a collection of botanical specimens—presumably for his own satisfaction for they would never be shown to anyone except the people who already knew them so well.

Axel and Lulluma had become inseparable and spent every waking moment in each other's company, apparently in a kind of blissful dream state. The others employed themselves more actively with their work, loves, and hobbies.

Only Nicky failed to find contentment in this Paradise and he became more moody and irritable as the days wore on. He had fallen a victim to one of those wild unreasoning passions common to such natures and its object was Rahossis.

If she had treated him harshly from the beginning he might not have taken it so badly, but she had been extremely kind. On those first two nights of feasting she had, on each occasion, become just mildly and happily tipsy on Tokay—or *Nektar* as the Atlanteans preferred to call it. She had been intrigued a little by his strangeness too and flattered by his unconcealed admiration, therefore she had shown no hesitation whatever in abandoning herself to his embraces and more, returned them with all the ardour suggested by her Titian hair.

Having twice tasted of these joys Nicky, somewhat naturally, expected their continuance, so he was surprised and hurt when Rahossis proceeded to treat his further advances with the utmost casualness once the feasts were over. Worse, she showed a decided preference for the impish and amusing Quet and it was quite evident that a serious affair was boiling up between them.

Nicky attempted facetious gaiety, prowled, sulked and postured, but all in vain. Rahossis treated him with the same friendliness she showed the others but simply could not be induced to favour him again with any special interest.

Whenever he did succeed in catching her alone she was always busy on some small task which, she declared, could not be put aside at the moment, and daily these frustrations were adding fuel to Nicky's passion.

It was in the early evening after work, but while there was still an hour to go before the nightly meal that, just a week after Sally's wedding, he at last found Rahossis alone and unoccupied, seated on the grass in front of her apartment.

"I suppose as soon as I sit down you'll find you've got

to get up and do something?" he said with heavy sarcasm.

Rahossis looked surprised. "No," she said, "I have nothing to do at the moment if you wish to talk to me."

Nicky sat down, put his chin on his knees; and muttered moodily: "Why are you so horrid to me now?"

Rahossis laughed indulgently. "I am not horrid to you. Be sensible my dear and you will become as happy as all the others here."

"Happy!" he exclaimed. "How can I be happy when you don't take any interest in me?"

"What is there to interest me in you?" she said lightly. "You seem like a rather spoilt child to me." Then, because to give pain was quite contrary to her Atlantean nature she added quickly: "I did not mean that, it is I who am too old now to appreciate your youth. Tell me your life story; I should like to hear it."

Nicky was pacified at once. He loved talking about Nicky Costello and plunged into the completely fictitious auto-biography that he knew so well; having forgotten already his confession of his true origin made to his friends in the bathy-sphere when they all thought they were going to die.

"I was rather a cute little chap I believe," he began modestly, "mop of golden curls you know and big eyes. Everyone used to turn and look at me in the streets. My father was in Real Estate an ordinary middle class business man—and ma was just a sweet homely woman. It's all owing to her influence that I am what I am to-day. She kept me straight as a lad."

"With exercises?" asked Rahossis brightening. "Perhaps you can show us some new ones?"

Nicky compressed his lips. "No, not exercises—prayers!" He replied in a faintly superior and snubbing tone.

"Oh—I'm sorry," apologised Rahossis meekly.

"I was never any good at my books," he continued with the gay laugh which reporters like to hear. "I'm afraid I wore the dunce's cap many times and *was* my bottom sore?"

"Was it?" asked Rahossis with polite interest.

This time he ignored the interruption; "My poor old father lost all his money one fine day and there was the family on the rocks—Nicky told them not to worry and got a job as an errand boy to a theatrical costumiers. Yes folks! You can all see what's coming. But stop a minute—father got ill, then mother got ill and little Nicky did his job by day and looked after the old folks, who had given him their lives, by night. Well—it's no use dwelling on unhappiness—there's enough of that in this little world—the old folks got better but meanwhile Nicky had walked into the Film Studios one day and asked for a part. There was a nerve you'll say—well something had to be done. No one can support three people on the few dimes I got for being an errand boy.

"The casting director helped me out of his office with the the toe of his boot, although he has to listen to me now, then little Nicky lost his way in the passages of that vast palace of sets and dressing-rooms and *quite* by accident he found himself in the back of one of the Caravans they were using for a big film for the new Juvenile Star—a kid called Coral Pacific.

"When she trundled on to the set Nicky hops on to the box and she catches sight of him—she was a passionate little creature and spoilt then—though she's got over all that now. 'Plumok' she yells at her director 'I want that boy in my scene instead of that scrubby little hobo you tried out yesterday.' She knew good stuff when she saw it.

"Then they discovered my voice," Nicky announced impressively. He always treated his voice as if it had been a second American Continent though the role of Columbus varied according to the public he was appealing to at the time. "They were amazed. Such a perfect crooning voice had never been heard before—and then of course I had to do my training—hard work there—at it all day, and studying all night to get through college. No one can say that film stars don't work for their living. But it is all worth it if we can give the great generous public even an hours relief from the problems which beset them—a little laughter makes life easier, and all the world loves a lover if the stuff is put over with genuine feeling and discretion—no hot stuff about Nicky Costello's films. Keep it clean was my old mother's motto and it still hangs over my bed."

"That reminds me," said Rahossis.

"What of?" he asked.

"To put an extra cushion on your bed—you seemed to be tossing about so uncomfortably when I walked past you early this morning.

Nicky did not consider that his poignant history of suffering and victory had been received with enough applause. "I wish my mother had known you," he said.

"I wish I had known her" Rahossis replied politely. "We should have been about the same age."

"Good God! Don't keep reminding me of that!" He exclaimed furiously. Then he glanced quickly at his companion's lovely face. He had just thought of a plan to interest her.

"Would you like me to sing to you?" he suggested and without waiting for her assent he sat down on the grass and drew her down too. Tilting his face towards the radiance of the earthshine he closed his eyes. Nicky had very fine eyelashes. Then he lifted up the muted cross between a tenor and alto, which he called his voice and started to croon.

Fortunately Nicky kept his eyes closed in growing ecstasy as he sang. "Dear Baby . . . God gave me . . . I'm holding . . . your hands!" Rahossis had never been called a baby before but she was always ready for a new experience. She was a little perplexed however when, having finished the last sob-note of "Dear Baby" he embarked on "In all the World . . . Mother-r-r-r . . . there's no one like you!" The tune of the second song was much the same as the first—both variations on about five notes and written specially for Nicky's particular talent.

He sang on—really enjoying himself now and plunging deeper and deeper into the part he had selected, being no psychologist, as most likely to soften and attract Rahossis.

Suddenly he ceased and buried his face in his hands; Rahossis jumped, for he had broken off in the middle of a long wriggle on middle C, and said anxiously. "Are you not well Nicky—what is the matter?"

"Matter?" he muttered and gave his famous hollow laugh; "the matter is that I'm miserable because I love you so—and you will never be mine!" The part did not quite fit but it served Nicky's purpose.

Rahossis looked relieved. "But I have been yours," she corrected him gently "Twice."

"Words! . . . words!" he exclaimed tragically, now visualising himself in the role of betrayed lover. "Rahossis—you are driving me to despair—I love you—I want you—we were made for each other. What is it that has come between us? You were so sweet to me only a few nights ago and now . . .! You are flirting with that man Quet—don't deny it!"

"Oh I just find him amusing" Rahossis said lightly.

"Don't lie to me! Not that! I could not bear it." Nicky

drew his hand across his eyes as the old cliches came back. "Tell me the truth—I am brave and I can bear that, although life will never be the same again." He groaned just as beautifully as he had in "All for Love". "I am only just a poor man who loves you—I've worked my way up from nothing—I know that—but I love you Rahossis. I love you more than words can say."

Rahossis was kind and generous to a fault and for the moment she was not bored. This was just like one of those romances which she and her companions were always following on their journeys—it was interesting to hear it at first hand. What odd words and gestures the people of the upper world use to make love—she thought. But Nicky was waiting there with a look like a hungry spaniel.

"Dear Nicky" she said, "I cannot always be alone with you here—the life we lead is so different from yours. She put up her hand and touched his face caressingly. He seized and kissed it, slipping into the role of the 'other' man like an eel into mud.

"Rahossis—dearest—you must leave all this—let's go away together. I'll take care of you I swear it. We'll start life anew. Just you and I in some place where no one knows us— It will be heaven to have you with me always. Poor little girl—you've had a rotten deal!"

Rahossis' expression had changed as these singularly inapt lines flowed from Nicky's beautifully curved mouth. His artistic temperament which always dominated his mentality at such times was his undoing.

She rose to her feet with dignity, pulled down her tunic and said coldly. "I think you are jesting. You know we could not leave Atlantis, even if we wished, and I am neither poor or a little girl."

Nicky blinked as he realised the mess he had made and Rahossis turned to enter her apartment.

She walked into her room and sat down on her bed, but he followed, flinging himself at her knees.

"Rahossis"—he cried, "I'm sorry—please forgive me— God knows I do love you and I'm nearly mad with wanting you. I can't sleep or eat—or think of anything else!" Then, without acting, he burst into tears.

Rahossis was horrified. She gathered him up in her arms as if he had been Ciston and held his head against her breast. "Darling" she murmured "there . . . there . . . there."

But no amount of petting soothed Nicky's sobs. He was on a good thing and he was going to stay on it as long as he could. So he sobbed and sobbed until poor tender-hearted Rahossis grew anxious. She gave him a drink of water but still he sobbed. "Come near me—let me love you . . . darling— don't leave me!"

His hands started fumbling at her tunic and she had not the heart to stop him.

If Nicky had not been so fully occupied he might have noticed his ears burning for several of his friends were discussing him just then.

Axel and Lulluma had begun to stroll hand in hand towards the jungle directly their work for the day was over, but Sally and the McKay were seated by the lake-side in the meadow, so they paused to speak to them on the way.

The newly-married pair were engaged in, what the Atlanteans regarded as a most curious pastime. Having discovered that neither of them were allowed to do anything but amuse each other during the period of their honeymoon, the McKay had collected an odd assortment of items on the first day that the Atlanteans went back to work; two long, tapering, bamboo canes, two lengths of yarn from the weaving shop, a couple of sharp bent nails from Nahou and some little pieces of silvery dress material provided by Lulluma. With the addition of a couple of pieces of cane for floats he and Sally had constructed a couple of rough fishing rods and had spent a good portion of the last three afternoons by the placid waters of the lake, trying in vain for a catch.

The Atlanteans had been tremendously intrigued, breaking off their labours and coming to stare over the kitchen garden fence at this strange spectacle of two lovers solemnly gazing at the water in which they had dropped a bent hook covered in dough with a tiny bit of tinsel above it.

To polite enquiries the McKay had replied that they were 'fishing'—which the Atlanteans regarded as a gigantic joke.

Nahou, courteous as ever, had offered to operate the concealed dragnet which would enable them to secure as many fish as they wished, adding that they could throw back any they did not require into the lake again, but when the McKay rejected the suggestion it became quite evident to their new friends that they could not be fishing whatever else they might be up to.

Atlantean opinion then became divided into two camps.

One school of thought inclined to the theory that the lovers could not be happy because they remained so quiet and that this offering of a small piece of dough on a string must be a propitiatory rite to some barbarous water God they followed. The other side postulated that there must be some queer hidden pleasure in the game which might add to the enjoyment of their own honeymoons if they could only find it out.

Lulluma inclined to the first belief. As she came up with Axel she paused beside Sally and eyed the rods dubiously for a moment. Then she stooped and said in a swift whisper: "I'm so sorry you're unhappy darling—is there anything I can do?"

"But I'm not unhappy!" Sally lifted her face in swift astonishment. "I'm having a glorious time. I never dreamed that life could be so good—surely I look happy don't I?"

"Yes," Lulluma agreed cautiously. "It is only seeing you spend so much time at this queer game you play that made me wonder if you were . . ."

"It was sweet of you to worry for me." Sally caught her hand and pressed it gratefully. "Sooner or later we'll really catch a fish—you'll see. The difficulty makes it all the more exciting in a way—but I *am* happy—divinely and deliriously so. Who could be otherwise in your enchanted island?"

The McKay, puffing contentedly at an Atlantean bamboo pipe, for he had now accustomed himself to their tobacco which had been introduced to him at his first banquet in the island, was explaining to Axel that they were getting plenty of bites but could not manage to land a catch owing to the indifferent hooks.

They both heard Sally's last words and Axel turned to her; "I know one person who is by no means happy and it is worrying me very much indeed!"

"You mean Nicky eh?" The McKay shot him a swift glance from under his shaggy brows.

"That poor boy hankers after Rahossis," remarked Lulluma.

"Hanker is a mild word me'dear," the McKay took her up. "I'm sorry for the lad of course as he's got it so badly, but he ought to learn to control himself. It's downright indecent for any man to make an exhibition of himself tagging after a woman with his tongue hanging out like that!"

"It's his temper that I'm afraid of," said Axel slowly.

"You remember the violent rages he used to get in with Vladimir about Camilla? And now he is positively consumed with jealousy because Rahossis prefers Quet. Well, Vladimir was so strong that he could afford to laugh but the Atlantean is quite a slim fellow so Nicky might go for him and then one of them would probably get badly hurt."

"You think so eh?" the McKay grunted, lifting his dripping line out of the water to inspect the bait. "Well, I promised the Admiral I'd keep you all in order and by Gad I'll tan that young man's hide if he starts creating any trouble here."

Sally laughed. "You *are* a bellicose person darling! How I dared to marry you I can't think—you'll be beating me next."

"That's it," he assured her with an adoring grin. "For two pins I'd cut off that long hair of yours so that you shouldn't look quite so attractive to anyone except myself."

Lulluma smiled and, catching Axel's hand, led him away. "I'm happier about them now," she said when they were out of hearing. "They do love each other an awful lot—far more than I'd supposed."

He nodded. "You needn't worry your sweet head about them—or those two nice pagans Vladimir and Camilla. They're both as happy as the day is long and the Doctor is as contented as can be collecting his specimens and talking ancient religions with Menes. It's Nicky who is going to cause trouble before we're much older."

"It is so difficult to know what to do in such a case," Lulluma said as they entered the jungle. "You see he is a very stupid young man—extremely conceited, and a bore—so how could any woman be expected to like him?"

"He's a fine strapping chap and very good-looking," ventured Axel.

She shrugged her plump shoulders disdainfully. "Who isn't? We're all of us that but one needs something else beside health and good looks to be really attractive in this life."

"Of course," he agreed as they sat down side by side in front of the statue of Priapus where he had first seen Danöe sleeping, "anyhow for people like ourselves, but this affair of Nicky's does raise a general problem. You seem to have solved the usual evils that wreck human happiness here—except this one thing—jealousy and unrequited love. What

293

happens if one of you falls in love with another who does not return that love. Doesn't that sometimes lead to tragedy?"

She shook her dark curls. "No, such a situation never occurs. You see time is on our side here. None of us can escape physically from our island and if one of us feels drawn to another who is having an affair with someone else we check our incipient passion and travel at once. If the affair is still in progress when we return or the person for whom our love is growing is asleep, we travel again—distracting our minds with new scenes and interests; but we meet at the harvests or the sowings and are free to develop our romance, if the other one is all over by that time. Often, the longer we have to subdue our longings the greater is the joy of their realisation in the end."

"Yes, I understand that," Axel gazed down upon her fondly as she stretched herself out on the grass with her hands behind her head. "By such cultivated restraint you may practically eliminate jealousy. Especially if you are quite certain of achieving your object in the long run, but what happens if you return time and time again only to find that the other person doesn't love you and is never likely to?"

Lulluma grunted. She did at times and Axel loved to hear the sound because it was a certain indication that she was in her happiest and most contented mood.

For a moment she stared up at him, a wicked little smile just lifting the corners of her full lips, then she said: "I'll tell you if you wish. In most cases just being together a lot during the harvest and a little fooling at the Festival is enough, but if that fails we resort to other measures. There are what you would call electric currents which pass between people and either attract or repel. Those have to be manipulated. It is part of the lore passed down to us from that antediluvian world which contained such an enormous store of wisdom. By a secret ceremony privately performed we set certain vibrations in motion and then concentrate our thoughts. Such means never fail and the woman who employs them will be sure of receiving a gift of flowers from the lover of her desire the day afterwards, or a man tender looks from the woman of his choice."

Axel nodded. "A love spell eh? Then you have made heaven on earth indeed. Not a single trouble is left to mar your perfect joy."

"You are happy here?" she asked softly.

"Yes—infinitely. It is like having been born again fully grown into a new and better existence—yet I would not be happy if it were not for you."

She shifted her position slightly and stretched up one bare arm to place it round his neck. Her breast was heaving gently against his side. "You do not know how I honour you for the restraint you must have placed upon yourself at those two Festivals," she murmured, "and all this week that we have been together."

"Honour," he repeated with gentle mockery, "but I would have something more. How I wish that I had been born an Atlantean."

"Why?" she enquired with a flutter of her dark curling eyelashes.

"Because they have qualities which would commend me to you in a different way."

She shook her head. "I prefer you as you are. Our life is so limited here in spite of our spirit journeys whereas you have really travelled and read much. You lack some of our special powers perhaps but your mind is deeper. I could laugh and talk with you for years; with our men only for a few months."

"Only talk?" he whispered as he caressed her hair.

"And laugh" she reminded him, her breath warm on his cheek.

He bent close above her and his voice trembled as he said: "Won't you teach me that secret sorcery Lulluma so that I can cast a spell on *you*?"

"My dear one," her eyes were moist and languorous, her breathing a little fast. "Forgive me that I made the test so hard for you; it was only because I wished our love to last. No spells are necessary between us two."

Three and a half weeks slipped by as though they had only been as many days and nights for the three pairs of lovers in that enchanted island. Almost imperceptibly the strangers from the upper world dropped into the easy carefree Atlantean habits; accustoming themselves to light meals, healthy exercise, dreamless sleep and the spirit of laughter which seemed to lurk behind every bush and tree.

The Atlanteans went no more upon their spiritual journeys for the time being. They were still far too interested in talking to and questioning the new settlers in their island to wish to observe their counterparts, with whom they could not speak, in the world above. In addition one of their harvest periods had come round, for which, in any case, they would have returned to get in their crops.

Lulluma and Axel alone refrained from helping since she had claimed from Menes an Atlantean honeymoon for them both. They held interminable conversations together in the gardens and slept each night in a recess of the jungle. At meal times they seemed dreamy and abstracted, only anxious to get away to one of their retreats so that Semiramis commented upon it; chiding Lulluma with gentle humour because they missed her deep chuckling laughter and feared that she had become serious for life. Axel could have informed them however that his warm passionate sweetheart had lost none of her divine merriment but reserved it for himself.

The McKay, Vladimir, Camilla and Sally had curtailed their life of complete idleness by their own wish and found the work allotted, which sometimes separated them for an hour or two, only lent fresh stimulus to their passion and gave a new interest to their lives.

Nicky had been passably good humoured for a few days after his last private encounter with Rahossis and she treated him on all occasions now with a special gentleness, but when the harvest time came he sank back into his previous discontented mood.

He prowled uneasily about the garden on his own, cast scowling looks at Quet, and alone among the people in the island behaved on occasion with downright discourtesy. The happiness of his friends, which they could hardly have concealed had they wished, drove him to silent frenzies of envy at their lot. Lulluma's passion for Axel particularly goaded him into sneers and bitter witticisms with which he fruitlessly endeavoured to irritate these two whom he termed contemptuously 'the turtle doves'. The thought that one of the beautiful Atlantean girls could surrender her every moment to 'that dry stick of a Count who was not even really handsome' which was his view of Axel, while another would not even grant him half an hour alone, was a never ceasing torture.

The island was not large enough for him to get clear of the others for any length of time, and he was constantly coming upon them in attitudes which did not shock him in the least but inflamed his jealousy and desire. His cup of misery was filled to the brim by the knowledge that he was a prisoner there for life.

For a few days he played up to Danöe. Partly in the hope of making Rahossis jealous and partly because he felt that a success with her would restore his self-respect and ease his feelings, although her slender golden beauty did not attract him half as much as more vital girls of the same type whom he had toyed with in the past at Hollywood.

Danöe, however, was having a purely platonic affair with Karnoum, her dark apparently boyish uncle, by whom she would bear her first child in a few years' time. She was by no means inexperienced already for Nicky had learned that girls did not reach even the physical age of twenty in Atlantis without having been initiated into the arts of love, but her relations with the Egyptian looking Karnoum appeared to be perfectly innocent. As they were both learning Spanish they spent a good portion of their time talking together in that language in order to practise it.

In response to Nicky's suggestions, Danöe turned an enormous pair of blue eyes upon him which showed mild surprise and, after what he considered the infuriating courtesies that all these people used, told him very sweetly that, she thanked him for his offer but would be too busy with her Spanish to accept it for some months to come.

"They're all a damn sight too highbrow in this place," Nicky told himself furiously. He forgot that, just as Camilla had become of no more interest to him than a bathing beauty now she could no longer attract him by the lure of her millions so he, robbed of his glamour as a film star, had little power to appeal to women on his looks alone. He had never been even a passably good lover in actual fact, since he was a hopeless psychologist and had never had to study women with a view to pleasing them. His easy successes in the past had all been temporary affairs with doll-like females who had become infatuated by his face and voice on the talking screen. Those casual conquests were an added handicap now for they had given him a completely false picture of himself and fostered both his impatience and conceit.

After his failure with Danöe he returned to Rahossis, upon whom the Danöe episode had had a completely negative result. She only noticed it to bless herself that she was rid of his constant spying whenever she was alone with Quet.

Once only did he succeed in getting her on his own during the harvest fortnight and that by invading her apartment in the middle of the night. She kept her temper remarkably well in the circumstances even allowing for the fact that she, and all her people, had been trained to a consideration for others as a first rule of their lives since, not content with breaking in and rousing her from her sleep he kept her up for a couple of hours with a repetition of all his old tricks.

She let him rave, posture, and weep but this time she was quite firm about the matter. Finally she told him that she had no intention of allowing him to make love to her any more, at least for three or four years to come, by which time he might have acquired some manners and a little sense. The possible time limit in her declaration shattered him more than any flat refusal. It silenced his weeping and sent him out into the night convinced that all the Atlanteans were stark staring mad and that this woman Rahossis could have no conception she was rejecting the world-famous screen star—Nicholas Costello whose fan mail was immense.

That check served to sober him for a day or two and both Axel and Menes, who were observing him shrewdly, felt that he had calmed down. He might then even have sunk into an apathetic despair had not the Harvest Festival Banquet come along.

At the Feast they were all assembled and ate heavily as before. By midnight the wine was passing freely and a joyous Saturnalia beginning. The lovers sat with arms entwined feeding each other titbits of dessert and pledging each other in the *Nektar* of the Gods. Camilla was lolling against Vladimir, both had approached nearer to the Atlanteans than any other members of their party in all but wisdom now, and Vladimir, who absolutely revelled in playing at being a cave man, had made a bedroom for them by arranging a platform in the fork of a high tree. Even Sally, safely embraced by the muscular arm of the McKay, had had as much wine as she could carry and no longer saw anything improper in the love dance which Peramon and Laötzii were performing as a turn in the unofficial cabaret.

Nicky squatted a little apart from the rest watching Rahossis and Quet with brooding eyes. They had not sat near each other at the meal but proceeded to do so shortly afterwards. As he watched every tentative movement in the age-old game they played together his jealousy flamed up into a burning hatred. In spite of Nahou's gentle remonstrance he insisted on abandoning the *Nektar* for that potent green liqueur with which they had been fortified on their exhausted arrival in the island.

At length Quet and Rahossis stood up, just a shade unsteadily, and left the Feast. Nicky rapidly swallowed a fifth portion of that fiery liquid which made his inside feel like a furnace as it went down, then he got to his feet and followed.

No one paid any attention to the departure of the three but Menes, who looked at Semiramis and then pointed to Nicky's form retreating in the shadows.

"That youth needs guidance and help. I will speak to him to-morrow and explain that he must restrain his desires for a little time. Then, if Rahossis still proves obdurate when her passion for Quet is ended you had best teach him the secret rites which will ensure her willing acceptance of him."

Had Axel been present and seen Nicky's state, he would not have left the matter until the next day but gone after him at once, in order to intervene if necessary. As it was he and Lulluma had left the party hours before, passing into the darkness as two silent shadows wrapped in a divine content.

Rahossis and Quet made their way to the jungle and finding a convenient spot sat down. Nicky stole after them, his drunken brain seething with chaotic thoughts engendered by his pent-up passion.

He'd show this laughter maker! he told himself. He'd show him who was who! Yes Sir—an' how. The dirty wisecracking Mexican dago—and that would learn Rahossis too. Every woman liked a man who was a man. Someone who wasn't afraid to fight for her. They loved that, damn their hard little souls. Particularly these savages. That 'ud get her for sure. He'd show her— Yes Sir and the world. Why the hell hadn't he thought of this before?

He nearly fell into the lake but recovered and stumbled on until, directed by their voices, he found Rahossis and Quet lying side by side in one of the jungle clearings.

Rahossis gave a heavy sigh as he appeared. "Oh, dear, it's *you* again! This is *too* much. Why must you follow me even here?"

"Want to talk to you," said Nicky thickly.

He had ignored Quet for the moment but the dark man stood up apparently in a high good humour.

"You wish to speak with Rahossis?" he said in the English which did not come at all naturally to him. "You choose a curious time. However—" he gave a shrug which was purely French and broke into that language—"*Messieurs les Anglais tirez le premier.*"

Nicky did not understand the jest and thought that Quet was carrying Atlantean politeness to extremes because he was frightened of a fight.

Actually the Atlantean was completely certain of himself *and* the situation. As he parted the bushes to walk away he said to Rahossis in their own tongue:

"This fool becomes a positive nuisance. I must speak to Menes about him in the morning. Get rid of him as quickly as you can and in the meantime I will bring fruit for our breakfast."

"Huh!" exclaimed Nicky with disgust on Quet's departure. "You see he's yellow. That's what he is—yellow. Good thing for him he cleared out when he did though—otherwise I would have shown him."

"You are an unpleasant creature and extremely stupid," said Rahossis quietly. "If Quet wished he could paralyse you with one glance from his eyes."

"What me!" Nicky did not take her words literally and only thought she meant that Quet could scare him with a look. He laughed contemptuously. "Jus' let him put his dirty head roun' the bushes again an' I'll show him! I'm not a feller to be trifled with. I'll show you too—by God I will."

Without further preamble he fell upon her.

Rahossis was big limbed and muscular. There was never the least likelihood that she would be the victim of Nicky's assault before Quet's return. Disdaining to cry out she fought her attacker off as he ripped her tunic from breast to thigh. But the panting struggle only lasted a moment. There was a rustling of the shrubs and Doctor Tisch appeared. In one glance he had taken in the full significance of the scene.

After copious potations of Tokay at the Feast he had suddenly remembered that there was one Atlantean flower which he particularly wished to see and that it only blossomed at night. He had collected his torch and come to the jungle in search of it.

"Why, Nicky!" he exclaimed. "What do you do! This is not right!"

Nicky staggered to his feet and confronted the little doctor. "Get to hell out of here, you dirty spy," he yelled, swaying drunkenly.

300

The Doctor held his ground. "But, Nicky . . ." he expostulated.

"*Get out*, you little rat!" Losing all control Nicky followed up his words with a smashing blow.

It caught the Doctor full in the face. He dropped his torch, staggered and fell, his head coming into collision with the trunk of a tree.

Little Doctor Tisch lay quite still where he had fallen. Nicky grabbed up the torch and flashed it on him. A trickle of blood was oozing from his temple.

Rahossis turned over on her face and moaned just as though she had received the blow herself. In a moment her moans had become a wild wailing.

Nicky, terribly sober now, propped up the Doctor's body and strove to rouse him, but he remained limp and silent. The blood fell in slow drops on Nicky's hands and it seemed to him that they fell in time to Rahossis' heartrending cries.

The Doctor was quite dead. In his fall he had cracked his skull upon the tree against which Axel had leaned when a little over a month before he had said so thoughtlessly to Lulluma:

"This is like Eden—to make it complete you only need the Serpent."

CHAPTER XXII

DEATH IN THE GARDEN

AXEL and Lulluma were sleeping peacefully, her dark head pillowed on his shoulder, when Rahossis' screams roused them to the awful knowledge that some terrible thing had shattered the peace of the island.

Without a word they sprang up and raced along the tortuous paths through the jungle towards the sound of that dreadful wailing. They found the small clearing and pulled up with a jerk in its entrance. One glance was enough to tell them what had happened. For a second they stood there silent, too overwhelmed to speak, then Axel gasped:

"Good God, man! What have you done? You've killed him."

Nicky still held the torch and was kneeling by the Doctor. "I—I didn't mean to," he stammered. "It was his fault—he tried to interfere but— Oh, God, I didn't mean to."

Lulluma was clinging to Axel's arm. Her eyes were distended with terror, then the beam of the torch lit the Doctor's head again.

"Blood!" she whispered. "Blood!" and her voice trailed away into a whisper.

"Beloved!" Axel sought to comfort her, passing his arm round her waist so that he could press her closer. "Don't look if it frightens you. We'll—we'll . . ." He broke off not knowing what next to say and she began to wail like Rahossis; just as though she were about to die.

The bushes rustled and Quet thrust his way through into the other side of the glade. He said something in Atlantean which neither Axel nor Nicky understood. His accent was harsh yet held a note of underlying terror. Only Lulluma caught the meaning of his exclamation.

"Blood!—blood has been spilled— Who caused this awful thing?"

He looked at Axel with dark fiery eyes and Axel made a helpless gesture towards Nicky.

"I couldn't help it," Nicky said heavily. "I only hit him,

then he fell and cracked his head against that tree. I never meant to kill him! It was an accident, I tell you."

Without a word Quet fixed his eyes upon him and held his gaze. To Nicky those eyes seemed to become Quet's whole body, the rest of it became shadowy and was swallowed up; the bushes and the clearing disappeared. Those eyes were forcing him down into the black depths of unconsciousness. He struggled for a second, whimpered and slipped to the ground beside the Doctor.

"Did—did you do something to him—or has he fainted?" Axel asked shakily.

"I have placed him so that he can bring no more evil among us for the moment," Quet answered in a hushed voice.

Danöe and Karnoum appeared. Immediately their glance fell on the Doctor's face Karnoum began to tremble and the girl added her wailing to that of Rahossis and Lulluma.

It was a dreadful sound. Axel felt that he had never heard anything so terrible. The high piercing note seemed to drag at his very heart-strings. Within five minutes every member of the island's population was gathered about the clearing and other voices had been added to that ghastly chorus.

None of these screaming women had ever had more than a casual friendliness for the poor little doctor and it was not for him they beat their breasts and tore their lungs in such uncontrollable grief and terror. It was because 'blood' had been spilled in anger.

Even Menes, when he arrived, seemed stupefied by the shock and quite incompetent to deal with the situation. In consequence the McKay took charge and the rest, as usual, accepted his orders without any question.

The Doctor's body and Nicky's unconscious form were carried back to the centre of the island. There, the wailing Atlantean women claimed the former and insisted on taking it into the temple. For a moment it occurred to Sally that, as a good Christian, the Doctor might not care to have pagan rites performed over his body, but even the McKay found it impossible to resist the distraught importunity of Semiramis and the females of her family. On learning that the burial would not take place until the following day, he felt that the temple was as good a place as any for the corpse to remain the night, so he let them have their way.

He enquired then what Menes wished done with Nicky, but the old man shook his head as though hopelessly bewildered.

Quet spoke to him in Atlantean and evidently told him what he had done to the evil-doer in the grove. Menes then made certain passes over Nicky's head and said:

"I have caused him to pass into a natural sleep. He will not wake until to-morrow night."

The McKay escorted Menes to his apartment. The male Atlanteans walked slowly away with downcast heads. Sally, Camilla, Vladimir and Axel remained in a silent stricken group beside the pool.

After a few moments the McKay joined them again.

"Well?" whispered Sally.

"The poor old Admiral's all to pieces," he replied tonelessly. "You see there hasn't been a murder here since 1066 —no, since the Flood I mean. All these people always die a natural death, so they're shocked out of their senses. Just listen to those women now!"

Piercing long-drawn cries coming from the direction of the temple made the night hideous. There was something about that eerie persistent wailing which made their flesh creep and the top of their scalps prickle.

Axel shuddered. "It is the spilling of blood which has affected them so profoundly."

"Oh, it's horrible." Camilla dabbed her eyes. "Just to think of the Doctor being dead now when he was laughing with us only an hour ago at supper."

"Yes," said Sally. "Yes, it's awful. He was such a harmless little man, but all the same," she added practically, "terrible as this is for everybody, he was our friend more than theirs. I don't see why they should be so utterly distracted. They must have seen bloodshed before on their travels in the upper world."

"Maybe, me'dear," the McKay replied, "and you've read of ghosts or the Devil appearing in stories, but you'd get a pretty nasty shock if Satan stood before you in the flesh one night—cloven hooves and all."

"I forgot that. Of course, they only see the people in our upper world as though they were acting in a sort of motion picture and the happenings there aren't truly real to them at all."

"No, only as stories for cocks and bulls," muttered Vladimir miserably.

They sank again into a tense silence. All five of them had been marvellously happy during these past weeks. They had accepted the life in this heaven that they had found so completely that it almost seemed now as if they had never known any other, and it had become unthinkable that any event should suddenly leap out upon them to mar their perfect joy.

"What would the Atlanteans do to Nicky?" "Could life in the island ever be quite so carefree and wonderful again?" Those were the thoughts which agitated them to the very depths of their beings, but they shrank from putting their fears into words.

Obviously there was nothing to be done for the moment so they took a despondent leave of each other and separated, but none of them was to get much sleep that night.

The keening of the women in the temple continued unabated and all the doctor's friends were saddened with the thought that they would never hear his guttural laugh again. They felt too, now, that they had never taken the trouble to be quite as nice to him as they should have been when he was alive. As Sally had said, he was such a harmless little man. His only vice was the apparently crazy desire to discover Atlantis, which had ended for them in this unique experience and, latterly, his eagerness to form a collection of the island's leaves and flowers.

Camilla wept passionately on Vladimir's broad chest when he had carried her up to that absurd tree-top home which had caused the Atlanteans so much amusement but which they had had such fun in making together. Sally wept too, in spite of all the McKay's efforts to comfort her with theoretical assurances that death was not a thing to be afraid of after all, and that where the Doctor had gone he had probably forgotten all about them now through being busy with the collection of another lot of flowers. Axel went back to the jungle, but he could not face his usual vine-hung couch without Lulluma and she was with the other women mourning for the dead. Like a lean ghost he roamed the island, haunting the scenes of his past happiness, while darkness lasted. Nicky the evil-doer alone slept peacefully, deep in the oblivion into which Menes had bade him pass by those signs of power made across his unconscious head.

In the morning everyone was astir early. Pale and exhausted, their beautiful faces haggard now from the stress of their emotion, the women came out of the temple. The Atlantean men crouched on its steps in dull apathy. None of them made any attempt to get themselves breakfast, so the

McKay ordered his party to pick some ripe fruit and serve it as though nothing had happened, but the Atlanteans refused to eat. The women, who all seemed to have aged ten years in a single night, flung themselves down where they were to sleep and the men sat unmoving, silent and heavy eyed.

Nicky slept on, a huddled figure beside the pool, the Doctor's blood still staining his guilty hands. After a little Sally could bear the sight no longer and strove to wake him, but Menes' hypnotic power held him in its spell. Failing in her efforts she washed his limp hands before them all, tidied his golden hair, and arranged him more comfortably. The McKay walked away behind some bushes while she did it in order that none of the others should see his face. He rated himself furiously because he was 'blubbing like a stupid kid' and such a thing hadn't happened to him in a quarter of a century, but he just couldn't help it, he loved her so much.

When he had cursed himself into renewed composure and Sally had completed her self-appointed task, he gathered his party together and led them off into the depths of the garden.

The flowers blossomed just as they had yesterday, some were fading but new varieties were bursting from their buds in those Elysian fields that held eternal Spring, but somehow there was a subtle difference. The spirit of death brooded over the secret enclosures. The leaves of the trees still hung motionless in the windless air, yet they seemed to whisper to one another: "Death and decay—death and decay."

The McKay halted in an open space and sat down on the grass. The others followed suit.

"Look here," he said, "I couldn't sleep a wink last night and I've been thinking. Quite apart from anything the Admiral may decide, we've got to make up our own minds what our attitude is going to be about Nicky's crime—and then hang together."

"Our own laws may not be perfect, but in this they are the only guide we have," suggested Axel.

"That's my view, but the point is—did Nicky commit murder?"

"I would interpret murder as a deliberate attempt to kill another human being," declared the Count, "and Nicky said this was an accident. I believe him too."

"So do I," agreed Camilla, "and anyhow he was tight when he did it."

"Of course he was tight, but that would not be accepted

as an excuse in any court of law," rejoined the McKay abruptly. "If you kill anybody when you're driving a car and you've had one over the odds it's manslaughter in the first degree, but this is worse unfortunately. We have to remember that Nicky struck a blow in anger and that blow caused the Doctor's death."

"He didn't mean to kill him though," protested Sally.

"Perhaps not¡ but the fact is that he did."

"He made a smashing most unfortunate as I might have done myself," said Vladimir, "but what do you think the Atlanteans will treat him to?"

The McKay shrugged. "It's impossible to say. They may have some form of trial. If so it's my view that we ought to let their law take its course. It's the usual thing to accept the decision of the courts in whatever country you happen to be, and this place belongs to the Atlanteans after all."

"If there is a trial I don't see how they can say it was anything but manslaughter," Sally argued, "but even if they did there won't be any question of—of an execution. They are far too gentle."

Axel backed her up. "They would shrink from that for their own sakes I am certain, but if they sent him to Coventry it would only be asking for more trouble, and in such a small place it is hardly practical to put him in prison with everyone taking turns at jailer. It is just possible that they might turn him out of the island though."

"They couldn't!" exclaimed Camilla.

"No—no," Vladimir followed her horrified protest. "I have never liked that Nicky but he has been through much with us. It would be death twice times out there in the black dark. I would wring his so stupid neck myself rather than he should suffer such awfulness."

"That's how I feel," muttered the McKay. "He is one of us so, rotten little blackguard as he is, we've got to do our best for him. The Doctor wasn't a vengeful man and I'm sure he would say the same if he were here to speak for himself."

"What will you do if Menes decrees some punishment for him of which we have not thought?" Axel enquired slowly.

"Providing it's humane things must run their course. Nicky will have to take his medicine, I'm afraid."

"Even—even if they do say it was murder and want to —to . . . ." Camilla's voice trailed away at the awful thought of the fair handsome Nicky, who had so often made love to her in his own conceited way, being led out to die.

"I think so, if it's a fair trial, although of course it's up to us to do every mortal thing we can to get him off. You see . . ." the McKay paused and then went on again more slowly. "I hope I haven't pushed myself forward, but in a way you seem to have looked to me as the leader of the party ever since we got stuck in the bathysphere, and the old Admiral appears to regard me in that way too—so I feel a certain responsibility towards you all. That's why I take that view. If the law here decrees that Nicky is 'for it' we can hardly say the verdict isn't just, so we have no real moral grounds for using force in order to save him. If we did the Atlanteans would be quite entitled to retaliate in any way they chose. Well, they at all events are completely innocent and they have been marvellously kind, so it would be the basest ingratitude on our part to start a scrap in which some of them would be certain to get pretty badly hurt; but there's worse to it than that. If it came to a showdown the odds are in their favour, so we might even have to kill some of them before we succeeded in getting control of the island; or they may have something up their sleeve, seeing the way Quiet laid Nicky out, which would make a mess of us—and *we've* got Sally and Camilla to consider. I'm sorry for Nicky, just because he's been with us from the beginning, although he's a vicious little brute, but my sympathies are with the Admiral and his pals. In any case though, even if I liked Nicky a lot better than I do, I couldn't advise the sacrifice of innocent lives to save him from justice, and I've no intention of imperilling the safety of the Atlanteans or our party in that way."

Axel nodded. "The thought of starting a civil war here is too horrible to contemplate and, as we should be the aggressors, totally unjustified. Whatever Nicky's punishment it will not be barbarous—we can be sure of that—therefore we have no possible right to interfere."

"Oh, poor Nicky!" Camilla suddenly burst into tears.

The conference ended then. Everyone felt that the McKay was right. They could do no more for Nicky than plead his jealousy and drunkenness as extenuating circumstances. There was nothing else to be said.

The leaden hours of the morning drifted by at last, but when midday came the Atlanteans again refused all offers of food. The others had no heart to cook a meal and nibbled at the fresh fruit without a thought as to its flavour.

In the early afternoon Lulluma awoke and Axel managed to get her to himself for a few moments behind one of the blocks of buildings.

She stared at him in dumb agony, her big eyes ringed by deep purple circles. On his questioning her she clung to him like a frightened child and became almost incoherent.

All he could gather was that the Doctor's funeral would take place at twilight and after that she saw everything "Black —black—black."

The island now seemed to have become unreal again. It was held in the thrall of a horrid silence. To all the McKay's party the time of waiting seemed interminable. At length the earthshine began to dim and Nahou approached them.

"Menes says that you may come to the temple if you wish," was all he said. Then he turned away as though reluctant to have further speech with them.

They stood up at once and followed him to the temple steps where the Atlanteans had already gathered, then the whole population of the island except Nicky, who still slept, passed through its golden doors.

None of the McKay's party had been inside the temple before. It was small but exceedingly magnificent. Only the dim light prevented their eyes being dazzled by the pure red gold of its walls and ceiling, while countless gems glittered dully in its furniture.

Two lines, each of six throne-like stalls, faced each other across the choir, but none of these were now occupied, the whole congregation stood bunched together just inside the doors while Menes, robed in white, occupied a position before the altar, which was quite plain, having only an inscription in Atlantean above it.

In the middle of the choir there was a gorgeous bier upon which lay the still form of the Doctor. At each of its corners stood a blue stone jar about a foot in height, and Axel guessed rightly that these held the brains, heart, liver and intestines which had been removed from the body by the women during the night. It was evident that they meant to embalm and mummify Doctor Tisch, hence the necessity for the immediate removal of these perishable parts, later his corpse would be soaked in bitumen, and this was only a preliminary service.

Menes muttered in Atlantean. The congregation bowed as

if in assent, then they broke into a doleful dirge. After that came an interminable litany, more chanting, more mutterings from Menes and deep obeisances from the rest. Next Menes sealed the nine openings of the Doctor's body, with ritualistic signs, so that no evil thing might enter into it.

Little Ciston came forward from the crowd and stood behind the head of the bier, Menes took up a position at its foot and began to ask questions in a loud voice to each of which Ciston made the same response. Axel's knowledge of Egyptian beliefs, which had been based on this even earlier religion, enabled him to guess that Menes was playing the part of the Forty-Two Assessors of the Dead, each of which would ask the departed soul if it had been guilty of some particular sin when it reached the 'other world'; and Ciston was taking the doctor's place by replying to each interrogation: "I am innocent." Then there was another litany, more dirges and further anointing of the body.

Sally, Camilla and Vladimir found it an incredibly wearisome business, so also did the McKay, and only a sense of respect held him rigid through the two and a half hours of what he considered senseless mummery. Axel's interest alone was held by following this ritual which had been practised when the world was young.

At last it was over. Menes made a sign and the Atlanteans suddenly changed their tone, bursting into a paeon of praise and glory as though the very gates of heaven were opening before their eyes.

Nahou, Quet, Peramon, and Karnoum lifted the four corners of the bier and followed Menes through a door at the back of the temple. Semiramis led the women after them, Tzarinska, Laötzii, Rahossis, and Lulluma, each carrying one of the four canopic jars. The others came in a little bunch behind.

They all descended a broad flight of stairs to the crypt, a great apartment, far exceeding the temple above in size. In height it was at least twenty feet and in breadth fifty. Its ends could not be seen, but were hidden in a sepulchral gloom as they ran towards the extremities of the island underground. Along the walls were ranged tier upon tier of great gilded sarcophagi, containing the mummies of all the generations of Atlantis which had survived the Flood.

Sally made a rough calculation—if a child had been born every twelve years there must be over nine hundred of them buried there—then, for the first time, she saw the Doctor's face.

His head had been shaven and the injury to his temple repaired so skilfully that under a gloss of wax it no longer showed. His features held a tranquillity and dignity which they had never displayed in life. Axel knew that every scrap of brain and mucus had been removed from the dead man's skull down the nostrils with delicate hooked implements, yet no trace remained to suggest that this skilful operation had been performed.

The bier was set down in the centre of the deep crypt below the altar, then they silently filed up the stairs. One by one the Atlanteans took their places on the twelve thrones which lined the choir until only Nahou was left standing. He made a gesture towards the temple door and said: "The service is over and we are about to take Council with the Gods."

The five friends passed out into the Atlantean night and Nahou closed the golden door with a clang behind them.

"Phew!" exclaimed the McKay. "Thank the Lord that's over—I thought it would never end."

"Just on three hours," said Axel as he walked down the temple steps beside him. "Anyhow they seem more normal now and much more cheerful."

Sally nodded. "I can't think they'll do anything really serious to Nicky, and the awful thing he's done will be a most terrible lesson to him. He will probably become a model of all the virtues in consequence, then after a time things will settle down again."

"Oh, I do hope so." Camilla squeezed her arm. "We've all been so wonderfully happy here."

"We'll be happy again, m'dear, once this tragedy's blown over. It's part of God's goodness that we're so made as to forget such things in time." The McKay spoke with a new confidence and they all felt a little cheered.

The Council of the Gods did not last long. In less than a quarter of an hour the temple doors opened again and the Atlanteans came out upon its steps.

There was a stirring in the shadows by the pool and Nicky roused at last as though he had received a summons. He saw his friends walking in a little group towards the temple and came up silently, unnoticed by them, in their rear.

Menes stood before the temple surrounded by his family. The McKay and the others halted at the bottom of the steps facing him and waited with strained expectancy for the pronouncement which he appeared ready to make.

After a moment he spoke. "On your arrival here from the upper world I was gravely troubled, yet I made no mention of my fears, for to cast shadows is to invite black thoughts which often breed evil actions. We accepted your coming only because in humanity we could not thrust you forth into the darkness again without a trial.

"Blood has now been spilled in anger by one of you, but he is only the instrument symbolizing the impurities which have not yet been eradicated from the natures of you all. Had he not struck this blow, sooner or later another of you would have committed a lesser or greater evil; for at our first Council, although we were allowed to accept you, the auguries showed me no state of permanence in your relation with my people.

"This is the judgment of the Council of the Gods, and from it there is no appeal. You have brought lust, and anger, and death, into the Garden, so you must go hence—even as you came—before the morning light appears."

CHAPTER XXIII

OUT OF PARADISE

THE McKay woke in pitch black darkness. He blinked to assure himself that he really was awake and then memory flooded back to him.

He heard again Menes' terrible pronouncement "You have brought lust and anger and death into the Garden, so you must go hence—even as you came—before the morning light appears."

He saw his friends distraught and pleading—the Atlantean women covering their faces in pity for them—the men firm and unbending, now that the awful judgment of the Gods had been given for the preservation of their own race from evil.

He recalled every detail of the scene when he had stilled the clamour by yelling for silence. The way he had reasoned and argued with Menes, insisting that he *simply could not* send them all out to die of starvation or be murdered by the fish eaters and finally—since the old man proved immovable —his ultimatum, that if one hand was laid upon himself or his friends to compel their departure he would blow the Atlantean temple down with dynamite.

After that something queer had happened. The McKay did not quite clearly remember what. Menes' eyes had seemed to grow very large and bright then his own knees had given way under him—the rest was blotted out.

He thought of Sally. A numb ache seemed to grip him in the stomach. Where was she? What in God's name had become of her? He rolled over and sat up.

"Darling!" came a swift whisper in the darkness. "Darling— Oh, thank goodness you've come round—are you all right?"

The numb ache faded. With unutterable relief he stretched out a hand and found Sally crouching there beside him.

"I'm all right dearest," he muttered. "But what happened to me?"

Axel's voice came from a few feet away "Menes hypnotised

you and sent you to sleep. He did the same with Vladimir when he tried to fight. The rest of us went quietly because it seemed more sensible to remain conscious so that we could collect food and things, before we left, than to be carried out. We're all here together.''

"Where's here?'' demanded the McKay.

"About two miles from the island. The Atlanteans escorted us this far and helped us in carting you along.''

"Two miles eh. We'll go back then and force an entry with the two bombs I've got left. Thank God I can feel them still in the pockets of my coat. I suppose some of you dressed me.'' The McKay struggled to his feet. "Come on—which way is it. To attack and take the place is our only chance of life.''

"It's no good,'' muttered Nicky. "I got the wind up after they left us here and tried to beat it back to the island. I could see the light in the entrance of this tunnel all right but I couldn't reach it. My head became swimmy and my legs gave way. Those devils are sitting there and they've put up some sort of thought-force barrier like the old man told us his people did ages ago to keep out the fish eaters.''

"They are not devils and they have every right to protect themselves from swine like you,'' said Axel with unusual fierceness. "If you do not speak of Lulluma's people with respect I will choke you.''

"And I with my so great hands will hold him for you Count,'' added Vladimir. "The cad pig who runs to make comebacks while our Captain and myself are unable to make defences for our ladies, because we are sleeping as though drug drunk.''

"I didn't mean to—I was frightened'' whimpered Nicky. "I don't want to die here in the dark—I don't want to die.''

"Shut up'' snapped the McKay angrily.

"You're brave—I'm not'' Nicky protested with a whining snarl. "I know you all blame me for this but what about the Doctor? Didn't he let us in for the whole business in the beginning? He's lucky to have got out of it so easily—that's what I say. We'll stagger round these passages for a few days until we've finished the fruit we've brought, then when we're too weak to resist them those filthy beast men will creep up and eat us. I can't face it. I can't—I can't!''

"Shut up damn you!'' roared the McKay. "Aren't things bad enough without our having to listen to your snivelling!''

314

"All right! All right!" Nicky muttered then he suddenly gasped "What's that!" and next second gave a piercing scream.

Vladimir had crept forward fumbling in the darkness and, as his hands touched Nicky, reached up and grabbed him round the neck.

"Help!" gurgled Nicky "He—lp! he's stran—gling— me."

Camilla had been the first to realize what was happening and she flung herself forward on the struggling pair.

"Vladimir. Stop!" she cried imperatively, wrenching at his great shoulders. "I won't have you a murderer—for God's sake stop!"

He obeyed her almost before the others had time to move and turning took her in his arms.

"There—my so beautiful" he soothed her "Our Public Cad Number One is frightened so it gives me pleasure to present him with something to be frightened for. If he opens his teeth again I will kick him as I have often thought to do with both boots of my feet—which someone has put on while I slept."

"We all got into our original clothes before we came away,' Axel remarked "and naturally we dressed you and the McKay too. We have our old weapons as well and enough food to last us a week."

"How about the torches?" asked the McKay. "They're more important almost than anything. For God's sake don't say you forgot them, or have the batteries run down?"

"No, we have them here. I'm economising light—that's all."

"That's sensible enough but isn't it risky to stay here without showing a flash now and then?"

"That is not necessary" Axel replied softly "we have one blessing at least though I would have robbed you of it if I could. Lulluma insisted on coming with us. Her mental faculties can penetrate this pitch black night and she will warn us in good time of the approach of anything evil."

"Lulluma!" exclaimed the McKay.

"I am here," her low voice came out of the impenetrable gloom close by. "I have not quarrelled with my people and have done my duty to them, giving a man child and a girl so, though they grieved, they could not refuse to let me go. Your

315

chances will be more than doubled by having me with you and, is it not said in your world above that a woman shall leave all and cleave unto the man she loves?''

"You are a daughter who would make proudness in the heart of Kings'' Vladimir declared while the McKay was left speechless with admiration at her courage but Nicky caught at the word 'chances' and muttered churlishly.

"Lulluma and Axel talked about *chances* early this morning before we left the island. I overheard them—but now we're out here they say our hopes are slender as a thread.''

"Slender!'' cried the McKay. "What in heaven's name d'you mean! Is there *any* chance for us at all?''

Axel heaved a heavy sigh. "You mustn't count on it please. The odds are so terribly against our scheme being practical, but after Menes' decree last night, when you were all down and out, I thought of it and Lulluma did the rest. She took me to the library—a place that none of us knew of before— in a secret room at the back of the temple. There were hundreds of books there—at least writings done with a fine iron point on sheets of copper.''

"Go on man'' urged the McKay.

"Well, we worked frantically all night there and at last we found a plan of the original Atlantean mine workings. You remember what Menes told us about Zakar's attempt to break out. This is the gallery that he travelled when he made his great effort to reach the mountain peaks still remaining above water that we call the Azores.''

Camilla trembled. "There is a hope for us then. There is a hope?''

"A faint one, no more. Zakar or his companions had actually used the map we found and marked all sorts of things upon it. The water-logged galleries and chambers are clearly etched in. This road to the upper world which he tried to clear had many notes beside it. Lulluma translated them for me. They show the places where he drove the beast men that he had under his control into clearing great falls of rock, sometimes several hundred yards in length. They show too the spot where tragedy overtook him. He was very near the surface then but the passage is still blocked. The Atlanteans of his own generation could not clear it, after he was killed, without slave labour but there is just a possibility that we might succeed by using our dynamite.''

"Good God man! Why didn't you say this before,'' the

McKay exclaimed. "Come on now all of you—which way does this passage run?"

Axel flashed his torch to the northwestward but his voice was still heavy with doubt as he went on. "I do beg you all not to count on this. Even if we can blast our way through the blockage that held up Zakar's friends, there may be others beyond which are quite impassable."

"No matter" cried the McKay. "I'll not throw in the sponge until I know myself we're sunk for good," and grabbing Sally's arm he began to stride along the tunnel.

"Better go steady" Axel advised as he followed with the rest. "We've got the best part of ten miles to cover before we even reach the place where the tunnel's marked as choked and every yard of it will be up hill."

The McKay checked his pace a little, but pressed on eagerly with a brief remark. "We'll rest for ten minutes in every hour we have to march."

For half an hour they progressed, almost in silence, through the long straight upward sloping mine galleries which turned at sharp angles now and again—flashing their torches every few moments—then Lulluma said:

"Be careful. We come to a great chasm soon here."

Axel's torch picked it up a hundred yards further on. It was one of the rifts in the earth where the land had sunk. Across a black gulf only a blank wall of rock showed ahead, but Zakar had made steps in the cliff face and clinging to each other in couples they descended into the crevasse.

At a depth of eighty feet or more the tunnel showed again, its entrance supported by great blocks of masonry. They entered it and pressed forward, coming to one of the lofty chambers shortly after.

Here they took their first rest, but Lulluma startled them just as they started off again by saying. "The beast men have been here quite recently. I can feel it. They are not far away."

Only the occasional flash of a torch stabbed the darkness as they tramped on, but they moved more warily now, filled with apprehension.

A broken section where the roof of a gallery had fallen in impeded their progress for a little and Vladimir swore loudly, having stubbed his toe against a sharp piece of rock.

Another chasm, this time of lesser depth, was negotiated, and then they entered a seemingly endless tunnel which sloped steeply uphill. A mile up it they paused to rest again, but they had hardly regained their breath when Lulluma pressed against Axel and whispered. "The beast men. They have crossed our trail and scented it. They are following us now."

McKay heard her and called for silence, but although they all strained their ears to listen they could not catch the faintest sound. The very silence of the grave brooded over those chill black catacombs untrodden by man for over a hundred centuries.

"Are you sure you're not mistaken?" he asked after a moment.

"I am certain" she insisted. "I hear with my mind which is more delicately attuned than any human ear. They are coming after us. The soft padding of their naked feet comes quite clearly to me."

"All right!" he said. "We'd best move on again."

After a further mile of uphill going the tunnel ended in another chamber.

"For God's sake stop" gasped Nicky as they entered it "the pace you set is frightful. We can out distance those brutes if they come up just as we did before. Let's fake a breather now."

The McKay knew that from fear of what lay behind them they must have walked the last lap at nearly five miles an hour in spite of the gradient. Sally was panting heavily beside him and Camilla in his rear. Of the women only Lulluma seemed unaffected. Common sense told him that he had *got* to suit the pace to the weakest members of the party. Reluctantly he halted and announced "Very well then, we'll take a spell."

They sat down on the rocky floor and endeavoured to control their laboured breathing but, before the ten minutes were up they were spurred on again.

Faint, almost imperceptible at first, yet gradually quite clearly they heard the steady pad—pad—pad of running feet approaching up the tunnel they had just traversed.

The flickering torches showed that the cavern they were now in had many entrances but Lulluma did not hesitate a moment. With Axel beside her she dived into one and almost unconsciously they all broke from a quick walk into a trot, as they followed.

The floor sloped upward again and it was heavy going. Nicky puffed and laboured in their rear in spite of his boasted fitness.

Another mile, or perhaps two, for they could only judge the

318

distances roughly, was covered, and the sound of following footsteps had died away when Lulluma suddenly exclaimed.

"Be careful—we are approaching another earth rift."

They dropped back into a rapid walk and, within a few yards, found that her peculiar gifts of judging direction and determining localities in the darkness from her memory of the mine plan, had not deceived her. A crevasse opened up before them.

This time it had no steps to descend in order to reach a continuation of the tunnel lower down. That gaped opposite to them, open and black in the beam of the torches.

In past centuries a bridge of stones had perhaps spanned the chasm but, if so, it had fallen away. The gulf yawned wide and deep at their feet.

"We've got to jump it" declared the McKay. "It's not much over two yards—a child could do it."

He was not far out in his estimate but eight feet is a lot when a slip means being dashed to death in a fathomless pit shrouded by darkness.

"Give us a lead Sally me'dear!" To ask her to go first was perhaps the most courageous thing he had ever done, but he knew that he had got to get the women over somehow and not even Vladimir could have carried their weight as well as his own in such a jump.

"Stand back" gasped Sally "and I'll do it!"

She took a run. The McKay's heart seemed to rise and choke his throat, while the others focused their torches on the opposite edge. Sally sprang high in the air, and landed a good four feet clear over the gap, barking her knees on the hard rock as she fell but in an ample margin of safety.

"Bravo!" called Axel "now the next; Lulluma darling you could jump twice that distance easily."

Without a word Lulluma took a flying leap and landed on the further brink, where Sally pulled her to her feet.

Camilla had one of the torches and, in flashing it round, noticed a jutting snag of rock waist high in the tunnel wall at their side. She swung out on it as Lulluma reached the other brink and next moment she was over.

Axel and the McKay followed. Only Vladimir and Nicky were left, the latter goggling at the crevasse in horror.

The Prince caught a glimpse of Nicky's face in the wavering torch light. "Now Public Cad Number One, do you jump or do I kick you" he said with grim delight.

"I—I can't" stuttered Nicky. "I'm weighted down—the stuff I'm carrying is so heavy.

"What stuff?" snapped the McKay from the further side.

"Food and—and when I overheard Axel talking to Lulluma of a chance to get away I—I took a few souvenirs."

"Souvenirs!" the biting contempt in the McKay's voice cut the darkness like a whip, but Vladimir had seized Nicky again and thrust a hand into his coat pocket.

As he pulled it out the torch light showed the dull gleam of gold between his fingers. Then as he opened them they saw in his palm a lump of the rich metal encrusted with precious stones.

"So that's where he disappeared to just before we left," Axel exclaimed angrily. "The dirty little thief was busy robbing the temple."

Vladimir hurled the gem studded piece of gold down into the abyss then he grabbed Nicky by the scruff of the neck.

"Do you go over dog-cur—or do I hurl you after your loot with one great tossing?"

Nicky wrenched himself free and leapt. He landed heavily on the further edge. The McKay jerked him to his feet and shook him.

"If you've got any more of that stuff you'd better get rid of it. You'll be caught for certain if you lag behind—and gold weighs mighty heavy."

"Don't I know it," Nicky panted, and obediently producing four more pieces from various pockets, he dropped them down the shaft.

Vladimir had crossed at a bound but clearing the gulf and the altercation with Nicky had lost them precious moments. As they started off they could all hear again that stealthy patter made by the herd that followed in their rear.

The going was harder than ever now since the gradient was still steeper but the McKay encouraged them as they ran by panting: "We're safe from those brutes now. They'll never be able to cross that chasm."

"Won't they" gasped Camilla a moment later. "They will —if they find that snag of rock—by which—I swung myself over."

"Courage," cried Lulluma in a low voice. "Have courage. We are not far now from the place where the tunnel is blocked —If we can only get through that. . . ."

Another hundred yards and they reached it. The roof had

320

fallen in and a heap of great stones barred further progress.

"Show all your lights," cried the McKay and he began to make a quick examination.

One large rock supported many others; there was a space beneath it but only a child could have wriggled through.

"That's the fellow we've got to shift" he said. "Then we can only pray to God that there are not others like it further on."

"Will you use both bombs?" asked Axel.

"No, one should be enough to smash this up. If I keep the other it means one more chance of getting through."

While the women held the lights the McKay placed the bomb and adjusted its detonator. The rest gathered all the scattered rocks they could lay their hands on and piled them round the opening to concentrate the force of the explosion.

"Now! back you go—all of you," rapped out the McKay. "A hundred yards at least. I'll be with you in a moment."

They had scarcely covered the distance when he came racing towards them.

As he clutched at Sally a blinding flame leapt out of the darkness. There were a thunderous roar which echoed down the tunnel for minutes afterwards punctuated by the clink and thud of falling stones.

On the McKay's word they dashed forward again. The big rock was shattered but its splintering had brought down all the smaller stuff from above and a great heap of debris now faced them.

Without a moment's delay they attacked the barrier, hurling the loose metal behind them. The task seemed endless but after half an hour a hole eight feet deep had been made below the larger rocks which were still jammed above.

"You must be quick" announced Lulluma tremulously. "The beast men were scared by the explosion, but they have recovered now and are crossing the chasm by the spur—one by one. I can hear their twittering as they mass on this side before advancing."

The workers redoubled their efforts tearing their nails and fingers as they wrenched out the jagged stones. The McKay lay on his face passing back the loose shale while Vladimir performed prodigies in increasing the size of the opening so that their leader could work more freely.

"Be quick—be quick!" cried Lulluma. "The herd are coming!"

321

The McKay gave a yell of triumph almost at the same moment.

"I'm through"—he called. "I'm through if only I can shift this blasted lump next to my shoulders."

Two terrible moments followed. They could hear the brutes now padding towards them, but Sally was terrified for the McKay. She feared that in moving the block he might bring down another fall of rock which would crush him.

"I've done it!" he shouted. "Down on your tummies— through you come." Then the beast men were upon them.

Axel pushed Lulluma down into the hole as he turned with Vladimir and Nicky to face the attack. They still had their steel levers which they had taken from the bathysphere and they used them savagely as the white leprous faces showed up in the torchlight.

The McKay, with his shoulders thrust into the far end of the passage he had made, grabbed Lulluma's hands and pulled her through, then Sally, then Camilla; Nicky abandoned the fight and wriggled in hard on Camilla's heels. The five of them waited with pounding hearts for the others.

After a moment Axel's head appeared and he held out his hand "Your gun" he gasped to the McKay "quick—give it me."

Bozo's pistol held three bullets, the part-reload that the McKay had kept in his pocket. He thrust it on Axel without a second's delay and the Count squirmed back through the hole to the far side of the barrier where Vladimir was fighting for his life against the score of skinny clawlike hands that sought to drag him down.

There were three deafening reports, then silence. Almost immediately afterwards Axel appeared again and Vladimir after him. The shots had temporarily quelled the herd and enabled them to get away before the foul creatures recovered.

"We'll remain here, knock them out one by one as they come through" muttered the McKay and he had hardly spoken when the first parrot-beaked brute thrust its narrow head through the opening.

Vladimir clove the head at a single blow, and it died without a whimper. The body was pulled back and another head appeared. They killed its owner too and a half dozen others that came after him. Then the attempts ceased but the clink and fall of rock could be heard from the side where the herd were gathered.

322

"They're enlarging the opening so that five or six of them can come at us together." said Axel. "We may slaughter half a hundred but they'll wear us down before we can kill one tenth of them."

"You're right. We'd best block the hole this end as best we can—then go on." the McKay responded. "It will take them some time to shift the whole barrier."

They did as he suggested, then marched up the hill again but their speed decreased in an alarming manner. Zakar had only cleared the tunnels as far as the point where he had met his death; from there on the whole floor was littered with masses of stones and rubble over which they stumbled, and in some places there were belts of debris shoulder high that could only be crossed by clambering on all fours.

These painful delays held a new menace, for where before they had been able easily to outdistance the herd by running, they could no longer do so. Once their pursuers were through the barrier the lead held by the hunted humans could not be increased again.

Another barrier reared itself up before them and their hearts almost stopped beating. For a second it looked as if they were finally trapped, but it was found that the stones did not quite reach the roof.

Lulluma had not spoken for an hour but, without her warning, they knew that their apparently implacable enemies were after them again. They could hear them slithering over the rocks behind and their horrid bird-like twitter.

The McKay scaled the new barrier and reported that they could get through under the roof as far as he could see. Utterly weary now the others hauled themselves up beside him and wriggled along over the sharp corners on their stomachs.

The blockage continued for fifty yards and downward-jutting rocks in the roof made the passage still more difficult. Before they had reached its further end they could smell the stench of the fish eaters entering it behind them.

Camilla dropped exhausted on the far side of the rocks. Vladimir picked her up, slung her over his shoulder and pushed on, leading now; Axel and Nicky were in the rear both sobbing for breath as they staggered up the steep stony uneven way.

Other passages began to branch off from the tunnel. They passed twenty openings in less than five minutes but Lulluma never hesitated, calling directions to Vladimir as she followed swiftly on his heels.

"I can't go on" yelled Nicky suddenly.

The McKay turned and flashed his torch upon him as he ran. His eyes were glaring, his face dead white and ghastly, his fair hair matted on his forehead.

"What the hell's the matter with you man," shouted the McKay. "Didn't you unload all that gold as I told you to?"

"No" sobbed Nicky. "No—All I could—but—but the rest's tied round my waist and legs—to—to distribute the weight. I've had no chance to—get—rid—of—it."

Vladimir was carrying Camilla. Lulluma ran with set teeth just behind them. The McKay had Sally by the arm and was still thrusting her on although she was half fainting. Axel was nearly done himself and finding it a terrible effort to keep up with the party. None of them could help Nicky now.

He gave a despairing cry and pitched forward on his face —picked himself up and lurched on again—but he had lost a dozen yards, and the beast men, their feet hardened to these stony floors were close behind.

A wild burst of exultant gibbering came as Nicky fell again, the stench of rotting fish was all about him, and then they were tearing at him with their talons.

The others were so desperately pressed that they did not realise what had happened until it was too late to attempt his rescue. While the front ranks of the herd ripped him to pieces the other humans gained a momentarily increased lead, but Axel's strength was failing.

Lulluma felt it instinctively and paused till he came up— then she flung out a hand to pull him forward.

"It's not far now" she breathed "It's not far now. We'll do it unless we are stopped by another barrier."

His breath came in choking sobs as he grabbed her hand and pressed it. "The chart of the mines—it weighs me down so. I'll have to drop it."

"What!—you took that?" she pulled up with a jerk. Her tone held indiscribable horror and reproach.

"Yes," his voice was thick and rasping as he halted beside her. "In case we lost our way—I—went back to the temple for it—afterwards."

Yet as he spoke he knew that he had not told all the truth. Even the slender chance that they might escape had filled

324

him with an overwhelming desire to bring something back to the upper world which would definitely prove the existence of Atlantis. The chart of the mine galleries was composed of twelve sheets of heavy copper delicately hinged so that it could be spread out like a map and, engraved upon it, were countless directions and phrases inscribed with the utmost care in Atlantean hieroglyphics; that lost language which Doctor Tisch had so stoutly maintained was the root of both Egyptian and the Maya of Central America—linking them to their common parent.

Just as Nicky's god had been Gold so Axel, through all his life, had worshipped Wisdom. The thought of needing the chart to find their way had been sufficient to excuse him to himself when he took it, because he did not know that Lulluma would prove so sure a guide, but now, as he faced her in the darkness, he knew that he would have told her that he meant to do so if he had not been impelled to the theft by a second motive.

"Give it to me" she said.

He pulled it from beneath his shirt where he had been carrying it and handed it to her.

A shout came from the McKay further up the passage. "Come on—what the hell are you two waiting for?"

"What—what are you going to do?" stammered Axel his heart contracting in a hideous fear.

"Take it back" she said simply. "I must. It is one of the sacred documents of the Temple."

"You can't," he cried "You can't. It's too late—the herd will get you."

"Come on!" yelled the McKay again his voice coming from a greater distance. "There's daylight ahead—daylight."

"I can" said Lulluma "I shall hide in one of these passages until the fisheaters have gone, I can travel more swiftly than they can and my senses will warn me if they are near. I *must* go back Axel."

The herd were pelting up the hill. Their gibbering filled Axel's ears, the stink of them was strong in his nostrils.

He grabbed Lulluma by the shoulders and tried to thrust her in the direction the rest of the party had taken, but she slipped away from him.

The McKay was holloaing, nearer again now. "Where in God's name are you?"

325

Half stunned by distress Axel groped for Lulluma in the darkness. He caught a whisper.

"Axel. If I get back I shall never—what you call marry again—bless you."

Then she had gone, diving into one of those side passages which she could discern but he could not.

He sank down on the ground and there, a second later, the beam of the McKay's torch found him.

"Lulluma's gone—gone back to her people," he gasped as the McKay hauled him to his feet by his coat collar.

With shrill cries of triumph the beast men launched themselves upon them but the McKay held the half conscious Axel under the armpit and was literally forcing him along as the herd clamoured at their heels. He knew now that daylight and safety lay ahead if only they could reach it.

Neither ever knew how they covered those last four hundred yards but in the latter part they were slipping and stumbling over seaweed.

Vladimir, carrying Love alone, had got Camilla up through a narrow gap in the rocks on to a long desolate shore lit by the afternoon sunshine.

Then he had dragged Sally out beside her. Now he returned into the entrance of the cave and grabbed Axel as he fell senseless.

The McKay scrambled up after them—then he turned and flung his last bomb into the opening. They heard the dull boom as the rocks lifted. The roof of the tunnel caved in and buried the first hundred of the beast men. The entrance of the passage seemed to tremble as though seen through a haze of heat then it dissolved into a mass of rocks, indistinguishable from those about it.

They had all reached the limit of endurance. Sally, Camilla and Axel sprawled senseless in a heap. Vladimir just witnessed the closing of the road that led downwards to Atlantis before his great legs gave way and he fell beside them.

For a moment the McKay stood there, his feet squarely planted, as he drank in the gentle breeze, the salt sea air, the blessed sunlight, then he pitched forward—unconscious but triumphant.

.   .   .   .   .

The following is an extract from a letter written some considerable time later by Count Axel Fersan on Pico Island to

326

Mrs. N. A. McKay—then in the United States of America.

Another season has passed and I am again compelled to abandon my search owing to the great gales which now sweep the beaches here.

You might well imagine that I know every yard of the desolate south and east coasts of Pico by this time, but when you and your beloved Captain come to stay with me next summer, as you have promised, you will appreciate the immense difficulty of my task.

The rocky promontories and innumerable coves all look so much alike that even I, who have spent so many weary months here, still find it hard to distinguish one from another except by continual checking on my map.

At times I utterly despair of ever finding the exact spot where we were picked up half dead by the crew of the fishing boat, and even that would be only a beginning since, in our delirium, we wandered, probably several miles, along the shore after the McKay blew in the entrance of the tunnel; but those black moods never last and I am already longing for our short winter to be over so that I can get down to my search again.

For the rest, owing to your splendid generosity, I live in epicurean comfort. The Roman Villa which you had built to my design is not large as you know but, now that its gardens provide a suitable setting, very beautiful.

The nine fruit trees which I grew from the stones we saved are doing well. They occupy a little sheltered court containing nothing else, just below my window. I tend them with a more devoted care than any horticulturist ever gave to a black tulip or a blue rose, since they are the only tangible thing remaining of our journey to Atlantis. When you are here they will be in blossom and recall to you with startling vividness the beauty and the fragrance of my dear Lulluma.

You will be prepared, of course, for a very quiet time. There is hardly an educated person on the island but *that* suits me, since it eliminates the necessity for a tiresome exchange of visits and wasting time among people who would probably have little in common with myself. However, I do not lead a completely useless life as, owing once more to your generosity, I have been able to do much for the fisher folk along the coast.

They think me a little mad owing to my obsession with

327

the foreshore but not entirely so. In fact they endeavour to ignore my eccentricity, with the natural politeness found among common people, and in all other ways have come to regard me as a sort of overlord.

Instead of carrying their disputes to the courts or resorting to private vengeance they have formed the habit of bringing them to me and accepting my decisions as a basis for settlement. In return I could always have as much free labour as I wished—if I needed it—and hardly a morning passes without a gift of fruit or vegetables being left at my door by someone to whom I have had the good fortune to be of assistance.

My last mail brought me one of those delightfully humorous effusions from Vladimir. He and his 'so beautiful Princess' beg me again to visit them in Bucharest in order to see my little godson but, great as is the temptation, I cannot bring myself to leave the island even for a month.

He tells me that plausible rogue Slinger is out of prison and that they met him a few weeks ago in Paris. When I am feeling very low I can still revive my sense of humour by thinking of Kate's rage when he realised how completely he had been fooled by two young women. No wonder you were so scared of his return, and so certain that he would come back vowing vengeance immediately he discovered that neither the carefully thought out letter to your lawyer nor the signature to the will itself were in the Duchess da Solento-Ragina's writing.

How infinitely wise you were my dear, after your first tragic marriage, to decide on changing identities with your cousin and how fortunate that you did so before Slinger came on the scene.

How marvellously too your plan to secure a husband who loved you for yourself, instead of a fortune hunter, succeeded. As long as I live I shall never forget the McKay's face when he learned that it was he who had married the real heiress to the Hart millions.

It is good to think of these things as I laugh little in these days.

My conviction that Lulluma got back safely remains unshakable. I believe that in all her spirit travels she comes to me here and at times I can almost feel the warmth of her beside me. But even if that is sheer imagination she was carrying enough fruit to satisfy her hunger and thirst for a week and I doubt if she had to remain hidden more than a few hours.

The herd would certainly have returned to the harbour for their next feed of fish and after that the road would have been clear for her to repass the barrier.

Immediate discovery after she had left us was her only real danger, but she was swifter of foot than the beast men and possessed those special senses, to guide her through that maze of tunnels.

She is living still—I know it—less than twelve miles distant from where I am writing now—safe in that secret island blessed by eternal Spring.

If I could once locate the wrecked entrance to the underworld, through which we returned to pick up the threads of our previous lives again, the rest would be easy. In company with a few stout fellows armed with machine guns those brutes which are neither animals nor men would prove no serious obstacle. Within four hours' march of this barren shore I should be able to look upon Lulluma's face again—the only thing I live for.

That I am so near her and yet separated from her by a barrier more difficult to cross than the seas from pole to pole causes me, at times, to go almost frantic with frustration, but my life is pledged to finding my way back to that enchanted garden where she dwells.

She was less than divine yet more than human and it never ceases to amaze me that one so infinitely gentle could be so splendidly courageous. For all those years she had known a faultless existence yet she abandoned it willingly in order to save us as, without her guidance, we would never have come through.

That she gave me her love, even for a brief season, has lifted me too a little towards the Gods.

I crave for the sound of her laughter as a man lost in the desert thirsts for water and, whether I find her again in this life or die here first, all that was my heart remains for ever with Lulluma.

This book
designed by William B. Taylor
is a production of
Heron Books, London

Printed in England by
Hazell Watson and Viney Limited
Aylesbury, Bucks